MASTERS OF WAR

A MAXX KING THRILLER

BOOK 2

JOHN H. THOMAS

This novel is entirely a work of fiction. The names, characters and incidents portrayed in it are the work of the author's imagination. Any resemblance to actual persons, living or dead, events or localities is entirely coincidental.

DEDICATION

Jon and Bill,

In the tapestry of my life, your threads are two of the brightest and most enduring. From the first moments I held you in my arms, you've filled my world with an immeasurable joy. This book is dedicated to you both, not just as a gift of words but as a testament to the love and pride I feel every single day. Pride in the men, husbands, and fathers that you've become.

This story, like our lives together, winds through moments of laughter, tears, growth, and uncertainty. May you find within these pages echoes of our own journey, and may it inspire you to write your own stories, to live your own adventures, with the courage, love, and passion that you've shown me.

You are my legacy and my heart. Here's to you, my incredible sons. May this book be an inspiration for you, lighting the way as you navigate the seas of life ahead of you.

PREFACE

Before diving into Book 2, I want to express my gratitude for joining me on this continued adventure. MASTERS OF WAR has been both a challenging and a richly rewarding journey. If you enjoyed THUNDERBIRD RISING, you'll know I relish weaving in surprises. What I hadn't expected, however, was for some characters to take me by surprise themselves. In this installment, several "minor" characters have not only insisted on a larger role but have practically written themselves into the narrative.

Their expanded roles, however, have come with significant trials. You'll witness some of the characters facing severe, life-altering challenges that will change their perspectives and responses to the world around them. Some of these characters have become reader favorites and have indeed shifted my original plans for the series. They will undoubtedly influence the direction of the story moving forward.

Many of you have inquired about the length of this series. I can confirm that it will be a trilogy, with potential for Maxx to star in additional, standalone adventures. The world I've created has deepened over time, much like our own timeline, necessitating a longer narrative than initially planned. Instead of ending it prematurely, I've chosen to tell the story in the manner it deserves.

Be assured, I have a clear vision for how Maxx's current episode will conclude. While I'm eager to reach that point, I'm even more thrilled that you've decided to travel this path with me.

EPIGRAPH

You will hear of wars and rumors of wars but see to that you are not alarmed. Such things must happen, but the end is still to come.

Nation will rise against nation, and kingdom against kingdom. There will be famines and earthquakes in various places.

- *Matthew 24:6-7*

PROLOGUE

MONDAY FEBRUARY 25, 2002

Maxx swallowed the double espresso in one gulp.

He side-eyed Gabby and asked, "Why do they make these servings so small? I swear a child could drink one of these and barely get a caffeine buzz."

"You've become quite the coffee expert since you replaced your whiskey habit with skinny lattes. I'm sure Starbucks will be calling you soon for advice."

"Why are you busting my chops?" He held up what looked like a miniature teacup in his oversized hands. "You have to admit, this size isn't meant for grown men. Tiny, teenage girls in size-two jeans is their target customer."

Maxx and Gabby had been in an exclusive relationship for a year. While the last seven months had been extremely tense and at times dangerous, it had made them closer than the average fresh couple. They knew they could explicitly trust each other in any circumstance. They were also an odd-looking couple, with Maxx at 6'4" and every inch an ex-soldier and Gabby a cross between a nerdy programmer and an aerobics instructor.

They were seated on the heated patio outside the coffee

shop near their condo on Capitol Hill. It was a rare sunny day in Seattle for February. They were willing to sit outside even if the weather was a chilly fifty-two degrees. The small tables were set close together, decorated with simple tablecloths and colorful clay pots of white snowdrops. The sounds of light chatter, the clinking of coffee cups, and the occasional laughter blended with the noise from the nearby street.

They'd picked this spot to meet with one of Gabby's friends who was familiar with the area. There was a steady blend of residents, nearby tech workers, and the occasional meeting of a coffee klatch. And no shortage of dogs sitting on the patio. Anyone unusual would clearly stand out from the normal routine of the Seattle neighborhood.

Maxx had relaxed his safety precautions as time had passed since their "run-in" with a group of Chinese spies in the fall. He and Gabby had become embroiled in a plot to steal ultra-sensitive data from her employer, TechCom. He liked to think they'd put any suspicion behind them but was cautious because of the aftershock of the events on 9/11. It seemed as if the country was heading into a protracted war in the Middle East. And less public but just as worrisome, a covert intelligence race with the Chinese simmered below the surface.

Hoping to improve the relationship between the US and China was why they were excited about this morning's meeting. They were optimistic about a breakthrough in the relationship between the two countries. Gabby's friend was the daughter of Dr. Xi, a high-level Chinese scientist who was categorized as a state enemy by the State Department and the lead on a highly competitive communication program at the Commission for Science, Technology and Industry for National Defense. COSTIND was the competitive counterpart to DARPA in the US. DARPA, or Defense Advanced Research Projects Agency, was a highly secretive agency within the US Department of

Defense tasked with developing innovative technologies for national security purposes.

Chao-Xing, Xi's daughter, used her Americanized nickname Connie while she was in the US. She graduated from Stanford with her PhD in artificial intelligence and then moved north to Seattle after graduation to work for TechCom. Even with her father's connection to the Chinese scientific community, she was too valuable for TechCom to turn down.

It was at TechCom that Connie and Gabby met. When Gabby had learned who Connie's father was, they had developed an immediate connection because of her interest in astrophysics. In the last six months, the two of them had been trying to broker an unofficial relationship between the Chinese and US to reach an agreement on a secretive project. Thus far, Connie had successfully convinced her father that Maxx and Gabby could be trusted.

"What's the plan for today's meeting?" Maxx asked after the barista brought him another double espresso.

Gabby furrowed her eyebrows, creating small wrinkles on her forehead. "I'm not entirely sure. When I ran into Connie last night at work, she said she had something important to talk to us about. She wanted to meet with us both as soon as possible, and this was the first time we could arrange."

"It sounds interesting, but I'm still puzzled about what it has to do with me. You two talk at work all the time. When we've spent time with Connie outside the office, you talk so much shop that I can hardly follow the conversation. And you know how smart I am."

Gabby snorted and rolled her eyes. "It's not about work or she would have mentioned it at the time. It must be something sensitive that shouldn't be overheard. Even the walls have eyes and ears in my office."

Gabby spotted Connie walking up the tree-lined sidewalk toward the café and waved her over. She looked like she was in early twenties, although she was closer to her mid-thirties, like Maxx and Gabby. Wearing a short, conservative hair style with a pants suit, she stood out from the rest of the younger, casually dressed tech workers. A pair of thick-rimmed glasses completed her distinct look.

When she walked to their table, Gabby gave her a hug.

Maxx said hello and waved to her from across the table. "Can I get you something? Keep in mind, they are very tiny servings."

"That's sweet of you, Maxx. I'll take a large black coffee in a to-go cup. I can't stay long."

Gabby and Connie continued chatting while Maxx stepped inside the cafe to grab Connie's coffee and a refill for himself. He enjoyed watching Gabby smile as she talked, waving her hands to make a point. It was a relief to see her regaining her easygoing nature after the trauma she'd been through last year. He'd seen plenty of combat in his life and still occasionally woke up in a cold sweat, reaching for the pistol he kept in the nightstand.

After he picked up the coffee, Maxx stepped up to their table and set down Connie's drink. Both Connie and Gabby broke out into loud laughter and avoided making eye contact. Obviously, they'd been talking about him. "Did I miss something?" he asked.

"Nothing really," Gabby said with a smirk.

"Mmm hmm. So what's the meeting this morning about, Connie? Gabby said you wanted to talk with both of us outside the office."

"First, I wanted to pass along a message from my father. He feels guilty about Haoyu killing your friend Scott, although he was acting against my father's orders. Haoyu lied about the situation and was told to only scare Scott. But he disobeyed my father and took matters much too far. Will you pass my father's condolence message to his family?"

"I'll tell Scott's father. Tell your dad not to expect a thank you card."

"I understand. It's a terrible burden for a parent to watch their child die."

"What about Maxx?" Gabby asked. "Haoyu also tried to kill Maxx three times!"

"That is true, but my father believed Maxx was an enemy agent, so those attempts on his life were justified." She shrugged, indicating that it was a closed subject to her.

Maxx scoffed. He'd never expected an apology from Xi and considered the score settled.

"Then I guess that's not what you asked us here to talk about," Maxx said as he looked sullenly at his empty coffee cup. He was glad to move off the topic, since Connie didn't know Maxx had ended up killing Haoyu. He hoped that she and her father at least felt a little guilt over the how much it had affected Maxx and Gabby but wasn't holding his breath.

"I've convinced my father to work with your government on this project," Connie said excitedly.

"That's fantastic news," Gabby exclaimed.

"He's finally agreed with me that it is best to set aside our nationalistic competition and address the situation together. There is too much to gain—and lose—he said. He's convinced others in the government to at least hear what you have to say. He believes we can find common ground."

"I'm certain we can make that happen," Maxx said. "Did he indicate where and when he'd like to meet?"

"He said that sooner is better, and he is thinking we could meet somewhere in the middle. Hawaii seems like a good place for a private meeting. Plus, you can work on your tan... You're starting to look like a ghost with a crewcut."

Maxx laughed. "Yeah, the big dark in the winter makes it hard to stay bronzed. If your father is comfortable with a meeting in Hawaii, I'll start making some calls."

Connie paused. "He does have one precondition before he agrees to meet. He wants written assurance that there is no remaining link between the US and Doctor Smith. He wants it in writing, and if there is any indication that Smith is involved, it's a deal breaker."

"I can understand his concern," Maxx said, "but I am confident that if anyone in the US knew the location of Doctor Smith, he would be a dead man. We want that guy out of the picture as much as, if not more than, your father. He dropped out of sight after he engineered the disaster on September 11th. The US government is determined to hunt him down."

"Do you think you can get me an official response today?" Connie asked. "Now that my father has been given the authority to share what we know, he's anxious to meet soon. He says there is a ticking clock. A clock with a figurative bomb attached to it."

"I'll try and get you a response by the end of the day. The government doesn't usually move that fast, but I know some people who are impatient to move forward. If you don't mind, I'll excuse myself now and start making some calls."

"Thanks, Maxx, I knew I could count on you," she said. "It's always great to see you."

Maxx sipped the last drop of coffee from his cup, kissed Gabby, and walked across the street to an empty bench in the little neighborhood park. He sat down on a bench that was catching some mid-morning sunshine filtering the trees and pulled his phone out.

He tried dialing a couple of numbers but didn't get anyone live. It was midmorning back in Washington DC, and they were probably deep into their meeting schedule. He left messages indicating that it was an urgent topic but couldn't leave any details for now. Maybe that would pique some interest.

While he was searching through his contacts looking for who to call next, he felt the hair on the back of his neck stand up. He'd learned through years of war to pay attention to a warning from his subconscious. He hadn't heard or seen anything that registered consciously, but it was an early sign that it might be time for him to fight or run.

Looking up from his phone, he tuned in to his surroundings. He could hear some kids playing on the swings behind him while their parents chatted. A quick scan told him that there wasn't anything happening behind or around him in the park. He shifted his eyesight to Gabby and Connie, who were still relaxed across the street on the café patio.

Lastly, he began to search the street. Traffic was normal. Slow but normal, mostly minivans and Subarus. No black cars with tinted windows.

As he looked past the traffic, he recognized the source of the danger. Although he hadn't seen her for half a year, and she looked very different now with short blonde hair and oversized sunglasses, he instantly recognized her. *Li Jing.*

It was no coincidence that she was here at the same time as Connie and Gabby. Li Jing was on the FBI most wanted list and had essentially disappeared after murdering Gabby's boss in the TechCom parking lot. She was focused like a laser on Gabby without making any attempt to be sneaky; she was homing in on the café like a missile that had identified its target.

Maxx stood up quickly. He was too far away to reach Gabby before Li Jing got there, so he yelled and waved his arms, frantically attempting to get Gabby's attention. He began to sprint toward her. *I'm not going to make it in time.*

Gabby turned her head and saw Maxx trying to get her attention. She looked confused at first. But when she heard him yell Li Jing's name and saw him point, she immediately began to react. She was licensed to carry a concealed weapon, and Maxx saw her reach into her purse.

When Li Jing heard Maxx shout her name and point at her,

she stopped moving toward Gabby. She waved to Maxx then ran in the opposite direction, away from Gabby.

Li Jing's change in direction didn't stop Maxx's momentum. He changed direction in the middle of the street and began running after her through traffic. He knew he could outrun her, and even if she was armed, he was willing to take the risk to catch her. She was much too dangerous to be let escape – especially now that she was obviously tracking Gabby.

There weren't very many people on the sidewalk at this time of the morning, and Maxx was quickly gaining ground. Despite Li Jing's head start and his plodding winter boots, he was going to catch her. This was a race he was determined to win. If he got close enough, a gentle tap would send her reeling onto the concrete where he could effortlessly disarm her.

As Maxx closed within the last hundred feet, Li Jing suddenly stopped at the intersection. She was surrounded by a group of people waiting for the light to change. He wondered how it would look if he bowled over a bunch of innocent people when he tackled her. Concerned, but not enough to slow him down. He was running like he was finishing the four-hundred-meter race at the state championships. With boots on.

Suddenly, a modified Acura roared up, causing everyone at the curb to jump out of the way, everyone except Li Jing. The passenger door swung open, and she effortlessly slid inside. As she closed the door behind her—with Maxx only fifty feet from success—she looked at him with a wide smile and shouted, "You forget something, Maxx!"

Li Jing pointed back toward Gabby. Laughing, she slammed the car door shut as the Acura sped through the red light and away from Maxx.

Shifting his focus from the vanishing car, Maxx spun on his heel and changed his direction back to Gabby. He didn't know what Li Jing had meant, but it had to be bad. Gabby was at least two blocks down the street, and there were too many people on the sidewalk between him and the café to see what was happening.

He was struggling to keep his breathing steady as he kept his pace at a near sprint. In his twenties, this would be another easy day at the races, but at thirty-four he wasn't in the same shape. Sure, he was in better shape than almost everyone else his age, but that was small consolation after running at full speed for a couple hundred yards. In boots. *Thank God I drank all that coffee*, he thought.

After getting through the next intersection, dodging cars and getting a clear view of the café patio, he could see the real danger. Gabby and Connie hadn't moved from their table but were still alert. Unfortunately, they were looking toward Maxx and not behind them.

Two men were walking quickly toward Gabby's table. As Maxx stared at them, they pulled pistols from beneath their leather jackets and held them down at their sides.

Maxx yelled, "Behind you, Gabby!"

It wasn't much of a warning, but it was enough to catch Gabby's attention. She'd kept her pistol under the table when Li Jing had first appeared, and it gave her enough of an advantage to catch the two men unprepared. They hadn't expected to face an armed target.

Gabby turned when the men were still a dozen paces beyond her and screamed at them to stop. Of course they didn't stop. They were professional killers motivated to finish a hit.

However, Gabby's shout did prompt them to raise their pistols, take aim, and fire. Maxx could hear the guns discharge, but it was impossible to tell how many shots were fired. There was too much noise around him as he cut through the patio tables and people scrambled to get out of the way. He was entirely focused on protecting Gabby and eliminating the threat.

It didn't look like Gabby had taken any hits, since she was

still crouched behind a large concrete planter and firing in short bursts like he'd taught her. But even from a distance, Maxx could see that Connie was slumped on the ground and not moving. He could also see that one of the men was down on the ground and rolling.

He screamed to his partner, "Kill her, kill her!"

The man still standing was continuing to move toward Gabby while taking cover behind the few cars parked on the street. He was not stopping his forward progress despite Gabby's shots to keep him pinned down.

With his focus on Gabby, the assassin didn't notice Maxx swing around the street side of the car.

When Maxx heard the gunman start shooting again at Gabby, he stepped around the trunk and swung a right hook using all his momentum. It was the kind of punch that would have stunned a professional boxer if he'd had gloves on, which of course he didn't. It was bare knuckle against the guy's jaw, shattering it. The guy fell to the ground like he'd been struck by lightning. The sound of his head slamming into the asphalt made it certain he probably wouldn't be getting back up for a week.

Maxx yelled to Gabby that it was okay to stop shooting, and he picked up the guy's gun and walked over to the first shooter. He'd stopped yelling at some point. Maxx rolled him over with his foot. Dead. *Good.*

Gabby's eyes were opened wide, her mouth set in a tight, straight line. She looked to Maxx like she was in shock and trying to process what had happened. The tears would come later, but for now she was focused and alert while she called Connie.

The coffee shop was chaos. Maxx walked back toward Gabby as he heard her calling Connie's name and trying to help her. Sirens were already echoing off the glass buildings in the distance, moving toward them rapidly.

It took Maxx a moment to notice that blood was dripping down his arm onto the ground as he walked. He couldn't feel any pain, but he could see a hole on the shoulder of his jacket. He pulled off his jacket to see that it wasn't a deep wound but would need some attention later. Right now, he needed to make sure that Gabby was okay.

Gabby sat on the ground with Connie's head in her lap. She was covered in blood, and it took Maxx a few moments to make sure that none of the blood came from Gabby.

"Wake up, honey," Gabby said as she gently shook her friend. "Everything will be okay. You're safe now."

Connie had been hit multiple times and had died quickly from what Maxx could see. It was difficult to believe that Gabby hadn't been hit in that melee when there were several other wounded people lying on the ground around her. While he felt terrible for Connie, Maxx was visibly relieved that Gabby had escaped unharmed – physically.

Maxx put his hand on Gabby's shoulder as she sat on the ground cradling Connie's lifeless body.

"She's already gone, babe," he said.

Her body hitched, holding back a sob. "I know, Maxx. Let me say goodbye to her."

He touched Gabby reassuringly and moved back a step to give her some space.

While he hovered nearby, a constant buzzing was the second thing that got through his sensory overload. With all the noise and activity, it had taken time to realize that the noise and vibration were coming from Connie's coat pocket. She must have been carrying a phone or pager.

Maxx carefully removed the pager from the dead woman's coat pocket. He was trying to silence the device when he inadvertently looked at the message. It was from a blocked number. "Tell Xi hello from an old friend! P.S. Your girlfriend is next,

Maxx. I'm saving you for last." *Connie, not Gabby, had been Li Jing's target today. And I failed to stop her.*

1

FALLACIES AND FEINTS

Miss Grey's phone vibrated again in her jacket pocket.

She'd been in the meeting without a break for the last two hours, and this was the second voicemail someone had left her. Taking out her phone would result in more than glares from the senior staff around the table. As a guest at the meeting, she was repeatedly told not to bring in any electronic devices. Obeying orders wasn't one of her strongest characteristics, so she'd put her phone on vibrate and dropped it in her suit pocket. It would be bad form if the others saw that she'd brought a phone into the conference room, let alone started taking calls or texting. The meeting would be wrapping up soon, and she decided to wait to listen to the voicemail.

Despite the annoying phone, she was absorbed in the conversation that was happening around the table, by video and on the phone. She'd been invited to the meeting because of her experience in the early days of the confrontation with the Chinese around the top-secret project, Thunderbird, named after the alien communication device that the US and China had been in a fight to activate. The race had resulted in the cataclysmic events surrounding 9/11.

September 11th was an inflection point in the United States. The shock was used by the government to address the national security questions raised by the communication with an alien civilization and the looming threat of conflict with China. Consumed by fear and outrage over what were portrayed as terrorist attacks in the heart of Manhattan, the population called for decisive action from its political leadership.

That action had been framed as the rationale to begin a considerable military effort framed as a global War on Terror. The broad, soft definition had allowed for a rapid expansion and creation of a foreign invasion force. While the president had framed the conflict as aimed at Al Qaeda and the Taliban, he was clear that "it does not end there." This military and intelligence expansion served two purposes that were lost in the details behind the stated justification. The invasion of Afghanistan less than a month after September 11th launched a sustained military campaign.

Afghanistan had been selected as the target because of the proximity to China's western border. It would be impossible to justify a military expansion into India, southeast Asia, or Russia. Access through Korea would be a slog but a plausible plan B if necessary. Channeling a conflict through Afghanistan and Pakistan on one front and pressing a naval interdiction from Japan and the Philippines would essentially keep China in both a land and sea war with limited geographic options for resources. The attack on Al Queda forces made this an easily justifiable location.

The hawks in the Pentagon and intelligence agencies who had been saber rattling for a preemptive war with China had grown silent after the debacle on September 11th. They were satisfied for the time being to focus on Afghanistan and Iraq. After the communication with alien civilization had begun in interest, the primary strategy at the highest levels of the government had been to focus on fostering the relationship with

Thunderbird without accelerating the competition with China. It also helped that China seemed to shift its focus away from Taiwan and creating a separate association with Thunderbird.

The initial communication with Thunderbird on September 11th led to a scramble within the government about how to respond appropriately. The US then received the updated communication files shortly thereafter. The communication from the aliens was dubbed the Lamba Files. They had been addressed to the Doctors Smith and Xi, also known as The Masters of War. The US had been unable to contact Smith after he had disappeared from New York. The US used every formal and informal channel to connect with Xi, but he had remained steadfast in his decision not to collaborate with the US.

The president participated in the second communication with Thunderbird and had relayed the fact that Doctor Smith couldn't be found, and that Xi had deferred any attempt to jointly communicate. The response had been less than cordial, but the aliens decided to proceed in discussions with the US and deal with China separately for the time being.

The first formal directive from Thunderbird had been to initiate the military buildup and the subsequent invasion of Afghanistan. They were explicit that the US was not to engage in a large-scale conflict and avoid a direct confrontation with the Chinese. The aliens initially suggested North Africa as the location for a buildup but had deferred the selection of the Middle East to the US. Naturally the US strategy of hemming in China in case of a future conflict wasn't mentioned by the president.

The reason stated by the aliens for the military and intelligence efforts masked by The War on Terror was to prepare for the possible invasion by the Others. They were clear that they considered the US and China to be the most capable global military powers that could engage an invasion in opposite sides of the planet. The US could battle in the Americas, China would shield Asia, and the two countries would work together to overlap in Europe and Africa. They thought it was odd that Russia or NATO were excluded from the alien plans, and any effort to explain it to the aliens was entirely ignored.

The aliens also ignored concerns raised about the abilities of the US to engage with an extraterrestrial hostile invasion. Thunderbird informed them invasions in the past had been focused on collecting and destroying the Thunderbird devices, in effect eliminating Earth as a watchtower. Historically, the Others sent small expeditionary forces, armed forces that could be defeated by the indigenous inhabitants if they worked together and prepared properly. After being defeated, the Others would move on to minimize the loss of limited resources.

In the event there was a protracted engagement, or the battle became too onerous for Earth, Thunderbird would help provide knowledge that would rapidly expand Earth's technical capabilities. But the current stockpile of nuclear weapons kept by the US and China meant that wouldn't be necessary. The Others wouldn't want to get into a conflict where they were targeted multiple times with that much energy. Thunderbird assured them it wouldn't destroy them or their transportation, but it would be a deterrent for further exploration. The Others were not interested in conflict with Earth or a protracted occupation. Earth was primarily a means of tracking down their real enemy—Thunderbird.

In contrast, Thunderbird said they did have a long-term interest in maintaining an interest in Earth. The primary benefit was a manned watchtower of an aligned intellectual species. Many of the people felt Thunderbird's view of humanity was that of a faithful watchdog. Humans weren't very advanced technically and of no threat to them—they knew they could count on us as faithful servants. Their only rule it seemed was that we didn't get in a position to cut off communication by fighting against each other. Therefore, they had positioned themselves through history as a god of punishment if humans lost focus on their primary purpose: To warn them if the Others landed on Earth.

That resulted in the current effort to encourage cooperation between the US and China. Their near-term objective seemed to be averting a war between the two countries and working jointly to intercede when the Others arrived. According to Thunderbird, they were also pushing the Chinese to align with the US.

For now, they were not forcing the issue, but they made it clear that cooperation was in Earth's and both countries' long-term interests. Leadership had no illusions that if Thunderbird felt that noncooperation was jeopardizing them in any way that they wouldn't hesitate to initiate punishment against one or both countries. The strategy to minimize the chances of the Chinese attacking the US was to make it clear that they were actively trying to engage China. Therefore if there was any blame, it would be solely on China's shoulders.

Miss Grey presumed that this was the reason she had been invited to the meeting. Every other attendee at the meeting was above her pay grade. She had largely been ignored before and during the meeting until the meeting agenda reached this topic. She'd made several attempts to provide input earlier in the meeting and had been soundly ignored. One of the hotshot CIA associate deputy directors, Barth Anderson, had openly rolled his eyes the last time she made a comment. *Pendejo.*

After a report from the State Department outlining their lack of success in reaching out to a wide array of formal contacts in the Chinese government and research industry, the vice president looked directly at her. "Miss Grey, thanks for participating in the meeting today."

"Thank you, Mr. Vice President Cheney."

He nodded. “I understand you were the agent who worked closely on the attempts by the Chinese to undermine DARPA’s efforts related to the Thunderbird device. What are your thoughts about why the Chinese are now stonewalling us about working together?”

Miss Grey had communicated her answer to this question several times in the last six months. There must be others in the room that had a contrary opinion, and he was voicing it to get the issue out in the open. That was fine with her. She was comfortable with her perspective, and wasn’t going to shy away from a fight now. The worst they could do was keep ignoring her.

“As we all know, Dr. Xi is the primary architect of the Chinese version of the Thunderbird program at COSTIND. He’s been competing with Doctor Smith for decades, and a great deal of personal and professional animosity built up between the two of them over the last twenty years. My source tells me that Xi believes Smith is still in charge of the Omega program despite our assurance that he is not.”

Barth coughed. “What sources do you have that we don’t?” he asked.

“I’ve been asked to not reveal my source at this point, but it is someone very close to Xi,” she said.

Vice President Cheney said, “Miss Grey, this is a sealed room, and I don’t think it’s out of bounds for the CIA to want to verify your source. Our national security and possibly the fate of the planet are dangling by a thin thread.”

“I’m not being disrespectful, sir. It’s only that I have given my word to the source that I wouldn’t divulge their identity until they gave me permission. If their name were ever leaked, it would burn them as a source and guarantee that Xi would never willingly engage with us.”

“I respect your judgment on this, Miss Grey, but I’m not

persuaded. I'll leave it for the moment, but I'll loop back to this topic."

"I understand, sir. The point is I believe Xi may be changing his position because of pressure from Thunderbird. I'm told they have been clear that they will hold China accountable if the Others are successful...and there will be punishment. This has Xi between an anvil and hammer, so to speak. While he doesn't trust the US, he does believe that Thunderbird and the politicians in his country see him as the wedge."

"He's survived many purges, and it's hard for me to believe that even the Chinese would eliminate him and risk causing a rift with Thunderbird."

"I don't believe they would kill him either," Barth interjected.

"It's not himself that is at risk. It's his daughter, Chao-Xing, who goes by Connie in the US. The threats are directed at her. If he fails, she will pay the price. With her in the US, there is nothing he can do to protect her if there is an official sanction ordered by the CCP."

"Well, why don't we pull her in? We can frame it as protective custody, but it's also a way to keep her close for our own purposes," Barth said smugly.

Miss Grey stared at him. "That's a guaranteed way to get Xi not to work with us. He already doesn't trust the US, and he'll see it as a threat no matter what you tell him."

The vice president put his hand up to halt the line of discussion. "We are not taking Mr. Xi's daughter into custody unless she requests it. I agree with Miss Grey that such an action would have negative repercussions for Xi and the Chinese government."

"We have been providing loose security, however. I have some contacts in the Seattle area who stay in close touch with her, and I've been augmenting with a small security team from the Department of Homeland Security. DHS is new, but we have some top-notch people."

"Is there anything else we could be doing to informally do to convince Mr. Xi to collaborate with us?" the vice president asked.

"I think focusing on the message that Smith is an enemy of the state. He knows that we, and specifically I, have no love lost for Doctor Smith. His trust in me when I tell him that Smith is out of the picture may be the most successful assurance we can give him."

A voice from the phone said, "And why does he trust you, Miss Grey?"

She knew that was the critical question and could guess why the speaker on the phone was asking. Of course, the woman on the phone already knew the answer, or she wouldn't have asked the question in this setting. In a meeting like this, knives were quick to be drawn.

"Good morning, Senator. He trusts me because his daughter has told him that he can," she said.

She could see the surprise register on several faces around the room. Even that fool Barth raised his eyebrows, having overlooked this critical piece of information.

Vice President Cheney spoke up, "Good morning, Senator Traficant. I wasn't aware you were joining us this morning."

"When I saw the agenda, I changed my schedule so that I could listen in, Mr. Vice President. Thanks for having me." The senator continued, "Miss Grey and I have been working together on this project before it was popular here in Washington. As some of you know, she was commended by the president himself for her efforts to stop Doctor Smith and get the contact with Thunderbird off on a positive foot. I strongly encourage you to take what she is telling you very seriously."

"Thank you, Senator, that's very kind of you," Miss Grey said. "As the senator knows, after September 11th, two of my colleagues in Seattle established a relationship where I was introduced to Xi's daughter, Chao-Xing. She is unaware of my exact role at the Department of Homeland Security but knows that I was the person who exposed Doctor Smith's attempts to start a war between the US and China by misleading our own government and Thunderbird. Not only is Chao-Xing grateful on behalf of her country, but she also knows that her father sees Doctor Smith as evil and as a mortal enemy."

"The important thing to know is that Miss Grey is actively working through a trusted informal channel to convince Xi that he can trust us," the senator said. "According to Miss Grey's confidential source, her relationship with Xi's daughter is causing him to improve his openness to join forces with us on this decisive project. I believe that, and you should too."

"Well said, Senator." The Vice President looked around the room and said, "Unless there are any other points to add to this topic, I'd like to move on to the next item of the agenda."

Everyone shook their heads, and few murmured no.

"Great. Thank you, Miss Grey and all of the visitors who joined us this morning. The next item on the agenda is for the standing committee only, so please show yourselves out."

Miss Grey and a few other people seated in the chairs around the edge of the room stood and made their way to the exit. She made certain to give Barth a half smile as she exited. It was a subtle sign that she had won that round. She was sure he'd find some way to get her back for embarrassing him, even if no one else had noticed.

After stepping out of the conference room, she quickly found an empty office she could step into. She closed the door but stayed standing while taking out her cell phone. There were several voicemails that she skipped over to find the two voice messages that Maxx had left her while she was in the meeting.

The first voicemail was cryptic but benign. Maxx had been

using this kind of messaging and texting since they had first started working together last fall. More than words, which really didn't say more than to call her back, he needed to talk with her. It was the tone of his voice. He generally lived up to the nickname she sometimes teased him with, *Steady Eddy*. The guy rarely got rattled or excited about anything. If he was excited, then it was some information that she'd want to know.

By contrast, his second message came about thirty minutes after the first. The contrast in his tone couldn't be starker. His tone was his normal flat communication, but what he said and the sounds in the background concerned her. She could hear sirens blaring in the background of his voicemail as he said to disregard the first message, but he still needed to talk to her ASAP about a recent development. She pressed redial on her phone.

When Maxx answered after a half-dozen rings, she could still hear sirens in the background before he said anything. *Please let him be okay.*

"Hey. I'll cut to the chase. Gabby and I were attacked by a couple of gunmen a bit ago. We stopped them. The police have one of them in custody, so we may get more information later. You may want to step in and take the guy out of local jurisdiction and into DHS."

"You're okay, right?"

"Yeah, we're both fine. But the person we were meeting with isn't fine. In fact, she's the opposite of fine. As in dead."

She could feel her stomach drop. "Who is dead, Maxx?"

"Connie. She took multiple bullets and didn't make it."

"Oh no," Miss Grey gasped. "How did it happen?"

"She or Gabby was the target. Li Jing was running the operation. We won't know until you talk to the guy the police are holding. That's why I was telling you that you may want to intervene."

"I definitely will. If it has anything to do with her father, then we'll want to get involved."

"It's all about her father. There was a text on her phone right after the shooting to tell Xi hello. It was a clear message to him not to get involved with us."

"A message from whom?" she asked.

"That's what we need to find out."

"I'm on my way now, Maxx," she said as she hung up and raced for the door.

2

FRENEMIES

Dr. Xi aggressively ran his hands through his thick, unruly hair as he stared at the black metallic cube sitting in the other room.

He was surprised he hadn't gone bald from the unconscious habit in the last few months. He was puzzled about many things since he'd escaped from New York last September. Things had seemed so clear at the time, but in the last six months he had developed the feeling that he was being pulled from one event to another. He no longer felt as if was the driver, merely a back seat passenger in a car sliding down an icy mountain road.

The lab where he was sitting was filled with instruments of every kind. They were constantly taking measurements from the cube-shaped device in the other room. To the naked eye, the device sat in the concrete chamber on an elevated platform, no signs of energy or movement. Even through the many inches of reinforced glass between the lab and the holding room, he still didn't feel comfortable. He'd seen firsthand the destruction that the device could unleash when triggered. He wondered if he'd even realize it was triggered before he was vaporized.

In the first forty years of controlling the device, they had learned very little about how it worked and what signals to monitor. However, in the last six months they'd finally decoded the instructions due to the advances with AI and information that an American spy had forwarded to him. The final pieces of information came directly from communication with the extraterrestrials.

As he watched the instruments, he could tell activity was happening in ways that they hadn't been aware of six months ago. There were no visible signs, and no telltale changes in the environmental factors that they traditionally monitored. But they had learned to measure changes at the subatomic level indicating the device was active. It was both a receiver and generator of signals that they hadn't been able to interpret. Precisely how much information was being transmitted had been difficult to determine since the instruments they had couldn't accurately measure such small changes in mass at the subatomic level. However, they'd determined that the inbound information was relatively small compared to the outbound signals. He'd surmised from the information that the device received a signal that triggered a predefined set of routines that were precoded into the device.

With all the monitoring instruments that they had added since he'd returned from New York City, they'd not been able to determine the end points of the communication to and from the device. They'd also had no success in disrupting the flow of information. Even though the lab and device were in a sealed environment buried beneath hundreds of feet of bedrock, it seemed to have no impact on the function of the device. Nothing blocked the flow of information once it was connected to a power source.

He had learned long ago that it required tremendous amounts of power to operate, but it didn't have to be physically connected to the power. Even if it was proximate to a natural power source such as geothermal, solar, or seismic, it could capture the nearby energy and utilize it. Whereas they had initially thought the device was not active because of the lack of external indicators, they now knew that the device was essentially in standby mode waiting for a power source. They had not seen it power itself up without an external signal, but he wondered if they knew enough to discover that kind of activity.

Deep in thought, he jumped when he heard his assistant clear their throat. "Dr. Xi, excuse the interruption, but there is a caller on your personal line. She says it's urgent."

"Unless it's my daughter, take a message."

"It's not Chao-Xing, but she still insisted that she speak with you. She says she has some very important news for your ears only."

"Fine, I will be there in a minute," he said with exasperation.

After he heard the door close behind him, he bent over the instruments. He made another adjustment to the signal receiver that they'd constructed. He'd been trying for the past month to divert the stream of data from the device to a separate instrument. He'd built the apparatus using information found in a subsection of the data file that had come with the device. Prior to the events in September, they'd overlooked it because they'd been in a sprint to prepare for the initial implementation. The arcane file hadn't seemed relevant at the time but now seemed important.

The information indicated the ideal conditions for data flow to the device, and he had been trying to see if he could capture and record the signal externally. An external copy of that function would allow them to decipher the data inflow without being concerned that they'd trigger an unintended response of the core device.

Xi wasn't positive about how or when the core device, which was referred to as Xinxi, had first been found. The early days were a closely guarded secret within the CCP, as it was somehow linked to the early days of the COSTIND. There was plenty of speculation about how the alien cube was discovered and then handed off from the early leaders to a group of scientists that could be trusted. Eventually a secret research division had been formed to handle the device and some other projects that were deemed crucial to the success of the future of China.

Eventually those early, strategic projects were combined into COSTIND, a black box organization that was designed to compete with the American formation of ARPA. Both organizations were highly secretive but superficially focused on advanced research projects. Xi was first exposed to the device in 1970 when he was assigned to the project as a research assistant after completing his PhD in astrophysics. He was confused about why he was assigned to the project until later it became apparent that his dissertation and research about extraterrestrial communication was directly relevant.

There had been little progress made in understanding the purpose and use of the device in the decade prior to his arrival. The constant turnover of unsuccessful project leaders hadn't helped in accelerating the project. It was considered a dead end by the time he was being promoted to senior-level positions. His reputation for considering innovative approaches to problem solving was a last-ditch effort. When he was assigned as project director in 1975, it was made clear that he was either going to make significant progress in the following year or he'd be be demoted and the project scrapped.

There had been considerable advancement in supercomputing capabilities during that period of time that allowed Xi to focus on the encrypted files accompanying the device. Although it was still unclear exactly how the device was intended to function, he had made a few assumptions that had resulted in a cursory understanding. He convinced others that the device was intended for alien communication, and a test deadline was set for July 28, 1976. Racing against the clock to save himself from demotion (or worse), and meet the July deadline, Xi had convinced the leaders in the CCP to test the device. The location chosen was in an underground facility in remote area of Tangshan.

Unsure of how the device functioned, Xi had the foresight to remotely position himself and the rest of the team for the initial trial. They had only been able to translate small portions of the manual, and while Xi had exuded confidence in his conclusions, he was not so egotistical to believe in his infallibility. It was likely that the device wouldn't operate at all, but on the other hand he didn't want to be responsible for an explosion that would kill himself and others.

The result of the test exceeded his imagination. He had never considered that there would be enough energy unleashed by the device to cause an earthquake with a magnitude of 7.8. Despite all the precautions, when it was initialized, the device triggered a disastrous seismic event. He would never rid himself of the guilt knowing that he had taken action that had resulted in the death of at least a quarter of a million people. For decades, he wasn't sure what had been the cause of the mishap. Even though he was not directly blamed by the politicians for the cause of the earthquake, they assumed it was a weapon that the Americans had covertly supplied them. A seismic trojan horse.

It had taken him over a year to excavate the test site, looking for remnants of the device to understand the cause. Underneath the tons of earth and rubble, he was shocked to learn that the device was unscathed. It had not only survived intact—there was not even a scratch on the smooth outer casing. This of course raised more questions about the development of the device and how it was possible to create such an artifact from elements that were unknown to them. Years of research followed that led to more questions than answers.

The initial premise that it was an American weapon were deemed unlikely. A major turning point for his research team occurred in late 1980. The working assumption that it was an American war device was answered with the explosion of Mount Saint Helens. What had at first seemed like natural massive eruption was determined to be the result of a device like their artifact. From several high-level sources, they had learned after the fact that DARPA had also been in possession of a similar device and was testing it at the time of the eruption. It was also made clear from the American sources that this was an unexpected event. The US government had been expecting a first contact communication, not a volcanic event.

That led Xi to the determination that they and the American's had possession of an alien device of some sort. And DARPA was under the impression that it was intended to be used for communication. Because of the relatively recent arrival of the device, they assumed it was from an active alien civilization. What they didn't understand was why the seismic events had occurred. They had gone in circles for years about whether it was intentionally detonated or due to an error. They had no evidence to support either conclusion, but no one was willing to undertake another test in China. After the initial information leaked from the US, DARPA had withdrawn their project into complete secrecy.

Instead of spending time on the endless debates without answers, Xi focused the team on two paths of action. First, trying to deconstruct the device in an attempt to reverse engineer it. They were partially successful but were still missing some key information about the physics that the device depended on. It was far beyond the understanding of known science. The second path of action was more fruitful: Deciphering the files supplied with the device.

By convincing the CCP to invest in technical capabilities focused on improving artificial intelligence that would generate immediate military benefits, Xi was able to co-opt the advancements to benefit his project. Using those advancements, in conjunction with the fruits of several covert programs embedded in American companies and universities, they were making steady improvements. The results were inadequate to convince anyone to test the device again but gave him hope that a useful application was possible in his lifetime.

The most significant event had happened in the last year, after decades of torturously slow progress. The rapid progress in 2001 that had led to the completion of the deciphered files had provided the information that they needed to understand how the device operated and where they had made errors in 1976 resulting in the disaster at Tangshan. It had also provided them with the opportunity to attempt to use the device, with low risk to themselves. Piggybacking off DARPA's efforts on September 11th in New York, they had planned to attempt to contact the aliens using the device without risking Chinese lives.

When the American's discovered Xi's plans to communicate using the device in Manhattan, his attempt failed. He had been lucky to escape New York with the Chinese device during the chaos occurring at the World Trade Center. No one in CCP intelligence had ever learned what the cause was that destroyed Tower 1 and 2, but they were certain it was related to the device. Of course, he had caused the detonation that brought down World Trade Center 7, but that had not been revealed to the public. As far as he knew, the events surrounding the devices and the subsequent communication remained a closely guarded secret.

He had only been back in China for a few days when they had received instructions from the aliens that was specifically directed to The Masters of War. It was generally accepted that included himself and Doctor Smith at DARPA. There had been attempts by the Americans to connect with him to coordinate a response, and he had resisted those overtures. He still harbored considerable distrust of Smith and did not want to be included in any coordination – knowing that at some point it was likely to lead to complications.

Following 9/11, he had worked long hours preparing the device for contact as the instructions indicated. In the initial communication the instructions were only to include himself and General Secretary Jiang Zemin. He presumed the Americans were operating under similar guidelines.

The purpose of the initial call provided the background about why the alien civilization was initiating contact and the expectation that they were to be coordinating with the Americans for preparation. Even though there were no overt cues, the conversation seemed to become more tense when the topic of cooperation with the Americans was broached. Xi had made it clear that his preference was not to work with the Smith under any conditions.

The Americans had reached out through formal and informal channels to encourage cooperation between the two countries. Xi had rebuffed all of the formal offers, and there was little that the Chinese government could do to force him to cooperate. The Americans had held out several olive branches in December. They even took the extraordinary step of granting permanent normal trade status despite no reciprocating concession on the part of the Chinese. None of that mattered to Xi.

The aliens made it clear that Xi was to remain their key contact, which left the Chinese leadership with few options. They couldn't remove him from involvement or even attempt to strong arm him into participating. The risk was too great that the aliens would stop the conversation completely or even initiate a form of punishment for crossing them. So the CCP kept the pressure on and convinced his daughter Chao-Xing to find ways to persuade him using personal pleas.

The last several months had passed quickly, as Xi worked long days preparing for the arrival of the aliens. Between meetings, he split his time working on the device in the lab and seeing his daughter when she was visiting. He was exhausted but had no choice but to keep pressing forward.

He had initially been motivated by his scientific fascination with the device and interaction with alien life forms. However, as the implications of failure grew with the imminent invasion, his motives changed from excitement to fear. Not fear of what would happen to him if he failed but fear about what that meant for Earth, and for the most important thing in his life: his daughter.

He was lost in thought when another knock on the door startled him. "Doctor, the woman is still waiting on the phone. She is becoming very unpleasant."

"Fine," he said as he shut off the instrument testing. He reluctantly followed his assistant down the hall to his office.

His assistant transferred the call to him once he was settled in his office. Spartan, with a few pictures of him and his daughter scattered between the papers and books. The story of his life was captured in a barren, square office.

"Hello, this is Doctor Xi. Who am I speaking with?" he said into the receiver.

"A voice from the past, Doctor."

The voice sounded familiar. Puzzled, he said, "I told you I would do as you asked. Why are you calling me again, Li Jing?"

"Because I don't trust you. I heard from a little bird that you were going to attempt to betray me. Again."

He could feel his face heat up with anger. Her accusation stung on many levels. Because they were true, and he couldn't undue the past.

"Continuing to threaten me is pointless. Tell me what information you have that I am not keeping my promise not to work with the Americans?"

"I suppose that's true. No more threats, it's time for you to be punished."

"There's nothing you can do to punish me," he said as fear ran like ice through his veins.

"I warned you before not to work with the Americans. I told you there would be consequences if you didn't listen to me. I'm calling to let you know that I left a message with your precious daughter. A personal message from Doctor Smith."

He felt all the air escape the room at the mention of Chao-Xing. "A message?"

"Yes, this is what happens when you cross him."

"What did you do?" he shouted. "What have you and that animal Smith done to my daughter?"

"Call her and ask her yourself," Li Jing said as hung up the phone.

3

AGENT OF CHAOS

Liu Yuxuan adjusted the knot on his tie for the third time in the last ten minutes. He had checked it in the rearview mirror of the car on the drive over to Zhongnanhai, and nothing had changed. He knew it was entirely nerves, but it was a rare opportunity for an administrative director to be invited to the CCP central compound, let alone to meet with the general secretary. He'd only seen Jiang from a distance and on television, so he wasn't sure what to expect when he was in the same room. So he'd pulled his lucky tie from the back of his dresser. He could only guess why he'd been invited to this meeting and pointedly told not to tell to keep it secret—not even to share with his wife—who he was meeting with.

He suspected that it might be related to the work that he was supporting Dr. Xi on the alien device. He wasn't a scientist, so he didn't understand many of the scientific elements of the project. But as an experienced bureaucrat, he did understand the nuances of politics within the party. He knew Xi and Jiang held semi-monthly meetings that were extremely secret, for which he had to make arrangements. He wasn't invited to those meetings, and it irked him as head of the program that he was excluded.

Yuxuan had taken the initiative to gain illicit access to the safe in Xi's office and read through the notes that were kept in his personal journal. At first, he'd thought it was Xi's prank, that they had been communicating regularly with some extraterrestrial civilization using the strange black device that was stored in the lab. He knew that the contraption was intended for some secretive purpose, but he'd been unaware that communication was happening routinely and why.

He became anxious when he learned the nature of the conversations were regarding the preparation for a possible invasion of Earth by aliens. It was one thing to think about communicating beyond the planet but something completely different to think they were planning on coming to Earth. He hated reading fiction, and this reminded him of the fanciful science fiction novels he had been forced to read when he was a schoolboy. He always imagined the aliens looked like giant bugs. Another one of his fears.

After concluding that this communication was in fact happening, he'd become intrigued by Xi's notes. They captured his unofficial and unexpressed thoughts following the meetings. It seemed that Jiang accepted the reasoning that the aliens proposed and intended to utilize the circumstances for the betterment of China. Even if those events came at the expense of the rest of the world. Xi didn't agree with the official position but went along with Jiang in public while harboring personal misgivings. According to his personal notes, Xi didn't like nor trust the Americans but was deeply suspicious of the intentions of the aliens. He believed that Jiang was accepting the alien positions without suspicion because their motives appeared to be aligned with his intentions of weakening the US.

Thinking about the situation for several weeks, Liu landed at a solution that he could use to his advantage. Initially, he'd thought that he could contact the security services and tell them that he had concerns about Xi's devotion to the party and Jiang. But in doing that, he would have to admit that he'd committed the crime of breaking into Xi's safe. If Xi wasn't punished for what he'd written, then he had no doubt he'd be ostracized from the program. It was possible that he'd even be killed because of his knowledge about the secret program.

Without any direct evidence of wrongdoing by Xi, and without openly admitting that he was aware of the detailed conversations, he had to approach the opportunity from another angle. After weeks of sleepless nights, he'd landed on a plan. He would pretend not to know of the specifics but write a position paper that supported the approach that he knew the general secretary was taking in the discussions. If his ideas went nowhere, at the very least he would know that he wouldn't be attacked for his conclusions, since they would support the chairman.

He'd written the support paper on the few days he'd had off at the new year. In short, he'd taken the position that while it was unclear if the alien's objectives were as they had stated, the greatest risk was to be found in outright disregarding their directives. That path was likely to result in the kind of cataclysmic punishment they'd already experienced at Tangshan. The devastation associated with the earthquake was still a sore point for the program. Another earthquake of that magnitude would place them in a weakened state regardless of what else happened.

On the other hand, preparing to repel an invasion wouldn't undermine their preparedness against the Americans. Nothing in the preparedness plan directly undermined their capability to resist an invasion if it came to that. In the meantime, they should be working on methods to disrupt the communication devices. In the near term, the greatest risk was to be found in the alien's capability to cause seismic activity, and if that could be circumvented that would give them time to prepare for the physical invasion.

As Yuxuan was finishing his light breakfast of tea and a steamed bun, there was a loud, insistent knock on his door. He rarely had visitors, so the intrusion, especially at this time of the morning, confused him. He slipped the last piece of sweet bun into his mouth as he cracked open the door.

In the hallway, two plain-looking men stood watching him peaking through the partially opened door. Despite their relaxed pose, Yuxuan felt the hair on the nape of his neck stand up. These were not his neighbors.

Still confused and now concerned, he cleared his throat and asked with a bit if a stammer, "Who are you looking for?"

One of the men stared at him a moment before answering, "You, Mr. Liu."

The other man pulled out a badge and showed it briefly to Yuxuan. "This is an official visit. Please stand clear of the door."

Yuxuan opened the door wider and stepped back into his little entryway to let them into his apartment. "May I ask what this concerns? I have an important meeting this morning and don't wish to be late."

"Yes, we know about your meeting. That is why we are here. We've been asked to escort you to the meeting with the chairman."

"That's not really necessary," he said. "I know the way to the chairman's office."

"It was the chairman's request, and he thinks it is necessary. He instructed us to search you and then bring you directly over. Would you like me to call him and tell him that you think it's not necessary?"

Yuxuan could feel his stomach roiling from the bun he'd recently finished eating. While he had nothing to be concerned about from a search, he felt sick thinking about the search extending into his apartment. If they did a thorough search of his home, he knew that he'd be tortured and killed.

"Are you alright, Mr. Liu? You look ill."

"I'm fine. I think the soft bun I ate is not agreeing with me this morning."

"If you're going to be ill, please step away from us. I don't want to have to clean off any mess. It'd make me angry."

The second man took a step back. "Please take off your clothes and hand them to my associate."

"All of them?" Yuxuan asked incredulously.

"Yes, all of them. Don't be shy. Neither of us are attracted to men. And you don't have anything we haven't seen before. And since we watched your wife leave, there is no need to be embarrassed."

Yuxuan quickly removed all his clothes down to his underwear, trying to tamp down his increasing embarrassment. This was not at all what he had envisioned when he'd been told that he was meeting with the chairman.

After searching through all of Yuxuan's clothes, one of the men ran several electronic devices over them. "I want to be certain he's not hiding any devices in the seams," the man said as he winked at his colleague.

"I'm not hiding anything," Yuxuan protested weakly, standing almost naked in the middle of his living room. It was difficult to hide the sheen of sweat covering his body. Luckily the windows were still covered, so no one in the building across from him could see inside.

After what seemed an eternity of being kept in the demeaning position, the men tossed him his clothes and told him to hurry and get dressed or they'd be late for his meeting. After the trauma of this morning, being late would be the final straw of humiliation. His earlier feeling of excitement had been replaced with dread. Perhaps that had been the intent of this visit – to remind him that he was not in control but always at the chairman's mercy. This visit was a stark reminder not to forget his place in the order of the state.

After he dressed and quickly brushed his hair, the two men hustled him out of the apartment. They took the stairs down to the street below, where a black sedan waited for them half on the sidewalk. No one was going to challenge their credentials; it was obvious that they were at the apex of the political system.

When Liu was pushed brusquely into the back seat, no one even gave them more than a passing glance. The passing drivers, pedestrians, and shop owners knew better than to show interest in the people getting into a black state car.

Yuxuan made no attempt to start any conversations. No one in the car paid attention to him or each other. The driver and his escorts silently watched the city pass by outside the tinted car windows, as if they were invisible. As his heartbeat slowed to a semi-normal pace, he began to focus his thoughts on the points that he wanted to make in his meeting with Jiang.

This surprise visit was a reminder that he was in a dangerous position. But the paper he'd written had largely reflected what he understood to be the chairman's position regarding cooperation with the aliens. Personally, he didn't agree with the position, but no one cared to hear that. Xi had been smart not to express his opinion. Perhaps someday Yuxuan's opinion would have value, but first he had to gain some credibility. And with a seasoned politician such as Jiang, that would best be created by agreeing with him and then demonstrating his value.

Liu's central objective in the initial meeting was to convince the chair that the most important element of the communication was to persuade the aliens to provide some new military technology to China. Technology that would be applicable in the pending invasion but that could also be used as a means of mutually assured destruction should the aliens be revealed later to be an enemy. He suspected that the aliens would easily identify the risk associated with giving China the means to later attack them.

That resistance could be solved by convincing the aliens that there was a greater risk in not giving them the weapons. And that is what Liu had proposed in the position paper he'd written --- a way to lessen the risk for the aliens in the near-term. It would be risky if the aliens suspected China was misleading them, but he suspected that was a risk that Secretary Jiang would be willing to take for a stronger long-term position.

After Liu passed through yet another security screening, he was seated in a small office by himself. There was still a long hallway between him and Jiang's office suite. There were no electronics that he could see, although he was certain there would be cameras watching him closely. Since there were no supplies visible – not even a pen and paper – he opted to close his eyes and mentally envision a successful conversation to relax himself and stop imagining alien bugs crawling through the streets of Beijing.

Yuxuan was much too stressed to even fall into a light sleep, so he immediately heard footsteps approaching in the hallway. The door swung open. One of the men who had searched him at his apartment stood by. An older man wearing dark-tinted glasses despite the fluorescent lighting scowled at him from the hall. Barely acknowledging Yuxuan as he stood up, the older man said, "Follow me." He turned and walked the other direction. The guard walked a step or two behind them both. It reminded him of a funeral procession.

The richly carpeted hallway was lined with portraits of many of the current and former party leaders, which only reinforced the anxiety that Yuxuan felt. This was place of immense power, and he was an interloper – a pawn. These eyes of the men in the portraits seemed to be judging him, and with every step he became more convinced that he'd made a terrible mistake in coming here.

The adjutant to the secretary knocked once and stepped inside Jiang's office, closing the door behind him. Liu was left to stand like uninvited guest. The security guard had stepped off to the side of the door to stand with the other men.

After a few uncomfortable minutes, the secretary with the dark glasses opened the door, motioned to Yuxuan to step in, and said, "Sit there, and don't speak until spoken to." He pointed to an oversized chair in front of Jiang's desk.

Jiang continued to read as Yuxuan sat uncomfortably and waited. The minutes ticked by slowly, as Yuxuan tried not to panic. He could feel the sweat forming on his forehead but dared not reach for a handkerchief to wipe it away. He didn't know how others would respond if he reached into his pocket, even if he did it slowly. He decided it was better to sit with his hands in his lap, try not to squirm, and hope none of the sweat trickled into his eye.

When Jiang finished reading the document, he made a couple notes and then placed it inside a desk drawer. He steepled his fingers and stared at Liu for several minutes. Liu tried to sit still and stop thinking how the sweat was building on his brow. He had never been tortured, but this felt like a light version of the experience. It was maddening.

Yuxuan jerked to attention when Jiang finally spoke. "What did you hope to accomplish by sending me this nonsense?"

This was not at all how Yuxuan had imagined the conversation going. He stammered, "Only for the betterment of our great nation."

"You think risking war with a stronger, more advanced civilization will better our country?"

"Yes, I do," Yuxuan said with a little more confidence.

"You are fool then."

"On many things yes, but I think not on this. We have some

leverage now, but in the future we will have none if we only do as they say."

"So you propose we create an event that causes the aliens to provide us with weapons to defeat their enemy. And then we can use those weapons to protect ourselves once the war between the aliens is won. Why would they be so foolish as to trust us?"

"They won't trust us, but it seems they fear their enemies more. We are like guard dogs that can be beat into submission if we misbehave. They will have little use for us once their enemy is turned away."

"You work with Dr. Xi at the XINXI lab?"

It was framed as a simple question, but Yuxuan knew Secretary Jiang meant something deeper. "We are colleagues, yes."

"And have you discussed this idea with him?"

"No, I haven't discussed it with anyone. I prepared the paper on my own for your eyes only."

"Do you think Xi would agree with your proposal?"

Yuxuan tried not to fidget and reveal his inner thoughts. "No, I think he would disagree. In my opinion, he trusts the aliens too much and does not think they would turn on us."

"Do you think I agree with you? Is that why you sent the paper directly to me?"

"I don't presume to know your mind, Mr. Chairman. I do trust that you have a long-term vision of what is best for our nation and therefore would be less trusting of potential enemies. Even if they present themselves as friends now."

Jinag scowled. "I don't necessarily agree with your proposal. I would first need to know what you would propose as the threat that would make the aliens provide us with more advanced weaponry. There is nothing in your proposal to answer this question."

"I intentionally excluded my idea. I thought it best to avoid a written record of it, which could be perceived as treasonous by some."

"Now that you have my ear, tell me this idea of yours."

Yuxuan took a deep breath. This was the moment he'd been waiting for. "We lead the aliens [Thunderbird] to believe that their enemies [the Others] are threatening to exterminate us if we don't stay out of the coming war."

The secretary could not hide his surprise and skepticism. His face was flushed with anger. "Why would they believe such a ridiculous claim?"

"Because we will trigger a seismic event of such magnitude that they will have no choice but to believe the proof."

"You want us to attack ourselves?"

"Yes, it will be a false flag to show the aliens that their plans have been leaked and that we need immediate protection if they want us to help to defeat their enemies. We can also blame the leak on the Americans, which will undermine their any relationship that they might be building."

"Who would do this? We'd need to find another communication device and someone that is linked to the Americans but wants to sabotage them."

"Yes, Chairman. I know just the person. His name is Doctor Smith."

4

PUPPETEERS AND PUPPETS

When Miss Grey stepped off the plane at Seattle Tacoma International Airport, it felt like a homecoming.

She'd spent last year in the Seattle area working on the case to stop the Chinese from infiltrating the top-secret program being run for DARPA. That had been a big career break, but still felt guilty about profiting personally from a terrible series of events. She'd often wished she could go back in time and influence a different outcome. If only she could stop the chain of events that resulted in that dreadful disaster on September 11th.

The Seattle mist provided a sense of cleansing from the beltway politics she'd been immersed in the last six months. It was hard to get any further from DC and stay in the contiguous United States. It felt like a world away from the DC swamp with the mountains and Puget Sound to remind her. The events of the recent past were entirely escapable though. Where in the past she had been able to directly walk through airport terminals, she now saw armed soldiers on patrol. Sometimes they still carried machine guns. Police cars stopped anyone that tried to park too near the airport. September 11th had been used as a reason to increase the security state, and it had other implications too.

Grey had talked to Maxx before boarding the five-hour flight from Dulles, arranging for him to pick her up at the airport. She'd had to pull some strings using her senior position at the newly forming Department of Homeland Security to get a last-minute seat on the full flight. She could have arranged for a private flight, which would have been immeasurably more comfortable than the coach seat she was in, but it wouldn't have gotten her here any faster. Instead, she worked on her laptop until the battery died then tried to catch a short nap.

When she walked out of the terminal, she texted Maxx to tell him at what door she was waiting. She hadn't had time to pack a suitcase and was traveling light with only her briefcase. She always carried some personal items in her briefcase in the event she needed to spend the night on the cramped little sofa in her office. She'd asked one of the junior agents at the local office to grab a change of clothes from a local store and leave them at the hotel where she had made a reservation.

Due to the extra security and the long line of cars picking up arrivals, she could see Maxx and his pickup truck inching toward her from blocks away. Rather than wait for him to creep through the traffic knot, she walked in his direction. Unexpectedly, she sensed that she was being watched. Trying not to be paranoid, she discreetly checked to see if anyone was paying attention to her. No one stood out from the crowd when she looked around. That was somewhat reassuring, but there were dozens of places where someone could see her, and she couldn't see them.

As Maxx pulled up to the curb, she climbed into his truck and smiled. "Good to see you trimmed back that stupid mustache."

"I'm glad to see that the coupon for the therapy sessions I

sent you for Christmas are improving your interpersonal skills."

She laughed. "I made my boyfriend use them. I never had a chance to go."

"That's shocking. Did the classes work for him?"

"Nah, we broke up. But enough about me, how are you doing?" she said as she raised her eyebrows.

"You mean other than getting shot?"

"Yes, other than that, Mrs. Lincoln. How was the play?"

As Maxx merged into the heavy late-evening traffic heading away from the airport, she watched him pause to consider his next statement. In the past, that kind of break in the conversation meant he had some bad news he wanted to share and hadn't worked out the details well enough to tell her directly. Maxx preferred a straightforward telling of the facts, like he was reading the bullet points off a PowerPoint slide.

While she waited, she reached over and changed the station on the radio. "You know I hate country, and I think you do that deliberately to irritate me."

"No, that's my favorite song. Leave it alone," he said.

"If it's your favorite, what's its name?"

"Something, something heartbreaking women."

"Not even close, but a worthy effort." She turned off the radio. "Quit stalling and tell me what you've been holding back."

Maxx took a deep sigh. "It's obvious that Li Jing was paying back Xi for something. I can only think it was to punish him for messing up the arrangement she had with Smith. But why wait until now?"

"I think you're thinking about this all wrong," she answered.

He rolled his eyes. "You don't think Li Jing was trying to punish Xi by killing his daughter?"

"No, if it was only revenge, I don't think she would have waited this long, and she would have been less subtle. Killing his only daughter is brutally cold, but if she was trying to make him pay emotionally, she could have kidnapped Connie and strung out her vengeance for a long time. That would have been emotionally devastating for Xi."

"If it wasn't for revenge, then why?" he asked.

"I said it wasn't only for revenge. I'm sure that was a side benefit for Li Jing. This is only a theory, but I believe the primary reason was to keep Xi from working with the US and Thunderbird."

"Why would she care if Xi was working with us?"

"I don't think she personally would, but there are a lot of people in the intelligence community who want to keep China out of the picture. And that's who Li Jing worked for when she got involved. Officially, we want to work with China, but there are powerful people behind the scenes who don't trust China and want to keep them at a disadvantage. Xi is the key to the Chinese program, and if he won't participate, then all efforts at cooperation are dead."

"Even though Connie was killed here in the US, Li Jing would have to convince Xi that she was killed at the direction of the US."

"With the emotional state that Xi will be in, I don't think that will take a lot of convincing. He was already reluctant to work with us because of his hate for Doctor Smith, who was our primary lead on the program in the past. Xi's default position is distrust of the US, and it will be fueled by knowing that Li Jing killed his daughter."

"That brings me to the other information I wanted to tell you in person," Maxx said. "The reason I initially called you is that Connie had told us that her father had a change of heart and was open to meeting with us to begin planning."

"Oh no," she exclaimed. "I wonder if that's the answer to your question about why this is happening now."

"That would explain why Li Jing was willing to come out of

hiding. If she'd gotten inside information that Xi was changing his mind about collaborating with us, then she needed to do something to change it back."

"Do you think it will work?" she asked, eyeing the bandage on his arm. "Or do you think he'd listen to you or Gabby, especially since you were with his daughter at the end, even risking your lives to stop it?"

"Honestly, I think Gabby shot me by accident. But don't tell her that. She is very upset about the attack and not being able to save her friend. Telling her that she shot me would only make her feel worse. A mere flesh wound," he said with a bad British accent.

Miss Grey rolled her eyes at Maxx's poor attempt at mimicking Monty Python. "Back to my question, do you think Xi will still meet with you now that Connie is no longer able to organize a conversation?"

"I can ask Gabby to question him. She wants to call him and let him know she was with Connie in her last moments and that she was talking about him. It might open the door to discussion about why we were meeting with Connie at the time. It's worth a shot."

"I know it seems insensitive to be pushing this topic with Xi when his only daughter was killed a few hours ago, but the stakes are so high. We are at such a critical point of dealing with Thunderbird and getting ready for the arrival of the Others that I think we have to try."

"I get it. But Gabby's the only one he'll listen to. Xi tolerates me, but he only trusts me because of my relationship with Gabby. If I push him, he'll shut me down." He laughed, "Or send another hit man after me."

"You're right, Maxx. Gabby is the key to connecting to him now that Connie is no longer able to act as an intermediary. Every other avenue we've tried has been a dead end."

The car grew silent.

"It feels like you're trying to tell me something. Stop hinting around it."

Miss Grey sighed. I really didn't want to bring this up, after listening to your point about Xi's connection to Gabby, but I need to point out something else I think you're overlooking. The timing was deliberate."

"Yeah, you already made that point," Maxx said.

"No, I mean the timing this morning. When Gabby was with Connie."

"Ji Ling wanted Gabby to watch Connie get killed. To scare her off?"

"No, Maxx. If Li Jing knew that Connie was meeting with Gabby, I think it was an attempt to take out both of them at once. Two birds, one stone. She could have gotten to Connie at any time, but to attack her with Gabby was intentional."

"I was there too. She would have known she'd have to get past me to get at Gabby."

"She did get by you, Maxx. The only reason her plan failed was because she didn't consider that Gabby would be able to hold off the assassins long enough for you to return from chasing her."

"You think she lured me away so she could have both of them taken out at the same time?"

"I do. It's obvious Li Jing was trying to lure you away, leaving Connie and Gabby unprotected. By removing both at the same time, any chance of convincing Xi to meet would be ended. Not to mention that it would be emotionally crushing for you to know that you were there and failed. Li Jing would love that kind of malicious plan."

Maxx's jaw tensed as he relived the event, knowing that Miss Grey was probably right. "That means that Li Jing, and whoever she is working for, has put a target on Gabby's back again."

"Yes, I think she's in real danger. More so now that Connie is out of the picture."

Maxx had been traveling slightly over the speed limit on the freeway but began to add more speed and weave in and out of the traffic heading north.

"Slow down. Where is Gabby now?"

"At the apartment. She was going to come with me to pick you up, but she's exhausted and wanted to rest."

"Then I'm sure she's safe. You have that apartment secured, don't you?" Maxx had told Grey that after several failed attempts by angry criminals to catch him at home, he'd spent a large sum of money adding intrusion proof doors, windows, and an impenetrable security system. That extra security had been worth every penny he'd spent, when last year the killer Haoyu had failed while hunting Maxx and Gabby.

"As long as Gabby had the doors locked and set the alarm, there's no way to get in. But I keep thinking of getting a guard dog instead of that cat."

"If Gabby's safe at home at Fort Maxx, you can slow down now."

Maxx snickered but didn't ease off the accelerator. "You thought I was speeding up to get home and protect Gabby?"

"Well, aren't you?" she asked.

"No, remember she was the one who shot the hired gun and me," he said as he held up his bandaged arm. "In her current state of mind, anyone who attempts to attack her is the person who is going to get badly hurt."

"Then why are you going so fast?" she asked in confusion.

"Because there have been a couple cars tailing me since I picked you up at the airport. I thought I lost them in the arrivals area, but no such luck. I was seeing if I could put some space between us and get off the freeway unnoticed."

"Whoever they are, they don't work with me. Either they

were already tailing you, or someone figured out you were coming to pick me up."

"I'm certain no one was tailing me while I was driving to the airport, so these mystery people must have known when you were arriving and had people in a position to tail you. You have the nicest friends, Miss Grey."

"I doubt they're my friends. More likely someone at one of the other alphabet agencies wants to know where I went to in a hurry. News had probably already gotten around that Xi's daughter was killed, and people will want to take advantage of the situation."

Maxx veered around the slower traffic and moved into the carpool lane. "By now, they'll have traced my license and figured out it's me driving. I can ditch them if you don't want to be tracked."

"I'd rather not have them stuck to our bumper. If you have time, I'd like to stop by the federal building before I go to the hotel. And I'd prefer that we have a few uninterrupted minutes to make a quick, secure call so we can pass along the information you told me about Xi wanting to meet."

"Okay then. Make sure your seatbelt is on tight, because there is an offramp coming up quickly. With my four-wheel drive, I can get off the pavement to the side of the line of cars where they'll get stuck for at least a few minutes. That should be enough time for me to drive out of sight on a side road."

Miss Grey turned in her seat and studied the cars behind them. "Maxx, there are at least three cars, and they are aggressively moving through traffic behind us. They aren't interested in only tailing us. They are making a fast move toward us," she shouted.

"Do I have another minute? We're almost to the exit."

"They're trying to cut us off from getting over. You better move fast."

Maxx focused on slowing his breathing and concentrating

on the traffic around him. He couldn't do anything about the cars behind him. They'd either catch up or wouldn't.

"We're out of time. Go now," she said.

He yanked the wheel sharply to the right and jammed on the brakes to avoid rear-ending the car that had opened up half a car length in front of a semi-truck. With only inches to spare, he yanked the wheel further to the right and shot onto the shoulder of the freeway. He could hear the truck behind him skidding to miss him as the gap closed narrowly around them.

He clipped the bumper of the car in front of them with an awful screech of metal, but it wasn't enough to make Maxx lose control of his truck. It did force the car into the vehicle in front of them, starting a minor pile up. He grimaced as he sped past the chaos he could see forming in his rearview mirror.

While he focused on not getting stuck on the shoulder, Miss Grey turned around to see what was going on behind them. It was chaos in the exit lane, but she didn't see anyone else following them onto the shoulder of the road. Yet.

When he got to the exit ramp, Maxx took a hard left, cutting through the stop light and causing another traffic snarl up that would temporarily shut down the exit ramp. He felt a little guilty about the number of collisions that he'd caused, but he was more relieved to have put some distance between them and whoever was chasing them. After crossing back over the freeway overpass, he drove far into the industrial area. He then felt secure enough to jump onto some service roads he knew would make it impossible to follow him.

Miss Grey finally turned back around and settled into her seat, letting out a big breath. "I don't know who that was, but they were willing to do anything to try and follow us. Luckily, that semi-truck driver was angry enough at you that he pinned them to the shoulder, and they couldn't move up behind us."

"Do you still want to go to the federal building?" he asked.

"No, I think we should find a safe place and think this

through first. If they were waiting for me at the airport, they might know I'm going downtown and be waiting for us there."

Maxx drove into the back of a mostly deserted area of low-rise industrial buildings. There was no way to see his truck from the road, and there was no activity in the parking lot. He kept the engine running and pointed toward the exit as a precaution.

"This is a good spot for now. Who were we going to call at the federal building?"

Miss Grey thought for a minute then answered, "Senator Traficant."

"Isn't she the person who helped you out when we were trying to convince the president that Doctor Smith was a traitor?"

"Yes, she is well connected in DC. She's been very vocal about the need for us to collaborate with the Chinese. She's fixated on jointly communicating with Thunderbird, despite the tremendous pushback from the Pentagon and intelligence agencies."

"But why would she want to talk to me? I'm not even involved. I'm supporting Gabby, and Gabby was simply helping her friend Connie."

"I wanted you to hear this from her, Maxx, but I'll give you a heads up because you and Gabby are friends. She has gotten intelligence briefings that Gabby is in danger because she is, or was, too close to Connie. There are powerful people in the US and China who don't want us to work together."

"You weren't guessing when you mentioned that earlier? You believe Gabby is a target?"

"All I know is what the senator told me, and she wants to talk to you directly. She's asking for your direct involvement, not only because she thinks it the right thing to do but to protect Gabby."

Maxx paused for a minute then started driving slowly out parking lot.

"I don't know that I trust any politician. I feel like I'm getting dragged into something I don't want to get involved with. Again."

"But?"

"I'm not going to take a chance and leave Gabby exposed," he said as he accelerated onto the road and toward home.

5

ROCK AND ROLL FIFTIES

Jane stretched out on the oversized king bed. Naked except for the thin sheet she had pulled up to keep from getting chilled as the light sheen of sweat dried. She grabbed a cigarette from the open pack of Virginia Slims sitting on the nightstand and effortlessly puffed on it while she thought through her next move. In the bathroom next door, she could hear the man whistling "Only You" over the sound of the shower running.

Even in the dim morning light peeking through the heavy drapes, she could see the exaggerated décor. It was evident that it had been originally decorated by someone with taste but had been ruined by a less tasteful masculine eye. James, of course. He'd made it clear to her the first time that he'd brought her here that this was his room. His wife rarely came to Washington DC, preferring to spend her time at the family farm. On the rare occasion she was here, she slept in another bedroom by herself.

Jane had been here occasionally over the last year but rarely slept over. Normally, James would make it callously clear that she needed to dress and leave shortly after they were done having sex. But last night he'd had a lot to drink and had fallen asleep before asking her to go, so she'd kept perfectly still until he was deep asleep.

"I thought you were going back to your place," he said when he walked out of the bathroom wearing a bright-red robe. James had been handsome a few decades ago but had put on too much weight and lost too much hair to be called attractive now. His appeal wasn't physical. It was his proximity to power in a city that thrived on the ability to manipulate and influence.

"Good morning to you too," she shot back as she pulled up the sheet to her chin.

"We've talked about this before. There are too many nosey neighbors looking for a snippet of gossip. It's better for both of us if you're gone before sunrise."

She tried a more conciliatory tone, as she stretched across the bed to distract him. "We both fell asleep after the cocktails. Sorry, hun."

"Be more careful next time."

"I will. When you're finished in the bathroom, I'll rinse off and take off."

He cinched the robe that was a size too small and strode out of the bedroom. "I'm done. I've got some work to do downstairs in my office, so you can let yourself out. I'll see you at the office on Monday."

She balled her hands into fists under the sheet. *I genuinely hate this man.*

Through a tightly clenched jaw, she said, "Thanks for everything." The sarcasm practically dripped off her lips.

Even though James was more than twice her age, she was very adept at managing his constant need to be in control. At twenty-five, she'd had a few discrete affairs with rich, powerful men both at home in Kansas and here in Washington. While she engaged them with her beauty and easy sensuality, it was her balanced personality that allowed her to manipulate men so easily. It never seemed to occur to them that someone so accepting would have ulterior motives. They were convinced that they were always the smartest people in the room. She was careful not to disabuse them of that belief.

Last night, after James had fallen asleep, she had taken the handheld Brownie camera from her purse and taken some pictures of her and James in various positions on the bed. She'd also wandered throughout the house to take a few posed pictures in other rooms including the bedroom his wife slept in. She'd learned early that a little insurance in black and whites went a long way if things didn't turn out the way she'd planned.

Last week, she'd located her next lover. She was busily laying the trap in her free time. Nothing absolute had happened, but she was sure that it would. She wanted to be sure that James didn't make things messy and muddle her next romance. Last night had gone as she'd planned, and a few sleeping pills mixed in his Manhattan had made sure she was able to work uninterrupted.

Once she was sure that she was going to be able to transition to a new relationship, she planned to meet James for dinner in a public place. She'd explain sadly that it was time for them to say goodbye and hope that they could stay civil and mature about the breakup. If it didn't, she'd give him a gentle reminder that she had enough evidence to make life difficult for him. She could escalate the separation if she needed to, but that had only happened once. The threat of going to the police with pictures and witnesses that support a claim of assault was enough to get people to quickly look for an easy exit.

After taking a brief shower, she brushed out her long blonde hair. She didn't want to leave the house with wet hair, which would get all frizzy in the humidity. She pulled a floral sun dress out of her overnight bag and slipped it on with a pair of casual black flats. She'd fit right in with the other relaxed Saturday shoppers at the market.

"Are you done up there?" James yelled from the bottom of the stairs.

She bit her tongue. "Yes, I'm about finished," she answered.

"Someone is on their way over, and they'll be here in a few minutes. If they get here before you're dressed, simply stay up there until they leave."

"I'm hurrying as fast as I can," she yelled back as she tried to finish brushing out her thick hair. She didn't want to get stuck up here any longer than she had to. Her skin was beginning to crawl thinking about spending another hour trapped in the house.

James was powerful member of the House. However, this was only his second term, and he still was learning how the game was played in Washington. His first term had gone poorly, and when it was time for reelection in the fall of 1954, he'd been desperate to find some help with the campaign. Jane's father, Jim Traficant, a powerful businessman in Kansas, offered financial backing in exchange for supporting legislation that he wanted pushed through congress. Jim Traficant's other condition was that James hire Jane as his staff lead when he won reelection.

Jane had been a supportive and dedicated team member during the campaign. When James had been reelected, she had left a position at one of her father's companies and made the transition to James's chief of staff. From there, it had been an easy transition from confidant to lover. Jane had made sure that she'd done enough planning that James's marriage was ripe for disruption. He was oblivious to the influence she'd had both in politics and his personal life.

Jane looked at her reflection in the mirror to make sure she looked presentable as she prepared to leave. When the front doorbell rang, she sighed in frustration and threw the hairbrush.

"Damn it, so close to making it out of here," she muttered angrily to herself.

The sound of the doorbell was still echoing in the downstairs hallway when it was followed by a loud knock on the front door. Clearly, whoever had come over to see James wasn't very patient. That was a bad sign.

"I'm coming. Calm down," James yelled as he moved downstairs toward the front door.

He might have been yelling partly for her benefit, she realized. She sat on the side of the bed and groaned.

Hopefully this will be over quick, she thought.

James threw open the front door with a loud bang. "You guys got over here faster than I thought. What's the rush?"

"We ignored the speed limit," one of the men answered with a slight New York accent.

"Like always," another voice added with a snicker.

"Come on inside then. We can go into the kitchen and grab a cuppa, and you can tell me what this emergency visit is all about."

"You alone?" the second voice asked as he walked inside.

Jane could hear the heavy front door close. "Only me," James lied.

"Good, because you've got a bit of reputation," the first man said.

"My wife is out of town," James said with a hint of irritation.

"Enough with the chitchat," the first man said clearly annoyed. "It's not a social call. Let's grab some coffee."

Jane could hear James and the visitors moving out of the foyer and toward the kitchen at the back of the house. The voices became quieter without the echo off the tiles in the foyer, but still loud enough to hear clearly when she stepped out into the hallway.

"So, David, what's this all about?" James asked.

"Did you read the report the CIA sent over yesterday?" asked the first man.

"It was kind of hard not to read it. The guy who delivered it sat in my office staring at me the entire time I was reading it. Then he took it back when I was done."

"What did you think?" the second guy asked.

"I think it was something you guys dreamt up while you were testing out LSD in the lab," James answered with a snort.

"I assure you that is not the case," David said. "Every detail has been double and triple verified."

Jane could hear an occasional cupboard opening and closing so she assumed that they were still in the kitchen. But the talking had stopped.

After a long silence, she began to wonder if she'd missed something.

Minutes later, James asked, "This device exists, and we have it?"

What device?

The second man chimed in, "Yes, it's in a secure location far from Washington, DC."

"Are there any plans to use it?" James asked.

"Nothing soon. That's why we're here. All your colleagues on the committee are pushing back until we do more testing. We need you to nudge them."

"Why would I pressure them?"

"Because we'd double our usual contribution to your retirement plan," David said.

"This is really going out too far on a limb. I think I'll pass this time," James said.

"It wasn't really a request, Congressman. Don't press your luck," the second man murmured.

"Alright, then make it triple and everyone is happy."

"Fine. Here's a list of who we need onboard and an advance. You've got two weeks to get us enough yes votes."

She could hear James sigh. "I'll get it done. Unless there's anything else, can I get back to my Sunday morning now?"

"Nah, we're square," said the second voice. "We'll show ourselves out."

Jane could hear the men walking toward the front door and closing it behind them.

After waiting a few minutes to make sure she could hear the men backing their car out of the driveway, she walked downstairs. James was in the kitchen cleaning up the few dirty dishes and dumping out the coffee pot.

"Is there any coffee left?" she asked. "I could use a cup before I take off."

He turned around quickly when she walked into the room, almost dropping a coffee mug in surprise. With his eyes open wide, he glanced guiltily toward the front door.

"Don't worry. They're gone," she said.

"They better be, or both of us will be in big trouble." James poured her a cup of coffee. "I thought you had left."

"I had planned to, but now I'm glad I stuck around."

"Those aren't people you want to get involved with, Jane."

"Who are they?" she asked innocently.

"They're the bad people who really run this town."

"There are lots of those, James. I imagine they'd say the same thing about you."

His face hardened. "Be careful. You're stepping on thin ice."

"Oh, I know. It's thin ice for both of us. That's why you're going to tell me why they were here."

"The hell I will," he said with menacing tone.

"I heard everything. What's this device that they were telling you about?"

He walked over and pressed his finger into her chest threateningly. "I'm warning you. Drop it and leave. And if you know what's good for you, don't mention this to anyone again. Not even me."

She had more leverage than he realized. She had compromising pictures and could easily blackmail him, but she wasn't ready to play that card yet. She didn't want him to know that she had accumulated enough hard evidence to create a scandal that would ruin him. She would save her ace card for another time.

"And I'm warning you. Don't threaten me. I'd hate for someone to find out about our little fling. And by someone, I mean my father."

His face turned red, and he took a step back. "You wouldn't do that," he growled.

"Don't test me, because I will. And my daddy will ruin your name forever. He'd never forgive you for taking advantage of me. Then he'll make sure some very bad people show up to teach you some manors."

She stepped away and sat demurely on a chair at the kitchen table. She crossed her shapely legs and rearranged the flowers in the vase.

"We can avoid all that nastiness if you will tell me what you know about this device. I promise I won't tell anyone else," she said with modest smile.

He sat down and pulled his chair next to her. He lowered his voice even though they were alone in the house. "All I know is that the Air Force recovered some technology that doesn't appear to be from Earth. I thought it was from the Ruskies, but it's not. The Air Force handed it over to a secret government program called Advance Research Projects Agency. They want approval to do some scientific trials."

She paused and tapped the table while she considered this revelation.

"And the people at ARPA are sure it's an alien device?" she asked.

"The scientists say the technology is way beyond anything we or the Russians could create. They've never seen anything like it before."

She raised her eyebrows. "Is it dangerous?"

"Unknown. They believe it's used for communication, but some people think it's a weapon – like a booby trap. That's why they're looking for political cover."

She had heard about this new agency being formed while having drinks with her contacts at the Defense Department. No one had any idea what this agency was working on, but there had been plenty of speculation. Theories ranged from new atomic weapons delivered by supersonic planes like the X-1 to manned space flight being developed by NASA. These ideas intrigued her, but she'd never been able to get concrete information on any of these secret projects. Before now.

"I need a copy of that memo so I can read it myself," she said. "Nothing personal, but I know how trustworthy you are. Or more to the point, aren't."

She could see the red creeping back into his face as his face twisted into an ugly scowl.

"I already told you everything I know," he snarled.

"Here's what's going to happen, James," she said calmly. "You're going to get me a copy of that memo, and I'll help you get the votes you need to get these guys off your back."

"I'm not giving you any money, if that's what you're angling for."

"I don't want your money. What I want is to be on the inside of this program. You help me get connected, and in exchange I will help you solve this problem. And of course, I keep my mouth shut about our little tête-à-tête."

He paused for a moment. "I never realized you were capable of this much deceit. You're not such a dumb blonde after all."

She smiled. "I'll take that as a compliment. Do we have a deal?"

"I don't like it, but we have a deal. But don't double cross me. And now that I know what a snake you are, I'll be watching you closely."

You still have no idea, she thought.

She stuck out her hand. "It's a deal then."

He raised his eyebrows and pushed himself back from the table. "I'm not shaking your hand. I hope you get what you want out of this, because you're way out of your league."

Jane stood and walked to the window where she could see her reflection. She straightened her dress and made sure her hair was in place, before turning and heading for the garage to get her car.

"This isn't what I want," she said. "It's only a means to end. Exactly like you."

"So what's the end?" he asked.

"I will be one of the most powerful people in the world. Senator, president, or whatever. The title doesn't matter."

He laughed disdainfully. "You're not in Kansas anymore, Dorthy. This is where the big boys play."

"Don't worry about me, James. I know more about how the game is played at twenty-five then you'll ever understand."

She knew that she'd have to keep him under her thumb. He was a rat, but an arrogant one. What he didn't realize was that the next lover she was arranging to replace him with was well connected at the FBI. It would only take a simple nudge to get James under surveillance and arrested.

"You can show yourself out," he said as he turned away.

"Thanks for the exciting weekend," she said as she walked out the garage door. "I'll see you at work tomorrow morning. Have that report ready for me."

6

OUT OF THE SHADOWS

Maxx parked the pickup truck in the garage under his condo building on Capitol Hill. He watched carefully for anything that seemed out of place. He was certain that they'd lost the tailing cars that had followed them from the airport. They might have had the foresight to send people to watch his office and home in the event they weren't able to catch him and Miss Grey on the freeway. He didn't have any idea who was following him, so he didn't want to make any assumptions about how smart or dumb they were.

He'd tried to call Gabby on her cell phone while they were driving, but she hadn't answered. She had told him before he left for the airport that she'd go home when she was finished at the crime scene. He speculated that she might have turned her phone off to relax. She might be with the police if they were doing extended follow up interviews. Since her car wasn't in her parking space, he figured that she was still sorting things out and hadn't made it back home. It was worrying but not yet alarming despite the news that Li Jing had been targeting her. He kept trying to reach her on her phone.

When Maxx and Miss Grey stepped off the elevator in his

condominium building into the carpeted hallway, he hesitated. He instantly sensed that something wasn't right. He put his arm out to block Miss Grey from moving any closer to his condo door while he stopped to listen. He reached for the concealed pistol under his jacket when the hair on the back of his neck stood up. His intuition had saved him more time than he could count, and he wasn't going to ignore his instincts now.

Miss Grey followed his lead and unholstered her weapon too. She turned to face the hallway behind them while Maxx focused his full attention ahead of them. Between the two of them, they had eyes on all the doorways and elevators on this floor.

"What's wrong?" she mouthed silently when he looked in her direction.

Maxx shrugged and shook his head. "I'm not sure," he whispered.

He began slowly moving forward staying close to wall. The door to his unit was on the same side of the hallway as the elevator exit, so it was hard to see without stepping out into the middle of the hall. He kept his breathing steady while he held the gun low and ready. He still wasn't sure what had triggered his subconscious, but between breaths he could hear the low whistle of air moving in the hall. He couldn't pinpoint the precise source of the sound, but it was an unusual noise in the normally quiet corridor.

The wood unit doors were spaced unevenly on both sides of the hall. The door to his unit was located at the end of the passage, which gave him an extra sense of privacy. Miss Grey stayed close to his side as he moved stealthily down the long hall, keeping watch behind them.

When he was ten feet from his door, he tilted his head out into the middle of the hallway to see around the door jamb. He could see from the edge around the door that it wasn't closed tight. The sound that he had heard was air blowing out from his condo, around his partly open door and into the hall. He had spent a lot of money upgrading the security on his condo, and that upgrade had included a solid core door and a state-of-the-art alarm system. The only way to keep the door open like that would be if someone had intentionally propped it open.

Maxx knew that Gabby would never leave the door braced open like that. Ever since the incidents last fall, she had been hyper vigilant about closing and locking the door. She would even set the alarm in "home" mode when she was home alone during the evening.

He turned to Miss Grey. "My door isn't closed," he said quietly.

"Should we back off and call for the police?" she whispered.

He rolled his eyes and snickered quietly. "Hell no. I'm going in. Try not to shoot me."

She blew out a big breath and gave him an unconvincing nod.

Maxx checked his pistol again and brushed the bead of sweat from his forehead. He took three giant steps toward the partly open door. Staying in a semi crouch, he stepped in front of the door and put his shoulder into the door. His weight drove it back. He heard the wall crack as the doorknob slammed into the drywall. He stepped inside his home with the pistol leading the way.

The lights were off, but there was a stream of afternoon light coming from the windows in the living room and kitchen. He could see everything plainly despite the gloom.

He pointed to the entry closet and small bathroom by the front door. Indicating to Miss Grey that she should clear those rooms then close the door behind them. He didn't want anyone slipping in behind them and catching them unprepared.

While she was doing a quick clearing of the space, he stepped forward into the kitchen. Empty. There was some food and trash on the counter. He knew that he and Gabby hadn't left the kitchen in this condition when they had left the house this morning. Gabby was a stickler for a clean kitchen, so someone else had been here.

After examining the kitchen, he paused to wait for Miss Grey to catch up. The hall to the two bedrooms and bathroom was on the right, and the living room was straight ahead. They had to make a choice. Stay together or split up. He waved her ahead toward the living room since they'd be able to clear it quickly. There was no place for an intruder to hide in that room.

When Maxx stepped into the living room, he spotted a man sitting on the couch, drinking a can of soda. He was very fair skinned, slightly balding with a moon face and paunch that was exaggerated by his slumped posture on the sofa. Dressed in cargo shorts and Birkenstocks with socks, he looked like he had wandered in from one of the nearby tech buildings. He didn't look like the intruder Maxx had envisioned, but he aimed his pistol as him anyway, keeping his finger off the trigger.

"Hey, Maxx," the man said with a slight tilt of his head.

"Do I know you? And how did you get in here?" he asked.

Miss Grey yelped when she walked into the room behind him. "What are you doing here?" she said.

"That's no way to greet a former colleague," the man said. "Sorry about the unexpected entry, but some of my friends from the agency let me in. They said to say hello. Hello."

Maxx raised his eyebrows quizzically and lowered his pistol slightly. "Can somebody fill me in before I shut this guy's smart mouth?"

The portly man on the couch waved his free hand toward Grey. "Go ahead. I'm only the guest."

"This is Mr. Green. He was the head of Team Tacoma." She was still shaking her head in disbelief as she sat down on the edge of a nearby chair.

"Was? What's he doing now?" Maxx asked.

"I don't know," she answered. "He died on September 11th. At least that's what everyone thought."

"Ta da," Mr. Green exclaimed. "Operational security and all that, you know."

"How did you escape? That entire floor was obliterated, and then the tower collapsed. No one could have survived that."

Mr. Green took a sip of the soda and slowly put the can on the end table next to him.

"All true. Fortunately for me, the senator had prearranged for the use of the express elevator. I walked right out of the communication room and on to the waiting elevator. I was on my way out of the building when the initial blast occurred. I missed it by a minute. After that, it was the senator's decision to keep my survival secret. As it turned out, that was a smart move when we later learned that Doctor Smith had disappeared."

Miss Grey had shown Maxx the massive Team Tacoma facility beneath downtown Seattle in September. She had revealed the extent of the project when they were trying to stop the Chinese spy ring that was hunting him. Even when she had revealed the details of Tacoma to him after 9/11, she had been careful never to disclose any names.

"Now that we see that you're alive, what are you up to?" asked Maxx.

"I'm still leading Team Tacoma," he said nonchalantly as he reached inside his jacket.

"Keep your hands where I can see them. She may trust you, but you're still a stranger to me," Maxx said.

"Sorry, sorry." Mr. Green slowly withdrew his wallet from the coat pocket. "I was going to show you my government ID."

"You don't need to convince me. If Miss Grey says you're good, I'll listen. Until then, you're just another spook who broke into my house and stole my Dr. Pepper."

Miss Grey took the wallet and flipped it to Green's ID. After studying his badge for a moment, she shrugged and handed it back to him.

"It looks legit, but I'll need more verification than that. I'll look into it later, but I'm curious about why you're here and telling Maxx and I that you're alive."

"The senator is extremely motivated to make sure the communication with Thunderbird is successful. She told me to work with you to get a meeting set up with the Chinese. She received intelligence that Xi is willing to meet."

Maxx arched his eyebrows. He and Gabby had only learned this news from Xi's daughter Connie this morning immediately before she was murdered. He knew Gabby well enough to know that she wouldn't have revealed sensitive information to the police even under duress. That meant either Connie's phone had been bugged or the senator had a source inside the Chinese organization.

"Where did she get the intelligence from?" Miss Grey asked, pressing the point.

Maxx rubbed his hands across the stubble on his jaw. Grey was thinking along the same lines as he was.

Green moved his eyes around the room as if he was thinking. "I'm not sure about that. Why does it matter who told Senator Traficant?"

"If there is a Chinese source on Xi's team that the senator is monitoring, it would be important for us to know so we aren't running blind," she said.

"I'm more concerned that it's not the Chinese but someone at Langley," Maxx said. "I want to know who all the players are on our team."

"Maybe the leak was your girlfriend. She probably blabbed to the police. They would have had someone from the FBI sit in on her debriefing because of her relationship to Connie and Xi."

Maxx raised the pistol an inch and stepped closer to Green.

"Keep talking, asshat. You've broken into my house, and now I'm feeling unsafe. Criticizing Gabby is all the motivation I need to put a bullet in you."

Beads of sweat appeared on Green's forehead as he leaned back, deeper into the couch cushions.

"Whoa, slow down, cowboy," he gulped. "My apologies. No offense intended."

"This isn't going to get us anywhere," Maxx said. "Forget the question about intel source for now. You'll only end up getting blood all over my furniture."

Grey interjected, "How is Maxx supposed to set up a meeting with Xi with his daughter dead? She was his intermediary with Xi. And I have no direct contact. The senator knows all this."

Mr. Green ran his fingers through his thinning hair. "I suppose she does. But she said to tell Maxx to use Connie's phone and call Xi on it. He will answer and talk to you."

"That's going to take a while. I'm sure her phone is locked up in evidence, and they aren't going to release it to me no matter how sweet I am."

"You're right. I'm going to reach into my coat pocket again, if you don't mind," said Green.

"Slowly using two fingers," Maxx growled.

Green pulled a flip phone from his pocket. "This is for you," he said as he placed the phone on the coffee table.

Maxx squinted and stared at the phone. It took him a moment to realize it was Connie's phone from this morning. "You didn't even bother to wipe off the blood, you ghoul."

Mr. Green shrugged. "It was dried by the time I got it. Anyhoo, the security code is written on the tape on the back."

Miss Grey picked up the phone gingerly and punched in the code. "I guess we should give Xi a call if he's expecting to hear from us."

"Dial the number for me, and we'll see if he answers," Maxx said.

Miss Grey scrolled through the address book on Connie's phone and selected the phone number for "Papa." After the first ring, she handed the phone to Maxx.

Maxx was convinced that the call was going to be sent to voicemail, but a man with a light Chinese accent answered in hesitant English, "Hello. Who is calling?"

"This is Maxx King in Seattle. Is this Dr. Xi?"

"Yes, it is. How may I help you, Mr. King?"

Maxx tilted his head to the side and squinted at Green. "I was told to call you to discuss setting up a time and place to meet."

The phone line was silent for moment. "Meet? No. This is a very difficult time for me personally. Perhaps we can discuss this in a few days."

"I understand, Doctor. I am sorry about your daughter. She was a wonderful woman. And it was a tragedy."

"What do you know about my daughter?" Xi said bitterly.

"I was with her when she was murdered this morning. My girlfriend and I were meeting with Connie for coffee when we were attacked."

"Ah. Then Gabby is your friend?" Xi asked. "So you must be the man who Haoyu was trying to kill?"

"Yes to both questions. Connie told us this morning that you were willing to meet and that you'd like me to call to discuss the arrangements."

"This is a very bad time. I've been up all night taking to your police and trying to make the arrangements for my daughter to be flown home."

Maxx was hesitant to push Xi too much, knowing that he was dealing with his daughter's murder. On the other hand, he knew it might be a while before they could talk again. With everyone feeling the pressure to get the US and China working collaboratively before the deadline, he was going to be press ahead. Even if he sounded like an inconsiderate jerk.

"I do understand this is a bad time, but this will only take a few moments. What if we plan to meet in Hawaii in a couple days? I'll work with the government here to get your daughter transported to Oahu. And then you meet us there and fly her the rest of the way home."

"You would do this?" Xi asked.

Miss Grey had moved closer to Maxx so she could hear both sides of the conversation. She nodded her head vigorously.

"Yes, I'll get it done. And when we are in Hawaii, we can spend a few hours between flights to discuss our common interests."

"I will make the plans to arrive in Hawaii two days from now. Send me the details, and I'll coordinate my arrangements. Obviously, we will need a secure meeting place, which I'm sure you can arrange in a private location. To be transparent, I am not committed yet to working with the US on this project. But I will listen."

"Yes, a remote meeting spot. I'll be escorted by a couple of other people who work for the US government. I am not officially a representative in the discussion."

Xi paused. "That will be fine only if it is not Doctor Smith. I do not trust him and still do not fully trust the United States. I'm sure you can understand why."

"I assure you, Doctor Smith is not working for the US."

"Good, that man is evil. I don't plan to bring anyone with me to the meeting. It will look suspicious if I am traveling with an entourage if the stated purpose is to collect my daughter."

"That's fine. We'll keep the group small. I'll email you the details as soon as I have them."

"Thank you for everything, Mr. King. I will see you soon," Xi said as he ended the call.

"I can't wait to hit the beach on Waikiki," Mr. Green muttered under his breath as Maxx causally slipped Connie's cell phone into his pocket.

***

Liu Yuxuan took off the headphones and placed them in his desk drawer. He was grinning from ear to ear, delighted with what he'd heard.

He had taken the not-so-extraordinary step to have Xi's phone tapped by the security team when he had been promoted to director of the XINXI program. He had never anticipated that the wiretap would be used for more than collecting small tidbits of information that he could use to influence the program for his personal gain. But Xi's latest call from the American – Maxx King – had given him the leverage he'd been waiting for.

He'd been concerned when he'd met with Chairman Jiang that he'd overstepped his ability to intercede effectively. To be successful, he needed to destroy Xi's credibility and undermine the US relationship. He knew that his idea of a false flag attack was a good one, but it was dependent on Xi's ability to get the Americans to trust him. They had to be convinced that the device had backfired and that Xi was to blame.

Now all he had to do was get invited to the meeting in Hawaii without letting Xi know that he'd been listening in on the call.

After a few moments of thought, he had the solution. He knew who could make it happen without raising suspicion.

He dialed the number on the private number he kept in his wallet.

"I need you to do me a small favor," he said when the woman answered the phone.

7

REVENGE BY THE DROP

"Time to go," Maxx said as he moved toward the front door.

"But it's cozy here. I was thinking of taking a nap," Green said as he yawned and overemphasized a stretch.

"You're leaving with us. And then I'm getting the place fumigated."

"No need to be rude," Green huffed. "You should get better security though. You don't want strangers waltzing in during the middle of the night."

"It won't happen again. Next time, I'll have a surprise waiting for you and your friends from the company."

Maxx was visibly irritated that one of the American intelligence agencies had been able to bypass his security system. He'd spent a lot of money to make sure that he and Gabby would be safe here. Now he realized it had been a false sense of security.

"Touchy, aren't you? If I can't stay here, how about giving me a ride down to the FBI office at the federal building? I need to talk to some people there."

"You wouldn't happen to know where Gabby is, would you?" asked Grey.

Mr. Green snorted. "I was wondering when you'd ask."

Maxx could feel the heat rising to his neck. He was really, really beginning to dislike this guy. *I shouldn't shoot him, but...*

"Just answer," Maxx said as he began to move the barrel on his gun in Green's direction.

"I'm happy to help. Relax, my friend. She's down at the FBI office. It'll be a twofer if you give me a ride down there. I'll even let you park in my special parking spot."

"Fine, you can sit in the back of the truck."

Miss Grey rolled her eyes. "Why is Gabby at the FBI office?"

"That, I don't know. After she finished with the police, the FBI still had some questions they wanted to discuss with her in private. My guess is that their interest aligns with our call with Dr. Xi."

The three of them moved out of Maxx's living room and to the elevators. Maxx was careful to lock the door and set the alarm behind them, whatever good that would do if the government wanted to get back inside.

They took Maxx's pickup truck with Grey in the passenger seat and Mr. Green huddled in the back trying to stay warm. Maxx laughed every time he could hear him yelp. He couldn't help but snicker when he went around a corner so fast that it threw Green sliding around in the pickup bed.

As promised, Mr. Green had a reserved spot in the underground garage at the federal building. From there they were able to quickly get through security. Green hurried off with a half-hearted wave.

Miss Grey showed her badge to a supervisor at the visitor entrance. Security had increased significantly since 9/11. Last year when she worked out of this building, she would have been able to easily breeze through the screening. Now they were faced with metal detectors and a thorough search. Miss

Grey was allowed to hold on to her weapon, but Maxx was forced to leave his weapon behind in a gun locker. Even though he was in a secure federal building, he couldn't help but feel slightly exposed after the day he'd already had.

Once they were cleared at the security entrance, Maxx and Miss Grey were escorted up a small conference room on the fourth floor and told to wait for the assigned agent to arrive. The conference room was the usual mix of cheap plastic chairs and laminated table. A vinyl floor that had accumulated years of yellow wax in the corners and off-white walls that hadn't been painted since John Edgar Hoover had led the FBI. At least there wasn't a camera visible. Maxx hated those things.

After a few minutes of silence, there was a solid knock on the door, and an agent in a rumpled white shirt and grey suit stepped into the room. In his thirties, he was already balding but offered a firm handshake and solid eye contact. Sporting a Mariners tie with the suit gave Maxx hope that he was going to be able to talk straight. He loathed dealing with the joyless Feds who wandered around the building.

The agent held out a hand. "Miss Grey. Maxx King. I'm Agent Hovis. Nice to meet you. I've heard a lot about the two of you. I can't say that I believe all of it though. How can I help you?"

"Thanks for meeting with us on short notice," Miss Grey jumped in. "This isn't an official visit, at the moment. We are looking for a friend we were told is here."

"Gabby Fisher. Gabrielle, if she's wound up," Maxx added.

Hovis laughed politely. "We are still in the process of interviewing her after the murder this morning. I understand that you were also there, Mr. King."

"It's Maxx, not Mr. King. Mr. King is my dad. Yes, I was there when Connie was killed. Both Gabby and I were interviewed by the police. So I'm confused why she is still here."

"Since we're on a first-name basis, call me Keith. Let me be clear. Gabrielle is under no suspicion, and there is nothing suspicious about her testimony."

"Does she have an attorney present?" Miss Grey asked.

"No, and she is free to leave at any time. The questions are related to Connie. I assume that you both know who Connie's father is?"

"Of course," Grey answered. "She's been very open about that. Her visa and security clearance were reviewed by several agencies when she moved here for school and work."

"So I was told. But something happened after 9/11 that raised her profile to a 'watch' notification. I don't have the details, but after her name was fed into the computer, it generated a demand to interview at our office, and I was assigned to follow up."

This line of questioning wasn't getting Maxx anywhere. It seemed this discussion was outside of Agent Hovis's knowledge about Xi's involvement with the Thunderbird device. Perhaps Xi had been linked to the attack at TechCom last September and suspected of terrorist activity.

Maxx stood up. "Let's get Gabby in here. I'm sure we can quickly clear this up."

Agent Hovis waved his hand at Maxx. "Have a seat. We will do that as soon as she is done with her interview."

Miss Grey raised her eyebrows. "What interview? You're here, so who's interviewing her?"

Hovis sighed heavily. "That's what I was getting to. The system triggered the 'watch' notice to several federal agencies, not only the FBI."

"I know it wasn't DHS, or I would have been notified," Grey shot back. "What other agency is here, Agent Hovis?"

The FBI agent rolled his eyes. "Central Intelligence."

"This is crazy," Maxx said with a growl.

"I suggest you take us to her right now," Miss Grey interjected angrily. "Either that or I'm going to start making calls. That will not be a contest you'll win."

"I'm not the bad guy here," said Hovis as he stood up and put his hands out. "I'll take you to Gabby and you can hash it out with the dude from the CIA. Simply a heads up, he's a real piece of work."

Hovis, Grey, and Maxx took the stairs up a floor. Maxx had thought the floor below was dingy and needed a cleaning. But this floor was literally a whole new level of decrepit. When Maxx pointed the dilapidated state, Keith told him that the FBI only rarely visited this floor. It was reserved for the exclusive use by some of the other transitory intelligence services. Most of the agents avoided the area completely because of bad vibes.

After winding through a maze of narrow hallways and empty offices, Agent Hovis stopped in front of a gray metal door with a tiny window that was slightly cracked.

"Don't say I didn't warn you," he said as he popped the door open and stepped inside without knocking.

"Get the hell out," a man barked.

"Sorry to interrupt, sir, but I have some visitors who are insisting that they speak with Miss Fisher," Hovis replied calmly.

Maxx could see the man over the top of Hovis's shoulder. He was wearing a Hawaiian shirt with a bright-red floral pattern tucked into chinos. It was completely out of place with his crewcut. He had a pair of aviator sunglasses dangling by a cord around his neck.

"I know that voice," Miss Grey said with a grimace.

Hovis started to introduce them, "Associate Deputy Director Anderson, this is—"

Anderson cut him off. "I know who they are, you moron. It's high and mighty Miss Grey and her sidekick Maxx King. I told you not to interrupt my interview."

"It's nice to see you too, Barth," said Miss Grey as she pushed past Hovis into the tiny interview room. "I should have suspected it would be you putting your nose into places that it doesn't belong."

While Grey and Anderson were busy making snide comments to each other, Maxx and Gabby made eye contact. She gave him a subtle wave and tired smile. He winked in return.

Maxx pulled up one of the heavy, gray metal chairs and sat down forcefully next to Gabby. "So what're we talking about?" he said to no one in particular.

"I'm following up with Miss Fisher on details regarding this morning's incident," Anderson said as he stared icily at Maxx.

"Cool," said Maxx. "Since I was there too, I'll be glad to corroborate whatever Gabby says. Then we can get out of this dump and go home."

"I don't think this topic involves you, Maxx. It is more connected to confidential information about Gabby and Connie's work at TechCom."

Maxx turned to Gabby. "Is that true?" he asked her.

"Not exactly," she said. "Most of the questions have been ambiguous, and I'm not going to divulge anything confidential to this guy anyway. Even if he's from the CIA."

"There you go, Barth. I guess we're done here unless you can be more explicit about what you're fishing for," Maxx said as he started to stand.

Director Anderson's cheeks turned a bright red. Maxx could see him working his jaw as both Miss Grey and Agent Hovis tried to hide smirks.

Anderson paused. He looked like he was struggling to get his temper under control. His hand clenched open and closed for a minute before he relaxed. It was completely silent in the room while everyone waited to see who would make the next move.

"All right. Let's restart this conversation to make it more

productive," Barth said as he took a seat at the table. "Why doesn't everyone take a seat?"

Miss Grey rolled her eyes slightly but sat down in the last chair. Agent Hovis leaned casually against the wall and picked at a piece of tape that was covering a hole.

Maxx lifted his head toward Anderson. "Bring us up to speed. Gabby and I were there when Connie was shot this morning. I've told Grey all about it, and Hovis heard it already during Gabby's debrief. What are we missing?"

"The missing piece is extremely confidential. Can I trust that everyone will keep this information in this room?"

Everyone nodded.

"It goes back a few months. After 9/11, we started watching Xi closely to see what his next move would be. We have some inside sources that are willing to give us some information, although he's working on a project that is locked up tighter than a drum. But we picked up on some personal issues that we had missed before."

"Personal like what? Drugs, women, money?" asked Grey.

"Nothing certain, but he has a relationship that he goes out of his way to hide from the CCP. About once a month, he evades his security detail and meets a woman. They never meet in the same place twice, and it's usually in public."

"If it's not sexual, is it a family member or friend he's keeping hidden from the government?"

"That's what we thought at first too. Likely family members he's trying to protect from the security goons. But when we went back into his records, we couldn't find any relatives that were unaccounted for on his or his dead wife's side of the family."

"So what?" asked Hovis. "The guy is single. Maybe it was a secret girlfriend."

Anderson shrugged. "No one saw any signs of a romantic

relationship. Nothing in the pictures or videos showed anything more graphic than a long hug."

Maxx could see Gabby tapping her foot under the table. Like him, she must be starting to feel that Anderson was stringing them along.

"Cut to the chase," Maxx said. "Who was she?"

"We didn't know. An old friend with no background as far as we could tell. Until one day she happens to be visited in her shop by someone we thought we recognized. A former employee of the CIA."

"Stop the theatrics," said Maxx. "Who was it?"

"Li Jing," said Anderson with a mug look.

"What the hell?" Miss Grey and Agent Hovis both said at the same time.

"Xi was working with Li Jing the entire time?" Gabby exclaimed. "That doesn't make any sense."

"No, I doubt it," Anderson responded. "We have Li Jing's DNA on file, and after we took a sample from the unidentified woman, we learned that they were related. Mother and daughter."

"And Xi is Li Jing's father, isn't he?" Maxx said.

"Bingo," Anderson said with a sly grin.

"That explains a lot," said Grey. "Li Jing is Xi's love child. And whether he knew or not, she's going to make him pay."

"He knew, "Gabby said as she looked down.

Everyone's eyes turned toward Gabby.

"How do you know that?" Maxx asked.

"Because he told Connie. Then Connie confided in me this morning after you had left the table. That's really what she wanted to meet about."

"I knew something wasn't adding up," Anderson exclaimed. "Why didn't you tell me about this before?"

"Because I wanted to talk to Maxx and Miss Grey first. You were being such an ass."

Maxx ran his hands through his short hair. He was trying to think through all the scenarios, at the same time trying to keep up with the conversation. Since Xi knew that Li Jing was his illegitimate daughter, was he feeding her confidential information? Was she working for him the whole time she was at Tech-Com? Could they trust Xi?

Miss Grey spoke up, "Before we get too far into the insults, Gabby, why don't you tell us exactly what Connie told you this morning?"

Gabby closed her eyes and furrowed her brows. "Her father called her yesterday to tell her that he was ready to talk with the US about working together. He wanted to move the conversation along because he was worried that he might be killed before he could make the connection and pass along some critical information."

"What information?" Anderson asked.

"He wouldn't say on the phone because he was worried that his phone might be monitored. When Connie pressed her dad about who was threatening him, he told her how he'd had an affair years ago with a coworker. Together, they had a daughter, but the mother had wanted to keep it a secret and had never told the daughter that Xi was her father. Apparently, the daughter had discovered the truth on her own and recently contacted Xi. She told him that she was going to make him pay for abandoning her and her mother."

Maxx interrupted her. "Connie was certain that it was Li Jing?"

"Yes, Xi verified the information with the mother. It is Li Jing. At first Xi assumed that she intended to blackmail him. But she made it clear that she wasn't looking for information or money. She wanted to ruin his life, not get bought off. He assumed she meant to kill him."

"That still might be her plan," said Grey. "But for now, Li Jing is content to make him suffer by killing Connie. And knowing that Connie was killed by his other daughter, because he had deserted her, must be a special kind of hell."

"In the meantime, Li Jing may let Xi stew awhile in his misery. She may even try to increase his pain. But eventually she will kill him. That's her ultimate objective," Anderson said.

"Then that's where we share common ground," Miss Grey said to Barth. "We both need to see Xi alive to find out what the critical information is and to ultimately forge cooperation between us and China."

"How do we make that meeting with Xi happen ASAP?" Anderson asked.

Maxx smiled. "That's where we can bring a ray of sunshine into the conversation. Xi has already agreed to meet. We simply need to protect him from his crazy daughter."

***

Li Jing sat in a dimly lit room, the only light emanating from a flickering candle. The flame cast dancing shadows on the walls. The room was sparsely furnished, with an aged wooden desk and a worn-out chair that creaked in protest as she shifted in agitation. The contours of her face were highlighted by the subtle exchange of shadow and light, revealing a determined jawline. In her, the darkness found its muse, and the night its silent champion. She was a portrait of introspection and hate.

Outside, the world was still, as if holding its breath. Waiting for her next movement. The night air was cool and damp, carrying with it the scent of pine from the nearby forest and the briny breeze blowing off the Puget Sound. The moon, a slender crescent, hung low in the sky, a silent witness to the tension and sense of satisfaction within. Killing her sister was regrettable but necessary.

In the shadowed corners of her mind, Li Jing wrestled with

thoughts as murky as the night itself. She contemplated the nature of her father's abandonment, the weight of her choices, and the path that led her here to this barren room. Each decision is a fork in the path of her life, and she pondered if she would ever find a bend that will bring her solace.

Doubt crept in like a persistent fog, obscuring the clarity she once claimed as her own. She questioned the morality of her choices, the steep price of her objectives, and the cost of the sacrifices she made along the way. The sacrifices that were yet to be made. The heavy silence of the woods was a stark contrast to the turmoil within—an obstinate battle between what was, what is, and what is yet to come.

8

SNAKE EYES

Miss Grey stared wide-eyed at the geothermal plant visible through the thick security glass.

She'd only been in this section of the Team Tacoma facility a handful of times, and it still seemed unreal that a structure this enormous could remain hidden beneath the city of Seattle. While the giant cavern had been formed by natural seismic activity tens of thousands of years ago, it had required an undreamed feat of engineering to build the plant. Without the energy, they would have had to build several nuclear facilities to generate the necessary power demanded by the technology center and alien communication device.

The last time she had visited the facility was the week before 9/11. In a time before she understood that this was the epicenter of the race to communicate with a civilization that existed in a distant galaxy. So far distant they were not even certain where Thunderbird lived. It seemed ironic that the link to the stars was buried so far below ground. It occurred to her that maybe it wasn't coincidence that so many ancient religions had developed a common theme to tie the sky above and the earth below. And here she stood by one of those gateways brought to life.

"It's glorious, isn't it?"

She jumped at the sound of his voice. She hadn't heard Mr. Green stride up behind her.

"It really is one of the wonders of the world," she said as she glanced at the huge cavern that housed the facility. "Especially when you consider its purpose."

"That's the beauty of the location. So close to the historical connection, but so modern in design, at the same time hidden from the rest of the world. I'm certain the aliens know of its location, but the people living hundreds of feet above are oblivious to its existence."

"I appreciate the invitation to visit, although I'm not sure why I'm here this morning. Especially after the conversation we had at Maxx's home yesterday."

"To be honest, it wasn't my idea. The senator wanted me to invite you to observe the meeting."

She looked sideways in confusion. "What meeting?"

She'd always been wary of Green. It seemed he always had a hidden objective and was toying with her. She had never caught him in an outright lie, but he regularly omitted critical information. He always tried to be the smartest person in the room. She hadn't yet figured out if the senator was aware of his deceiving behavior or if she was in on his attempts to keep her in the dark.

"We've been having consistent communication with Thunderbird over the last six months, and this is where we coordinate the calls. We know the device is secure here and have the necessary power. We'd like to you to observe the meeting."

"I'm honored but still puzzled by why you want me to observe."

"I don't want you to. The senator wants you to. You'll have to ask her yourself. She doesn't feel the need to tell me her reasoning."

"I'll do that next time I talk to her." *Maybe she doesn't trust Green after all.*

"Anyhoo, let's head over to the communication center," he said casually as he began walking quickly down the large tunnel bored out of the volcanic rock. "It's almost time."

"Any instructions on how I should act in the meeting?" she asked. "I don't want to create an intergalactic incident by mistake."

Green stopped outside the door and put his hand on her shoulder. "Here are the instructions, darling. Don't say or touch anything. You only need to sit there, look pretty, and keep quiet."

She could feel the color rising into her cheeks as she took a step back and out of his reach. *Es un poco capullo.*

After taking a second to calm herself, she said, "Your boss asked me to be here, so I'm here. But don't call me darling or touch me again or I'll hurt you. Comprende?" She stared at him with a tight grin, but her eyes flashed danger.

Green's normally droopy eyes opened wide as he moved out of her arms reach. "No need for threats. I didn't realize you were that sensitive."

"I'm not sensitive, or I wouldn't be in a line of work filled with type A men. I'm telling you there's a line you don't want to cross."

"Got it," he said with a bit of smirk.

When she entered the meeting room, it was not what she was expecting. She knew that the device was the communication portal based on the videos captured during the initial contact on 9/11. She had envisioned that the device would be in the room with them. Instead, it was placed in an adjoining room behind a clear wall of glass.

The device was a cube of smooth sinister metal about the size of an oversized refrigerator. The metal object didn't reflect any of the bright lights in the room, seeming to absorb the light instead. Its dark frame stood out in stark contrast to scientists in white lab coats bustling around it. She shuddered as she thought about what the object might represent, a completely foreign civilization in a strange universe. She didn't fully trust their intentions.

Green pointed her to a set of plastic chairs against the wall opposite the glass wall. The partition separated the conference room from the room holding the device. If not for the visible scientific chamber, she could be seated in a conference room anywhere. Instead of the usual bank of whiteboards, she was staring into a sterile lab that held one of the greatest discoveries the world had ever seen. The shadowy container looked so sterile and yet menacing.

Grey took a seat against the far wall, as Green had directed her to. A couple of the others in the room glanced at her occasionally, but no one came over to introduce themselves. It seemed like identities were on a need-to-know basis. And it was clear from the way that she was disregarded that no one wanted to know her.

She noticed on the table near Green's chair there was a timer counting down. With less than three minutes remaining, she watched a handful of people quickly file into the room. They either sat at the table or took a seat along the wall. Grey did a quick head count in the room. Eight people including Green and herself. There was a somber air in the room, and if there were any conversations, they were hushed and brief.

When the countdown clock reached zero, all the scientists filed out of the device chamber, securing the door behind them. The lights dimmed. Mr. Green cleared his throat to get everyone's attention, even though every person in the room was already looking at him.

"Thank you for your attendance for today's communication with Thunderbird. We have several people listening in from remote locations, but they are all muted. As a reminder, only I will speak unless you are directly addressed. Is everyone ready?" asked Green.

After a series of nods, Green pressed a button on the keyboard in front of him. "Device is activated at 15:15 UTC."

Miss Grey could feel the low pulse of the machine as it went active. The lights in the secure chamber changed colors from white to all colors of the spectrum as the device seemed to throb. She didn't see the device move as much as she felt the pressure build deep insider her. She concentrated on remaining calm despite the unique sensation. Everyone else in the room looked slightly bored, as if they had been through this sequence enough times that it was routine.

Without any preamble, Miss Grey felt and heard the aliens begin the communication. The sound was flat, emotionless, and even though the sound surrounded her, it felt distant. She couldn't have spoken even if she tried. She could barely take her eyes off the device even though it sat motionless. Never had she felt such dread.

"Thunderbird initiating contact," an alien voice intoned.

"This is Director Green from the United States," he responded with a slight tremor in his voice.

He must be feeling something is wrong too, she thought.

"We know," Thunderbird responded. "What other humans are participating in this communication?"

Green proceeded to mention everyone in the room by name and title. Miss Grey could feel all eyes turn toward her when her name was mentioned at the end of the list. It gave her an extreme sense of uneasiness now that she was no longer partially anonymous.

He avoided mentioning any names of people who might be listening remotely.

The oversight did not go unnoticed. "Who are the people listening to the call who are not in the room?" Thunderbird asked. It sounded more like an accusation than a question.

"Is it a problem that other senior people are listening in? We've done this on other communications, and it's not been an issue for you."

"It's not a problem now," the voice answered. "They have all been disconnected except the one who calls herself Senator Traficant. She can remain connected to the communication. We have also disabled all your recording devices."

Miss Grey could see Mr. Green's face turn a shade of white. He must not have been aware that the aliens could detect their electronic measures. And he surely had not intended to reveal that the senator was eavesdropping on the call.

He stammered, "Now that I know it's a problem for you, I will make sure that I announce those details at the beginning of the call."

The line was silent.

"Did we lose our connection?" Green said after a few seconds as he looked warily at the device.

"We are still connected," the remote voice answered. "Proceed with the information that was requested."

Mr. Green cleared his throat. "Um, we are still not engaged with the Chinese team, despite all our effort. However, we are making progress. They have finally signaled that they are ready to meet and begin cooperative planning."

Miss Grey tried to keep a straight face. That must be why she had been invited to attend, in case there were questions about the recent conversation with Xi. But Green had misrepresented the situation. There was no way she could honestly corroborate his statement.

"This lack of cooperation has been raised as concern for many of your solar cycles. Perhaps we have not been clear about the risks you, your people, and your planet face."

"No, no, you've been very clear. We face an extinction-level event if we fail to protect the planet from your enemies. But we cannot force the Chinese to engage. Perhaps if you put some pressure directly on them, they'd be more responsive."

"Do not presume to tell us what to we should do, Director Green. We are the masters, and you are the servants. Do not forget your place again, or we will provide you a violent reminder."

Green was turning whiter by the moment. "Please except my apology. We will increase our efforts. Trust me, we will not fail."

"We do not trust you. It is your nature to deceive. We do not wish to reset your planet, but we will if necessary."

"You have two solar cycles to jointly contact us. If not, we will begin the resetting process."

Miss Grey put her hand over her mouth to stifle a gasp. Two days to convince Xi and recontact Thunderbird was insane. They weren't even meeting with Xi until late tomorrow, and he was far from convinced of the need to collaborate with the US. She slumped in her chair, feeling like the weight of the world was on her shoulders. She could accept her fate, but the thought of her family dying because of her failure was almost more than she could bear.

Green's face was ashen. Through clenched teeth, he said softly, "We need more time. Please."

"No more time. Our enemies will arrive on your planet in the solar cycle you call March 1. If we do not hear from you and the Chinese that you are prepared to work together, we will destroy the planet on that date."

"We are prepared for their arrival, although we don't know where they will arrive. Can you at least tell us so we can have adequate military response?" Green pleaded.

"We will inform you on our next communication that includes the Chinese leaders. We know you have nuclear weapons capabilities that can reach anywhere in the world within hours, so you will have plenty of time to prepare."

"But we wish to avoid using large-scale nuclear weapons. We would prefer to use more tactical weapons deployed by our special forces to keep the population from panicking. To prepare takes at least twenty-four hours, especially if your enemies are arriving in a remote area of the planet."

"That's your choice. We do not care how you succeed. Either you destroy them, or we will destroy the planet to keep it from them."

"Is there any more that we need to know at this time?" Green asked.

"No."

Miss Grey could feel the throbbing of the device abruptly cease. The communication cube in the other room went dark. Everyone in the room let out a collective sigh. Green slumped forward and put his face in his hands.

The stillness in the room held for a moment, until the speakers built into the conference room table began to hum to life.

"Director Green, can you hear me now?"

Green lifted his head off the table. "Yes, Senator, we can hear you."

"I've been trying to break into the conversation for the last five minutes. I heard every word, but my microphone was disabled."

"Then you heard their instructions and warning."

"I did. Everyone, please leave the room except Director Green and Agent Grey. Now," she said with an edge in her voice.

After everyone had grabbed their bags and papers and closed the door behind them, Miss Grey moved to the table. She took a seat a few feet from Green so she could use his microphone if necessary.

"The room is clear," Green said.

"Miss Grey, this next step is on you. You must convince Xi of what is at stake. He is going to be emotionally distraught from the loss of his daughter yesterday, but you need to convince him that we must work together, or all is lost."

"Maybe you should contact him prior to traveling to the meeting in Hawaii to buy some time," Green interjected before Miss Grey could respond.

"No, he'll be more receptive in person," the senator snapped. "I can ask the president to contact the secretary general to prompt him, but Xi needs to be handled in person."

"I agree," Miss Grey said. "If we call Xi now, he's going to be suspicious that we're pressuring him. He's going to need to trust that the threat is real and that we will work together as partners. That's only going to happen face to face."

"Director Green is going with you to Hawaii in case there are any technical issues to cover. I'd recommend that Maxx and Gabby accompany you too, so that there is a personal connection. Are they up to speed on what's happening?"

"They're aware in general of what is happening, except for the timeline that we heard a few minutes ago."

"I'd keep them in the dark about that if you can," Traficant said.

"Why?" asked Grey. "If we're conveying the deadline to Xi, then they're going to find out eventually."

"Okay, use your discretion. But we need to keep them focused on getting Xi to help and not spinning off on a personal agenda. I need to update the president. Contact me if there's anything else that comes up."

Miss Grey hesitated but leaned in before the senator disconnected. "I will do everything to convince Xi. Assuming that I'm successful, will we have time to prepare for the alien incursion on Friday?"

"I know you'll do your best. We have some intelligence to

indicate where the invasion will be, even if Thunderbird isn't willing to tell us. Operation Anaconda is being prepared for what comes after."

Mr. Green raised his eyebrows as the line went dead.

What does that mean? she thought.

9

IN HIDING

Agent Hovis reread the summary that he'd written of the meeting last night and scratched the irritating stubble on the back of his neck.

As many times as he rewritten it, there were too many sections that didn't make sense. He'd tried to keep up with the conversation between Director Anderson, Agent Grey, Maxx, and Gabby, but they all seemed aware of inside information that he didn't have. He'd been assigned as the task force lead in the local office to capture Li Jing after the murder of Connie Xi, but it seemed she was only a small part of a larger conspiracy. Li Jing had been on the FBI's most wanted list since last September, and this was the first solid break they had in finding her.

What he couldn't get his head around was that the murder was completely related to a personal vendetta with her estranged father. It was too on the nose. He didn't fully discount the personal motive, but it didn't answer the question of why Li Jing had initially been put on the FBI's list. She was wanted for espionage and as the potential killer of a TechCom employee before she'd went into hiding. Neither of those crimes were connected to her father in any of the reports that he had access to. Of course, none of those reports had detailed that her father was the infamous Dr. Xi either. There had to be inside information that was not in the official record. Top secret government knowledge was missing.

Keith was still wearing his rumpled suit from the day before but had removed his tie and hung it over the back of his chair. It had been a long day and a half, and he'd not had more than a few minutes of sleep. He was leaning back in his chair, and his eyes were beginning to close when his desk phone rang. He grimaced and reluctantly picked up the phone after the third ring.

"Hovis. What's up?" he said.

"Is that how you answer the phone there at the FBI? Seems like a pretty relaxed atmosphere during a major investigation."

"It's only the back line. How can I help you, Director Anderson?"

"I have some good news for you. Hot off the CIA press."

Keith was doing his best to keep from rolling his eyes. This Anderson guy had been a pain in the ass from the first moment he'd barged into his office yesterday.

"Thanks?"

"Try and put a little more enthusiasm in your voice, Agent. I've got a lead for you on the location of our mutual interest, Li Jing. She's still in your neck of the woods."

Keith sat up straighter in his chair. "That is good news. Is it a solid lead?"

"As solid as the US dollar, my friend. We traced a satellite call to a number that we know she's used. The call was encrypted, so we can't be 100% certain, but we think it's better than a 50/50 chance it's our gal."

"If you're not sure it's her, what about the location?"

"The nerds at the National Security Agency were able to triangulate some signals from a few satellites in the area. It's in a three-block radius near Mercer and 9th Avenue. Do you know that area?"

"South Lake Union. Yeah, it's a neglected commercial area. Lots of abandoned buildings and a few boats to hide in. I'll head over there with some agents and get some help from Seattle PD to go door to door."

Anderson snorted. "Are you trying to catch her or scare her away?" he asked disdainfully. "I don't want her to know we're able to track her phone. She'll vanish, and we'll lose our chance. She doesn't know you. Go over there and start poking around and see if you can get a firm location. Then we'll bring in the troops and eliminate any chance she has to escape."

Hovis didn't like the way this news was being pitched to him. It was too informal. But it was better than sitting at his desk waiting for a miracle. They had lost Li Jing's trail yesterday morning when the car she was in disappeared from the downtown traffic cameras. After her getaway car jumped on I-90 heading out of town, the trail got sketchy. The highway patrol tracked the vehicle as far as Mercer Island, then it had seemingly vanished. She could be anywhere by now.

"Alright, we'll do it your way, Anderson. I don't like it but keep your cell phone handy. You're going to be one of the first people I call if I spot her."

"Definitely. I've got a team of heavy hitters on standby. She was trained at Camp Peary and was assigned to the Special Activities Center. She's as dangerous as they come. But we want her captured alive if possible. We have lots of questions we want to ask her."

"I saw that detail in her file. I'm not planning on confronting her on my own."

When they ended the call, Keith went to the bathroom to

change into some casual clothes that didn't scream FBI to anyone who noticed him. Jeans, sweatshirt, and a pair of Nikes would do if he needed to get dirty. He couldn't do much about hiding his government haircut, so he put on a SuperSonics cap he kept in his desk. The hat always made him feel a couple of inches taller.

Rather than taking his car, he hopped on one of the metro buses that ran every five minutes outside the building. The buses were free downtown and would drop him off a couple of blocks from his target area. He'd pulled up a map from the office library and planned out a rough search grid to follow. He wanted to be sure to eyeball each of the buildings in the focus area that Anderson had mentioned. That meant a lot of walking in circles unless he caught a break.

Keith stepped off the bus as it neared Harrison Street. The stop was in a largely neglected area of Seattle. Even though it was only blocks from Lake Union and the Seattle Center, it felt like it was a world away. The streets were dirty and narrow, running straight between low-rise or single-story buildings. The poorly maintained brick and concrete buildings housed trades, warehouses, and construction businesses that needed to be near downtown but couldn't afford the rent. The area was busy with employees coming and going during the day but largely abandoned at night. It was a perfect place to hide without having to worry about the police or nosey people getting into your business.

While he rode over on the bus, he'd come up with an idea to get a lead on Li Jing's current location without raising too many questions. It wasn't uncommon for small businesses in the area to have problems with people not paying for work. Collections were always a challenge when people paid in cash to avoid leaving a trail or paying taxes. It was a sore point for many of the business owners in this area. The Seattle Times had written a series of personal interest articles about the financial struggles of the local businessmen. The problem would be a relatable topic of conversation, allowing him to ask questions with minimal suspicion.

He stopped at a concrete two-story building that housed a sand and gravel business. The peeling paint and eroding structure looked like it hadn't seen a good day in the last decade. There were a couple of the men working and cussing at each other in a garage bay, so he bypassed them and went straight to the front office. The dusty glass door was propped open with a brick. The door opened into a small front office lit with hanging florescent tubing. A middle-aged woman with an out-of-date beehive hairdo sat behind a metal desk typing on computer with a huge, yellowed monitor. The sign on her desk read, "Harriet."

When Agent Hovis entered, she stopped typing and looked up over the top of her cat eyeglasses that were from the same era as her hairdo. He would have bet money she was around when the building was freshly built. "We're getting ready to close. May I help you?" she asked.

"Hi, Harriet. I'm doing some follow up on overdue accounts for T&J Hardware a couple blocks over." He'd spotted the sign on the bus ride.

"No matter what Tom told you, we don't owe them any money," she snapped at him.

Hovis chuckled a bit nervously. "Sorry to create any confusion. They aren't saying that you owe them money. They're looking for a company owned by a Chinese woman who was doing a concrete job on the other side of town. She bought some tools on credit. Now she's disappeared without paying."

"We don't have any Chinese women who work here either."

"No, of course not. Tom was only wondering if this woman might owe you money too. She told him she was working on a concrete job."

Harriet paused and wrinkled her forehead. "No Chinese

woman owes money that I know of. And I would know since I do the scheduling and billing. When was this?"

"Last week."

"Definitely not in the last week. Tom was wrong. He's got his nose in everybody's business. If anyone knew this lady, it'd be Tom, so I'm not sure why he sent you to talk to me. Probably wanted to irritate me. He's such a jackass," she huffed.

Keith smiled at the jab. He wondered if Tom and Harriet had some history. "Sorry to bother you then. Have a good evening."

When he stepped outside onto the sidewalk, he headed back to T&J Hardware. Tom must be the "T" in the T&J. Harriet had inadvertently given him the next hint.

After walking a half-dozen blocks on the dirty, cracked sidewalks, Keith was glad to see the entrance to the hardware store. The inside lights were on, although there was only one car in the front lot. Hopefully the car was Tom's and he hadn't left for the day.

"Is Tom in?" he asked as he walked up to the bored girl at the checkout register.

"Yeah, I think so. Do you want me to page him?" she asked as she looked at him with disinterest over the top of the magazine she'd been reading.

"No thanks," Hovis said. "I'll check his office." He thought about asking the clerk if she'd seen a Chinese woman around here but decided that was pointless. He'd get more information from Tom in a private setting. The salesclerk didn't seem particularly observant nor interested.

The clerk went back to reading her magazine while Hovis wandered to the rear of the store. He was sure he'd find the offices near the stockroom and delivery dock.

Walking through the half-empty aisles to the back of the store, Keith was curious how a business stayed open without any customers. He hadn't seen one person in the store except the clerk at the front counter. He didn't expect the store to be jammed, but he thought there'd be at least a couple of the local businesspeople shopping.

He felt bad about the lack of customers. His parents had owned a small business, and he knew how tough it was. Feeling nostalgic, he grabbed a set of box cutters off the shelf. He was tearing down some old wallpaper at home, and it would come in handy. He put the tool in his pocket, planning to pay on his way out of the store.

After stepping through a pair of wooden swinging doors in the back, he found a set of closed doors next to the restrooms. Figuring that at least one of the doors had to be an office, he rapped on the one that looked the most promising. A sign taped on the door that had been changed from "office" to "orifice," which was a strong indication he was in the right area.

He heard some rustling of papers, and someone walking toward the door. "Damn it, Darlene. I told you not to bother me when I'm trying to do the books," the man grumbled as he swung open the door.

A gray-haired man with a square head and three days of patchy beard hair stood in the door. He stared slack jawed at Agent Hovis for a moment before saying, "Hell, you aren't Darlene." He wiped off his hands on his overalls and stuck out an oversized hand. "Name's Tom. Who are you?"

"Nice to meet you, Tom. I'm Keith Hovis." He'd almost slipped and said Agent Hovis but caught himself at the last moment. "Harriet down the street said I should talk to you."

Tom scrunched up his nose like he'd smelled something a little overripe. "I have no more business with Harriet. We're square."

Hovis waved his hand. "I don't know anything about that. Do you mind if we grab a seat?"

"Okay, but make it snappy. I need to finish these books and close up."

Tom lifted some old, musty binders off the guest chair and set them on the floor. He brushed off most of the dust of the plastic seat and then slid back behind the desk with a loud sigh.

"Have a seat. I'd offer you something to drink, but I'm fresh out."

"That's fine. I don't think I'll be long. Harriet told me that you have an ear to the ground and seem to know about everything that's going on in South Lake."

"Nothing illegal though," Tom said as he eyed Keith warily.

"Oh no, nothing like that. In fact, I'm helping Harriet out with some collections. This Chinese group had them do a small job near the ballpark and then skipped."

"Not the first time that's happened. Did she give you a name or description?"

"That was the unusual thing. She said it's a woman boss. Pretty Chinese lady. Feisty as hell. Goes by the name of Jing or something like that."

Tom leaned back in his chair and rubbed his chin. He was concentrating so deeply that Keith could practically see him thinking. "I haven't met her myself, but I hear there's some real looker hanging out with a group over by the old boat house. Doing some remodeling, I heard. Although they haven't been by here."

This is sounding promising, Keith thought. "Do you know which building?"

Tom looked at him a bit sheepishly. "My memory isn't what it used to be. Get old, and you'll see. Sometimes the smell of money jogs my memory though."

Hovis laughed. "Sure, I get it." He took out his wallet and put a twenty on the desk. "Does that help?"

"It's a little clearer. Try one more. That'll probably do it."

Keith placed another twenty on the desk and put his wallet back in his pocket. He raised his eyebrow to make it clear to Tom he wasn't going to get any more money.

"Ah yes, now it's coming back to me. About three or four buildings to the east of the old boat house you'll see a group of storage sheds and houses. They're clustered between the street and the pier. Some homeless people were living in the buildings that were left open. Rumor has it that this Chinese group has cleared out a couple of the buildings and doing some work on a crab boat they tie up at the pier during the off season."

"And this woman is staying there?" asked Hovis.

"I don't know for sure that it's the woman you're talking about. But there's lots of scuttlebutt that this good-looking woman is a crazy bitch. Everyone avoids the place now." He shrugged and held up his hands to indicate that was everything he knew on the topic.

Hovis stood up and brushed the dust off the back of his pants. "Thanks for the information. Very helpful."

Tom didn't stand but stuck out his hand. "Glad I could help. Let me know if you find her. I like to keep tabs on things around here."

Keith shook his hand. He nodded in agreement, although he had no intention of coming back here. It was too depressing.

He had intended to pay for the box cutter on the way out, but the salesclerk was gone when he got to the front of the store. After a moment of hesitation, he left a five-dollar bill on the register to cover the cost. *An extra contribution to help Tom with his medical condition*, he thought as he tucked the blades in his back pocket. He made sure the front doors locked behind him on his way outside.

Keith walked through the mostly empty streets. There were still lights on in few of the buildings, but most of the people that worked in this area had already left. There was a dull light in the sky, but with the heavy cloud cover, it was getting dark quickly. He was running out of time tonight to do much more.

He had his Bureau-assigned pistol on a clip inside his belt to keep it concealed. He doubted that he'd need it, but it did give him a measure of reassurance. There were no bars or clubs in this area, so assault and robbery were rare events.

As he headed toward the lake, he could see the cluster of structures that Tom had mentioned. He'd never paid much attention to this block because the small buildings blended into the background of the larger construction surrounding them. It was an odd mix of a dozen small buildings and abandoned homes. Bobbing in the lake, he could see a few small fishing boats.

Crossing the street, he dodged the few cars that were passing through the area. Other than the occasional streetlamp, there were plenty of shadows to mask his approach to the block. It wasn't that he expected anyone to be watching him, because the place seemed deserted. He couldn't see a single light on the block, only the dark outlines of the buildings defined by the even darker lake behind them.

He walked steadily through the space between the decrepit buildings, trying to stay on the portions of the sidewalks that were still passable. Junk was piled in random mounds with a narrow path that he could navigate without tripping or running into a dead end. He could hear the occasional scratching of critters moving through the debris. It smelled like something had died in one of the piles of rubbish.

After a half hour of looking into the occasional open door or broken window, he decided that this was a pointless exercise, especially in the dark. If he'd been thinking, he would have grabbed a flashlight from the hardware store. But he had been operating without a clear plan, so he was winging it. Better to call it quits until he went home and grabbed a flashlight.

Turning back toward the street, he felt a presence suddenly appear out of a nearby shadow. He couldn't see anything plainly in the dark but felt the air movement. Something heavy swung toward his head. He wasn't fast enough to completely avoid being hit. The blow caught him on his shoulder, causing a bright flash of pain. Even on his shoulder, the blunt force was hard enough to bring him to his knees.

The last thing Agent Hovis saw was a rat scrambling away out of the corner of his eye. Then his forehead smashed into the broken concrete of the sidewalk as he blacked out.

10

STATE OF MIND

Keith felt like he was waking up riding an out-of-control carousel.

He was unable to recall where he was and how he'd gotten here. The pitch-black room didn't provide any clues. He had a foggy recollection of walking through a hardware store, but his memory was hazy after that. He couldn't puzzle out why would he be on a merry-go-round in the dark.

Lying flat on his back was making him nauseous. When he tried to sit up, he found that his arms and legs were held down. His only option was to stay prone.

He could taste the bitterness rising in his throat but valiantly fought the urge to vomit. He continued to spin and sluggishly came to the realization that he wasn't really spinning at all. The motion was only in his head. Even though it burned his throat, he swallowed the bile building in his mouth. Forcing himself to relax, he tried to stop the room from spinning.

He must have passed out again. When he woke, he realized that the spinning motion had slowed down considerably. *It's like a kid's carousel,* he clumsily thought.

"That makes no sense," he muttered.

A bit of the mental fog had cleared while he was unconscious, but there were large gaps in his memory. He could effortlessly recall leaving a store and walking toward Lake Union from the hardware store. After that, he had a patchy recollection of falling face first onto the sidewalk. He couldn't recall why he'd fallen over, but it seemed like an important detail.

His head throbbed. He wondered if his skull was fractured, but his hands couldn't reach it to determine if the crack was real or imagined. The pain was nearly unbearable. That could mean he had a concussion. Or worse, his brains were leaking out. He made a mental note to check his head as soon as his arms were freed. Of course, if his brains were spilling out, it wouldn't matter because he'd be dead soon.

"Help me," he croaked through the adhesive tape over his mouth. He'd tried to yell, but it was barely louder than a muted *hmmm-mm* sound. That minimal effort brought back waves of spinning and nausea. He paused to catch his breath, trying to relax and get the room to stop twisting. At the moment, drowning in his own vomit sounded infinitely worse than his brains slowly leaking out.

For a few beats of his pounding heart, he focused on steadying his breathing and slowing his pulse. He was slightly claustrophobic, and this position was making him panicky. Keith gingerly tested the cord that was tied around his wrists. It felt like old fashioned rope. Maybe twine, but not nylon. Not metal, which felt like a piece of good luck. His eyes were fully adjusted to the dim lighting by now, but it was too dark to see anything but the faint outlines of the bindings. His hands didn't feel like the ropes were cutting off circulation yet. But it would be impossible to untie in the dark.

Carefully testing the cords on his legs, he found that the movement triggered another dizzy spell. Even though his legs weren't pulled tightly against the bindings anchored to the footboard of a bed, he couldn't get them near enough to his hands to reach the knots. Running out of ideas on how to free himself, he moved in every direction he could. He tested the limits of his position on the lumpy mattress trying to ignore the bouts of nausea.

Rolling on his side, he could feel that his gun was missing from the holster. Not that his gun would do him any good with his hands tied and stretched over his head.

He considered, then quickly discarded, the thought of waiting to see what happened next. Waiting wasn't in his nature. Yelling for help was also likely to attract whoever had secured him to the bed.

With a flash of momentary clarity, he recalled placing the box cutters in his back pocket. Pressing his lower back into the bed, he sensed the small metal tool was still there. They must have missed the small cutter when they tied him down. Things were beginning to look up. But it was impossible to bring his hands down to his pocket more than a few inches.

Even though his present position made his legs cramp, he used his heels to inch himself toward the top of the bed. This motion at least provided enough slack in the rope holding his arms to move his hands so he could feel the metal headboard.

The right side of the bedrail didn't reveal anything to his fingertips but the smooth metal frame. However, on the left bed pole, he'd discovered a loose screw. Loose enough that it snagged the rope if he twisted it carefully. *Hot Damn*.

Patiently, Keith began to work the rope over the screw. Ignoring his pounding headache, the cramps in his legs, and the occasional digging of the screw into his knuckle, he focused on the sawing motion. Back and forth. The movement was all he allowed himself to concentrate on, blocking out all the other sensations. The repetitive motion gave him something to engage his mind to reduce the rolling waves of nausea.

He lost track of time, but it couldn't have been more than an hour before he felt the final strand of rope on his wrist give way. His numb hand dropped to the bed. Despite the throbbing ache in his shoulder, he hastily worked his free hand behind his back to take out the box cutter. With the razor blade, it was easy work to free his other hand and legs. He carefully removed the tape covering his mouth to breathe freely. Doing a quick pat down, he verified his holster was empty, and his phone and badge were indeed missing.

When he tried to stand, he almost fell over. The exertion of removing himself from the lashings had weakened him enough that he had to carefully lower himself to the floor. Crawling on his hands and knees, he moved over the rough wood flooring until he reached the wall.

Lowering his face to the floor, he could see a sliver of dim, yellow light. Keith made his way over to the light. It was shining through a tiny crack under the door. He pushed himself carefully up the doorjamb to avoid making himself dizzy again. Finding the doorknob gave him another moment of hope, until he realized that the wood door was locked.

The knob wouldn't turn. He couldn't feel any way to unlock the door. He must have been locked inside by whomever had captured him. He tested the hinges with his fingertips, and they were unmovable. Someone had installed this door and secured it to keep the occupant locked inside. He wouldn't be surprised to learn that the room was soundproof too. He probably wasn't the first person to be kept here.

He crawled around the perimeter of the room to determine if there were any other exits. The only other exit was a small window, but it was tightly covered with boards. Trying to pry the wood boards off the window was a dead end.

The only way out of the room was through the locked door.

He moved to the door and crouched down on the hinge side. He was going to have to wait for someone to enter the room then try to subdue them.

He settled into a crouch behind the door, trying to stay focused. He imagined he was fighting a concussion, and it took all of his concentration to stay alert. He pinched himself repeatedly and scraped his hands across the splintered wood floor. If he dozed off, all his effort to get untied would be for nothing. Whoever had tied him up would be much more careful the next time. If they didn't kill him first. Every moment he was stuck in here lowered his chance of getting out alive.

He'd lost track of time when he heard the lock quietly rotating in the door. He slowly stood up, feeling the pain in his legs. They had become numb, and the feeling of pins and needles made him want to scream. He bit his lip to avoid making any sound. He didn't want to reveal his location behind the door. He also slid a half step to the left in case they tried to pin him behind the door when they entered the room.

As if they had read his mind, the person burst through the door with a bang. They must have anticipated that he might escape the restraints. Or they were paranoid. Either way, he was prepared to respond with as much violence as he could muster.

He stepped around the hanging door with his arm extended, slashing at the person in front of him. He immediately felt the razor-sharp box cutter connect. He couldn't tell where he'd cut the intruder, but it was more than skin deep. When they pulled away from him, his cutter was yanked from his blood covered hand. A howl of pain told him that it was a solid strike. And from the sound of the scream, it was clear that the person was a woman. For some reason, he hadn't anticipated that his captor was a woman. The realization caused him to pause for a fraction of a second.

The thump of a heavy object hitting the floor shortly after his box cutter landed jolted him back into the fight. He brought his coiled body around the front edge of the door. He swung his fist at the person, trying to follow through with the momentum. It was a knockout punch, but because of lack of depth perception in the dim light, it only grazed her. Nevertheless, it gave him a sense of her location. He followed through with a series of jabs that caught her with her arms lowered.

As the woman started to fall forward, he pulled her into the room and threw her aggressively to the ground. She went face first into the floor, and Keith jumped onto her back, pinning her down and knocking the air out of her. She was trying to protect her arm when she fell and landed on her shoulder. From that position, she wasn't able to roll away. Her blood was making the floor slick. She was trapped.

"Get off me," she yelled while trying to catch her breath.

He couldn't see much detail with the dim light coming through the open door. But it was enough to convince him the woman was pinned down and losing blood quickly. He grabbed her arm and forcefully pulled it behind her back. He was trying to stop her from scrambling around and stop the blood flow at the same time. Now that he had the upper hand, he wanted to keep her alive. And get some information.

"Stop moving around," he barked. "I'm trying to stop you from bleeding out."

She hissed something that he couldn't understand. It sounded like an Asian language. *Chinese*, he thought.

"Li Jing, stop," he said.

Keith could feel her body stiffen. *Got her.*

He leaned over and grabbed the box cutter and a piece of rope lying on the floor. He tied a piece of rope around her upper forearm as a temporary tourniquet to staunch the bleeding. He used another piece of the rope to tie her hands behind her back. She was breathing heavily, but at least her shrieking had changed to quieter explodes of cursing.

"Calm down," he said, trying to defuse the situation. That was the wrong thing to say. She grew agitated again.

"You are so stupid," she snarled in English. She tried to roll him off her. Although she was viciously strong, he outweighed her by at least fifty pounds. Despite her thrashing, his training prevented her from dislodging him. She eventually grew tired and kept still.

"You don't know what you're getting involved in," she said.

"I know that you knocked me out. Let's start there, and you explain the rest," he said.

"You were here to arrest me, weren't you?" she asked.

"Yes, and now seems like a good time for me to read you your rights."

After he had recited her rights, he asked, "Would you like to continue?"

"If it'll get you off me," she said.

"I'll get off you, if you sit up with your legs in front and with your back toward me. I want to check your wound anyway. Do you have my phone or a flashlight so I can see?"

"No lights," she said as he kneeled off to the side. She sat in the position he had told her to.

Her wound was dripping blood, but it was no longer gushing. He cut off some of his shirttail to use as a temporary bandage. "Alright, talk."

"You need to get me to the hospital," she said.

"I will as soon as you tell me why you're in Seattle. And don't tell me it's the coffee."

She groaned. "I don't know how much you know. I saw that you are only FBI, so I doubt that anyone has explained much to you."

"I know that you are wanted for the murder of Dale Phi and Connie Xi. Isn't that enough for now? Did you come back to kill Connie Xi?"

Li Jing banged her heels on the floor. "Not only that," she yelled. "I admit I did get some pleasure out of knowing she's dead. Dale was simply business. But both needed to die for a bigger cause, one that's bigger than you and me. That's why."

"You're sounding crazy right now," Keith said as he shook his head.

Now that she was subdued, he'd lost interest in continuing to interrogate her in this dark, dirty room. He wanted to get up and leave. He needed a way to get her into a more contained environment. Without a phone, he was going to have to yell and hope help would arrive or carry her to the street and flag down a passing car.

"I wish I was crazy," she said. "The truth is more insane than anything I could make up. If you don't let me go, a lot of people will die. And you'll be responsible."

"Die because of what?" he asked.

He felt her lean forward and shake her head. "What if I told you that aliens are going to arrive on earth in the next week? And the plan is to start a war with them? Isn't that worth stopping?"

Keith couldn't help but laugh. "Nope. You're certifiably nuts."

"Do you remember the man they used to call 'the master of war.' Doctor Smith."

"Vaguely. He and a scientist from China had some mad scientist feud going on to build the best weapons. But I read that Doctor Smith died during September 11th."

"That Chinese scientist is my father. Dr. Xi Jianguo. I now work for Doctor Smith. He didn't die. He escaped."

Keith's jaw dropped. He sat in silence to process this information. He knew she was telling the truth about her father being Xi, because Anderson had revealed that secret last night. Could she also be telling the truth about Doctor Smith? And what did that have to do with aliens?

"If Smith is alive – and I'm highly skeptical – what is he working on that will stop this war?"

"It's the same technology that he and my father have been working on for decades. The question of how to successfully communicate with alien civilizations. They've both solved the problem but are still competing."

"Competing? Is Smith working for the United States, and Xi working for China?"

"No, Smith is talking with the aliens. The US has its own program. They are trying to work with Xi."

"Okay that sounds completely mad. And even if I believed any of it, it doesn't explain why I should let you go. How are you helping Smith?"

"Because I must stop my father from succeeding in starting this war. That's why I killed my half-sister. Connie had convinced my father that the Chinese and US should collaborate to fight and defeat the aliens. This would lead to a global conflict that would kill millions, if not completely devastate the planet."

"And what is Doctor Smith working on?"

"Doctor Smith is trying to convince the aliens not to invade Earth and to peacefully cooperate. He wants the world to welcome the extraterrestrials as potential allies, not as conquerors. It is the best chance to stop the annihilation of Earth."

Keith had heard a lot of excuses from people during his ten years with the FBI. This wasn't even the first time he'd heard people use aliens as justification for their behavior. And he'd lost count of the number of times he'd heard variations of "the devil made me do it." But this explanation was on an entirely new level, because Li Jing was not only brilliant but was in extreme pain. People in pain didn't make up a story that was this complex.

None of that mattered though. Even if any of her explanation was true, she had confessed to two murders. If he'd wanted to give her any breathing space at all, she'd undercut it. She would have to explain this conspiracy theory to everyone back at the office, though he doubted that she'd be at the FBI offices very long before the CIA intervened. There was no chance that Director Anderson was going to let her out of his control.

As he was trying to figure out how to get her back to the FBI office, Keith heard soft footsteps in the other room. He lowered his voice, almost whispering. "Are you here by yourself?" he asked Li Jing.

She didn't lower her voice, but she also didn't call for help as he expected she would if she had partners in the area. "No, I'm alone."

The sound of the cautious footsteps on the wooden floor drew closer. They were coming toward him. He would be an easy target if he sat here waiting. He should try and find the object that Li Jing had dropped when she had entered the room. It was likely a gun. But if it wasn't a weapon, then he'd have moved away from Li Jing. He didn't want to give up any leverage, and she would lie if it was in her best interest.

"Go back outside," he yelled to whomever was in the hall. "I'm a federal agent and I'm armed."

"Help me!" Li Jing shouted. "He's lying. This man has a knife and is going to kill me."

The other man stepped into the room. Keith could only see a dim outline in the doorway. "He's not going to kill you, Li Jing. Are you, Agent Hovis?" the man asked.

Keith jumped up. "Director Anderson?"

"Yep," he answered. 'You didn't answer my calls or texts. I started to wonder if you'd run into trouble. I heard Li Jing screaming and followed the sound."

"I'm damn glad to see you. She knocked me out then took my gun and phone. I didn't know how I was going to get her back to HQ."

"It's all good, Agent. I don't have your phone, but I have your gun. It was out in the hallway."

"I wounded her, but she's weak from blood loss. Call an

ambulance and get some police to cordon off the area. She may have some friends looking for her."

"No, we're not going to do that," Anderson muttered. "I'm walking out of here with her alone. No ambulance, no police."

Li Jing moaned. "Don't let him take me. He will kill me," she said.

Hovis set his jaw. "Anderson, I know you want her for your reasons, but we need to do this by the book. You're in my jurisdiction, and that's how it's going to go down."

"I disagree, Agent Hovis, but I'll let you get your way until we get to the office. After that, she's mine."

"That's fair. Now help me get her up."

Anderson walked slowly over to where Li Jing was on the floor. "Did she tell you why she was here?" he asked.

Before Keith could answer, she cried out, "I told him that I was here to punish my cheating father. Isn't that enough?"

Hovis bent down to take Li Jing's wounded arm to help her up. He felt Anderson step behind him to grab her other arm.

But he didn't help at all. Keith heard the movement a fraction of a second before he felt the contact on his already aching head. Everything went dark. Again.

11

SOMEONE SAVED MY LIFE TONIGHT

Maxx had been following Agent Hovis since early this evening.

He had been driving home, exhausted after the crazy week, and had taken the back way through South Lake Union to avoid the rush hour traffic. Highway 99 was blocked for a mile in both directions because of an accident on the bridge. Taking the side streets was faster and less stressful.

While he was sitting at a stop light, he watched Hovis walk into a store. He was moving like he was in hurry and looking around like he was looking for someone.

It could be simply coincidence that he was dressed like a civilian and moving through this part of town, but Maxx didn't trust coincidences. Now that he knew Hovis was the agent from the Seattle office assigned to watch Li Jing, he was intrigued. It was also odd that he was walking, didn't have a vehicle, and was operating without a partner. It might only be personal business, but with the search for Li Jing heating up, it felt odd.

Maxx pulled into a vacant lot across the street from the store and turned off the engine. He kept a book under the seat of his truck and took it out while he waited. In the past six months, he'd become intrigued with the history of Seattle—there were so many secrets. He thumbed through the pages while checking regularly for the reappearance of Agent Hovis.

It wasn't long before Hovis stepped back out onto the street. Maxx followed him discretely a block at a time. The setting sun was throwing long inky shadows, but Maxx kept his headlights off to avoid attracting attention from Hovis. He didn't need much light, as it was obvious that the FBI agent was walking directly toward the Lake Union waterfront. *Curious.*

When the agent crossed the main street, Maxx lost him in the dark complex of buildings. Sitting at the stop light, he couldn't do much other than watch Hovis disappear into the shadows. Maxx drummed his fingers on the steering wheel while he waited for the light to change and the car in front of him to move out of the way. By the time car moved, he'd lost sight of him and decided to find a nearby place to park his truck and follow on foot.

It took him several minutes to find a nearby parking lot that had a space big enough for his truck. He walked toward where he'd last seen Hovis, beginning to question what he was doing here. Hovis wasn't doing anything particularly suspicious other than walking around in a rough neighborhood. Maxx began to wonder if he was letting his imagination get the better of him. It was getting late, and maybe he was chasing shadows.

Maxx looked into several of the buildings, but they were all abandoned. Strewn with junk, it didn't look like a place that Hovis would be hanging out unless he was looking for someone or something. He didn't see any lights. It was getting extremely dark as he moved further from the road. He had forgotten to grab a flashlight from the glovebox and was getting concerned about stepping on a needle, or worse.

He was trying to listen for the sound of movement but couldn't hear anything other than ambient noises. It was challenging to hear anything past the sounds of the road and the boats moored at the nearby dock.

Suddenly, a high-pitched screaming came from the buildings on his right.

It didn't sound like Hovis. Someone was in pain...a lot of pain. He moved quickly in the direction of the sound. But he couldn't move faster than a slow jog because he kept tripping on the piles of debris and the broken concrete of the sidewalk. He cursed himself again for not bringing a flashlight. He was concerned that he might break an ankle trying to get there.

As he drew close to the building the screams were coming from, they abruptly stopped. The sudden silence was more ominous than the screaming. He slowed his pace. It was past dangerous. He was carrying his weapon, but it was less than optimal in the pitch darkness. Without a clear target, he wasn't going to start shooting. Too many things could go wrong.

As he poked his head around the corner of the building next door, he was surprised to see two people bolting out of the building he was heading toward. They were about thirty yards away, so he couldn't see enough detail. It looked like a large man and either a small man or a woman. The man looked taller than Hovis, but he wasn't certain. The smaller person was clearly hurt from the way they were moving, hunched over holding their arm against them. And keening in pain.

Maxx held his pistol down at his side. He moved toward them cautiously. "Hold up. I'm here to help," he yelled.

When he shouted, they stopped suddenly and looked in his direction. But they didn't stop for more than a moment and then began running in the opposite direction. They seemed to be familiar with the surroundings because they moved much quicker than he was. They quickly disappeared in the dark alley. The sounds of their footsteps faded rapidly.

From the sounds of the retreating footsteps, it sounded like they were moving in separate directions. There was no way he was going to chase them. It was too easy to get caught in here with multiple people who may or may not be armed.

Instead of chasing them, he moved toward the building they had exited. He didn't want to leave the area in case there was a person inside that was hurt and unable to move on their own. He'd left his phone in the cupholder of the truck when he'd parked. He could either go get it and call for some help or do a quick search of the building then call afterward.

"Screw it," he muttered as he walked into the dilapidated house.

Scanning the small living room and what looked to be a kitchen area, Maxx moved forward warily into the run-down dwelling. The old wood floors creaked with every step. There was no way to be covert in here. Abandoning caution, he moved rapidly into the narrow hallway.

Keeping an eye on the room behind him, he investigated each of the small bedrooms. There was junk and a few mattresses that smelled of urine and weed piled in the corners, but the two bedrooms were otherwise empty.

The bathroom as so foul smelling that he didn't even bother to go inside. He nearly gagged from the stink and pulled the door shut. That only left the only open door at the end of the hall.

He popped his head around the corner of the entrance. He noticed a person slumped on the floor next to a ratty bed. The window had all been covered, so it was completely dark except for the filtered light coming in from the hall behind him.

Maxx edged over to the person and nudged them with his foot. He could hear soft breathing, but they were unconscious. He turned the body over slowly. He could see enough of the person's face. Hovis.

He did a quick search of the FBI agent's holster and pockets. All empty. Squatting down, he picked him up with a grunt.

Hovis was alive but unresponsive, deadweight. Maxx carefully put him over his shoulder.

He backed out of the room, carefully walking back the way he'd come.

"Okay, buddy," he said to Hovis. "Let's get you to my car and call 911. There ought to be an interesting story when you wake up."

Hovis silently concurred.

***

In the dimly lit room, shadows danced on the walls, casting eerie shapes that seemed to move with a life of their own. Gabby sat at the center of her bedroom, her eyes wide with a palpable sense of dread. Her hands trembled slightly as she put on one of Maxx's oversized t-shirts. A symbol of the intimacy of their relationship, it brought comfort and served as a fabric shield against the encroaching twilight.

Gabby's fear was not of the tangible kind—no aliens in the closet or killers at the door. At least at the moment. It was a deep-seated, all-encompassing anxiety that had begun to gnaw at her since the events leading to September 11th. Her mind was a tangle of worries, each turn leading to another dead end of doubt and uncertainty. The fear of not being able to protect Connie, of losing Maxx, and of the unknown future that had once again been pressed into her life. It all loomed over her like a storm cloud.

Her breathing was shallow, each lungful of air a struggle against the invisible weight pressing down on her chest. The room, her safe space, now felt like a cage, its walls closing in with every passing second. Gabby's eyes darted around, searching for an escape but finding none. The ticking of the clock on the wall was a cruel reminder of time slipping away, each tick amplifying her worry that Maxx should have been home by now.

In moments of clarity, Gabby knew that her fears were irrational, that the scenarios playing out in her mind were unlikely to happen again despite the violence that kept finding her. In the grip of anxiety, logic was a distant memory, overshadowed by the overwhelming tide of emotion. She wished for the past when she could face the world with confidence, when her steps were sure and her heart was light. Those days seemed so long ago.

Despite the darkness, there were moments of light. Gabby found solace in trivial rituals—making a cup of coffee in the morning, playing with her cat Buttercup, or snuggling up to Maxx's back, listening to the sounds of his light snoring. These acts, though seemingly insignificant, were lifelines that kept her anchored, reminders that there was still beauty to be found. And that despite the fear, she was safe.

Gabby's journey had not been one of dramatic battles or heroic triumphs. But without her agreement, her battle had become that last fall. Since then, it had become a quiet, daily struggle against an unseen enemy, a testament to her strength. She had learned she was a warrior and could survive events that would break most people. But now she was left fighting for a sense of normalcy in a world that was not normal. She yearned for the strangeness to end and return to the ordinary life she'd lost.

As the evening wore on, Gabby's breathing began to steady, the t-shirt that smelled like Maxx providing a small measure of comfort. She knew that the fear would return, that the shadows would once again dance on the walls. But for now, in this moment of calm, she allowed herself to hope that one day the shadows would recede, and she would step into the light, unafraid. A warrior at heart.

12

ONE OF THESE THINGS (IS NOT LIKE THE OTHERS)

OCTOBER 2001

Doctor Smith pulled the thin fabric drapes together tightly, making sure to cover any gaps.

He pushed the dented wooden table in front of the door to his hotel room, blocking the entrance. The locked door and heavy furniture wouldn't stop someone from getting into the room if they were determined. There was nothing that would stop the kind of men who were chasing him if they wanted in the room. He knew those kinds of men, because he'd hired many of them in his life. The table was only meant to keep out nosey hotel staff or errant maids.

It was a cheap room in a cheap hotel in a city with a name he couldn't pronounce. The room was dusty and hadn't been thoroughly cleaned in days, if not weeks. The thought of getting in the lumpy bed made him slightly nauseous. Last night, he'd just gotten on top of the covers and tried not to let his imagination run away from him. He needed to hide, and this would be far down the list of places his enemies would expect him to be.

He'd checked into the hotel last night, using a fake Spanish passport and the local currency. Rather than speak in Spanish, he'd pretended to be a mute. The clerk at the front desk had given up trying to communicate with him and resorted to miming actions. His ruse worked better than he'd expected. Other than some minor irritation over his request for a room on an upper floor, the clerk had overcharged him. He considered it a minor bribe and willingly paid to get out of the lobby and into a place with some privacy.

Carrying his battered suitcase up the stairs, he had found the room and settled in before dark. He was exhausted, hungry, and tired after traveling for the past week. He'd prepared several travel routes and was proud that he'd had enough foresight to lay some false trails and options in case his primary plans were interrupted. He'd anticipated the disruption in air travel after September 11th and had chartered a boat to get out of New York. It had been expensive but worth the cost to escape the US as quickly as possible.

Most of the precautions were focused on delaying transportation into the US and Europe, so the police and border guards found little interest in a small, bookish salesman heading toward Jerusalem. When he'd reached Spain, he'd changed his appearance, passport, and destination to Dubai. From Dubai it had been a private car out to his final destination – a small desert city that saw few tourists but frequent western scientists working in the oil industry. No one had given him a second glance when he hauled his battered suitcase from the market to a hotel outside the central section of the town. He was invisible in plain sight.

While he was secured in his cabin during the ship's Atlantic crossing, he had colored and cut his hair. He'd purchased a first-rate fake beard that matched the color of his new hair. He'd switched from his usual pair of glasses to colored contact lenses. He missed his glasses, but without them he looked much different than whatever photos the CIA and Interpol would have distributed.

Lastly, he'd tossed his clothes over the side of the ship and used the clothing the captain had been instructed to have aboard. He looked like a businessman on his last dime. Inexpensive shoes, several aged suits, and some white shirts that were more yellow than white. A cheap silver wedding band completed his new disguise. He hated seeing himself in the mirror, but he fit the part of a poor traveling salesman or low-level clerk.

He lifted the tattered brown suitcase onto the bed and lifted out the dirty clothing. The floor of the suitcase hid a false bottom that he carefully removed. The inner lining was shielded so that it could pass through a metal detector but wouldn't survive a thorough physical inspection. Fortunately, none of the checkpoints he'd passed through showed the slightest interest in doing a thorough search of him or his suitcase. The compartment contained the only two items that he'd brought with him when he had escaped from New York.

He powered on the satellite phone. He'd charged it during the long car ride so it had a full battery, which should suffice until he got to his next destination. He dialed one of the few phone numbers he'd memorized. After making the connection, he counted the dial tones and got to ten before she answered.

"What's your favorite color?" she asked. This question was their prearranged identification. Her question meant she had not been caught. If he answered incorrectly, she would destroy her phone and proceed with their backup plan.

"White, of course," he answered.

"It's so good to hear from you, Doctor," Li Jing sighed with a hint of relief. The satellite was designed to encrypt their call. Nevertheless, they always avoided names and locations.

Smith, trying to minimize the connection time, jumped to the reason he'd contacted her. "Were you able to make contact with your father?"

"Yes, he is aware that I have uncovered his secret and could expose him. He is willing to do as we ask to avoid the embarrassment."

"It's important to make sure that he doesn't reconsider. Your sister will be the penalty he will pay if he betrays us."

"He will do anything to protect her. I'm certain he will delay working with the Americans to keep her alive."

"You have done well, my little rose. We are ready to move to the next phase. I will contact you in several weeks with instructions."

"You honor me, Doctor. Together, we will make the unbelievers bow low before us."

With a tight-lipped smile, Smith disconnected the call. He needed devoted collaborators, and Li Jing was nothing if not devoted. He was not as certain as she was that Xi could be blackmailed. He might bend to their pressure for a short time, but eventually he would try to outsmart them. They had been enemies for decades, and he knew Xi better than his own daughter.

He carefully secured the satellite phone back in the hidden slot. He then lifted the second device from the other slot. The object felt remarkably cool in the stifling heat. The metallic cube was roughly the size and shape of a Rubik's cube, but the similarity ended there. It was a deep-black hue that seemed to absorb any light around it and never changed temperature regardless of the environmental conditions. He imagined it was akin to staring into a small version of a black hole. The device was a miniature version of the Thunderbird device. That memory caused him to shiver.

The small piece of equipment was his most prized possession. He doubted that there were other similar devices – he was sure that he had been chosen. Chosen for what, he hadn't determined yet, but he felt it in his heart. His entire life had been building up to this moment in time, and only now was he beginning to see the edges of a life larger than he'd imagined. A role in history that far surpassed his expectations.

The small cube had appeared on his desk on September 11th. He'd been staring intently at some of the scientific equipment when he felt a shift in the air. He felt the hair on the back of his neck stand, and when he turned around, the contraption was simply there. He didn't know how else to describe the circumstances, but having a solid object materialized in the middle of your desk makes one question their perception of reality. At first, he'd thought it was his imagination reacting to the stress of the moment. But picking the object up had convinced him that there was a meaningful purpose.

The events of the hours that followed the appearance of the device were nerve-racking. He'd thrown the device in his briefcase along with his laptop and a stack of confidential files and escaped the floor in the World Trade Center at a jog. The subsequent explosions at the World Trade Center and his rapid escape from New York had left him little time to consider the source of the device, the intent, and his role.

The ship he had arranged passage on was waiting for him at the industrial port. It was a small transport vessel that was on its return leg back to the Mediterranean with a hold full of automotive parts. The cargo was crated before loading, and therefore the ship only required a skeleton crew. The captain had given him a single berth that was stark but clean. Other than the small bed, a metal desk, and a chair, the only other item was a floor safe. The captain assured him that he was the only person on the ship who knew the combination, so he was free to use it to store valuables.

After he was convinced that the ship was in international waters and heading for a small Spanish port, he was able to relax. He'd placed the contents of his briefcase in the safe, locked the door, and fallen asleep. Despite his anxiety and the bright light streaming through the small porthole, the rocking motion of the waves had lulled him to sleep.

He must have been asleep for several hours, because when he woke, the golden light from the window filled the berth with shadows. He had the uncomfortable feeling that he was not alone in the room but couldn't see anyone in the small space. The hair on his arms tingled again. He felt something nearby despite his eyes not detecting anyone or anything. The ship continued to rock back and forth, making the shadows dance with the motion of the waves. The motion that had put him to sleep a few hours ago now felt strangely unsettling.

As the seconds slowed to a crawl, it felt as if time was suspended despite the movement of the light through the window. Everything seemed to be suspended in slow motion as he tried to pinpoint the source of his unease. He'd never had such a disorienting experience. He questioned if he'd been drugged while he slept.

He walked unsteadily to the door to make sure the lock was still engaged. It was, and he felt a little less distressed as he moved to the door. *Maybe it was only my imagination after all*, he thought with a bit of relief.

However, as he moved back toward his bed, he could feel the sense of distortion growing stronger with each step. Time slowed, shadows swayed, and he felt a presence reaching for him. The sense of something pressing into him was so strong that he once again glanced around the room. His eyes settled on the safe.

With his hands trembling, he twisted the combination dial on the safe. He was having difficulty recalling the sequence as the numbers. His thoughts became jumbled when he lost focus. He had to restart several times, as his thoughts became muddled with random numbers and equations. The combination had seemed so simple when he'd locked the safe earlier. Now it felt like a herculean task to recall.

When he finally heard the lock pop open, he wiped away the sweat that had beaded on his forehead. He felt like he'd been running through a dense fog. He swung the door back and stared into the pitch-black recess of the safe. It was impossibly dark, apart from the strange device. It seemed to be drawing in all the light in the room and yet was still sharply visible.

When he picked up the device, it stunned him. Despite his attempt to drop it, he was unable to release it from his hand. It was adhering to his hand as if it had been glued to his palm. Trying to pry it away with his other hand only made both hands stick.

There was no sound in the room except the sound of his heavy breathing. All the background sounds of the engines, the creaking of the hull, the slapping of the waves faded into the distance. And yet somehow he could hear the device making a low cacophony of foreign sounds. Bass rumbles that sounded like words in a language that his mind couldn't quite process.

Until suddenly he could understand, even though rationally he knew he shouldn't be able to. He might as well be able to find meaning in the sound of the wind.

"We are the Others. You will help us."

He tried to speak, but his response went unheeded. It didn't seem to acknowledge his attempt.

"In seven of your solar cycles, we will contact you. Be at this location," it rumbled again in the sounds that weren't words. A series of coordinates appeared, etched in the metal of the device.

He found that he'd memorized the latitude and longitude even though he didn't recall thinking about them. They'd been infused into his subconscious. Instantaneously memorized, the coordinates then vanished from the device. The metal was cool, almost cold, and dropped from his hand to the metal deck.

Exhausted, Doctor Smith slowly lowered himself to the

edge of the bed. Although the entire experience couldn't have lasted more than a few minutes, he felt as if he'd been running in sand for hours. He was slick with sweat and wiped his hands on the wool blanket.

As the tendrils of fog in his mind slowly began to clear, he carefully lifted the device off the floor and placed it back in the safe. Back on the bed, he'd quickly fallen asleep. He had strange, vivid dreams every night since that event. Although he knew he dreamt, he could never recall what happened in his subconscious after he opened his eyes.

Since that disorienting episode, he had made his way to the coordinates that pressed into the recesses of his mind. He was like a kite in the wind being pulled constantly toward the time and place that the device had shown him. Any attempt to change his course or delay his travels had met with such resistance that he found it futile to fight the pull.

That brought him back to the present moment.

Sitting on the edge of the bed in a dirty room in a no-name hotel in a city with a name he couldn't pronounce, he knew it was time. The device had led him here, and he had come. He didn't know exactly what was going to happen next, only that he would discover the next step on the path that he'd been chosen to take. The feeling was exhilarating, but at the same time it was frightening. He knew he couldn't resist the tide of history. For someone who had been careful never to cede control, it felt as if he was sitting in a runaway car and watching the cliff speeding ever closer.

He turned on the small clay lamp next to the bed, to chase back some of the gloom. The dim yellow light only pushed the shadows back to the corners, but it was better than sitting in the darkness. The lamp light kept his fear from taking over and erasing the calm that he was trying to hold to. He picked up the small, metal device and held it in both hands. Running his fingers gingerly over the edges, he let his mind wander.

As he was letting his thoughts float back over the events since he'd first started on this project, he struggled to keep his eyes open. The long days, heat and stress were taking its toll. At first, he didn't realize that the lamp light had changed hue. The colors seemed richer and less yellow. The light radiated like the golden light of the setting sun. *It's happening again.*

The cube, which had already been slightly cool to the touch, now felt cold. It was a stark contrast to the intense temperature in the room. Nevertheless, his hands slicked with cold sweat. He tried to watch the hands on his cheap watch. He'd planned to time the episode, but the hands on his watch moved erratically. One moment, the watch hands were moving forward, and then suddenly they'd stop and reverse direction. It made no sense to use his watch when it was affected by the device. But that also meant he too was being affected by the passage of time. Was he aging, caught in limbo or growing younger?

Beyond the physical effects that he was experiencing of the light, temperature, and time, he once again sensed a presence in the room. Like the experience on the ship, he knew there was no human presence possible. The room was small, and there was no place to hide that he hadn't previously checked. He was the only living thing in the room—and yet there was a sentient aura nearby. No, not nearby. As close to him as the device in his hands. He could almost imagine an invisible being pressing against him.

The outside sounds of the small city faded into an eerie silence. He could only hear his own breathing and the pulse of his racing heart. Then the rumble of the foreign sounds began, like summer thunder in the distance. Except there was a pattern to the sound, which he knew would make sense if he stopped trying to actively decipher the meaning. Like a language that was buried in his subconscious, the meaning would become clear when he stopped trying to process it into a contemporary language.

"It is time for the next step on your journey. Are you prepared to listen and obey?" the drumming sound asked.

"I am," Doctor Smith whispered.

"We are coming to your Earth. Our enemies plan to stop us. With your help, we will prevail. When we are successful, we will give you power and knowledge beyond your present ability to understand. You will no longer be a servant but a master. You will be one with the Others."

"Yes, yes," Smith murmured. "A master."

"Follow the path to the next place. There you will find a device that will allow for effective communication. You will need to prepare quickly, for we arrive in five of your lunar cycles.

"Only trust the two others for now. You know who they are because they have been led to you, as you have been led to us. One will never betray you, even if their life is in danger. Our enemies have many humans who will help them. Their schemes are a mystery to us, as you will be a mystery to them."

They know about my two collaborators, he thought.

A new set of coordinates glowed briefly on the device. The numbers faded away as the device warmed slightly and the alien presence grew distant. He glanced briefly at his watch. As close as he could tell, it hadn't been more than a minute since he'd sat down. *How was that possible?*

Exhausted, Doctor Smith slowly pulled his feet on the bed. He turned on his side and curled with the cool device pressed closely to his chest. As the light returned to the dim yellow, he closed his eyes and dreamed of a bright future.

13

ALOHA - BACK TO FEBRUARY 2002

Miss Grey stepped off the plane at the private terminal at Honolulu International Airport in Oahu. She took in a deep breath of the fresh tropical air and removed her sweater.

They had departed from Seattle very early this morning using an unmarked Department of Homeland Security jet. That allowed them to bypass security as well as bring the coffin containing Xi's daughter. Keeping that promise had been more of a bureaucratic challenge than she'd expected. They had flown west with the sun, making it to Hawaii shortly after breakfast. She'd read briefings on the plane between naps. The break from the cold, rainy weather in Seattle was a welcome relief.

Maxx and Gabby had arrived at Boeing Field shortly before they boarded the plane. Maxx had bags under his eyes and was in a foul mood. When she asked him about what had happened, he brushed off her questions. Gabby didn't seem willing to shed any insight on the situation. She shrugged and broke eye contact when asked if she knew the details.

Her answer was curt. "Maxx was working late last night."

Mr. Green was the fourth member of the US coalition. He had sat alone in the rear of the plane. While sitting alone, he had actively avoided any conversation with the three of them. She had urged him to spend some time preparing for the conversation with Xi and the Chinese delegation, but he brushed off her attempts. Eventually, she stopped trying to engage him and made her own preparations.

Anderson was slated to be the fifth member of the team but had reneged. Director Anderson had sent her a text indicating that a more urgent matter had arisen requiring his immediate attention. She couldn't imagine what was more urgent than this meeting, but she was relieved nevertheless. He said that he expected her to handle it and looked forward to reading her written report shortly after the meeting concluded. She had thought about answering with a "screw you, I'm not your secretary" response but decided she didn't care enough to bother.

Outside the terminal, the group met the vehicle that had been arranged to transport them. A gray passenger van with US government markings stenciled on the door pulled up to the curb. A large, muscular man with a military haircut walked quickly toward them. Although he was clearly a soldier, he was wearing a pair of khakis and a bright-blue Hawaiian shirt.

The driver stuck out his hand and eyeballed the group. "Aloha. Captain Holt. I presume you're Mr. Green, Miss Grey, and your two guests. Where's Professor Plum?" He grinned broadly.

Grey groaned at the bad joke. She shook his hand firmly and introduced herself. "I'm Miss Grey. Since we're keeping a low profile, let's drop the rank and go with Mr. Holt for today."

"Yes, ma'am," he said with a more relaxed grin as he shook hands with the rest of the group. "Jump on in and let's get going. Traffic is the usual cluster this time of the morning."

"Is someone here to take Connie Xi's casket?"

"There's a specialized crew unloading the coffin from your

plane. They'll follow behind us in another vehicle. They have instructions to load the cargo directly on your visitor's plane."

"We are we heading?" Maxx asked from the back seat.

"We're heading up to K-Bay," Mr. Holt said. "It's about twenty miles away on the Mokapu Peninsula."

"Why so far away?" Mr. Maxx asked. "There must be a place closer where we could meet."

"Yes, sir. But your foreign guests requested a more remote location where they could land directly and bypass the civilian airport. Command selected the Marine base at Kaneohe Bay. We refer to it affectionately as K-Bay."

"Do you know if the foreign team has arrived yet?" Mr. Green asked.

"Yes, the two gentlemen are waiting in a secure building near the airfield. The CO cleared out a space for you all that has plenty of secure communication equipment if you need it."

The rest of the drive on H3 through the lush countryside was a chance for Holt to give them a quick review of the island. It wasn't the busiest highway but offered some stunning tropical views. He asked a few probing questions about their backgrounds and purpose of their meeting, but no one offered any information to enlighten him.

After passing through several security checkpoints, they headed toward a plain-looking three-story building painted faded yellow. The bay and lush green cliffs loomed in the background. The runway jutted out into the bay. Completely isolated from any land access. Secure and offered no chance of the Chinese visitors being seen by prying eyes.

Parked a short distance away, close to the air traffic control tower, was a midsize jet. Gleaming white, it was devoid of any markings except the tail number. Holt told them that was their guest's jet. Despite the high fence surrounding the gate, there were several security teams close by to ensure no one wandered by.

Holt pulled the van into a parking spot in front of the building and jumped out. He took them inside the concrete block building. "This is your stop. We didn't know how long you plan to stay, so I've set up in an office by the front door. I'll be waiting for you there. Now if you'll follow me."

Leading them down a series of hallways with gleaming tile floors and white walls covered in photos of helicopters, he stopped outside the meeting room. There were a couple marines in uniform standing beside the door. "We've arranged for food to be brought over from the mess hall, so you won't go hungry. If your meeting continues into the night, we'll arrange a place to sleep. Good luck with whatever you're doing," he said with a wink. He opened the door and ushered them inside.

Dr. Xi stood at the large window looking over the runway and the blue tropical waters. When Mr. Green's group entered the room, he nodded slightly. "Finally, we meet, Mr. Green. I have heard many things about you and the program you have run." He had dark circles of fatigue around his eyes that contrasted with his casual attire.

The other Chinese man in the room stood and held out his hand. Wearing a black suit and white shirt that looked like it had been recently ironed, he introduced himself, "I am Director Liu, Doctor Xi's colleague and the administrator of the communication program. It is a pleasure to meet with all of you."

Each of the Americans stepped forward to shake hands and introduce themselves. When it was Gabby's turn to shake hands with Xi, he gave her a gentle hug. "Thank you for all that you have done for my daughter. She spoke highly of you."

Gabby hugged him a second time and brushed a tear from her cheek. "I'm so sorry. It is a tragedy, but she would be proud to know that we have taken this step to meet on her behalf."

Xi turned to Maxx. "I have already apologized for Haoyu's attempts to kill you. I'm sure you understand why I considered you to be the enemy. I hope now that we will be able to be on the same side of history."

"Bygones," Maxx grumbled. "But I'm going to catch the person responsible for killing your daughter and attacking Gabby. I won't be as nice as I was to the last person who attacked us." Maxx felt Gabby jab him in the side with her elbow. He looked at her sheepishly when he remembered that Connie's killer was Xi's estranged daughter.

Xi nodded. "Don't fret. Li Jing must be brought to justice and pay her debt. I will harbor no resentment toward you."

Mr. Green pulled up a chair at the head of the table. "I like chitchat as much as the next person, but we need to get this meeting started. People are counting on us to figure out how to work together. And we have a deadline looming in a couple days."

"You are correct," Xi said, taking a seat next to Director Liu. "We have a big responsibility and much to discuss. Will you please tell us what you would like to accomplish today, Mr. Green and Miss Grey?"

Mr. Green wiped a bead of sweat off his forehead. "We have been routinely communicating with the alien civilization, Thunderbird, since September. They have instructed us to work together with your nation to prepare for the invasion of their enemies. An invasion is expected within the week. If together we are unable to stop their enemy, they have warned us that they will reset the planet. We don't know exactly what 'reset' means, but we've interpreted it to mean they'll trigger a series of cataclysmic events. We assume they have the capability to act on this threat. We are treating it as a legitimate global threat."

Liu, with a look of shock, leaned over and whispered quietly in Xi's ear. Xi shook his head and said, "This is indeed disturbing news. Before we proceed further, we want to be certain that Doctor Smith is no longer with the United States on this project."

Maxx coughed to get everyone's attention. "Dr. Xi, when we talked on the phone a couple days ago, I told you that the US is in no way longer connected with Doctor Smith. He has disappeared following the debacle on September 11th and is considered a criminal by the US government."

"Maxx is correct," Mr. Green said with a nod. "Doctor Smith is an enemy of the state, and we presume that he is dead."

Maxx coughed again. "That's not exactly true. Mr. Green may not be aware of this information yet, but Doctor Smith is alive."

"That is of no matter, although I do wish to hear the good news of his death," Xi said. "As long as he is not working with you, then we will proceed."

"Well, I know this is going to come as a surprise, but it does matter that he is alive. Not only is Smith continuing to work on a similar communication project, but I've learned he is in contact with the adversary aliens – the Others."

Miss Grey's eyes opened in surprise. "Learned this from where, Maxx?"

"I was waiting until we were all together to let you know that I had an incident last night. Agent Hovis was kidnapped briefly by Li Jing. He was able to free himself and hold her temporarily. While she was restrained, she admitted that she was working with Doctor Smith."

Dr. Xi and Director Liu both stared at Maxx with his mouth agape. After gasping, Liu asked, "Did she say what they were doing together?"

Maxx shook his head. "Hovis, an FBI agent, was struck in the head a couple times and now has a mild concussion. His memory is spotty, so he wasn't 100% certain of what Li Jing told him. What he recalled was they were working on a communication project to keep the Others from invading. He doesn't know anything about this project, so he thought she was lying, or he imagined the conversation."

"Did he indicate how Smith is communicating with them?" Mr. Green interjected. "We know the communication apparatus he built was destroyed on September 11th. How would he get in contact with the other civilization even if he did have a replacement device?"

"No, he didn't have any information about the device. Li Jing admitted to killing Connie and was frantic to get back to Smith so they could save the world. He thought she was crazy."

"Why did she kill my Connie then?" Xi asked softly. "My daughter had nothing to do with this project."

Maxx sighed. "She told Agent Hovis that she killed her to stop you from working with us. That together the two countries were going to cause a war against the aliens who were coming in peace."

Miss Grey scowled at Maxx. "If we'd known about this earlier, we could have asked Li Jing all these questions ourselves. Is she being held at the Seattle FBI office?"

"No, she escaped after Hovis detained her."

There were several gasps in the room. "How did that happen?" Grey asked.

"Hovis can't recall. He was unconscious when I found him, and the ambulance took him to Harborview. The emergency doctor said he had two separate blows to the head. When Hovis regained consciousness, he said Li Jing had knocked him out the first time. But he was completely blank about what happened after he'd talked to Li Jing."

"Lovely. So she's back in the wind," Miss Grey said. "Hovis is lucky to be alive."

"But Li Jing must not understand what is really happening. Doctor Smith is lying to her if she thinks the aliens are coming here in peace," Green said. "The two alien civilizations are at war, and we are caught in the middle. We have picked a side by helping Thunderbird. It sounds like Smith is cooperating with Thunderbird's enemy to prevent our two countries from cooperating."

Xi stood halfway out of his chair. His face had turned a bright red as he raised his voice at Miss Grey. "If Smith is trying to stop us from working together, then he is mistaken. The enemy of my enemy is my friend. Have no doubt that he is my enemy. He is an evil man and will always choose to be on the wrong side of history."

Everyone stared at Xi. Liu looked at the ground in embarrassment before Xi took several deep breaths and sat back down.

After a few moments of silence, Green looked at Xi and asked, "So where do we begin?"

Liu stood up and straightened his tie. Bowing again to the group, he said, "Now that we understand that we are dealing with a greater risk that we first imagined, I would like to suggest that we agree to share our plans."

Mr. Green raised his eyebrows. "What plans are you proposing that we share, Director?"

Liu paused before answering, as if he was thinking. However, he looked down at his notes, which gave the impression that he wasn't speaking off the cuff but had planned this request. "I'd like our generals to share their plans to respond to the invasion. China is prepared to respond, but it would be more effective if we aligned our military efforts."

Miss Grey looked back in forth between Liu and Xi with a look of puzzlement. "Are you authorized to speak on behalf of the military? We are not. We can pass your proposal to the chain of command, but that idea is outside of out purview."

"We cannot speak for the military either," Xi said as he glared at Liu. "We are authorized to only address the communication device."

Director Liu turned a bright shade of red. Lowering his

eyes, he avoided looking at Xi, as he sat back down. "My apologies, I misspoke. Dr. Xi, where would you like to begin?"

"I believe there are several roads that we can take together. The most obvious is the device itself. We are willing to share all that we know about the origin and operation of the machine," Xi said.

Mr. Green nodded vigorously. "We are utilizing the original machine that was delivered to us in 1957. Any knowledge about the construction and function of your device and ours can only help. We also have the documents from Doctor Smith's attempt to build a replica. I hate to admit it, but he made some brilliant advances in our understanding the technology."

"Then we are in agreement to collaborate on this point," Xi responded. "My recommendation is that there is no need to mention this element of our collaboration to the aliens. We don't know if they would approve, but it is better to ask for forgiveness than approval."

"Since we have learned about Dr. Smith's involvement in leading a hostile program, I imagine that we should pool our efforts to stop him and his collaborator, Li Jing."

"We can agree with that joint action too," Miss Grey said. "This activity has been under my direct control at Department of Homeland Security in conjunction with the FBI. I can get Agent Hovis to work together with your representative."

"Thank you. I have already spoken with the director of the Chinese police on this matter. Because of the political implications, they have requested that an objective third-party represent our interests. Someone we can trust who will not let politics get in the way of success."

Miss Grey looked puzzled. "Do have someone in mind, Dr.?"

"Yes, we have decided that our representative will be Maxx King."

Maxx stopped looking out the window when he heard Xi

say his name. "I'm not an official representative of the United States. I'm honored that you trust me, but I don't have any authority here."

Xi ignored Maxx and turned to Miss Grey. "Is this something that you can arrange, getting Mr. King the appropriate authority?"

Grey chuckled. "I certainly can. I'll discuss it with him on the flight home. Right, Maxx?"

He glared at her. "We'll discuss it, Dr. Xi. I'll let you know after we chat."

"Good, good," he said. "Finally, the last point of collaboration should be our joint communications with the extraterrestrials. I believe it would be more effective for us to present a unified voice in our dialogue with them."

"Thunderbird has been pressing us for the last several months to engage with you in preparations, so that should please them," Mr. Green said.

"Who is Thunderbird?" Xi said as he furrowed his brow. "This Thunderbird has never requested that we work together with you. They have only asked us to be prepared for their arrival and to aid in their defense."

The Americans paused whatever they were doing and gaped at Xi. Mr. Green was the first to break the awkward silence in the room. "The aliens. That's what they told us to call them at the initial conversation in September. What did they tell you to call them?"

"They said that they are known as the Others."

"Oh my God," Gabby whispered. "We've been talking to two different civilizations this entire time."

"What does this mean..." Liu barked.

Xi held up his hand, stopping Liu. "It means that, although our devices seem similar and may use similar technology, we have been unknowingly communicating with both sides in this war."

"They have been using us as pawns to fight their enemies… and each other," said Miss Grey.

"Pawns, but we can be so much more," Xi said as he took a small chess board out of his briefcase. He opened his case further and removed a set of pieces carved from onyx and jade. "I believe we can use this misdirection to our advantage."

He set the jade pawns on the board. "These are the white pawns. They represent the people of Earth," he said with a cunning grin.

14

EVERY PAWN IS A POTENTIAL QUEEN

Senator Traficant's staff pushed ahead of her, clearing a path through the crowded hallway of the Russell Senate Building.

The senator had received a text message from Mr. Green on her personal phone over an hour ago. "We are leaving K-Bay soon. Call me ASAP."

It meant he had news that couldn't wait until their scheduled call. She'd left him explicit instructions not to bother her unless he had good news. She was in no mood for failure when they were only days from success. She didn't like Green and his irreverent sense of humor, but he was still a useful pawn in her political game. Plus, he gave her plausible deniability if anything went seriously wrong with the Thunderbird device.

She'd been on the Armed Services Committee hearing and as the subcommittee chairperson was unable to break away mid-meeting. At the moment, she was mostly interested to learn the outcome of the meeting with the Chinese delegation in Hawaii. A climax was quickly approaching in the Middle East. There would always be an endless stream of bureaucrats to berate in these committee meetings.

As soon as she could gracefully exit the hearing room, she'd signaled her staff to clear the way through the corridors. She'd make the occasional nod or wave to someone who mattered, but mostly she kept her head down and powered forward. Her aides would have an ultra-secure conference room ready when she arrived.

The room was a designated SCIF located in the brick-lined basement corridor. She'd had the Sensitive Compartmented Information Facility built during a long past crisis to accommodate confidential deliberations with the national security advisory team. The soundproofed, electromagnetically shielded communication facility also served as an ideal location to hold private conversations. Discussions she wished to keep away from the prying eyes at the National Security Agency. The super-secretive tech-savvy goons at the NSA were always listening in on the world's communications, even hers. She'd been in this game long enough to know where all the traps were hidden. Many of the traps were designed for her benefit. There were too many people in this town who would turn in their own mother to get a step ahead.

When she entered the secure conference room, her aides quickly established the protected communication equipment and closed the solid door behind them as they silently exited. They knew better than to ask any questions when she set her jaw.

She dialed the number that Green had texted her. From the area code, she guessed that he was sitting in an office at the Marine Base at Kaneohe Bay. They'd need to keep the conversation tight since his end of the conversation wouldn't be secure. It was better than talking on his cell phone, but not by much. Any sensitive keywords would get trapped by the NSA filters and passed along to the CIA.

He picked up on the second ring. "I was beginning to wonder if you got my message."

"Busy day here in the heart of democracy," she said with a heavy note of sarcasm. "I presume you've got good news."

"Very good," he said. "Xi committed the Chinese to working with us. He'd like to join us on the upcoming calls with Thunderbird. We're also sharing information on device research. We decided to create a clean data room where we can exchange information."

"That sounds promising. I presume you'll schedule a joint call with Thunderbird as soon as you're back at the facility in Seattle. Will Xi join you there?"

"Yes, he's going to fly back to Seattle with us. He'll send his daughter's body on ahead to China. He's paying his respects to his daughter now, and then we'll be leaving shortly."

"Perfect," she said. "Is that it?"

He took a long pause. She could tell he was hesitant to tell her something. *Just once I'd like it to be easy.*

"There is a bit of bad news. Actually, a couple bits. Doctor Smith is alive."

She furrowed her brow. "That's not exactly a surprise, since we didn't recover any evidence of his body after the attack on September 11th. Do we have any intel where he's at?"

"I don't know that yet. What I learned is that Li Jing told the FBI that she is working with him."

"That woman keeps showing up in the most peculiar places. I may have misjudged her survivability. What is she doing with Smith?"

"This is the strange part. She said they are working on a device that is communicating with the Others. They are trying to stop the conflict with Thunderbird."

She could feel a headache coming on with the sudden pressure behind her eyes. "I should have known that he'd find a way to complicate things. He made a mess of the first contact with Thunderbird and is willing to once again put the plan in jeopardy."

"Agent Grey said they would work with the FBI to make finding him a priority. She understands that we need to stop him before Friday, even if she doesn't fully grasp the reason why. She's confident she can get it done."

"That man needs to be put down. Keep me posted," she said.

He coughed to stop her from hanging up. "That's not the most surprising news."

"There's more?" she said incredulously.

"It turns out that Xi has not been communicating with Thunderbird for the last six months. He's been talking to the Others."

The senator took a deep breath to calm herself. "You're telling me that we assumed that both the US and China were communicating with the same extraterrestrial civilization, and we were actually talking to different groups?" she said.

"Thunderbird and the Others use similar technology, and we thought they were the same. Both devices were discovered around the same time in the 1950s, and we've both been operating under a mistaken assumption this entire time."

She took a moment to think through this revelation. "And the Chinese are still willing to work with us and Thunderbird?"

"They are willing, and Xi even proposed a plan to use this confusion to our advantage."

"You can tell me about this plan when you get back. Right now, the important thing is that the Chinese are willing to partner with us and buy us some time with Thunderbird. Now I understand why they were threatening us if we didn't get the Chinese to cooperate. They knew their enemy was engaging China all along. We keep silent about them talking to the Others until I figure out how to use this information to our advantage."

"I hear you. I'll arrange the communication with Thunderbird, and we can talk then."

It took every ounce of her control not to scream with frustration after she disconnected. Even though the room was soundproof, she struggled to maintain control. It wasn't yet a major setback. It was a problem to be manipulated and defeated, like the many hundreds of setbacks – big and small – that she'd beaten over the last fifty years. She hadn't risen to power by giving up when the road became steep and rocky.

Taking a moment to catch her breath, Jane leaned back in the leather chair. She straightened her jacket lapels and made sure her hair and makeup were perfect. She wasn't going to let that moron Doctor Smith get in her way again. She'd underestimated him once before, and he'd almost destroyed her chance to connect directly with Thunderbird. Of course, she had known that his work at DARPA would fail, but she thought she'd finally ended his interference on September 11th.

What she hadn't counted on was that he'd been prepared for her duplicity. By planting explosives in Team Tacoma's work area, he had killed many of the team's experts and buried the communication device under the collapsed towers. It had taken weeks for them to recover the device and make it operational once again.

And now the thorn in her side was back. Not only had Smith escaped, but he was also working against her directly by engaging with the Others. She didn't doubt the information from Li Jing was accurate. He would betray the US and Thunderbird to reassert himself as an invincible agent of chaos. How he had managed to connect with the Others wasn't important, only that he be stopped before he could interfere with her plans.

What mattered most now was contacting Thunderbird to let them know what she'd learned. They likely were already aware that the Chinese had been communicating with the Others, which would explain why they had been placing so much pressure on the US to collaborate directly with China.

She'd always wondered why they'd ignored her pleas to pressure China—because they had no direct contact. They were counting on the US to make the bridge without alerting the Others.

But this news about Smith's work would be a revelation to them. If the Others were using Smith as a knight-errant, it would be a huge blow to Thunderbird's plans to prevent a successful invasion. She decided that she couldn't wait for Green to connect with them using the normal channels. At the risk of exposing her direct dealings with Thunderbird, she needed to signal to them that something urgent had arisen.

Lifting her briefcase onto the table, she entered the code into the lock. It was a lock that the CIA had assured her was impenetrable. Any unauthorized attempts to open the case would result in an explosion that would destroy the contents, apart from the small metal cube made of materials that weren't found naturally anywhere on Earth. The device was indestructible but also of no use to anyone but her.

The small cube arrived in 1957 along with the much larger communication device and data files. These items were recovered by the military at the base commonly referred to as Area 51 and placed into storage while the government had formed the top-secret research team. The device had sat dormant for several years with no progress. Eventually the program was mothballed and placed into a storage facility at a black site at White Sands.

The turning point came two years later, when she was conducting an onsite visit to the facility. She was visiting to decide whether to defund the project or try a new tack. During the visit, the small cube had reacted to her presence. She was in a room with several project scientists at the time, but none of them had experienced the same sensations that she had. Time slowed, light patterns changed, and she could hear or sense some form of external communication.

While it was an overwhelming experience for her, the other people present saw and felt nothing unusual. After it became clear that the events went unnoticed, she elected to keep the effects a secret. She was afraid if she mentioned the episode to anyone else that they might question her sanity or assume she was using hallucinogenic drugs. And keeping secrets had always worked in her favor.

At the conclusion of the meeting, she had recommended that they decommission the venture. The team was then reassigned to other projects. The communication device and data files were placed into long-term storage and buried in the bureaucratic record keeping. After an adequate amount of time had passed, she returned to the facility to smuggle the small cube out. She had been using the cube as a personal connection device ever since.

After years of trial and error, she was able to use the cube more consistently for communication. It provided her with enough information that she was able to guide the formation of DARPA and reactivate the communication program with Doctor Smith as the lead. After her election to the Senate in 1980, her power base had continued to grow using the bits of information that she periodically gleaned from the cube. Unfortunately, the information was not always complete. That partial information – and Doctor Smith's unwillingness to listen to her – had led to the disaster at Mount Saint Helens.

Now she was much more careful with the information that she obtained from the cube. Time had been on her side, so she had been reluctant about taking large risks. Until time had become critical with the pending arrival of the Others. Thunderbird had then begun pressing to advance the progress on the communication device for broader two-way communication with the United States government. She'd been pressured by the aliens to push the breakthroughs last September. She had covertly supplied the breakthrough to the Jet Propulsion

Lab that had led to the data key being "suddenly" decrypted after forty-three years.

She wrapped her hands around the cube. The lights began to shift in the room. The fluorescent bulbs began to flare a deep shade of blue in the corners. She closed her eyes to focus. The cube grew noticeably cooler. It wasn't uncomfortably cold, but temperature changes were always the second physical sensation that the device was activating. Time began to slow until she felt as if she was floating weightlessly in a void. She had tried a depravation tank once, and it was a similar experience, except now she could feel the presence of another life force.

"You summoned us," the voice said. She'd learned that only she could hear the voice, but it sounded like it surrounded her. It filled the emptiness around her.

She'd also learned that cube didn't hear her thoughts but sensed her emotional state. Consequently, she forced herself to feel anxious about the information she'd learned from Smith. She repeated the words "something bad has happened" repeatedly to herself. Saying the words increased her apprehension.

"You are afraid," the voice intoned. "Do not worry. We will not harm you."

They had misinterpreted her emotion. She cleared her mind and tried a different approach. Anger. Desperation. "Must kill Doctor Smith" she repeated passionately to herself.

Since the time really was irrelevant to her in this state, she waited.

"Your enemy has been found again. What has he done?" the voice asked, although it knew she could not answer.

"The Others," she repeated to herself. With the words came feelings of wonder, anxiety, helplessness.

"Then we must talk. Soon." the voice responded.

Slowly, Jane again became aware of her physical surroundings. The increasing warmth of the cube, the leather chair, and a faint smell of ozone in the air. She opened her eyes and looked at the atomic clock on the wall. Only seconds had passed since she had removed the device from the case from her briefcase.

She felt slightly better now that she'd alerted Thunderbird that something was afoot. That should encourage them to coordinate communication as quickly as possible. She texted Green to make sure that he was setting that connection immediately.

A loud knock on the door startled her out of the last seconds of her reverie.

"Who is it?" she said testily as she rapidly snapped her briefcase closed to hide the cube.

"It's Director Anderson."

What was he doing here? She doubted that her staff would tell him where she was without checking with her first. She never trusted him, even though he was working for her. She had enough leverage to put him in a federal penitentiary for life. There was more financial upside for him by staying on her side of the line. But occasionally men like Barth had to test the flame to make sure it was still hot.

She pressed the electronic door lock. "It's open."

Looking every bit the part, he strutted into the room. With his slightly long surfer blond hair and deep tan, he looked like he'd recently returned from a month in the Caribbean. He was wearing a Brooks Brothers suit, a white cuffed shirt, and Bally loafers to blend into the power players at Langley. At least he had retained enough sense of style not to get to the level of Tommy Bahama shirts and chinos like Green.

"I thought I might find you here," he said with a smirk. "I presume someone was updating you on the kerfuffle the FBI had last night with Li Jing?"

"It wasn't a kerfuffle, you ass. It turns out she is working with Doctor Smith."

He kept on smirking. "I'd heard that piece of news. Sadly, I didn't have a chance to let you know."

"But she also escaped, so we didn't get a chance to interrogate her," she said. "What a disaster."

"Not entirely," he said, pulling up a chair. A little closer than was comfortable for her. She could smell his cheap cologne. "It's better that she escaped, otherwise she'd be held indefinitely by the FBI. We don't have time to sort that out. We've got two days to track down Smith before..."

She squinted at him. "You had something to do with her escaping, don't you?"

"You should thank me. Yes, I made sure she escaped. I need her to lead us to Smith, and she can't do that from an FBI holding room. We know he's somewhere in the middle east. Probably Iraq or Afghanistan, but that's TBD since we don't have enough ground intel to confirm. The biggest risk is that she gets caught or killed before she leads us to where Smith is hiding."

"Isn't it a bigger risk that you lose her trail?" she asked in confusion.

"Nah, I injected a tracker into her while she was out. Then I woke her up and chased her away. The only glitch in my plan came when that gorilla-looking, ex-special forces guy, Maxx, found the FBI agent too quickly. She almost didn't escape."

She wrinkled her brow. This was getting too chaotic. "Who knows that you helped her escape?"

"She does obviously. Also, the FBI Agent Hovis and Maxx King."

"Isn't she going to be suspicious?" Jane asked.

"Nah, we used to be a thing on some projects for the CIA. She thinks I still have an interest in her."

"You're a disgusting man, Barth. You let her think that while you're using her?"

He grinned broadly. "All for the good of the country, ma'am."

Jane shook her head in disgust. "What about the other two?"

"I'll take care of them. They're going to be assigned to track her down. I already arranged that. And gosh it would be terrible if somehow, they got killed. A real tragedy."

"Make sure they stay silent," she said. "I don't want to know how you do it."

15

COMING TO KABUL

Doctor Smith moved quietly through the stuffy granite tunnel, gliding through the inky darkness.

A huge rock chamber appeared far ahead at the mouth of the tunnel. To his right were the cramped living quarters of the facility workers. There were dirty blankets pinned to the wall to provide some privacy, but most of the attempts at privacy had fallen into disrepair during the previous six months. When they finished with his project, the temporary workers would pack up their meager belongings and move to where the Taliban told them to go.

Ahead, the long narrow corridor ran between the rough-hewn stone walls. Smith could see the wooden door to a room carved from the rock. Previously it had been the home of a Taliban warlord, but now his own temporary residence. Further along the tunnel, in the chamber, was the black metallic device where the scientists from Iran were stationed.

Past the open chamber was the underground waterfall. It had been diverted to power a small hydrogenator to provide power to the device. The tunnels behind the falls had been formed from the lava tubes. The Taliban used this system of tunnels to transport weapons hidden from the foreign militaries that prowled the skies above.

In the mid-1980s, at the peak of the Taliban's resistance to the Soviet invasion, several hundred men had lived and worked in these tunnels. The underground town had expanded to service the resistance, storing weapons and transporting supplies using the underground river. Later, the power generation had been added courtesy of the CIA.

However, to everything there is a season. After September 11th, when it appeared that the Americans would soon be taking their turn in the mountains of Afghanistan, the tunnels became reactivated and the mine reopened. The facility was prepared for a yet-to-be-determined project. That was when Doctor Smith moved in. With assistance from the Iranian government, he claimed the tunnels for his project on behalf of the Others.

And the Taliban had allowed him to settle here with the alien device while they prepared for the coming war with the Americans.

But now he was doing what he was destined to do. This time, he would not run.

Smith walked into the domed chamber naturally created in the granite. Large enough to easily hold one hundred men and their equipment, it was largely empty now. In the center of the hollow was the large metallic cube with thick black power cables snaking to the power plant. The glow from the portable light stands along the edge of the cavern did little to illuminate the device. It looked like a dark, unnatural wound in the natural space.

"Doctor Smith, will you please come here?" one of the men in a white lab jacket said in broken English.

Smith had required that all the men on the device team wear the jackets, making them easily distinguishable from the soldiers here to protect the device. No one except him and the "white coats" were allowed near the device or power equipment. The penalty for getting too close to the device without permission was a quick death. He made no exceptions.

The man who called to him was Faraj, his right-hand person here in the cavern. He oversaw the operation of the device during the rare times that Smith was sleeping or temporarily outside of the tunnels. Wearing pants and boots form the Iranian military, he wore a threadbare Bruce Springsteen t-shirt underneath his lab jacket. With wiry black hair and a thick, graying beard, he looked like the rest of the men. However, Smith knew he was frighteningly intelligent and was zealously dedicated to the project.

Faraj had come from a small, poor village in the nearby Kush. He had seen most of his family die when an errant Russian artillery round had landed in their home. Since then, he had vowed to commit his life to repelling the foreigners from his homeland. He'd gone to Oxford with a scholarship then returned to Iran and joined the military. He'd been hand selected for this project because of his physics and engineering expertise and his devotion to the cause.

"Why did you send someone to wake me?" Smith asked as he rubbed sleep from his eyes. It was 3:30 in the morning, and he'd only slept a few hours.

"I am most apologetic, Doctor," Faraj said without looking the least bit apologetic. "There was an urgent message relayed to us on the radio, and you were asked to call this number."

Faraj handed Smith a slip of paper with a number written in pencil.

It wasn't a number that Smith recognized. That was unusual. He only had a handful of people who tried to contact him. Anyone trying to reach him would call a number in Kabul, which was then relayed via shortwave to the small camp at the foot of the mountain. From there a runner would bring the information to the tunnel. Due to delays in communication, it could be hours before he could return a call from the satellite phone.

"Thank you, Faraj. I will call them," Smith said. "Since I'm awake, has there been any change in the device while I slept?"

"It is still in the same passive mode. Standby, it seems. It is not the typical device sequence we see before communication. And we can find no reference to this mode in the files that you provided."

"I assume it is related to the upcoming events. When the Others want us to know why, I imagine they'll tell us."

There was so much that Doctor Smith didn't understand about the plans of the Others that he had to take a number of actions on faith. When he was given the small cube, he took each step of the journey as it had come, accepting that he was being led to greatness. Certainly, he expected to be tested, but he'd never waver. He was confident that he was on the right side of history.

When he had traveled from New York to the Hindu Kush, he had not known what he'd find. He never suspected that there was a communication device at the end of his travels. No one had an answer to how it had arrived at this location. They simply accepted its sudden appearance.

When the device first appeared after September 11th, the Taliban believed it was a trick of the United States. Eventually accepting the miraculous appearance was a sign from Allah, they had contacted the local imam for guidance. The imam had received a vision.

The vision told him that the object was a tool given to them for the upcoming war. He was told to be patient, that a learned man would arrive to teach them how to use it. Then Smith walked fearlessly to the entrance of the cave holding the miniature version of the cube.

That was all in the past. Smith walked quickly, following the long set of tunnels to the entrance overlooking the valley. It was an awe-inspiring view. Not only was it a place where nature's grandeur and human history intertwined, but he believed where the future of humanity would be written. And he was one of the authors.

From his vantage point, he could see a vast expanse of jagged peaks and deep valleys. The air was crisp and clear, offering panoramic views that seemed to stretch endlessly. The full moon cast dramatic shadows across the landscape, highlighting the textures and contours of the mountains. In the distance, he could see the scattering of lights from small villages clinging to the mountainsides, with terraced fields adding a touch of human presence to the otherwise wild scenery.

Dialing the number from the piece of paper, he waited for the connection. He marveled at how a place rich in history and culture was linked together by the human technology in his hand, in the satellites above him, and the alien technology deep in the cave.

When the line finally connected, he heard a familiar voice, "Good morning, Doctor."

It was Liu Yuxuan, the administrator of the XINXI device program. He'd initially recruited him to spy on his nemesis, Dr. Xi. But Liu also gave him a means to funnel information in to and out of the CCP. He was an ace up his sleeve.

"Liu, I have told you not to reach out to me unless there was an emergency. What's wrong?"

"I apologize for the request to speak with you, Doctor, but I felt I must warn you. The Americans and Chinese have learned that you are alive."

"A minor inconvenience. The Americans cannot stop me now. We are too close to the finish."

"They are trying to follow Li Jing to your destination. I don't know this man named Maxx King, but everyone seemed very confident that he would stop you and Li Jing. Even Xi thinks very highly of him."

"I have met him. He is dangerous, but I am well protected."

"But it is not only the Americans who are searching for you. Xi has also committed China's cooperation with their communication plan."

He cringed. "Then that part of our plan has failed. I was hopeful Li Jing would persuade her father not to work with the Americans."

"She failed, and now they are planning to follow her to you."

"They will not be able to find me before it's too late," Smith said. "I will not fail this time."

The caller paused. "Do not get mad at me, but I have also been asked to remind you that the Chinese have requested additional weapons from the Others. They believe they can win the war against the Americans but are certain they will prevail with a technical advantage."

"Do not pester me with such minor details," Smith barked. "The Chinese have a direct connection with the Others they can use."

"You are right, of course. And they have asked, but so far their request has been ignored."

"Then they have their answer," Smith said. "This is not my problem. Be ready to fight when the Others arrive. It will be soon."

"Victory will soon be ours," the caller said and cut the line.

Smith stared out across the valley. He was beginning to see hints of light in the eastern sky as he reentered the dark cave. Only a few more sunrises and the world would be changed.

Holding the phone, he hesitated to turn it off. He wanted to call Li Jing and warn her about the Americans, but it was a risk that he was not willing to take. She had known what this project entailed and had still committed to its success regardless of the cost. She had been dedicated enough to even kill her own half-sister. He would have to let it play out and let her deal with the people hunting her. He had no doubt that the Americans would kill her if they caught her. So be it.

Most importantly, he needed to contact the Others to warn them that the Chinese were now aware they and the Americans had been communicating with different civilizations. And now the Chinese and Americans planned to join forces and collaborate with Thunderbird. This was a very dangerous development so close to their arrival.

He walked back to his room and closed the rustic wooden door. Unlocking his battered case, he removed the metallic cube and sat on the chair. He could feel the temperature of the device drop as he closed his eyes and focused his thoughts on Xi. *Danger and betrayal.*

***

The Department of Homeland Security jet carrying the team back from Hawaii landed at Joint Base Lewis McChord south of Seattle around 7:00 p.m.

The unmarked Gulfstream had originally been routed to Boeing Field close to downtown, but there had been a conversation on a secured line between Miss Grey and her supervisor during the last hour. She had told the group that they would be landing at the military airbase and then split up from there. Mr. Green and Dr. Xi would have a team from DHS security escort them up I-5 to the DARPA facility. Everyone else would remain at the airfield for a debriefing.

The military police took Miss Grey, Maxx, and Gabby from the special guests' terminal to a plain-looking concrete building in a remote area of the airfield. Miss Grey informed them that it was used by federal agencies when they were working on joint projects with the military. Surrounded by barbed wire and a gate manned by heavily armed military police, security was clearly intended to deter random visitors.

As they walked through the door, they found a familiar face waiting for them. Agent Hovis sat inside. Looking better than the last time Maxx had seen him, he was wearing a bandage on his head and still looking peaked. He got to his feet a bit shakily and weakly shook their hands.

"I'm surprised they let you out of the hospital," Maxx said as he put a large hand on Keith's elbow to steady him. "You looked like crap when I left last night."

"I was released against medical advice," Keith said with weak laugh. "I'm feeling a little better now but am still have some gaps in my memory."

Miss Grey walked over and looked closely at the heavy bandage on Hovis' head. "No recall on how LI Jing escaped?"

"It's a blank, and thinking about it only gets me agitated. The neurologist said I may recover those memories with time. But focusing on it won't help."

"You're lucky that Maxx came along when he did," Miss Grey said. "He probably scared them away."

Keith laughed nervously. "I owe him one. Or two."

"Don't worry about it," Maxx said. "You can take me out for taco Tuesday someday."

"Don't fall for it." Gabby smirked. "He'll empty your wallet."

"It's great to see you're out of the hospital, but what brings you here?" Maxx asked.

Miss Grey interrupted. "I spoke to the assistant director, and he suggested that Agent Hovis meet us here."

They went into the small conference room and grabbed a seat around the cheap folding table. Maxx was too large to fit in the plastic chairs, so he stood leaning against the wall. Outside the high window, they could see the occasional cargo plane take off or land.

Maxx looked at Miss Grey with a raised eyebrow. "So why

are we meeting in this dump instead of DARPA or the fancy FBI digs?" Maxx asked.

"This stays between us for now," Miss Grey said. "I'm concerned that we may have some people who aren't fully aligned with our objectives."

"Who?" Gabby asked innocently.

"Name names," Maxx said. "I hate these secret squirrel games you Feds are always playing."

"I'm not going to say until I have firm evidence, but we're getting some concerning signals that the CIA is running a side operation. We all experienced it the other night at the FBI headquarters when we learned that they have been tracking Xi and Li Jing but not sharing the information."

"And Anderson was the one who gave me the information that Li Jing was near Lake Union," said Hovis.

"That's scary," Gabby said. "Anderson gives me the creeps."

"Me too," Miss Grey said. "The point is we met here because I know this location isn't on the CIA radar and they are expecting us to be downtown."

"That doesn't make me feel all warm and fuzzy, but I get it," Maxx said. "My second question is, what are we meeting to talk about?"

"We've located Li Jing. She's on a Turkish Airlines flight to from Los Angeles to Kabul, Afghanistan."

"Why Afghanistan?" Maxx asked. "That seems like jumping out of the frying pan into the fire."

"We don't know, but we need to find her and stop her. And since we are trying to avoid relying on the CIA assets stationed there, someone else needs to go. Someone that I trust and is familiar with how to operate in the area."

Gabby looked startled. "You mean Maxx? Don't you have someone else who can go?"

"I would if I could. But I talked it over with the main office, and everyone thinks that Maxx is our best option. He's outside the CIA loop, knows Li Jing, and is familiar with the area because of his deployment in the Middle East when he was in special operations."

"It'll be okay, Gabby," Maxx said as he walked over and gently put his hand on her shoulder. "I don't like it either, but Miss Grey is right. I'm going to go."

"I'm going too," Hovis said. "I've been assigned as your wingman, so you have a connection with the FBI and DHS."

"I appreciate the offer, but you're really not in any condition to do this kind of operation, Hovis," Maxx said.

"You're right, but he's who you have," said Miss Grey. "He'll be able to call in the calvary if it's needed, but I don't expect that. What I expect is for the two of you to track Li Jing down, arrest her, and bring her back to the US. You'll have presidential authorization.""That authorization won't mean anything if we get twisted up with the Taliban," Maxx said.

Miss Grey nodded. "There is a quick reaction force that will be supporting you. An A-team of Green Berets is already on their way over that will be around if you call. They'll have Special Forces Operational Detachment Bravo backing them up if it really turns into a cluster."

"Okay, then it sounds like we have a plan. I'll pack some bags and get going," Maxx said.

"No time for that, Maxx. We'll have a kit and weapons waiting for you when you arrive. Your flight to Bagram Airfield leaves in thirty minutes. And I have a special surprise waiting for you there," she said with a wink.

16

WADING THROUGH LIES

Xi sat in the back seat of the black Suburban with dark-tinted windows.

The driver and the passenger in the front seat hadn't said one word since Mr. Green had handed them a piece of paper that Xi assumed included their instructions. Mr. Green hadn't been inclined to talk to him either, only answering questions with a murmur or as little information as possible. So Xi watched the scenery stream by as they headed north on I-5 on the busy freeway leaving the military base and driving through a mix of commercial zones and undeveloped wooded areas.

After about forty-five minutes of silence, he was startled when the driver abruptly slowed down and pulled over to the side of the freeway. "Is something wrong?" he asked Green.

"No, but I need you to put this on for the rest of the drive," Mr. Green said with a thin smile. He handed Xi a soft piece of black cloth. "We're getting close to Seattle."

Xi took the cloth and turned it over in his hands. "Why do you want me to wear this?" he asked with a note of consternation. In his experience, nothing good ever happened while blindfolded.

"We're going to an extremely confidential facility. It's in everyone's best interest if we keep the location secret."

Xi pulled the hood over his head. It smelled like a combination of men's cologne and damp earth. Green helped him secure the hood lightly around his neck. The material was dense enough that it was pitch-black. The material also made breathing a challenge. He tried to control the rising sense of panic.

He could feel the vehicle accelerate as it merged back into the traffic. He attempted to get a sense of the distance and direction by counting the minutes between turns. After several redirections, he realized the driver was going in a circular route. His novice attempt to maintain a sense of direction was pointless.

After an indeterminate amount of time driving on the freeway and in city traffic, he felt the car tilt steeply downward. The sound of the car's engine became muffled, and he guessed they were entering in an underground garage. The slope seemed to go on endlessly as they descended with turn after turn. It felt as if they'd gone deep underground, passing through several gates.

At last, the car stopped. He felt the driver exit, open his door, and help him to stand.

Green took his elbow and guided him forward. "We've almost arrived, Dr. Xi. Sorry about the extreme discretion, but you'll soon see why this precaution was necessary."

They stopped for a moment while an entrance was unlocked. It sounded like a heavy metal door as Mr. Green grunted with the effort. They passed out of the garage into an enclosed hallway, and Xi could hear the door close and lock behind him.

"May I remove this blindfold now?" Xi asked no one in particular.

"Only a few more minutes, Doctor," Green answered. "I'll

remove it when we get on the elevator."

Walking down the long hallway, Xi could hear several distinct footsteps on the tile floor. Three pairs of shoes plus his. The air conditioning hummed softly in the background, masking the occasional muffled sounds of people talking in the rooms they passed. Beneath the strong smell of the hood and the lighter smell of floor wax, paper, and paint, he sensed a musty odor of rock and minerals.

They paused in the hallway as the sound of machinery grew louder. The doors of the elevator slid open, and Mr. Green guided him on to the lift. When the doors closed, he felt someone carefully untie the hood and lift it over his head.

He blinked his eyes to adjust to the bright florescent lights of the elevator. He was surrounded by two guards and Green, as if he were a threat. There was nothing to see in the elevator, which was controlled by a card reader, and there was no evidence of what floor they were on. It felt as if they were descending, but he wasn't certain because of the disorientation from wearing the thick hood for so long.

"Welcome to my office," Green said with tight grin as he stepped off the elevator in the tunnels hewn from stone. "Not much to look at, but it has a hell of an intercom system."

"This is where you maintain the device to communicate with the aliens?" Xi asked.

"Yes, this is the primary location," Green said. "It's easier to protect and do our research on the device and extraterrestrial communication here. Being deep underground seems counter-intuitive, I know."

"We have a similar facility in China for our device. The greatest challenge was establishing the infrastructure for the required power."

"We don't have that issue here. It has a convenient, naturally sourced power supply."

"And this is where we conduct the communication with

Thunderbird," Green said as he opened the door to the conference room and escorted Xi inside.

Xi could see the device behind the thick, transparent wall across the room. The large cube was similar in size and shape to the communication device he had maintained in China. They had always assumed the Chinese-held device was identical to the device in the United States, but he could see several differences that indicated they were not identical, the immediately visible difference being how the device responded to light.

Xi had observed the Chinese device back in his lab for endless hours. While the cube seemed to absorb the surrounding light, it had an underlying greenish tint that occasionally rippled. It was a slight hue that always reminded him of the sunlight beneath the ocean.

However, the device here in the American facility had a bluish tint beneath the deep black. He didn't know the cause of the color difference, but it seemed to be an innate characteristic of the device and irrespective to the surrounding lighting. It seemed that the two alien civilizations had utilized similar technology and design but had made some alterations that might be meaningful beyond the difference in hue. He'd ask Green about this distinction when they had time.

Green had Xi pull up a seat next to him at the table. He could see Green then connecting a remote communication session with a connection to "Senator Traficant." Then the power-up sequence with the device was initiated. It was a sequence he had participated in many times with his communication device, but he always felt anxious before the device could be connected. It always felt as if he was playing with supernatural abilities that he didn't understand.

Xi felt the result of the connection in the pit of his stomach before he heard the sound.

He'd often wondered what the aliens would sound like if they weren't filtered through the communication device. For the first time, he realized that while he was hearing the communication in perfect spoken Mandarin, the other people in the room seemed to be hearing the voice in English. The device was somehow translating to each listener's natural language simultaneously.

"We are listening. What is the purpose of this communication?" the alien voice asked.

"We are here to give you an important update," the senator spoke up to answer before Green could speak.

The tone in Senator Traficant's voice made Xi uncomfortable. It sounded disingenuous to his ear.

"The deadline approaches quickly. We presume this is related to saving your planet. Speak."

"We have learned that Doctor Smith is working with the Others to support their invasion," Senator Traficant said.

"We will consider this development in our conflict plans, although it was expected that they would attempt to find allies on your planet. They will still fail."

Green leaned into the microphone. "The Chinese have also agreed to work together with us. Their representative has joined us for this communication."

"That is wise of them. Xi, you are now aware that you have been communicating with our enemies."

Xi looked down sheepishly. "Yes, we did not realize we were communicating with a different civilization - the Others - until the Americans informed us of our misunderstanding."

"The Others are a very deceptive culture. However, they will soon realize that you are collaborating with us," Thunderbird said. "Expect retaliation."

"We are expecting some retribution," Xi said with a nod. "Unless we convince them that we are only pretending to work with the Americans to undermine them once the invasion begins."

"Why would you do this?" the aliens asked.

"Because they would then delay attacking our country and turn their forces on the Americans. This misdirection will allow us to surprise them. It's a gambit I have used successfully in the past."

"And what reward do you expect from us in return for your allegiance?" intoned Thunderbird.

"We would receive some of your more advanced weaponry. That will allow us to surprise and destroy them quickly," Xi said.

"We have already supplied you with a biological weapon that the Others are unprepared for."

"Consider this to be an insurance policy in case that strategy fails."

"We will consider your proposal," Thunderbird said as they terminated the communication.

***

Li Jing stepped out of Toyota pickup into the high desert sun of Kabul and swiped her brow.

She had flown from Seattle to Kabul. After landing, she was immediately picked up in a dull-gray pickup by her Taliban contact. She hadn't had time to adjust to the Afghani weather after the cool, moist Pacific Northwest weather. She had been all over the world and always despised arid climates. She settled into the cold front seat of the dusty pickup for the long drive. With the bright sun shining through the window, it felt like sitting under a sun lamp in a refrigerator, but it kept her awake.

She knew that the Americans had to be close behind. She had used a fake passport and bought several tickets to various locations across the globe to mislead them. But that effort would only buy her a few hours of misdirection. Since September 11th, the intelligence agencies had put significant resources into facial recognition technology and linking disparate data sources. All this capability would be directed toward finding her.

She had to get to Smith.

It was more than a mission objective. That was the rationale he'd used when instructing her to come to his location in Afghanistan. The Others would be arriving very soon, and it would be the beginning of a very stark global conflict, centered in the Middle East. The travel to this part of the world wasn't going to get any easier for a long time. Smith had been firm that he needed her with him.

But she had to admit, she secretly hoped it was more than an alignment around mutual objectives of hurting her father and undermining the Americans. Smith had never directly told her that he wanted a romantic relationship, but she had sensed it. The way he sat close to her during meetings, the occasional hand on her arm, the softened tone of his voice. What else could it be?

She had initially brushed it off as the fantasizing of a lonely woman in her mid-life. But once she had seen the signs, she couldn't unsee them. And certainly, he trusted her with his life, and she had been willing to kill for him. While she had relished his order to kill, she had sensed it created a deeper bond between them, one most people could never imagine. And now they were joined together in a plan that would affect everyone on the planet. Together they held millions – no, billions – of lives in their hands.

As she climbed the last hill to the cave, the thought of seeing him again made her stomach flutter. It was as if she were a schoolgirl once again and flirting with an older teacher. Forbidden, exciting, and a temporary reprieve from the darkness that threatened to consume her.

"Li Jing, you made it," Smith said as she walked out of the bright sun into the mouth of the tunnel.

The cool air and the sound of his voice sent shivers down her spine. "Doctor, it is lovely to see you again," she said softly as she firmly shook his outstretched hand. "I came as quickly as I could."

"Do you think they tracked you here?" he said in a conspiratorial tone.

"I have no doubt they are trying to find me, but it will be impossible for them to follow my trail from the airport to this location. I'm not sure I could even find my way again."

"It won't matter if they don't find your route within the day. After that, they will have much more pressing concerns."

Li Jing nodded. "I'm anxious to see the device from the Others. Is it active?"

"Follow me," Smith said as he moved deeper into the faintly lit tunnel.

When she walked into the cavern holding the large device, she breathed in with a slight gulp. The device seemed like the American communication device she'd worked on previously with Smith, but for some reason she had never imagined that it would be so familiar.

"I'm confused, Doctor. Is this the device you built at DARPA?"

Smith chuckled. "Of course not. That device was destroyed in the tower collapse on September 11th. It may look the same, but they are very different devices beneath the outer shell."

"I've never seen one of the devices operate. Does it always pulse like this?" she asked.

"It has been doing this for the last few days. I'm not certain why. I'm presuming it is related to imminent arrival of the alien owners of the device. But that's a guess."

He stepped back and his tone changed. "While you were traveling here, I was able to communicate with the Others. I let them know that your father is now working with the US."

Li Jing stopped short. "I failed then," she said softly. "I did everything I could to prevent this, and it wasn't enough. I killed my sister for nothing."

"It was always a gamble," Doctor Smith said as he placed his hand gently on her shoulder. "You did what had to be done. It didn't stop Xi, but it delayed him long enough that the US and China won't have enough time to adequately prepare."

"Thank you, Doctor, for your trust. I promise I will make it up to you."

"While it's concerning to learn of their collaboration against us. There is another bigger concern. China will soon realize they were communicating with the Others and not Thunderbird. The opportunity to sow confusion will be lost when they start plotting with Thunderbird."

"I know my father well enough to know that he will try and use this knowledge against the Others. He is very clever."

Smith sniffed as if he smelled something pungent. "I don't underestimate my enemies, Li Jing. He is not that cunning. I will outwit him, as I always have."

Faraj stepped from the shadows into the dimly lit chamber. He walked hesitantly toward Doctor Smith and Li Jing.

He limply shook Li Jing's outstretched hand. "I am Faraj, Doctor Smith's primary assistant with the device."

Li Jing stepped forward, quickly closing the distance between them.

"You were his primary assistant," she said smugly. "I am Li Jing, and you will now be his second assistant."

Smith laughed. "There is enough work for everyone and no need for quarrels. Both of you will report to me."

Li Jing stared at Faraj intensely until he looked away nervously.

"Of course, Doctor, we all are here to assist the Others," Faraj said.

"Now that we are all clear on the pecking order, what is that you wanted to tell me?" Smith asked Faraj.

"Should I contact Tehran with the arrival information?"

"Yes, they need to be prepared for their approach. I expect the Americans to attack soon after, and we will need their assistance."

Li Jing raised her eyebrows. "When will they be arriving?"

"Tomorrow after dark," Smith said with a tight grin.

"Then I have enough time to greet the Americans following me with a surprise Afghani welcome," Li Jing said with a wicked grin of her own.

17

KAHWAHTEA AND BITING BULLETS

Maxx looked out the window of the C-17, anxiously feeling like he was descending into a bad dream.

Landing at Bagram Airbase was not just a routine flight for him. It was a vivid reminder of the years he'd spent in the Middle East. The C-17 Globemaster was the military transport of choice due to its ability to take off and land on short, austere runways. The airbase was larger and more complex than most, but it was symbol of the complications of military operations in Afghanistan. Landing at the remote airbase felt familiar and yet more ominous since September 11th. Bagram looked like the military was digging in for a long fight.

One of the flight crew was walking the length of the cargo area of the plane to make sure that all the passengers were buckled in. He made sure that Agent Hovis's webbing was snug while he slept. Hovis didn't even budge while he was jostled around. He continued to snore loudly as he had for the last two hours. The seating in the cargo hold wasn't full, so both Hovis and Maxx could take turns stretching out across an empty seat. Maxx had slept for brief sections of the flight, but the seating arrangement was so uncomfortable for his oversized body that he couldn't stay still for long. He'd learned to sleep any chance he had, even when the conditions sucked, but this was a test of his commitment to getting some rest.

"Welcome back," the airman said to Maxx with a wide grin and thumbs up.

"I couldn't stay away," Maxx said. "I was longing for the smell of burning tires, jet fuel, and gunpowder. Other than east LA and Oakland, it's hard to find that smell in the States."

Outside the small, round window on the door, he'd glanced out to admire the rugged terrain of the Hindu Kush Mountains surrounding the base. In some ways, it reminded him of the mountain ranges surrounding Seattle, but more dangerous. The approach was usually quite dramatic, with steep descents and tight turns necessary to navigate the mountainous landscape. And the occasional missile or gunfire. He was glad his stomach was empty.

The runway at Bagram was long. Designed to handle heavy military aircraft, it was always busy since it had been secured last October and protected since then by the 10th Mountain Division. The landing was often bumpy due to the high altitude and the wind shear. The pilots were performing a tactical landing, and it felt like an express elevator down. It was meant to be quicker and steeper than usual to minimize exposure to potential threats from hostile gun fire.

On the ground, the sprawling base surrounded the landing strip. With a mix of modern and older Soviet-era structures, it seemed like a city sprung up from the dust with no plan or future. The airfield was bustling with activity, with Humvees, fuel trucks, and ammo shuttling back and forth to the aircraft. The base was becoming the central hub for U.S. and coalition forces, and it reflected the odd blend of cargo aircraft and helicopters.

As the plane began to slow down and head for one of the arrival terminals, Maxx shook Hovis awake. It took several aggressive shakes before the snoring stopped and he was conscious enough to push Maxx's hand away.

"We're here, Sleeping Beauty," Maxx said. He offered him a container of warm water he'd grabbed out of one of the open crates. "Better stay hydrated, because I'm not carrying you around."

Hovis poured some of the water over his head and took a mouthful. "I hope I can still walk after sitting here. Maybe we have time for a massage?" he said hopefully.

Maxx snorted. "The only massage you're going to get is when you're tossed around in the Humvee."

"I'm beginning to think I was lied to. Miss Grey told me this was going to be an exotic, relaxing getaway."

The plane rolled to a slow stop, and the engines shut down. Maxx unbuckled himself and began to collect his gear. "Grab your gear, princess. Time, tide, and formation wait for no man."

"What are you talking about?" Keith said belligerently. "I thought we were going to spend a couple days here gathering intel?"

"Nope. We're going to keep moving. We need to catch up to Li Jing, or she'll disappear into those mountains."

Throwing his rucksack over one shoulder, Maxx strode off the ramp at the rear of the plane. He'd been expecting the cold, but stepping back into the sun reminded him how intense the winter sunlight could be at altitude. The wind was biting as he pulled his jacket tighter around him. They'd only been able to bring what they'd been carrying when they boarded the plane. Clothing from the mild early spring weather in Seattle was not going to be adequate. They were expecting to be kitted up now that they were in the country.

"Hovis, stick on my hip," Maxx yelled over the commotion on the runway. "We won't be here long."

A Humvee pulled up next to them as they were walking

toward the divisional headquarters building. "Sir, are you Maxx King by any chance?" the driver asked.

"I sure am. Who's asking?"

"Specialist Howard, sir. I was told to retrieve you and your companion and take you to an assembly point. There are some people waiting to meet you."

Maxx and Keith jumped in the back seat.

"It looks like you guys are staging an operation," Maxx said with a look of concern. "Anything I should know?"

"Nothing that will affect you, sir. There's something happening in a day or two, but it's going to be focused on one of the nearby valleys. I heard we're going to open a can of whoop ass on the Taliban."

"We'll be sure to stay out of the way."

"Smart," he said as he pulled up in front of a low-slung metal building sitting away from the runway. "Here's your stop. sir."

Maxx and Hovis climbed out of the vehicle and rapped on the door to the building. "Anyone here?" Maxx said as he opened the door and peered in the dimly lit interior.

"Back here," a gruff voice yelled from the back of the building.

"Look who finally showed up," someone said as they walked into the bunk room in the back.

A large black man jumped off the top bunk and attempted to grab Maxx from behind.

"What the hell?" Maxx said as he spun, bringing his ham sized fist around. But he stopped his swing before the punch connected.

"Glen," he roared as he returned the bear hug. "What is your ugly mug doing here?"

Glen laughed as if that was the funniest thing he'd ever heard. "I heard you were going to get in trouble, and I had to see for myself."

"But we barely landed. How did you know we'd be here?"

"Your friend Miss Grey. She called us while you guys were meeting in Hawaii and arranged for us to get on a special flight from McChord to Kandahar. She wanted it to be a surprise, and from the look on your face, it worked."

"Who's us?" Hovis asked from the doorway.

"Us is me and the big ape hugging Maxx," a voice said from one of the bunks.

"No way! Andres," Maxx snorted. "I'd know that accent anywhere."

A small Hispanic man sat up on the edge of the bed and straightened his shirt collar. "Good to see you, Maxx. It's a shame we had to come all the way over here for a reunion."

Maxx turned to Agent Hovis. "Did you know about this?"

"Absolutely not," Hovis answered with smirk. "I'm not sure what this is."

"Well, you've now met two of my best friends. Glen and Andres. We were in the Special Forces together and all live in Seattle. We all retired from the military, except for unusual projects that we get roped into."

Andres laughed. "We met Miss Grey on another special project last fall, and this seems to be the next gig for our little band."

Maxx coughed loudly. "Dude, that is the understatement of the year. The two of you have been in a hot and heavy relationship since you laid eyes on each other."

Andres laughed. "That's true, but not a necessary piece of information now. I came here to help you, you big oaf."

"And who are you?" Glen said as he eyed Hovis.

"Special Agent Hovis. FBI. I've been tracking a fugitive for six months now. Maxx and I have tracked her here and are trying to arrest her and bring her back to the US."

"I have to be honest that I'm not a big fan of Feds. But if

Maxx says you're okay, I'll let it slide. So long as you carry your own weight."

"Yeah, he's a good guy," Maxx said as he put a hand on Keith's shoulder. "He can link us back to the Feds if we need any resources and can't get a hold of Miss Grey."

"I can carry my own weight. I wasn't in the military, but I know how to do my job."

"What job is that, Agent?" Andres asked with genuine interest.

Hovis shrugged his shoulders. "I've been assigned to the Critical Incidence Response Group. That's why I was assigned as the special agent on this case. My expertise is in criminal investigative analysis and the training of our undercover employees."

Glen walked over and shook Keith's hand. "We're just busting your chops. CIRG is impressive. Glad you're on the team."

Both Glen and Andres were already dressed in a mix of standard uniforms and non-standard civilian clothes. Both men had on camouflage pants and black, long-sleeve t-shirts, but that was where the similarities ended.

Andres had put on a pair of black trail shoes and heavy wool vest over several layers. Being average height and build, he could easily blend into any background. With his longer hair, full beard, and brown skin, he looked more like a native than a full-time archaeology professor. The students in his classes liked to refer to him as Indiana Jones for his background in special operations.

Glen, as solidly built black man at 6' 2", would stand out anywhere. He, like Maxx, was built like a professional football player. He had opted for a Fu Manchu beard and mustache. He didn't look military wearing a Carhartt zippered hoodie and vest. He looked more like he'd walked over from one of the nearby construction sites. All he needed was a tool belt and John Deere baseball cap to complete the outfit.

Maxx looked them over quickly. "We didn't have the chance to grab any clothes before we flew out. Did you see any gear around that we can use while we're here."

Andres pointed to some lockers against the wall. "They said we can take anything we need from the stuff that's in there. Hopefully it's in your size, Maxx."

Maxx and Keith popped open the lockers and pulled out all the clothes that they thought might fit. Maxx had a hard time finding a shirt his size but was able to squeeze into some standard issue pants. Keith had plenty of options being ordinary size and looked like he blended in except for the short hair. Maxx slipped on a boonie hat to hide his buzz cut. Luckily, he had been wearing reasonable boots when he left Seattle, because there was nothing in the locker close to his size-fourteen feet.

None of them looked like they'd fit in with the Army troops stationed here, but they'd blend in fine with a group of special operators in the field. Once they had weapons and were moving with a unit, they wouldn't warrant a second glance. Except Maxx and Glen for their size.

"Anyone say anything about weapons?" Maxx asked.

"They said we'd all head over to the armory when they got back from the afternoon briefing. They have some standard issue weapons they'll release to your guys if Mr. FBI Agent will sign for them. The sergeant said they have all the paperwork but need Hovis to give some ID and sign. He said don't lose them though, because Hovis will get a big bill from Uncle Sam."

"I'll sign for them," Keith said with an easy grin.

"Don't too excited, Hovis, until you see if the weapons work. The stuff was probably left over from Vietnam."

"I'd be happier if we never had to see if they work at all," Glen muttered.

"Speaking of working, can you give us more intel this assignment? Miss Grey said you'd brief us when you arrived," Andres said.

Hovis finished lacing up the used pair of boots he'd found in the cabinet. "The person we're tracking is an ex-CIA agent who has gone rogue. Her name is Li Jing and is wanted for several murders. She is extremely dangerous. Do not underestimate her, as she will not hesitate to kill."

"I think I dated her," Glen said with a belly laugh.

"This is no joke," Maxx said as he stared Glen down. "A couple days ago, she tried to kill Gabby. And she kidnapped Agent Hovis. Luckily, he was able to disarm her and escape."

"Sorry man, I was kidding around," Glen said sheepishly.

"But that's only half the issue. She is also linked to that operation from last fall. The guy who started that whole mess is here and kicking things off again."

"That's crazy," said Andres. "I thought that was the end of things on 9/11."

Maxx shook his head. "No, it's even worse than it was then. We need to capture them before they link up. It could be bad. Real bad."

"Has Maxx arrived yet?" a voice yelled from the front door.

"I'm back here," Maxx answered loudly. "Who's asking?"

"It's Sergeant First Class Zeller," the man said as he walked into the bunk room. "I was told to grab you and your team and head over to the armory. Is this everyone on your team?"

Maxx watched Zeller stroll into the room like he was out for a walk in the park. He spoke with a heavy southern drawl. Mid-thirties and was dressed in a mixed outfit of camouflage and civilian clothing like they were. The only thing that stood out was the salt in his beard and the fatigued look around the eyes.

He looked every part the senior noncommissioned officer down range.

"It is. Where's your team?"

"We don't have a full operational detachment assigned to you. We have split the team so there's only six of us working with you, and the other five guys are waiting in the Humvees outside."

"Yeehaw, let's get this party started," Glen said as he picked up his pack and headed for the Humvees.

Outside, they made quick introductions between the two teams. To Maxx, it looked like many of the seasoned special operations teams he'd worked with in the Army. Lots of confidence, beards, and experience. Hovis was awkward and stood out as the only one in the group who hadn't been in this kind of environment before. Maxx never let him get too far from his side.

The group laughed and caught up about past units as they made the quick drive across the base to the armory. They drove by lots of activity, as engineers worked to secure the airbase. It was clear they were preparing for a large influx of personnel and equipment. Hovis sat next to Maxx, who was looking out the window with a look of surprise. Watching the news back home, there had been no indication that this buildup was going on, but he could see the tension building. This was no small state of war.

When they reached the armory, Agent Hovis and Sergeant Zeller went inside to finish the paperwork to release the weapons. Zeller's team grabbed a couple cans of ammo and headed over the target range to get in some practice while they waited.

After several minutes, a couple of the armory staff came out carrying the weapons for Maxx and his team. They each received an M4 with a suppressor, M9 pistol, tactical vest with extra magazines, and a knife. The M4 carbine was compact version of the M16 with several features added for close-quarters combat. The M9 had been the standard issue military handgun since 1985 and felt like an old, reliable pair of shoes. Hovis also had grabbed them each a set of bulletproof ceramic plates to put in their vests. But Hovis was the only one who put them on.

They grabbed more cans of ammo from the back of the Humvee and began to fill the magazines. They pulled the vehicles over the range and sighted in their weapons to make sure they were accurate and working smoothly. Even though the Bearded Bastards would be capable of handling any trouble they might run into, Maxx, Glen, and Andres were going to be fully prepared for a firefight.

Hovis took a little longer getting used to the rifle. He scrunched up his face in concentration as he got used to working the weapon. After shooting a few hundred rounds on full auto, he was wearing a slight grin, like a kid who had recently figured out how to ride a motor bike.

When the last of the ammo had been expended, Zeller signaled the team to group with him.

Taking a knee, he passed around a piece of paper with Li Jing's photo. He said, "The mission is to capture this target. Alive. She's a US citizen, and Agent Hovis has a warrant for her arrest and signed extradition papers. Everyone clear?"

All the heads nodded as they looked at her picture and passed it on.

"We don't expect any resistance, but she's dangerous, so don't underestimate her ability. Treat her like every other combatant we run into, and hand her over to the FBI agent when she is secured."

Maxx nodded. "Do you have any intel on where we will find her?"

Zeller pulled out a map and pointed to a section of Kabul.

"She was spotted heading into this section. We've taken down a few Taliban in that area, so we're familiar."

"Sounds straightforward," Glen added. "Smash, grab, and go."

"Unfortunately, not as straightforward as I would like," Zeller said as he scratched his graying beard. "She was being tailed by someone we want to avoid. It could get a bit messy."

Maxx look puzzled "Who would try to tail her other than us?"

"Someone we were told to avoid. Our spook friends from the 'see eye of a.' Langley must have an interest in her too," he said with a frown.

18

THE HUNTER BECOMES THE HUNTED

Driving through Kabul on the cusp of war was a surreal experience.

The streets were filled with a mix of military vehicles, local traffic, and pedestrians, all navigating a city under constant tension. Despite the chaos and threat of impending war, it seemed that life went with little change for most of the residents. They passed through markets bustling with street vendors and children playing soccer in the streets. The contrast of daily life against the backdrop of war created a unique atmosphere, where moments of normalcy and beauty could still be found amidst the uncertainty and approaching danger.

With their convoy of three Humvees, Zeller and the team were frequently changing course to avoid security risks. No one wanted to get caught in a dead end. Checkpoints and security barriers were a common sight, reminding Maxx that no one was safe here even in a small convoy of heavily armored vehicles. He could hear the constant chatter between the drivers of the three Humvees as they frequently adapted their route to threats and rumors of threats.

Maxx and Hovis rode in the backseat of the second vehicle

of the three. It smelled like stale sweat, oil, and diesel. Unfortunately, it was a combination of odors that was all too familiar. Sergeant Zeller was in the front seat assisting with the navigation and clearing them through the US and coalition checkpoints with minimal delays. During the brief pauses of radio chatter, Maxx questioned Zeller about the interaction with the CIA that he alluded to earlier.

"You're sure that Li Jing is being followed by Langley?" Maxx asked Zeller during a moment of relative silence.

"Affirmative. One of my guys speaks fluent Pashto and hangs out around Sarai Shahzada, seeing what news he can pick up."

"Sarai is the money market?"

"Yeah, we've found that a little bit of money moving around seems to loosen the lips. Yesterday, there was a lot of chatter about a special guest coming in. A woman. It's unusual for a woman – especially a foreign woman – to get that kind of attention."

"We keep our eyes open for activity among the regular intel sources," the driver added. "All the locals know who works for the agency because they pay top dollar. It didn't take long to hunt down what kind of information they found interesting enough to buy."

Maxx paused for a moment and knitted his brow. This wasn't a huge complication, but it was concerning that the agency was going after Li Jing and not looping them in. Miss Green had told him that Director Anderson was read in on the mission. He had agreed with Maxx and Agent Hovis leading the hunt, but now it looked like he was running an operation on the side rather than cooperating. He didn't trust Anderson, and this maneuver didn't help.

"But what kind of information is the CIA trying to buy?" Maxx continued.

"They're trying to find out what she's been up to since her

plane landed. They had tailed her from the airport but lost her outside of town. Now she's been spotted again. They're hoping she'll lead them to Doctor Smith. If they wanted to take her out, they would simply go in hot."

"Do we know where she's heading?" Maxx pressed.

"Not exactly. We know which of the Taliban factions are helping her, so that narrows down the choices. What we do know is the general direction she's heading into the mountains. That will limit the roads we have to keep under surveillance. We'll set up at an intersection where two of the roads joined. We have another squad watching the other two roads, in case we're wrong."

"I'd think we'd be easy to recognize. It's not like we blend in with these vehicles."

"We're going to switch over to a couple pickups if we catch wind of her. Two men will stay back with the Humvees. It's not like we're going to get in a firefight with her Taliban escort. They'll be in civilian cars. Once we grab her, we'll hightail it back to the Humvees and head to Bagram. Easy as pie."

Zeller's confidence made Maxx uneasy. *No easy day...*

"It doesn't worry you that the Taliban are willing to help this Chinese woman? It seems unusual to me."

"Under more typical conditions, it would be extremely strange. But since the new year, they've been developing lots of new and strange relationships. Al Qaeda has networks that go all over the world, but we don't know where they begin and end. They've been up in mountains – up to no good I'm sure – but we have a hard time getting any reliable intel."

"That sounds like it might be connected to the work we know Li Jing is involved in," said Hovis. "She's in cahoots with Smith. We'd like to get our hands on him too. The mountains would be a good place to hide out."

"They're dug in deeper than a tick on a hound in those

tunnels," Zeller drawled. "We know where they are but can never get deep enough to clean them out.

The driver laughed. "They simply pop up somewhere else, like whack-a-mole."

Maxx couldn't tear his eyes from it. He was in awe as things outside his window changed in a matter of seconds. He was astonished how quick things turned—calm to chaos, laughter to screams, daylight to darkness. Of course, none of that was articulated in his head, it was only a feeling, shock and horror and awe, like you might feel for an instant when you're in a spinning car and know you're going to crash into the—

BOOM!

The blast—an IED—struck to the right of the front of the lead Humvee, sending up a great black spray of dirt and asphalt. The bicyclists along the road screamed, and the shopkeepers in the market across the street cringed away from the impact.

Oh, heaven help them, it wasn't done. He saw the wheel and part of the axle emerge from the cloud of dust, howling overhead, angling toward the rest of the squad in the trailing vehicle. The driver might have had time to see it rocketing toward them, but not enough to get out of the way.

Maxx watched it with a gaping mouth, even as he instinctively ducked and braced himself against the back of the front seat. The flying wheel caught the front windshield and seemed to obliterate it on its way to the car behind them and then a third, rolling and bouncing. As it tore through the street, it spat out mangled humans, cars, and motorcycles behind it so that metal and flesh were all mixed together.

Zeller's driver, clinging to the twisting steering wheel, managed to turn his horrified face to Maxx, eyes wide and mouth stretched, screaming, "IED!" It was as though he couldn't see the carnage with his own damn eyes.

The pieces of the Humvee ground to a halt in the street, and all those frozen, tar-slow people alive but hurt started thrashing like white water. Everything happened too fast to keep track of.

Someone screamed something, and it might've been Zeller or someone else, but it didn't seem to matter, because then everyone was yelling so loud that Maxx almost didn't hear the firing of the enemy assault rifles. He could tell from the deep, resonant "boom" they were firing AK-47s, the go-to weapon for the Taliban. The bullets started hitting the windows and armored door next to him.

The radio squawked, "Target is in the red pickup, coming up to the intersection. NOW."

"Ah shit!" Maxx barked as the spidering glass swelled in his vision. Bullets were hurtling out of the gray cloud of smoke and dust. He barely got his weapon up and the safety off before a rocket-propelled grenade went flying by so close that he felt the blast shake the heavy vehicle. He followed the trail of the RPG, essentially a shoulder-fired missile, with his eyes, thinking that it was heading right for the Humvee behind them. The Humvee that Andres and Glen were riding in.

When he turned, it was a bloom of fire, the blue color of the Camry behind the third Humvee vanishing in the blast. But then the Toyota driver and the big, bearded passenger came shooting out of the flame, the car's rear end lifting like it had been shot out of a cannon. The whole right side of driver's face was a charred mess, but he barely slowed down, focused on getting as far as he could from the car that had become a raging furnace.

His vehicle was the last one operational in the convoy now, and everyone was dismounting from the first and third Humvees. He could see the majority of Zeller's squad, Andres and Glen getting away from the cars and looking for cover in the buildings along the road. He breathed a sigh of relief.

Hovis was hunkered down as low as he could get in the seat, wide-eyed and yelling "no, no, no," repeatedly to no one in particular.

The driver of Maxx's car veered around the lead Humvee and pulled up to block the intersection in front of them. Zeller was yelling into the radio to try and get some support when Maxx saw the pickup truck carrying Li Jing trying to slide by them.

Zeller's men disappeared behind cover, taking defensive positions. There was too much smoke swirling around the car to see clearly. Maxx coughed, blinked it the irritant out of his eyes again, and adjusted his rifle to the side, hunched low in the seat trying to get his door open. The lock was stuck.

Bullets and RPGs. *Where were they coming from?*

Eyes up. He peered through the gloom and thought he saw Li Jing's pickup ahead, trying to ease through the traffic jam. Several cars full of Taliban trying to clear the way and keep the Americans pinned down. Maxx had a choice to make, stay here and fight or push Zeller to follow Li Jing when her vehicle cleared the intersection.

Li Jing.

She was the reason they were in this mess. The Taliban was only trying to keep them pinned down to give her time escape. The rest of the team would be okay without him and Hovis. He hated the idea of leaving them, but she was the mission.

Where was Li Jing's car? Maxx's eyes scoured the edges of the intersection, looking for that flash of red somewhere in there. And he realized, almost as an afterthought, that he wanted to spot the car—wanted to be the first one to get to her so he could finish her. He knew they wanted her alive, but he was furious. He had one hand already making sure he had the selector set on full auto.

He didn't spot her truck, but now he could clearly see the man who was shooting at them. Crouched in the bed of a nearby pickup and taking time to aim as if he had all the time in the world. Beard, white robes, headband and AK-47 to complete the standard outfit. He looked like a hundred other men Maxx had fought and was standing right next to a guy loading another RPG. The casual way these guys were trying to kill him really pissed off Maxx.

No chance he was going to let that rocket hit him. The bastard Haji might've got a few kills by sending RPGs when people weren't expecting them, but now that he could see where the shooter was placed, it wasn't hard to spot where they were aiming. He stepped outside the door, watching the launcher start to point at them. Staying behind the safety of the armored door, Maxx placed several rounds into the head of the guy placing the rocket-propelled grenade launcher on his shoulder before the other shooter spotted him.

Before dropping dead, the guy must have pulled the trigger on the RPG. It went off course and split right down the middle of the parked cars, slamming into the road right where they'd been, then skipped, slamming into a parked car. The civilian in the driver's seat couldn't get out of the way fast enough, then pieces of his car went flying in all directions. The people in the nearby market ran, not interested in getting involved, but the car and anything near it were burning.

Good thing Gabby wasn't here to see how close that was.

A glimmer of red caught his eye to his right. He couldn't help but glance at it. For a brief second, he saw that face, that almond-eyed, familiar face, peering at him above the door on the pickup truck blocked in the traffic. And then she ducked and disappeared.

"Li Jing!" Maxx snarled, boots down, rifle up, diving clear of the Humvee as he fired at the guy with the white robes still crouching in the pickup bed. He was less relaxed now that Maxx was fighting back.

Maxx slid to a stop behind a parked car. Checking his M4 to make sure he still had most of a magazine. Breaking it open with one hand, he pulled a spare magazine out of vest to replace it with a full one.

Li Jing seemed to realize her attempt to hide wasn't sufficient and screamed at the driver of the pickup to try and push through the sidewalk stalls dragging crates, pottery, and fabric behind her. People scrambling in all directions to stay out of the way of the red pickup.

The shooter was running directly at him, but Maxx was beyond being careful at this point. He could move faster and was good at running and evading. You could be the fastest guy in all the world, but you still couldn't outrun a well-placed bullet.

He was midway to getting the fresh magazine loaded, but he was gaining ground on the Haji too fast. He made a quick decision, seated the magazine, and let the rifle drop on the sling. Maxx drew the knife from his vest with his free hand. It felt so fluid, but that was what rage and killing did—you went in normal, and you came out the other side a killing machine. A machine that didn't need to think, only act.

Gripping the knife, he reared back as far as his shoulder would allow, jumping on the hood of a parked car, waiting for the right moment as he sprung toward the man. He spotted Maxx leaping and tried to backpedal away from him, raising his rifle, but it was too late at that point. Maxx swung the knife with everything he had, with every bit of fury. It all came out in one big thrust of muscle and brawn, and the six-inch blade sliced across the neck of the Haji, sending blood spraying in all directions.

His momentum forced him on top of the Taliban before he had even fallen to the ground. It was a bloody jumble of arms as legs as the two of them crashed into a cart of vegetables left standing next to the parked cars. Maxx was still stabbing the man even as they slid several feet to come to a messy stop. Blood everywhere made it hard to stand.

Maxx's boots fought for traction in the dirt and blood. He pressed the man away and held the knife overhand ready to strike if the man tried to engage him. He couldn't see the man's rifle for a second. There was such a jumble from the turned-over cart, but then he spotted it under a parked car. The man was on the ground, like he wanted to get up and keep fighting but couldn't figure out how with his hands holding his neck.

Maxx could see the Talib was never going to make it his feet again. Dark eyes, staring at him but not really seeing him. Blood soaking the ground around him. Hands grasping his throat. Legs thrashing slowly.

Maxx stopped right there, standing over him. Knife in one hand, rifle in the other. Dust blowing in his eyes. Sweat running dripping off the tip of his nose.

He wasn't a merciless man, but he wasn't quite himself at that moment. All the anger that had been building since Gabby had almost been killed by Li Jing's men was raging inside him. He wanted to make them hurt, but there was no point to be made here. The man was only seconds from death. The one he really wanted to hurt was Smith. He was the one who had started Li Jing on this path. Everyone else was merely a soldier doing their job.

With Li Jing and Smith, it was personal.

"Ah well," he said to the Haji. "You're probably nearly dead anyways. Some might consider this merciful, giving you a final few moments." He turned on his heel and started running back toward where he had last seen the red pickup.

As he jogged back to the Humvee, breathing heavy, face spattered with dust and blood, a mess of the fight behind him, still surrounded by halo of smoke, he was surprised to find that he was feeling better than he had any right to. Except his knees, which always seemed to hurt.

He pulled his cell phone from his pocket and saw that it had been ruined in the fight. He tossed what was left onto the floor of the Humvee and grabbed a canteen.

"Hovis, come with me," he yelled as he leaned out of the car door that he'd left ajar only a few blurred minutes before.

Zeller was still in the Humvee trying to coordinate support on the radio, when Maxx poked his head in. He looked at him with eyes wide. "Where are you going?" he asked incredulously.

"We're going to see if we can get to Li Jing on foot, since you're stuck here in this mess. If you get unstuck, head in that direction," Maxx said as he pointed toward the intersection. "I saw her a few minutes ago but lost sight of her again. She's here."

"How will I locate you?" Zeller shouted as Maxx and Hovis jogged off between the burning wrecks blocking the road.

"Follow the sound of gunfire," Maxx yelled back with a wicked grin.

19

FALSE FLAGS [OR THE SETUP]

Liu's smile fell from his lips a split second before the pistol butt smashed into his right ear.

He crumpled to the floor in a heap, conscious but too dazed to understand what had happened. While he curled on the ground, General Secretary Jiang's bodyguard stepped in to deliver a vicious kick to his side before he was waved off.

"That's enough, Mr. Fu," Jiang said as he tapped his fingers on the ornate teak desk. "I think the fool understands the lesson. Sit him in the chair."

Liu groaned loudly as the bodyguard lifted him into the seat as easily as if he were a child. He couldn't think clearly but knew he'd crossed some line that he'd misunderstood. He felt a trickle of blood sliding down his neck.

Liu removed a dirty handkerchief from his pocket and dabbed at his ear to curb the flow of blood dripping on his shirt collar. He was trying to buy a few moments of quiet to clear his head.

Jiang chuffed. "Would you like to try this again, Mr. Liu? I'd encourage you to not try my patience. Mr. Fu will not be so gentle next time."

The secretary general's office was meant to reflect a sense of harmony. Sleek surfaces of dark, lacquered wood, dimly lit, saturated tones of red, black, and gold. Its Zen-like aesthetic was in sharp contrast to the emotions that were whipping through Liu.

"My apologies, Chairman," Liu said with a stammer. "I meant no disrespect. I was merely speaking plainly."

"Too plainly for my taste. Tell me if you have obtained a commitment for weapons from these Thunderbird aliens."

Liu tried to take a deep breath despite the ache in his side. He wondered if his ribs were cracked. "I have not, Chairman. I told them that their enemies were threatening us and made the request. They were noncommittal."

"And what will it take for them to commit?" Jiang asked with a glare visible behind his thick, oversize glasses.

Liu was more careful with his wording this time. Reminding the chairman what they had agreed to before had been a poor choice. "If they believe we have been attacked by the Others, I think they will give us what we ask for, superior weapons technology to defend ourselves."

"So it is your opinion we should proceed with this fake attack to pressure them?"

"Yes, Chairman. If they don't provide us with the weapons, we still may get them from the Others."

Jiang glared at Liu for a few moments longer. Liu could imagine the distrust rolling off him in waves. He feared another warning sign from Jiang to the bodyguard that was standing too close behind him.

"Have you a proposal for this false attack? Keep in mind that the plan fails, you will bear responsibility for the result."

Liu's mouth was dry. He took a moment to wet his throat so his voice didn't crack.

"I understand, Chairman. If the plan fails it will be the result of my stupidity. Therefore, I'd propose that we stage a false attack in an area the has little population and infrastructure. It will look more devastating than the reality. We can claim it was only a sign of their intent."

Jiang pursed his lips. After a moment of consideration, he waved for Liu to continue.

"I suggest we convince the Others to trigger an earthquake in Kunlun. The Kunlun fault is very unstable and likely to cause a powerful earthquake. There is a very small population nearby and few high-rise buildings. An earthquake of a high magnitude will generate a lot of attention with little death or infrastructure destruction."

Jiang slapped his hand on his desk startling Liu. "I like it," he exclaimed. "When can they make it happen?"

Liu blew out a sigh of relief. A momentary reprieve. "I haven't confirmed the date with my contact. He is directly coordinating with the Others. I wanted to obtain your approval first."

"Now you have my approval. Contact this Doctor Smith character and make the arrangements as soon as possible. I want those weapons, Mr. Liu," he said with an implied threat.

Jiang's eyes were like dark pools staring at him from the shadows. In the dim light, it was impossible to read his emotions, but he felt like he was sitting in a cage with a hungry tiger. Any wrong move would result in an attack.

Liu gulped before responding. "I will tell Smith that we need the earthquake to be triggered as soon as possible. I'm unsure how they will be able to cause an earthquake in a specific area without a communication device. No one has ever explained to me how they cause these events."

"This is your problem to work out with Doctor Smith. I trust you are properly motivated to make it happen."

Liu placed his hands on the chairs of the arm to stop them from visibly shaking. "Consider it done, Chairman. Then we will have the challenge of convincing Thunderbird that we are at risk of more attacks and need their weaponry to protect ourselves."

"Can Xi help with this problem?" Jiang asked. "He has been in contact with Thunderbird for several days now. And the Americans seemed to trust him too."

"This is all true, Secretary. However, Xi is not aware of this plan. I have intentionally not shared this part of the plan with him so that he does not accidentally or intentionally reveal our intentions. He still believes that we are intending to help the Americans repel the invasion of the Others."

Jiang steepled his fingers together on the desk as considered the challenge. "This is true. We must keep him in the dark for now. Eventually, we may remove him from the middle of the relationship. But for now we need him to continue misleading both the Americans and Thunderbird. Once we have the advanced weapons from Thunderbird and the Others, it will not matter."

Liu sat silently waiting for directions. He still felt Fu standing close behind him. He didn't want to lapse again and risk taking another blow to the head.

After a few moments of silence, Jiang put his hands on his lap. "We need Xi to convince Thunderbird that we are indeed threatened by the Others. It would be more believable if this came from someone other than you, since he doesn't know that you have a connection with Smith. His distrust of Smith will overshadow anything you tell him."

I know all this, Liu thought but was careful not to show his impatience.

Secretary Jiang tightly smiled, which was unusual for him. "Tell Xi that the threat of an attack by the Others came from his daughter, Li Jing."

"Oh yes," Liu exclaimed. "He knows she is crazy enough to do anything to get him to stop working with the Americans.

The Americans and Thunderbird will believe him, because he will believe it himself."

"Time is short, and it is not on your side," Jiang said as he pushed a button to open the door to his office. "Now go clean the blood off your shirt."

***

Liu stepped outside the Xinhua Gate into Beijing. Jiang's guards had unceremoniously escorted him through Zhongnanhai to make sure that he didn't wander around the compound unattended. It was a not-so-gentle reminder that he was an outsider.

He pulled his jacket tighter. It had been an unseasonably warm day for late February but was cooling off quickly. There were plenty of taxis at the nearby stand, and he didn't have to stand outside in the cold. It was a quick ride back to his apartment. He'd used a few extra yuan to encourage the driver to take some shortcuts.

When he walked into the apartment, he made certain that his wife wasn't home from her mother's. He wanted privacy for his call with Xi and didn't trust his wife not to try and listen in. She was always looking for tidbits of gossip to share with her siblings.

Taking off his suit and tie, he slipped into a pair of loose-fitting cotton pajamas. He made sure to put a bandage on his ear. The blood had soaked into his shirt collar and handkerchief, so he placed them in the wash. He'd have to come up with an explanation for his wife – he'd never hear the end of it if he told her the truth about getting hit by Jiang's guard.

He calculated the time in Seattle. 6 a.m. Good. He'd enjoy waking Xi up and ruining his day. He couldn't be too quarrelsome with him directly, but he was passively aggressive as often as he could. He looked forward to the day that Xi was no longer a sharp pebble in his shoe.

"Why are you calling at this hour?" Xi mumbled as he answered the phone on the third try. The first two times had gone to voicemail, but Liu wasn't going to be ignored.

"I understand it is very early, Dr. Xi, but it is urgent that we speak." Liu tried to keep the irritation from his voice. "We are both on unsecured phones, so please be careful not to say too much."

Xi cleared his throat. "Yes, of course. Perhaps we should arrange to speak on a secure line. I could go to the embassy and take the call from there."

"We don't have time for that. This is an urgent matter. As you know, the deadline is quickly approaching. Just be careful not to say too much."

Liu could hear the exasperation in Xi's voice. "Fine. What is so urgent?"

"We received a call at the lab a short time ago," he lied convincingly. It was your second daughter. She insisted on speaking with you. When I took the call and told her that you were unavailable, she flew into a rage."

Xi was silent for a few heartbeats, although Liu could hear him breathing heavily. "Jing is not well mentally, so I trust you did not tell her where I was."

Liu needed to tread lightly. He didn't want to give too much information to Xi, or he might become suspicious. He needed to keep the lie as simple as possible. "She seemed confident that you were at the lab and were avoiding her calls."

He could hear Xi's sigh of relief. "Why was she calling me then?" he asked.

"She said she knew you are now working with the Americans and had warned you not to do that," Liu continued with the misdirection. "She added that the punishment was going to be out of her hands now."

"How does she know that I'm working with the Americans?" Xi wondered out loud.

"She didn't say. But the most important part of her message was that you were going to be punished. In fact, she said the entire country would pay for your stupidity."

"She's been threatening me for a long time, but I don't know what to make of this new threat. What do you think she meant?" Xi asked in a worried tone.

Liu took a breath before closing the trap. "She said the Others were going to send a warning to everyone since you would not listen. They will give us a taste of what is to come if we continue on this path with the Americans and their enemies."

"Are you sure these aren't the ravings of a mad woman? It is one thing to try and kill me or set of a bomb, but this sounds much more threatening."

"It may be the rants of a lunatic, but I don't want to take that risk, Dr. I spoke with the secretary general so he would be appraised of her threat. His directive was that I should call you immediately."

"You took this craziness to Jiang," Xi gasped. "What did he say?"

"As you know, he is not one to take a threat lightly. The threat of an attack only encouraged him to strengthen his resolve to act. He wants you to put pressure on Thunderbird to supply us with some of their weapons if they attack us directly."

"We've already requested that several times," Xi said. "They've ignored our requests. Until there is an actual attack, I don't think they'll listen."

"The secretary general thinks an attack is imminent now that we have been warned. I was clear with your daughter that we are not changing our position to work with the Americans, unless you think we should withdraw our support for the

Americans." Liu knew Xi was committed to this path but wanted to hear him say it.

Xi answered immediately, "No, we have committed to support the Americans in repelling the invaders. If we withdraw our support now, we risk losing them as allies. We must stay on this path."

Liu looked at his reflection in the hallway mirror and smiled. He knew that Xi would lock himself into this position because of his misguided convictions. It had already cost him one daughter, and now it was going to cost him his last child.

"I agree," Liu lied effortlessly. "That is why Jiang recommended I call you immediately so you can give advance warning to our American allies and Thunderbird. We are confident we are going to be attacked. We need the alien weapons to protect ourselves now."

"I will contact them now. And I hope this attack is not too destructive," Xi said anxiously.

***

Faraj peeked around the door to Smith's tiny bedroom. It was a barely a wide space hewn from the tunnel wall, but by adding a rickety door, it had become a private area to sleep and think. Smith was on the lumpy mattress stuffed with rags trying to catch a few hours of rest.

"Doctor Smith, there was a call on the satellite phone for you. It was our Chinese friend. I told him to call back in ten minutes."

Smith arched his stiff back and pulled on his boots. He couldn't remember the last time he'd slept for a few hours at one time and didn't bother to take off his clothes anymore.

When he stepped out of his room, he looked toward the chamber that held the contraption. "Has there been any change in the device?"

"No, Doctor, or I would have woken you," Faraj said. "It still appears that it is in standby mode. It can't be too much longer."

"Their calculation of time is different than ours, but I expect their arrival imminently. It's very exciting," he said with a thin-lipped grin. *More exciting than you realize.*

Smith stepped outside the mouth of tunnel. It was still light out, but he could see the shadows starting to form on the side of the higher peaks. He had spent most of his days inside the cave and missed the feeling of the bright sun on his face.

The phone vibrated to let him know that a call was coming in. He always got a little uneasy when the phone rang. It harbored a deep suspicion that the Americans would someday locate him and would call him before a cruise missile arrived. His luck didn't need to hold out forever, only a few more days until the Others arrived. After that, the Americans would be on the defensive.

"Hello, my friend," he answered with a hint of sarcasm. Liu was far from his friend, but he enjoyed teasing him. Smith hoped he'd be able to cut the fool loose soon. He still needed him now, so a little courtesy couldn't hurt.

"Doctor, it is good to hear your cheerful voice. Things must be going well."

"Yes, they are. Do you have some good news for me?" Smith said to cut off that line of conversation. Liu was a busybody, and his endless questions irritated him.

There was a long moment of silence on the line. "Not good, no," Liu said. "I tried to sway Xi away from working with the Americans as we had discussed. But he remains committed. More than ever since his first daughter has died."

Smith was agitated by that comment. Li Jing had overstepped her authority and killed Xi's daughter, and this was the result he'd feared.

"That is unfortunate. The water she has spilled is impossible to get back. What other idea do you have to change his mind?"

"I have discussed it with the general secretary, and he says it is time for us to get some help from our friends. If they can send a signal to trigger an event at Kunlun, then Xi will be convinced to be more cautious. He'll tell the Americans we need time to reevaluate our position."

Smith could tell that Liu wasn't telling him the complete truth. There was a tone to his voice that reeked of distrust. There was some piece of this puzzle that he was missing.

"And you think that event will be enough to sway Xi?" Smith asked doubtfully.

"Yes, but we are also worried about Thunderbird attacking us if we withdraw our support. Will you request the special weapons from the Others again? We would be much more secure in taking this step if we were sure we could protect ourselves."

Ahh, there is the missing piece, Smith thought. *They are trying to play both sides.*

"I will ask them again," Smith lied effortlessly. He had no intention of asking again. He would send the attack to Kunlun as requested but then would force the Chinese hand.

"Thank you, Doctor. It is urgent, so I will call you to hear what you learned in a few hours before the attack on Kunlun."

"I will talk to you then, my friend," Smith said as he ended the call. He had no intention of talking to Liu again any time soon. Hopefully never.

Smith intended to contact the Others and initiate the attack on Kunlun as Liu requested. But the damage would be made to look like a natural event. No one will believe it was an attack by the Others. Then they would know if the Chinese would follow through and stop helping the Americans and Thunderbird. Their plot would be made plain.

Smith hummed to himself as he walked down the mountainous path. In the dimming twilight, he made his way toward the small village at the base of the mountain. Li Jing would soon be here, and he wanted to be there to greet her.

20

TWISTED

Maxx and Keith wrapped the checkered scarfs around their heads, trying to blend in with the Afghani men walking down the dimly street wearing keffiyehs.

The traffic was still stop and go in this area despite the late hour. It seemed everyone was busy preparing for the escalation in the conflict.

Almost all the men were carrying weapons, so Maxx and Keith's weapons didn't stand out. Their dress, an odd mix of uniform and civilian was designed to blend in with the population. Their biggest concern was that neither of them looked the least bit Middle Eastern. Hence the keffiyehs that the Green Berets had given them to partially cover their faces.

They used hand signals when they needed to communicate, because no one would be speaking English in this part of Kabul. Maxx knew a few words in Pashto, but his American accent would be an immediate giveaway. It was better not to say anything and keep moving at a pace that kept them from standing out from the pedestrians.

They had followed Li Jing's red pickup for several blocks after it sped away from the previous ambush. Now her truck was back to inching along the narrow road. Maxx and Keith were getting closer, despite their moderate walking pace.

Maxx didn't think they'd be able to capture Li Jing, but he was okay with that. At this point, he was set on her killing her rather than trying to take her alive. He hadn't told Hovis about his resolve, but Keith would find out soon enough when the bullets started flying. Maxx had decided that it was going to be her or him – winner take all.

They could turn around and go back to the ambush, but they'd probably never find her again in time. He didn't like the situation – it sucked – but there wasn't a better option that he could see. *Suck it up, buttercup.*

Maxx was quickly walking up the sidewalk on the passenger side of the target truck. Hovis was slightly behind him to make it less obvious that they were together. It also allowed him to watch behind them and to the left. Someone could have followed them from the ambush location. They were far outside the wire, and there was no calvary.

What they hadn't counted on was Li Jing getting lucky. As they stepped under one of the rare working streetlights, Maxx caught a glimpse of her in the side mirror of the truck. She made eye contact with Maxx for a brief second and then ducked down again.

"Did she recognize me?" he angrily muttered to himself.

He got the answer to his question several heartbeats later when the red truck slammed on its brakes and the passenger door flew open. Li Jing bolted out the door and looked briefly in Maxx's direction before running into a side market. She disappeared around the corner into a large alley off the main road.

Maxx didn't have time to signal Hovis about the sudden shift in action. He took off at a run to the mouth of the alleyway where he'd seen Li Jing disappear. Fortunately, no one else jumped from the truck, so it might be a foot race instead of a gun battle. He made sure to keep some pedestrians between himself and the truck as he ran by to make certain he had cover on his flank.

The alley was lined with carts and tables pushing out from the shops. Vendors displayed their goods, ranging from fresh fruits and vegetables to colorful textiles and handcrafted items. The market was lined with a variety of stalls, each illuminated by hanging lanterns or small electric lights. It was surprisingly busy for this time of the evening.

Maxx moved discretely through the busy market, moving through the narrow pathways. He was trying to follow Li Jing's shawl when she shifted quickly amongst the crowd. Fortunately, she was wearing a blue head covering instead of the conventional black, so she stood out slightly, giving Maxx an identifiable target.

Navigating through the market required constant alertness and agility to dodge people, carts, and stray cats. Despite the hustle and bustle, Maxx noticed that the occasional shopkeeper was staring at him a little too long. Something was making him stand out from the crowd. It was uncomfortable as he felt the eyes on him as he passed quickly through the tight pathways.

Occasionally, he would lose sight of Li Jing in the mass of vendors and customers. But he continued to press ahead until he was able to catch sight of her scarf again. She hadn't bothered to look behind her for a long minute, so Maxx picked up his pace. She must have concluded that she had lost them somewhere in the crowd and was making her way to a nearby safe house.

He was intensely focused on her back, when he felt Hovis place his hand on his elbow. When he made eye contact, he nodded to a quiet doorway off the alley. Maxx shook his head and pointed back toward Li Jing. He was trying to make it clear that they didn't have time to break off the chase. Even a few minutes for a private conversation would mean that Li Jing would likely be lost in the crowd.

Hovis shook his head irritably at Maxx. He motioned again vigorously toward the doorway. Maxx was tempted to ignore Hovis's forceful signals and continue without him, but after a brief moment of indecision, he rolled his eyes and stepped out of the passageway and into the empty entryway.

"Make it quick," Maxx whispered heatedly. "We have about thirty seconds before we lose her again."

"I know you're the expert here, but we're getting too far from any backup," Keith whispered back.

"It happens. Let's give it another five minutes, and if we haven't caught up by then, we'll head back."

Hovis looked at Maxx with a squint. "And what happens if we catch her in five minutes? How are we going to get her out of here. Have you looked around us?"

"What's your point? You think that we won't be able to subdue her and exfil?"

"Be realistic, Maxx. Are you going to carry her out over your shoulder? We'll be dead before we travel a block. And no way do reinforcements get here in time to help. We're too far away."

Maxx roughly rubbed the stubble on his jaw. "True. What if we take her out? I think I can get close enough to use a blade, and we exit before anyone realizes we're the bad guys."

Keith raised his voice slightly into an angry whisper. "That isn't the objective. We don't have authorization to murder American citizens. No way am I helping with that."

"Damn it, she needs to die or she's going to kill someone else. I'd cross that line, but I can't do it alone, Hovis."

"I'm not going to help kill her, Maxx. I'm not," he said insistently.

Maxx turned away to search down the alley for Li Jing. He spotted her a block ahead stepping into a stall selling carpets. "Fine, let's follow her for another ten minutes. If we don't get a break, we'll turn back and see if we can get help from Zeller's team. Fair?"

"Fair enough," Hovis said as he took the point position and headed down the corridor. Maxx clenched his jaw and followed behind him.

With Hovis in the lead, Maxx couldn't keep track of where Li Jing was going. His task was to watch for threats to the left and rear. With the change in positions, he could see why Keith had been getting nervous. Even though no one was obviously following them, it was clear that they were generating a lot of interest as they passed through the market. There were always several men watching their progress.

The hair on the back of his neck stood up when he saw a couple of the men break eye contact and take out cell phones. It could be coincidence, but Maxx never trusted coincidences. They were getting into a jam.

He started to reach for Hovis's shoulder, when he suddenly increased his pace. The change in movement surprised Maxx. He had to take several large strides to keep from losing contact. Keith then quickly swung right into a doorway, heading inside a dim hallway.

Maxx knew they were in trouble. He should have warned Hovis not to follow her inside any buildings, but it was too late now. The mistake was made. *Boxed in.*

Leaning inside the doorway, he watched the street to make sure no one was coming in behind them. It was still clear of obvious threats, but it didn't matter.

Two men with turbans and AK-47s stepped out of the shadows and aimed their rifles at Keith and Maxx. Keith didn't have time to react. He'd be dead before he even swung the muzzle of his M4 around.

Maxx's odds of getting the guy pointing the rifle at him were fifty-fifty because he'd been expecting something before he had stepped into the building. But Keith would die, and then it'd be two on one in a hallway, surrounded by a lot of unfriendly men with weapons. His first instinct was to fight, but he wasn't going to put any pressure on the trigger unless they fired first.

He assumed if they had wanted to kill them that they would have started firing immediately. Not that it was a good sign, but it was better than the alternative. Getting shot with automatic weapons in a narrow hallway was a guaranteed death sentence. Anything other than that was a reprieve, even if it was only a momentary delay.

"Put your weapons down," one of the Afghani men said in English. "Now!"

Maxx lowered the muzzle of his rifle without hesitation. "Do what they say, Hovis."

Hovis stood frozen with indecision. Maxx couldn't see his eyes but guessed right now they were rapidly trying to understand the trap he'd led them into.

"Listen to him," the man shouted at Keith. "You will surely die if you don't."

Keith slowly lowered his rifle.

"Now put them on the floor. All of them."

Maxx took out his pistol and placed it on the floor next to his rifle. He kept his knife in his pants pocket. Not that it would do any good in a situation like this, but maybe another time. Keith followed his lead, laying both of his guns in the small pile at their feet.

The man said something in Pashto. Two teenage boys ran into the hallway, grabbed the weapons and ran back out. "Follow me now," the Talib said, waving his rifle at Maxx.

With the English-speaking man leading the way, they opened the wooden door at the end of the hallway and stepped outside. With a wave of his hand, he motioned to Maxx and Keith that they should follow.

Stepping through the door, Maxx realized they had cut through the buildings to a side street running parallel to the market. Here it was quiet and dark, with several other Taliban soldiers waiting in the bed of dented white pickup.

Parked behind them was a red pickup, the same truck they had been following for the last hour since the ambush. Sitting in the passenger seat was a woman with her head covered by a blue shawl.

"Nice to see you again, Maxx and Agent Hovis," the woman said with glee. "I was beginning to get worried that I'd lost you in the market."

"Li Jing. I'd say it's a pleasure to see you too, but it's not," said Maxx with a frown.

Li Jing laughed. "My friends will help you into the back of the truck after they tie your hands and feet. Isn't this like old times, Agent Hovis?"

Maxx could see that Hovis's face was ashen. When he made eye contact with Maxx, he looked crestfallen. Guilt was written all over his face. He didn't bother to respond to Li Jing's dig.

She said something to the men in Pashto. The soldiers laughed lewdly as they pushed Maxx and Hovis into the back of the pickup. They managed a few kicks and punches while they zip tied Maxx's legs and hands together. He didn't respond, which only seemed to agitate them. He wasn't going to give them any satisfaction.

As rough as they were with Maxx, the men didn't pull any punches with Keith. They hit him in the stomach so hard it knocked the wind out of him. He pitched face forward onto the dirty truck bed. With his hands already restrained, he couldn't do anything to slow his fall and landed headfirst on the metal. He let out a loud yelp, which resulted in more laughter from the men.

Watching them hit Keith only made Maxx angrier. Something Li Jing had said had triggered them. He wasn't worried about himself; he'd be able to hold his own. It wasn't the first time he'd been beaten. But Keith hadn't yet recovered from his previous fight with Li Jing.

It wasn't a fair fight, and Maxx hated watching him take the violent beating. He knew there was nothing he could do to stop it. And anything he said would only prolong Keith's suffering.

People in the buildings along the street started to take notice of all the shouting. After several minutes, Li Jing yelled at them angrily. She must have told them to stop, because they gave Keith one more kick and sat down in the truck bed.

Sitting in the back of the pickup surrounded by the angry men, Maxx tried to clear his thoughts. It was hard to focus while sitting on his zip tied hands. They passed by several bustling markets that were closing down. Vendors were packing up their goods. Occasionally, he'd see groups of men gathered around small fires, sharing stories and laughter. All of them oblivious to the coming war. Or maybe they knew and were enjoying their last moments.

The roads were a mix of smooth and rugged, with some of the streets showing the wear and tear of years of conflict. The jostling was painful. Keith moaned whenever they ran over a particularly large pothole.

The air was becoming bitterly cold, and there was a sense of calm as the hustle and bustle of the day faded away. There wasn't much Maxx could do about their situation. He didn't want to focus on the dire nature of the shitstorm they now found themselves in, so he focused on the location surrounding him. If this was going to be the end, he was going to savor the final moments of his life. It had been a good one. He was far from perfect, but he felt that he'd done far more good than bad.

The smell of the street food lingered in the air, a blend of spices and grilled meats reminding him that his stomach was empty. The city, with its mix of ancient and modern architecture rushed by, bathed in the soft glow of the occasional streetlight.

In the distance, the mountains surrounding Kabul created a majestic backdrop, their silhouettes stark against the night sky. The stars above were bright and clear, offering a serene contrast to the city's lights below. After several minutes, it was obvious they were leaving the city behind them and heading toward the foothills. Once they left the city, there would be little chance of escaping.

The silence from the inside of the truck cab was broken with the sounds of a muffled conversation. With the sounds of the engine and road, Maxx couldn't tell what was being said even if it was English. But Li Jing's voice was distinct enough to be identifiable. It sounded like she was having a tense conversation with the driver. They weren't yelling, but they were agitated about something.

Twisting uncomfortably toward the front of the truck so he could see the road ahead, Maxx could see a series of lights. From the arrangement of the lights, it looked like several Humvees were blocking the road. A coalition checkpoint.

The pickup slowed down and pulled to the side behind a partially burned-out hut. The white pickup pulled up beside them. They both turned off their headlights.

The driver of the second pickup jumped out and came over to Li Jing's window. She rolled it down, and they began talking, occasionally pointing in the direction of the roadblock. After reaching some sort of decision, the second driver gave instructions to the rest of the men in the trucks, and they took defensive positions around the building. Maxx noticed they were careful to stay behind cover. They must be worried about being spotted by the men manning the roadblock.

Maxx was curious what Li Jing planned to do. They couldn't go forward into the roadblock or they'd be killed or captured. The only options were to either turn back to the city and try to find another route or sit here and hope the soldiers at the roadblock left. Knowing the time pressure Li Jing was working within, he didn't see her showing patience for long.

Li Jing finally stepped out of the truck and walked over to where Maxx was sitting. She had a satellite phone in her hand and was dialing.

Li Jing brought the phone to her ear. "Hi. I stopped before the old intersection. There's a blockade, and I don't have enough men to fight my way through."

After a moment, she nodded and brought the phone up to Maxx's ear. "It's for you."

"You wanted to speak with me?" Maxx said into the phone receiver.

"I've got some good news and some bad news. Which do you want first?" the man said.

"You know I'm going to kill you Doctor Smith, so it doesn't really matter."

"Don't be rude, Maxx. The good news is that I'm too busy at the moment to kill your girlfriend, Gabby."

"And the bad news?" Maxx said.

"I thought it would be obvious. I'm going to kill your girlfriend."

21

WORRIED LIFE BLUES

Miss Grey leaned back into the sofa cushions as she watched the seaplane accelerate and then take off from the smooth water of Lake Union.

She had been seeing Andres over the last six months. They had been introduced by Maxx and Gabby during the initial Thunderbird incident last September. Both of them coming from large, conservative Hispanic families involved with the military and federal government had provided for long nights of conversation and sipping tequila while they got to know each other. While her path had led to the DHS, he had chosen an academic career after serving in the military.

Andres had purchased the houseboat on Lake Union after he'd received tenure at the nearby University of Washington. Nestled along the shore of the tranquil waters, the houseboat exuded charm with every creak of its wooden frame. Its weathered, sun-bleached planks painted a robin's-egg blue and a miniature, sloping roof crowned with a rustic chimney, evoked a storybook simplicity. Floating on the lake added an additional layer of magic.

Inside, the space was cozy, adorned with vintage maritime decor. Every corner whispered stories of Andres's past life in the military. The windows, framed by faded curtains, offered panoramic views of the lake's gentle ripples, and outside, a tiny deck big enough for two invited endless sunrises over the Cascade Mountains. He enjoyed rowing and sailing on the lake and nearby waterways. Living directly on the lake offered him a unique connection to the community and the natural habitat. Andres had chosen the houseboat seeking simplicity, a connection to nature, and a different pace of life, where the view from his living room changed constantly.

Miss Grey had fallen in love with the tiny home. It had taken her a few anxious nights to get accustomed to sleeping on what she considered to be more boat than home. But over time it had become her favorite place to spend her time when in Seattle. Not only because of the views of the water, mountains and surrounding city, but because it represented her life with Andres. The relationship had started with plenty of passion but had become anchored on a much deeper level in the last few months.

She typically didn't stay on the houseboat alone, but Andres had convinced her to stay when he made the sudden trip to Afghanistan. She felt a bit guilty about how that had materialized, but it had been his idea, so it was difficult to turn down his offer.

While on the TSA plane returning from the meeting in Hawaii with Xi, she had contacted Andres to let him know that she was going to tied up for an indeterminate time in Seattle. When she had mentioned that Maxx, one of Andres's best friends and former colleague in the military, was going to be leaving for a special mission to Afghanistan, he pressed her for details. Andres quickly offered to help Maxx if she could arrange to get him a flight. He'd even suggested that he'd recruit another of their friends to assist, Maxx's friend Glen.

Feeling slightly guilty about how she had pushed Maxx into going to Afghanistan, having Andres assist him was a good compromise. This ensured that Maxx would be supported by two of his friends and former Special Forces buddies, along with a Green Beret team based at Bagram Airbase. It wasn't the ideal situation but the best that she could do on short notice and still keep the effort to track Li Jing confidential.

Those arrangements unfortunately meant Andres had flown out on a military transport before she had landed. To help fill her need for conversation, she'd contacted Gabby to come over for lunch. She made some sandwiches and a small salad with the contents of the refrigerator. She'd even cracked open a bottle of chardonnay from Chateau Ste. Michelle, a local winery.

She hadn't had much of a chance to connect with Gabby since the events had spun up at the beginning of the week. It had been one rushed event after another. She had sensed that Gabby was struggling to adjust with the tragic death of her friend Connie and the sudden departure of Maxx. She considered Gabby to be a friend and someone that she could talk openly with. But she'd detected that Gabby had been struggling with the events of the past week and wanted to hear her concerns.

She was watching another seaplane take off when she got a text message from Andres. "I'll call you in five minutes on the land line in my office. Will you be able to pick up?"

She quickly texted back a quick yes and moved down to Andres's small office in the back of the house. He used the room for work when he wanted to get away from his workspace at the university. She kept the door closed whenever she visited, because the room was a chaos of books, papers, and charts. The messiness was a stark contrast to the way he organized everything else in his life. She shook her head at the contradiction.

She lifted a stack of papers off the creased leather chair and set them in an empty spot on the floor. The mix of smells was a curious reminder of Andres, paper, leather, and his favorite cologne. If she closed her eyes, she could imagine that he was in the room with her.

She drifted off for a moment, until the desk phone rang. He had told her that the phone and office had been checked for surveillance devices, but she never trusted that completely. After September 11th' it had been clear that the alphabet intelligence agencies were frequently monitoring phone calls based on select locations and keywords. If she was a betting woman, she'd put money on the fact that his phone was a source of increased interest once it become known that they were in a relationship.

"Hi, honey, it's great to hear from you. Is everything okay there?" she said as she picked up the phone.

After a few seconds of delayed connection due to his location, he answered. "Hey, babe, I'm glad I caught you. I only have a few moments before we head back into the wild. The good news is that we were able to find our target."

"That's great," she exclaimed. "You're on your way home with her in tow?"

"Not exactly. We got blindsided by an ambush, and she escaped. We're all fine other than minor injuries. But the bad news is that Maxx and Agent Hovis took off chasing her, and we're trying to link back up with them. I wanted to give you a heads up that we're hot on her trail. And if you hear anything on the news or through other channels, we're good. Not to worry."

She relaxed in the chair, feeling some of the tension drain away. "I'm glad you're okay. I'm going to see Gabby shortly and will let her know that Maxx is doing okay. He might have called her by now."

He paused on the line. "Probably not. He doesn't have his phone on him, which is why we're having a hard time reconnecting with him. Both he and Hovis left their phones behind during the ambush. Tell her not to worry about him. We'll complete this mission shortly and be home soon. Miss you."

"Be safe, hun, miss you too," she said and disconnected the call.

It was difficult to tell from the short call if Andres was being completely forthcoming about the events in Kabul. He had made it sound as if there wasn't anything too worrying, but he'd made the effort to call her at midnight in Kabul to tell her everything was okay. In retrospect, his tone seemed off. He was more concerned than he'd let on.

The doorbell rang, and she got up, closing the door to the messy office behind her. She'd have to take him at his word and stop trying to read hidden meaning into the call. She brushed her hair back behind her ear, put on a smile, and opened the front door.

"Come on in and relax. I'm so glad you could get away for lunch with me," Miss Grey said as she gave Gabby a hug. "I know it's not the fancy food you can get at the café at TechCom, but I have a bottle of wine. That is if you don't mind sharing a glass during the workday."

Gabby laughed. "I won't tell if you don't. To be honest, a glass might help take the edge off. I've felt off all week, and the jet lag from our quick trip to Hawaii didn't help."

"Help yourself. The bottle is on the counter breathing. I'll whip up a salad. Are you okay with some salmon on the salad?"

"It sounds a lot better than the Snickers bar I have in my purse."

After Gabby had poured a glass of chardonnay for Miss Grey and herself, she found a spot on the couch. She relaxed into a spot soaked in the late-winter sun. She took off her slip-on shoes and curled her feet up under herself.

Miss Grey made small talk while she finished preparing their lunch. It wasn't fancy, but it helped distract her from the difficult conversation that was coming. She didn't want to tell Gabby about the call from Andres and the news about Maxx missing until she was in the same room. Gabby looked tired and more vulnerable than usual, and she wanted to be cautious about how to share the news with her.

She set the plates down on the glass coffee table in front of them and sat on the sofa. "Eat up. You're looking a little thin," she said with wide smile.

"It's been difficult to keep my appetite up this week," Gabby admitted with a sigh. "This week has brought back a lot of bad memories I thought I had put in the past."

"It has been a lot of pressure. Not a typical week in the office for me either. Have you had a chance to catch up with Maxx since he left?" she asked hopefully.

"He left me a voice message when he landed in Kabul. Unfortunately, I was in the shower, so I missed talking to him. Have you heard from him or Andres about how the search for Li Jing is going?"

"Actually, I spoke with him right before you arrived," she said sheepishly. "He said that they had located her, but she'd managed to evade them." She purposely left out the fact that there had been the surprise attack. Since no one was hurt, she didn't see the point in concerning her unnecessarily.

Gabby looked at her wide eyed. "Did Andres say anything about Maxx?"

"He said that Maxx and Agent Hovis were tracking Li Jing and felt positive about their chances of capturing her." She felt guilty about leaving out the fact that they'd lost contact with Maxx, but that it would only agitate Gabby further without more detail.

"That's good, I guess. I know Maxx is capable of handling himself in those situations, but I can't help but worry about him."

"He's more than capable. There's no one I trust more in a

situation like this. With Andres, Glen, and the team of Green Berets backing him up, I'm sure he'll get the job done and be home soon."

Gabby set her glass down and looked out the window pensively. "But that's not the end of it, is it? I mean, all of this is leading to something big in the next day or two. And I know Maxx well enough to know that he'll lean into whatever needs to be done regardless of the risk."

"You're right. We don't know what happens next. Take it one day at time and stick with the people we trust. We've went through terrible times last September, and it all worked out by trusting each other."

"That happened so fast I really didn't have time to think about it. But here we are again six months later, and it feels worse than ever. Watching Connie die brought it home for me. There are bad people out there, and I'm not sure they'll stop until Maxx and I are out of the picture. We didn't ask for any of this."

Miss Grey took Gabby's hand. "I understand this is a lot to deal with. But you're strong and have a solid relationship with a man who will do anything to protect you. The two of you are as strong as anyone I know."

"But Maxx isn't here, is he? I've been thinking about this a lot over the last two days, and I want out. When Maxx gets back, I want the two of us to pack up and disappear for a while. Until this thing with Thunderbird resolves itself. I don't want to be in the middle anymore."

Miss Grey raised her eyebrows. "And if it doesn't resolve itself?"

"Then it doesn't really matter does it. At least we'll have each other when the world comes unglued."

Miss Grey was quiet for a moment while she considered how to respond to Gabby. She needed Maxx to stay involved to see this through to the end, but she also couldn't ask Gabby to set aside her fears, because she was right in assuming that both she and Maxx had targets on their backs.

"Let's not make any hard choices until Maxx and Andres are back. Then we'll get out the barbecue and talk this out over some steaks and beer. If that's how you and Maxx feel, I will do everything I can to help you. Sound fair?"

Gabby smiled and squeezed Miss Grey's hand. "Only if you promise to tell me your first name."

Miss Grey laughed loudly. "It's a deal, chica."

There was a solid knock on the front door as they both laughed. They couldn't pretend not to be home because whoever was outside would have clearly heard them laughing.

Miss Grey walked over and looked out through the peep-hole on the door before opening it. She cursed under her breath. "What is he doing here?" she muttered.

"I know you're in there," the man said forcefully. "We need to talk, Grey."

She cracked open the door wide enough to talk but not to let him in. "What do you want, Director Anderson? You could have called me."

"It's not you I want to see. It's her," he said as he tilted his head toward Gabby.

Gabby shook her head. "I have nothing to more to say to you."

"I think you do. I know your boyfriend is in Afghanistan on some misguided adventure. But I need to get to him before he interferes in something he doesn't understand. Can you call him, because he's not answering his phone, and the Green Beret team seems to have lost track of him."

With a sigh, Gabby pulled her phone from her purse. She dialed Maxx's cell. The call went right to voicemail. "Babe, call me back when you get a chance. It's important," she said.

Anderson glared at her as he turned and walked away. Over his shoulder he said, "If he calls back, tell him to call me ASAP.

You both are in way over your heads, and I've lost my patience with your meddling."

***

Gabby sat at the edge of her desk, the gray afternoon light of her small condo casting long shadows across the room.

Her fingers nervously twirled a strand of her long, dark hair as she stared at the encrypted laptop on her desk. The screensaver displayed a radiant image of the Space Needle, a memory of happier times. But beneath that screen was a labyrinth of codes, secret communications, and the weight of a world teetering on the brink.

The Omega Project had started innocuously enough, a project management position at TechCom that promised innovation and change, something that would benefit the world, but she hadn't understood there was a dark side. She'd first realized the implications in the week before September 11th when she and Maxx had been drawn deep into the conflict between the US and China. But as months had passed since September 11th, Gabby had been able to put those horrific events into the past, until three days ago when she had watched her friend gunned down while sitting next to her having coffee. She felt like she was being slowly pulled into another nightmare from which she couldn't escape.

Gabby was no spy, no scientist, only a bright young woman with a knack for coding and a strong desire to make a difference in the world. But now as she pieced together the full scope of the project, the reality crashed down on her. Being stuck between two extraterrestrial forces trying to control the world was overwhelming. She'd been able to deal with the stress while she was not in imminent danger. It was a problem to be solved without worrying about her or Maxx being hurt. It was a noble cause, but the pressure, the secrecy, the potential fallout if apprehended—it had become too much.

Of course, Maxx was involved up to his neck too. He had been her anchor, her confidant, and now her co-conspirator. He believed in the cause, perhaps more than she did. But lately even his resolve seemed to waver. They hadn't had much chance to discuss the change in the last week. He had hastily left for Afghanistan, leaving her to deal with pressing fears and growing doubts. She wanted out but wouldn't leave Maxx to deal with it alone.

"I think we should quit," Gabby had said on the flight back from Hawaii, her voice barely above a whisper. "This isn't what we signed up for. We're not heroes, Maxx. I'm just...scared."

Maxx had looked at her, his eyes reflecting the same worry but also a stubborn hope. "If we leave, who takes our place? We're in too deep, Gabby. If not us, who?"

But tonight, alone with her thoughts, Gabby felt the walls closing in. The project, and the communication with the aliens that called themselves Thunderbird, was supposed to be their salvation, a beacon of hope for humanity. Instead, it felt like a sword hanging over her head. She thought of the encrypted messages, the late-night calls, the constant fear of surveillance. What if they were caught? What if their families became targets?

Her phone buzzed, snapping her out of her reverie. It was a text message from Miss Grey. "Meet me at 0800. Secure location."

Gabby's heart raced. She had only left Miss Grey a couple hours ago after Director Anderson had dropped in unexpectedly to threaten her. Another meeting meant more decisions, more commitments. She looked at the photo on her nightstand, her and Maxx standing on the deck of the ferry, carefree, before all this. She wanted that back. She wanted out.

With trembling fingers, she dialed Maxx's number. "We

need to talk," she said as soon as it went to voicemail. "I can't do this anymore, honey. We need to find a way out."

The world might be on the brink, but for Gabby, the immediate battle was for her and Maxx's freedom, their chance at a normal life, away from the shadows and the secrets. Whatever happened after that would be out of their hands.

22

DEAD ENDS

Maxx's vision narrowed down to a single point.

He could hear Smith continuing to talk through the satellite phone, but the words were a constant drone that he couldn't process. After Smith had told him he was planning to kill Gabby, rage had taken over, and he was seeing everything through a haze of red. It was impossible to listen when he kept imaging all the ways that he wanted to hurt Smith. No, not hurt. Kill.

"Maxx, are you still there?" Smith asked multiple times, each time progressively louder.

After the third or fourth inquiry, Smith penetrated the red haze. "I'm here. I was thinking about the best way to kill you and your girlfriend Li Jing."

Li Jing giggled in the background.

Doctor Smith sighed. "Fortunately for me, you'll never get the chance to live out your fantasy. Li Jing is going to take care of you shortly. I wouldn't give her any ideas if I were you...She's been itching to execute you ever since she led you into that ambush."

"Then why am I still alive?" Maxx said to Smith as he turned to glare at Li Jing.

"Because I wanted to make sure you knew that you'd effectively killed your girlfriend. If you'd stayed home, you could have protected her. Maybe you would have had a chance to save her. But since you've chosen to chase me halfway around the world rather than protect her, I'm wanted you to know that you failed to achieve both objectives."

Maxx could feel the fury rising again. This time his anger was mitigated by the ache he felt for Gabby. He had screwed up, and that hurt more than the knowledge that he was probably going to die soon. He'd made the wrong choice, and the woman he loved was going to pay for his mistake.

"Yes, I regret not being there for her. But if there's more to life than this, I will be waiting for you in hell, Smith. I will accept any punishment, in this world or the next, to watch you burn."

"You give yourself too much credit, Maxx. Love will never win over hate. But that wasn't the only thing I wanted to tell you. That was the hook."

"Nothing else you could say would surprise me," Maxx shot back.

Maxx heard Li Jing giggle in his ear again. He tried to shrug her off, but she pressed tighter, bringing the tip of her knife to his throat.

"I doubt that very much. The sad part is that all of this is for nothing. You've not only gotten yourself and your girlfriend killed, but you've done it for a lie."

It was Maxx's turn to laugh. "Since the first time we met, everything you've ever said to me has been a lie. My only wish is that I could go back in time to the first time we met. If I'd known then what an evil person you were, I would have painted the walls of the conference room red with your blood."

"Water under the bridge. But I told you the truth about

Gabby dying. Someone is on their way now to take care of my little side project. Now I'm going to tell you the hardest truth of all. You think you're helping the good guys to stop me and save the planet."

"That's what this is all about, isn't it?" Maxx said. When you and the Others are stopped, the world continues on its merry way. I'm the tip of the spear. If I fail, the American and China military are coming in behind me."

"Ah, you're sadly mistaken. I thought you were smarter than that. That bitch Senator Traficant isn't doing this for the good of a noble cause. She has her own reasons, and none of them lead to the world-saving event that you've convinced yourself of."

Maxx was stunned into silence for a moment. *Why would Smith lie to me when I'm going to be dead soon?*

"What other objective could she have?"

"I don't know all the details. She's a cunning little weasel, but she has a special deal with Thunderbird. She's been working with them for decades, and this is her big payoff. She only has to stop the Others by any means necessary, and she wins. So you're only a pawn in her game, Maxx. Just like Mr. Green, Miss Grey, and everyone else she has dragged in."

Maxx felt his stomach roll. All of this had been for nothing. He'd not only been used but had brought in others thinking he was on the right side of history. Not only had he failed to stop Smith, he had led them all to doom. And Smith was going to kill the person who had trusted him the most.

His last shred of hope dissipated like his warm breath into the cold, night air.

***

Li Jing watched Maxx deflate. He pushed the satellite phone away with his shoulder after Smith's last words.

"Are you done speaking with him, Doctor?" she asked.

"Yes, I told him you're going to kill him now. I only wish I could be there to watch you do it, but I need to stay near to the device. I might hear from the Others at any moment."

"You don't want me to bring the prisoners back to the tunnels?" Li Jing asked. "I thought we were going to use them as hostages to bargain with the Americans."

"Change of plans, my rose. I need you to get back here quickly in case things begin to happen soon. You won't get through the roadblock with two American prisoners. You need to kill them and leave their bodies behind. Don't draw attention to yourself."

She looked perplexed at the lights of the roadblock in the distance. "You're certain the Americans will let me through the blockade?"

"They will send a signal to you when they are in place. Three long flashes of light mean you must move quickly, or you will miss your opportunity to pass. We have a friend who will let you pass without questions if you're alone. Tell them your name is Jane Smith.

"Kill them and be ready to move soon," Doctor Smith ordered. "Do it quietly. Don't alert the Americans at the road-block, or you'll never get through."

The call ended, and Li Jing signaled to several of the soldiers to make sure Maxx was restrained in the bed of the truck. With his hands and feet bound with restraints, there was little that he could do, but she wasn't going to risk him doing anything to intervene while she was focused on the other American. The FBI Agent.

"You don't have to do this," Maxx said to her as he readied himself for what came next.

She ignored him and told the Taliban soldiers to gag Hovis and drag him out of the bed of the pickup. She pointed to a rusty, broken pipe in the ground next to the abandoned building and instructed the men to secure him.

Hovis was still dazed from the beating he'd received earlier. His eyes were unfocused, but he tried to follow her motion as she ambled over to where he kneeled on the ground. If he hadn't been bound to the pipe, he would have tipped over and curled into a fetal position in the dirt.

"It's been a while, Agent Hovis. But fate brings us together again. And we're back to how we first met a few nights ago. This time, I won't give you the chance to escape. You betrayed me once, and I never give second chances."

Keith mumbled something into the rag stuffed into his mouth. She waved dismissively, ignoring anything he had to say.

"I was going to put a bullet in the back of your head. Nice and quick. But I've decided that since fate has played a hand in our rendezvous, I'll even out our relationship. Karma and all that." She blew him a kiss.

She removed the blade from the sheath on her hip. Tiny flecks of light reflected off the edge of the blade as she waved it under his chin. She slowly took his arm tied to the pipe and sawed the blade through the sleeve of his jacket from wrist to elbow. The fabric hung from his elbow, exposing the skin of his forearm.

Moving the blade up and down his arm, she placed long, shallow cuts. He tried to jerk his arm away when she hit a nerve, which only made the blade dig deeper. "Stop thrashing," she said as she held his arm tighter and drew another long cut. She was being careful not to end his agony too quickly. She wanted to make sure that he suffered like she had. More than she had.

Blood began to flow more freely as she dug the edge of the knife a little deeper with each turn. She was purposefully trying to avoid a vein, but his thrashing made it difficult. She was watching his eyes grow wider with each cut, which made her smile grow broader.

Turning to Maxx, Li Jing held up the bloody knife so he could see it clearly. “I hope you’re watching, because you’re next. I have something special planned for you.”

When Maxx shrugged and winked, she lost her focus and lowered the knife too close to Hovis. He lowered his head and whipped his neck across the edge of the blade. She felt the tug of the tip as it sunk deep into the muscles of his neck.

She jumped back in astonishment as the artery began to spurt onto her pants and the surrounding ground. She’d clearly underestimated him. Even in tremendous pain, he was willing to drive himself onto the knife to end the torment. Her face contorted in anger, knowing that he had deprived her of the chance for retribution. He hadn’t paid a high enough price for hurting her. But someone was going to pay.

Jing swiveled toward Maxx, certain that Hovis was already dead. She signaled the Taliban to bring Maxx over to her. She was in a malicious mood and looked excited about moving on from the warm-up.

She turned back to cut the restraints holding Hovis to the pipe and kicked him out of the way. He was on the ground surrounded by a dark patch of bloody soil. Useless to her now. She heard the soldiers behind her muttering softly as they removed Maxx from the pickup bed.

Suddenly, one of them shouted. A noise loud enough that she spun around in time to see that Maxx was standing on his feet. The fools must have cut off the ankle restraints to make him walk instead of carrying him over.

Maxx lunged at the soldier on his right and headbutted him hard, the crack of bone echoing off the walls of the abandoned building. The man dropped to the ground senseless.

The other soldier, the one still holding the knife used to cut the binding on Maxx’s legs, reacted quickly, stabbing at Maxx, who twisted at the last instant to avoid the potentially fatal thrust. Catching the soldier off balance, he didn't pull back as Li Jing expected. Instead, he stepped into the blade and lifted the restraint between his wrists, severing the plastic zip tie in a single, violent motion.

Without any restraints, Maxx was freed. She watched in disbelief as he immediately pivoted and began running toward the distant lights of the roadblock. She thought momentarily about chasing him but realized it would be pointless without being able to use lights or a weapon. He could run and hide for quite a while. And she needed to get back to Smith.

Using hand signals, she angrily directed several of the soldiers to chase after him. She reminded them again not to use their rifles or lights or she would personally kill them. She wanted Maxx dead, but more importantly she needed to get through the roadblock while she had the opportunity. After that, she didn't care what the Taliban did with him.

***

Li Jing watched the blockade for the signal while her mind dredged up the past. *Three long flashes of light.*

For the thousandth time, she recalled the day her father had left, as if it were a scene frozen in time. A pivotal moment that didn't merely close a chapter but seemed to rip out entire pages from her life's story. As a young girl, the initial shock was like falling into an abyss where reality lost its grip. "How could he?" she would ask herself, replaying every interaction, every promise, as if by dissecting the past, she could alter the future. Where he had stood as a pillar of strength, there was nothing but emptiness. Where they had been a family, there was only her and her mother left to grieve. Not even a photograph of him to remind them of what had once been. He didn't even leave his name, so there was nothing tangible to anchor herself to.

As she matured, the anger followed, not merely a fleeting emotion but a persistent fire. A fire that consumed any good memories. She was angry at him for his departure, at herself for her naivety, at her mother for protecting him. This anger was her shield, guarding her from the vulnerability that had led her to such a dark place. Yet beneath this shield was a battlefield of betrayal, where each memory became a weapon against her own heart. A potential weapon against anyone that would dare betray her again.

Through her teen years, depression enveloped her like a dense fog, clouding the path ahead. She grieved not for him but for the imaginary family life he had taken with him. Days melded into one another, each a stark reminder of her loss. Her mother struggled to maintain a home, but they were outcasts in her village. Her self-worth felt diminished by his exit, as if his leaving was a commentary on her value, her lovability. It was a dark passage, where the light at the end seemed more illusion than promise.

Gradually, acceptance dawned, a quiet realization that life would continue, with or without him. Rebuilding wasn't about erasing the past but weaving vengeance into the fabric of the woman she was becoming. She embraced the hatred that simmered in her heart and filled it with visions of how she would make him suffer as she had suffered. Her dreams of revenge filled the emptiness, allowing her to explore parts of herself she had overlooked. She learned to cherish her ability to cause pain for others, finding strength in her loneliness.

Years later, the echoes of his abandonment still resonated in her approach to relationships. Trust, once freely given, was now a commodity she offered sparingly, if at all. Yet there was a newfound strength in this wariness, a self-reliance forged from necessity. She had built barriers, but also pathways to unhealthy connections. She realized that even in the absence of love, she could build a strong bond with a man. Someone that shared a deep passion for vengeance, not love.

She viewed that chapter of abandonment not as a defeat but as a profound lesson in resilience. It taught her the depth of her ability to hate, to suffer, and most crucially to find a soul as tortured as hers. Through the echoes of abandonment, she had found Doctor Smith.

It wasn't a relationship built on romantic or sexual attraction but on a mutual foundation of hatred and revenge. She was attracted to his strength and mind, but she was drawn most to their shared hate for her father. They both hungered to destroy the world that had betrayed them, and for this reason she would do anything for him.

And she trusted Smith not to betray her. Because he of all people would understand the depths to which she would go to make him pay for any betrayal.

Three long flashes. It was time to go.

23

THE TRUTH IN THE MIRROR

Senator Traficant glared at Mr. Green. If looks could kill, he'd be buried under six feet of concrete.

They were locked in a fourth-floor office in the Team Tacoma building in Seattle's Pioneer Square. Team Tacoma had bought one of the historic buildings a block off the main intersection during the 1980s under the guise of a remodel. They then were able to construct the massive underground storage space and primary power source for the Thunderbird device. It had taken them the better part of a decade to complete the project while avoiding raising public awareness. The construction of several skyscrapers in the adjacent downtown corridor had provided a plausible explanation for the constant presence of tunneling and construction equipment.

Sitting in the conference room overlooking the rainy street, they hadn't been able to reach agreement on how to proceed with the approaching interaction with the Others. The Pentagon was prepared for combat action in several positions around the Middle East, with the focus on Afghanistan. They knew Smith and the Others' device were located near Kabul. The Joint Chiefs were awaiting direction from the president.

And the president, while getting advice from multiple sources, was waiting for Senator Traficant to make the final decision regarding the location for the initial combat. It was a fluid situation.

Senator Traficant leaned forward aggressively. She was tired of arguing. "Regardless of what we've heard from Smith or the Others, we should proceed with an aggressive action."

Green had leaned back to make some space between the senator and himself. "I am less trusting of the motivations of Thunderbird than you are. I think we should at least attempt to hear from the Others before launching an aggressive military attack."

"Based on the direction given to us by Thunderbird, it makes no sense to risk agitating them by delaying or giving any credence to their enemies. The worst that could happen would be that we get beaten by the Others and have to request additional assistance. It might make America look like weak allies to Thunderbird, but there are worse positions to be in," she concluded.

Green nodded as if to concede the point. "But once we're at war, the Others wouldn't see any value in trying to find a diplomatic resolution. We have one shot at compromise. Yes, Thunderbird would likely see this as a disloyal move."

"If Thunderbird concludes that we aren't loyal to them, it's likely they will go ahead and reset the planet. It will keep Earth from falling to the Others. It's what I would do," she said with a shrug.

"But I think a possible outcome is that we avoid making Earth a battleground for an interstellar war that we don't understand," Green said.

Once again, they had reached the same impasse.

They had used the AI systems at DARPA to run various scenarios over the past week and hadn't come to any clear resolution. The results of the simulations didn't change much regardless of the path they chose. Unfortunately, any series of decisions led to a 50% chance of the Earth being destroyed. The other outcomes were evenly split between success for Thunderbird or the Others and the Earth surviving but under alien control. There was less than a ten-percent chance that the Earth would survive and the US would remain an independent nation.

Xi had remained neutral. He provided observations and objective support or criticism for both options but was adamant that he was only an observer and wasn't going to intercede in their decision-making process. They only topic in which he provided firm guidance was related to China's role.

It was impossible for Xi to state unequivocally that China would or wouldn't intervene in supporting the United States in either option. While the official position was that the US and China would act as allies in repelling the invasion by the Others, he was not convinced. He was not part of making China's decision and had no definitive knowledge of the military's offensive position. It was his opinion that they would certainly act defensively, but that was as far as he would vocalize a strong opinion. Consequently, they had factored his opinions into the situational analysis, leading to the low probability of global success.

What became clear through the argument was that the longer a delay went on, the probability of success increased. The more time the Americans had to prepare a military response or act as a deterrent, the more likely they were to convince the Others and Thunderbird to let them be. They all agreed that time was an element of the situation they couldn't control. From all the signals that they'd received, it seemed certain that the Others were going to make an appearance in the next day – two at most.

Trying to shift the conversation to a less controversial topic, Green raised tilted his head and looked at Xi. "You've seen how much the potential outcome of success depends on whether your country aligns with us or not. Since you're unsure what they will do, is there anything you can do to convince your leaders to support us?"

Xi paused and spread his hands. "First tell me what they would support you doing. Will you immediately attack the Others or will you try diplomacy first?"

"We've been over this. We don't know yet," Green answered.

"My answer depends on the initial path your country chooses. If you attack the Others immediately, I think my leaders will wait to observe the results. Once the implications are clear, they will decide. Until then, they will take little risk. Remember, we are new to this communication with Thunderbird. You may trust them, but we do not. And we are skeptical of your country's motives after years of competition."

"What if we take the path of diplomacy?" Senator Traficant asked cynically. It was obvious from her tone that she didn't support this option.

"We are more likely to join you in this approach. It would be an easy choice for us, as we have a direct communication link with the Others and have an established, although unclear, relationship. Granted it was built on a different understanding of their intentions. It is hard to know if they were misleading us as Thunderbird has stated or if our assumptions are based on our naiveté."

"Are you worried about the possibility of retribution?" Green asked Xi.

"Certainly. But retribution from whom? We have asked for guarantees from Thunderbird, and they have not responded. The Others have never made any threatening statements to us, so I think that is of low risk. That may change once they learn with are working with you and Thunderbird."

The senator shook her head. "This isn't helping us sort through the options at all. If we can't count on your country to stand by us in attack, we must assume that they won't. I know neither of you trust Thunderbird to stand by us in a conflict, but I do."

Green sat back in his chair and squinted at Traficant quizzically. "Why is that, Senator? I'm a little surprised by that statement. You always hedge your bets depending on the political winds, and here you are making a bold statement of support."

The senator's face took on a light shade of red. She was not accustomed to being challenged so directly by underlings.

"Mr. Green, my reasoning is quite clear. They have never misled us in any way. They have demonstrated their capability to easily destroy us and yet elected not to take hostile action on September 11th. They had every reason to create a bigger disaster in New York after Smith had brought us to the precipice of disaster despite their clear warnings."

Xi leaned forward. "Is that a guarantee of how they will behave in the future? We don't know what their reasoning was for their inaction, but I think it's unwise to assume they will always act in our best interests until we are certain of their motives."

Traficant scoffed, "They're an advanced alien civilization that can destroy our planet on a whim. I doubt we will ever understand all of their motives, but at this moment they seem to be aligned with us. I think we should – no, must – take them at their word."

Xi pursed his lips and looked out the window to break eye contact.

After a short pause, Traficant relaxed. "I understand both of your perspectives and will consider them. However, we don't have the luxury of time nor inaction. I still have to decide, but in the meantime I think we can provide Thunderbird with some evidence of our commitment to assist them. It may buy us goodwill. Mr. Green, please prepare a data set that includes our current military preparedness for the looming invasion."

Green looked at her quizzically. “Senator, you already have that information available through the SCIF.”

“Of course,” she responded. “What I meant to say was, could you prepare that information for Thunderbird and prepare to transmit the data to them?”

Green turned pale. “Senator, I don’t have the authority to do that. It’s a breach of our agreement with the Department of Defense. That information is not to be shared outside of Team Tacoma.”

“You have the authority based on my direction. If you disagree, send me a memo to cover yourself.”

“Yes, ma’am,” Green stammered. “I don’t agree with you, but I’ll do it.”

The senator nodded. “Thank you, I knew I could count on you to the smart thing. Now, if you will excuse yourselves, I have an urgent call I need to take. Let’s reconvene in an hour and then agree on a path forward that I can communicate to the president.”

After Xi and Green had shut the door behind them, the senator grimaced as she dialed a number from memory using her private cell phone.

“Good afternoon, Senator. I’m glad you called,” Anderson said as he answered.

“You said it was urgent. I’ve got a tight timeline, so make it snappy,” she said with thin tone of agitation.

“Yes, ma’am, it is urgent. We’ve got a bit of a situation, and I thought you would want to know as quickly as I could. I presume you’re aware that the Maxx character and FBI Agent Hovis were sent by the Department of Homeland Security to track down the spy Li Jing.”

“Yes, I read that in the report from Miss Grey. As I recall, you told me you were going to take care of the situation, keeping them from interfering with your search for her and Doctor Smith. Did I get that right?” she said.

"That's correct. What Grey didn't know at the time of her report was that they located Li Jing and initiated a firefight. They were then captured by her and her Taliban allies."

"That sounds positive. Why the urgency then?"

"I'm getting to it," he said shortly. "She was able to kill the FBI agent, but somehow the Taliban allowed King to escape. He's in the wind now, but both the Taliban and my assets are trying to locate him and make sure he doesn't make it back."

She grimaced and rubbed her forehead. "I don't like the sounds of this, Anderson. You assured me you had this under control."

Senator Traficant had been growing weary of Anderson's lack of ability to problem solve, lately. He had become more pushy and less reliable. For now, he was a necessary evil. But she was determined to replace him as soon as she had the opportunity.

Anderson coughed nervously. "Li Jing escaped and made it through a coalition checkpoint outside Kabul. She's on her way to Smith apparently. I have a tracker on her vehicle, so we'll be able to intercept her after I am certain she has reached Smith's location."

"The clock is ticking, Mr. Anderson. I need to know Smith's location so we can get the military to intervene before the Others arrive. If we can interrupt their arrival, we will be in a much better position with Thunderbird and not dependent on the Chinese to help."

"I understand, Senator. I have a black ops team waiting at the airbase as backup, in case the military can't respond quickly enough or is concentrating on the alien arrival. I'll make sure to get to Smith and Li Jing."

"It sounds like you only have one loose end. I'd focus on that if I were you," she said curtly as she began to disconnect the call.

She could hear the irritation in his voice when he interjected, “Thank you for the advice, senator. But I believe I have two loose ends. That’s why I’m calling.”

She was beginning to lose the little patience she had left. *He’s always got some hidden agenda.*

“If it’s about Miss Grey, I already have told you several times not to take any action until I give you explicit authorization,” she barked. “I’ve been comfortable with you blocking her when she gets too close to restricted information, but that’s the limit.”

“It’s not Grey,” he said, “although I think one day you’ll regret not letting me remove her completely from this project. She’s like a bloodhound once she gets wind of something that doesn't smell right.”

Since last September, Anderson had been pushing to get Miss Grey pulled from the Thunderbird project. She had initially believed that it was a simple case of professional jealousy, but in the last month it had become evident that it was more complex. She was beginning to think Anderson saw Grey as his potential replacement.

“Then who is this other loose end you want my permission to remove?” she asked with genuine curiosity.

“Maxx’s girlfriend, Gabby. If he figures things out, I think she’ll be the first person he calls. And she’ll immediately go to Miss Grey. I think we should take her off the board before either she or Maxx has a chance to make this situation any more complicated.”

Traficant chewed her lip and shook her head. This situation in Seattle was already becoming too messy for her liking. Uncomfortable questions were starting to come from the White House. She just needed a few more days and then any possible intervention from Miss Grey wouldn’t matter.

“Do it. But make sure her demise can’t be tied to Thunderbird, or you’ll set off too many warning bells. Make it look personal.”

"I know the right person for the job," Anderson said with a chuckle as he hung up the phone.

***

Mr. Green's private lab at the Team Tacoma facility was alive with activity, equations scribbled across whiteboards and the hum of computers analyzing data from the deep reaches of space. He sat at his desk with his head in his hands.

His classified team had been making progress in the last week, inching closer to creating a universal language that might be understood by Thunderbird and any other intelligent life form out there. But then came the shocking request from Senator Traficant. Her voice, smooth yet with an undercurrent of calculation, suggested a shift in the project's focus. Unknown to the rest of the team, she ordered him to relay some top secret information regarding the military capabilities of the United States. She didn't explain her rationale, but sending out a broadcast of the country's sensitive data rather than waiting for contact from Thunderbird was an enormous breach of protocol.

This wasn't simply a redirection; it would be a perversion of the authorized mission. He understood the appeal for Senator Traficant, envisioning the headlines, the public awe, and the political capital she could gain. This had been her pet project for more decades than he'd been alive. Yet he knew that this level of alien interaction, if it were to happen, wouldn't be about an equal partnership but about giving them enough information to control America's military. They would have access to everything, including nuclear capabilities and launch codes.

The weight of the choice loomed over him. He could comply, ensure he stayed in the senator's good graces, and perhaps even advance his career. Or he could stick to the original path and ignore the command, risking everything. He wanted to speak with Miss Grey, the closest thing he had to a confidant and colleague. He knew she found him annoying and a first-class smart ass, but she had always remained professional even when he didn't. Her expertise in the politics of the situation would be crucial, and her moral compass as true as he had ever encountered. He trusted that the integrity of our project would be worth more to her than any political gain.

Doing nothing was a calculated risk. The other option was to leak documents detailing Senator Traficant's interference, hoping to galvanize political support for the original mission of the project. The backlash would be immediate. Government agencies and her enemies would swarm, opinions would be split. Some would hail him as a hero of patriotic integrity, while others would accuse him of irresponsibly endangering the project and by extension humanity's chance to save the planet from probable extinction.

Senator Traficant's career would take a hit, her intentions questioned. As for him, he'd be removed from official duties. Or worse. He was not naïve to the implications of crossing such a powerful person. But the project itself would be saved, reorganized under different leadership but hopefully dedicated to its original scientific goals. Of course, the implications for the relationship with Thunderbird were unknown because of how closely they hid their intentions.

Regardless of the outcome, he felt convinced that he wouldn't regret his choice if he trusted Miss Grey. He would have stood for what he believed in, for the purity of science over political maneuvering. Team Tacoma would continue, free from the shadows of political ambition, seeking to save Earth. Allied with a civilization that might help them thrive in the universe and beyond.

As the phone rang, he realized that he'd settled on a path

forward. If nothing else, he needed to let Miss Grey know there was a dangerous plan looming that would affect her.

24

HAOYU'S GHOST

Gabby wrapped her scarf tighter around her neck as she stepped into the gray expanse of Gas Works Park on what was turning into a bleak winter day.

The Seattle air was thick with the chill of impending rain, and the park, usually bustling with life, now whispered with the cold breath of solitude. Instead of going back to work after leaving Miss Grey's houseboat, she had decided to go for a walk to clear her mind.

The towering structures of the old gas plant loomed ahead, their skeletal forms casting eerie shadows on the frosty ground. Gabby's boots slipped on the damp grass, as she approached the old boiler house, its walls, usually vibrant with graffiti, appeared muted under the overcast sky. The structure now served as a shelter, but today it looked more like a relic from a forgotten world, its open sides offering little protection from the biting wind.

She walked up the Great Mound, her breath forming clouds of mist before her. From this vantage point, Gabby could see the skyline of Seattle, ghostly and distant, separated by Lake

Union's steely waters. The contrast between the living city and the dead industrial remains at her feet felt stark, almost like standing at the edge of two colliding worlds.

Two colliding worlds was how she'd felt trapped lately. She was caught between the mostly normal world that still clung to a city that hadn't changed much since 9/11. But underneath she could feel the tension of a building conflict and the uncertainty of the collision with alien worlds. It felt like she was living in a waking dream she couldn't escape. If Maxx were here, they would be able to find solace in their relationship. But being alone darkened her hope that things would work out.

Descending the hill, Gabby moved toward the play barn, where under normal circumstances children's laughter would ring out. Today, however, it stood silent, the old exhauster-compressor building looking more like a mausoleum than a place of joy. The wind howled through its empty windows, a mournful sound that sent shivers down her spine.

An elderly man, almost blending with the gray surroundings, caught her eye. With his cap pulled down to keep the rain off his face, he nodded toward the structures as he walked by. His gravelly voice almost lost in the wind, he said, "They say this place remembers, you know."

Gabby felt a chill run up her spine that wasn't from the cold. Or maybe it was the man's odd greeting. She considered the layers of history, the residual energy of lives once lived in the shadow of these giants. Lives that had seen things she couldn't imagine.

As the first drops of heavy rain and an occasional snowflake began to fall, Gabby decided to leave, the park taking on an even more foreboding atmosphere. A few pellets of snow seemed to attempt to cloak the industrial skeletons in a guise of purity, but it only accentuated the sense of desolation.

Walking away, Gabby couldn't shake the feeling that she

was being watched, not by the place itself but by someone. The park on this somber winter day felt less like a place of recreation and more like a reminder of forgotten times, its silence speaking volumes of the city's past, now fading beneath a veil of mist. The old man had vanished into the light fog. She couldn't see anyone else wandering in the park but still couldn't shake the feeling of being observed.

She doubted that Anderson had followed her after leaving Grey's. She'd looked for him and any cars that might have followed her to the empty parking lot, but she'd been distracted as her mind had wandered. It sent another shiver up her spine as she imagined the creepy Mr. Anderson watching her from the shadows.

Gabby reached into her purse to make certain that she had her pistol. The cold steel offered her some comfort that didn't supersede her intuition. She began to walk faster toward the parking lot, trying to outrun the fear tightening her chest.

"Gabby!" someone yelled.

She was surprised by the sudden noise. She turned in circles, searching for a familiar face.

"Over here, silly," the woman yelled again. She couldn't see who it was because the person was standing in the inky shadows of the old barn. The light mist and snow limited visibility in the gloomy park.

"Come get out of this terrible weather for a moment," the woman said as she motioned her to come over to the building.

Gabby had felt that she was being watched and was relieved to find out that it wasn't Anderson. Her tension diminished knowing someone she knew was here on this desolate afternoon. The place seemed slightly less ominous as she ducked her head and headed for the open door.

As she walked into the darkened building, she could see the woman sitting at one of the benches on the far side of the barn.

Wearing a heavy raincoat and a large bucket hat, it was difficult to make out who it was. The woman waved again. "Over here."

The play barn was a welcome respite from the drizzle, its robust wooden beams and industrial framework standing resolute against the grey sky. The patter of rain on the roof created a rhythmic backdrop. The blend of aged timber and modern play structures took on an eerie hue. The dim light filtered through the clouds and into the windows, casting long shadows across the concrete floor. Droplets of rain sneaked through the occasional crack, contributing to the damp, earthy smell that mixed with the scent of wood and rust.

As Gabby pushed closer to the seated woman, she still hadn't recognized her. All that she could see clearly was a hint of a smile that peeked out below the brim of the rain hat. Her hands rested on her lap with a Nordstrom shopping bag sitting on top of the table.

"Thanks for spotting me," Gabby said as she stepped closer. "I was surprised to find another person I know here on such a dreary afternoon."

"I was hopping I'd run into you," the other woman said. "This is a great place to talk privately."

Gabby tilted her head in confusion. "You were expecting me?"

"Yes, silly goose. I didn't come all this way to sit by myself in this creepy old building."

The woman reached into the bag on the table and pulled out a pistol. Aiming it at Gabby, she motioned to the bench across the table. "Take a seat and let's chat. Don't bother yelling or running, because I won't hesitate to shoot you. Neither of us want that."

Gabby's stomach was doing summersaults. She was frozen for a moment as fear took control. She would have turned and ran if the woman didn't have the pistol pointed directly at her with her finger on the trigger. At this distance, there was no way to avoid being shot.

She inched closer but still hadn't sat down. "What is this about? Do I know you?"

"I'll answer the second question first," the woman said as she removed her hat and shook out her short brown hair.

Gabby gasped. "Natalie," she said with a hint of anger creeping into her voice.

"Ah, so you do recognize me. That's wonderful," Natalie said with wide smile. "That will make this so much easier."

"Yes, I recognize you from the pictures Maxx destroyed, although you look like you've aged a lot in the last couple years," Gabby shot back.

"Now, now, don't be a bitch. Have a seat. I wasn't kidding when I said I would shoot you. After that snarky comment, it's very tempting."

Natalie had been Maxx's girlfriend before Gabby. They'd shared an apartment and even been partners at home and in Maxx's security business. According to Maxx, they had a good relationship that lasted for a year or two until they started to go their separate ways. They finally broke up when Natalie found someone else and dumped Maxx. He was over it by the time he and Gabby had met, although he occasionally still referred to her as his "psycho ex."

The breakup was painful, but the hardest part for Maxx was when he discovered Natalie had been siphoning off clients and embezzling funds from the business. When she left, she had taken most of the money from the bank and left him on the hook for a lot of the outstanding debts. To add insult to injury, she had started rumors that he had been physically abusive. The experience had almost destroyed him financially and emotionally – leading to his past drinking problem.

The worst part of her deviousness had led to the traumatic

incidents of last fall. She'd secretly been working with the Chinese killer, Haoyu. He'd hired her to do some research into Gabby and her boss at TechCom. That contract had resulted in Maxx being caught up in events that almost cost both of their lives. Maxx had expressed suspicion that there was more to the connection between Natalie and Haoyu's plans, even if he couldn't prove it.

And here she was again. Alone in a deserted building with a gun.

Gabby slowly lowered herself onto the bench across from Natalie. She set her purse on the bench next to her out of view below the tabletop.

"Now that we're friends again, do you want to tell me what this is about?" Gabby asked while trying to watch Natalie and not the barrel of the gun. "Would you mind pointing that elsewhere. It is making it hard to focus."

"I do mind," Natalie said. "I'm sure by now you've realized I was working with Haoyu."

"Yes, that's old news though. Why wait until now to bring it back up?"

"I'll get to that in a moment. I never trusted that guy. He was always playing both sides. I sent him your direction knowing that Maxx would get involved. It was good for a laugh knowing the two of them would be going at each other tooth and nail. My money was on Haoyu outdoing Maxx, but you can't win them all," she said with a cheeky laugh.

Gabby could feel her face flushing. The terror that they had lived through was only a sick joke to Natalie. She was more evil than she'd realized.

"Anyway, good times," Natalie continued. "The reason I mention Haoyu was he had told Maxx he had a present for me. That was right before Maxx shot him with that big, stupid gun of his. You know the one. He keeps it in the nightstand on his side of the bed." She gave an exaggerated wink.

Gabby could feel the bile rising in the back of her throat. This bitch was baiting her with personal details. "How do you know Haoyu told him that?" she asked, trying to keep her voice level.

"Funny story. Apparently, Maxx forgot to tell me what Haoyu said, but I heard about it from a friend, someone who has access to the transcript of their final confrontation."

Gabby shrugged. "That doesn't mean anything to me, sorry."

"Here we are six months later, and I finally get my present. Kind of like a delayed Christmas."

This was sounding like the ranting of crazy person. "Congratulations. What was the present?" Gabby asked.

Natalie smiled and waved the gun around. "This. Isn't it a beauty?"

"It's nice, but it looks like most pistols. Is there something special about it?"

"Of course, that's why it's a present. It's totally untraceable. It has no serial number and has never been registered. It's literally a ghost gun. And since Haoyu's now dead, it's a ghost's gun. That is really funny, don't you think?" she said with a giggle.

Gabby simply stared at her. *She's nuttier than a fruitcake.*

After Natalie's laughter faded, she sighed. "That's why I'm here. Haoyu gave me this ghost gun so I could kill Maxx and no one would be able to trace it back to me. I was going to make it look like it was you — you know, a murder-suicide kind of scenario. Jealousy can be so cruel."

"Sounds like a great plan, you psychopath. One minor detail, Maxx isn't here."

Natalie rubbed her jaw as if she was thinking. "True, but I decided to give myself a different present. I decided I'll kill you and leave some evidence pointing to Maxx. That way, he only suffers. Killing him lets him off too easy, the way he treated me."

Gabby howled. "Treated you? If anything, he was too nice. He thought you were misguided. But I see who you really are —-the devil with a pretty face."

"You think I'm pretty?" Natalie said with a toothy grin. "You're not only saying that because I have a gun pointed at you, are you?"

Gabby's heart was beginning to race again. Natalie was crazy, had a gun, and didn't seem to have any reluctance about tormenting her. It still struck her as odd that she'd run into her in this desolate place at this time of day. *It couldn't be coincidence.*

"How'd you know I was going to here? Either you're incredibly lucky or were following me," Gabby said.

"I'm very lucky, but this wasn't luck. The same friend who told me about Haoyu's final gift told me you were here. They're very interested in you. That way I don't waste my time following you around on all your petty errands. When my friend called and said you were wandering around at Gas Works Park, I hustled right over."

Gabby raised her eyebrows. "Why are they that interested in me?" She didn't have any enemies other than Li Jing that she knew of. And Miss Grey had told her they'd seen her in Afghanistan."

"They want to know where Maxx is. They said if you told me, I should let you go. If not... Well, you get the picture," she said as she admired the gun.

"Maxx is in Afghanistan. Where exactly, I don't know."

"That's the best you can do?" Natalie said with a sigh.

Gabby tensed. "That's the truth. He's on a special mission out of the country, and I haven't heard from him in days."

"I'd really prefer to shoot that big gorilla you call a boyfriend, but if you don't help me, I can't help you. Last chance, I'm getting bored."

"Who is asking? At least tell me that," Gabby said.

"No, but I'll give you a clue. Let's see how smart you are. You already know I was double-crossing Haoyu and the Chinese. Who do you know who would be trying to get rid of the Chinese and Maxx at the same time?"

"Doctor Smith and Li Jing?"

"Hmm, yes, that's true. But not them. You're warmer than you realize though. Sadly for you, I'm done with this guessing game. Where's Maxx?"

Gabby smiled.

"What are you smiling about? You don't believe I'm going to shoot you now?"

Gabby shifted her eyes over Natalie's right shoulder.

"I'm not falling for that old trick," Natalie said with a shake of her head.

At the open window, the old man Gabby had passed in the park earlier was standing with a gun pointed at Natalie's back.

"Special Agent Williams from the CIA," he yelled. "Put the gun down, Natalie Mason!"

Natalie's head whipped around to look behind her. As she turned, she shifted the gun to aim at Williams. "No, you old fool!" she shrieked.

Before Natalie could turn all the way around to get the gun directly pointed at Williams, he fired twice, hitting her.

"Why?" Natalie said as she dropped the gun, slipping down to the ground into a puddle of blood that was quickly pooling beneath her.

Gabby sat shocked for a moment, unsure if she should move away or stay where she was seated. "Twice in one week," she mumbled under her breath.

"Call 911 and stay where you are, Miss Fisher," Agent Williams said as he disappeared from the window after he waited a moment to make sure that Natalie was still.

Gabby dialed the phone number.

"This is 911. What is your emergency?" the woman's voice said when the call was picked up.

"A woman's been shot. I'm at Gas Works Park inside the Playland building," Gabby said as her voice began to shake.

"I'm sending help now, ma'am. Please stay on the line. Are you safe now?"

"I don't think so," Gabby said as the tears rolled down her cheeks.

25

A MATTER OF TRUST

"Miss Grey, I'm sorry to bother you. Someone tried to kill me again," Gabby said between sniffles.

Miss Grey stared in shock as she pressed the phone tight to her ear. "Are you safe now?" she asked incredulously.

"Yes, the police are here. And Agent Williams from the CIA."

"Agent who?" Miss Grey asked in surprise. "Never mind that. Where are you, and who tried to kill you?"

Gabby took a deep breath. "I'm at Gas Works Park. I went for a walk after I left your house. I ran into Maxx's ex-girlfriend Natalie. She wanted to know where Maxx was. When I told her I didn't know, she said she was going to kill me. But Agent Williams told her to surrender, and when she pointed her gun at him, he killed her. It all happened so fast. I'm still shaking," she said in rush.

"That's terrible," Miss Grey exclaimed. "Stay where you are, and I'll come get you. Don't go anywhere with the CIA agent. There's something very strange going on."

"The entire incident was surreal. Agent Williams said that Director Anderson had told him to watch out for me. Thank goodness he did, or Natalie would have shot me. She is crazy. Insane actually," Gabby said between sobs.

"I'm heading over now," Miss Grey said as she walked out the front door and climbed into her car. "Did Natalie say why she was looking for Maxx? Did it sound personal?"

"She hates Maxx but said the person who wanted to know where Maxx is also set up Haoyu. And she said it wasn't Doctor Smith. Who else could that be, Miss Grey?"

"I don't know and am still trying to process this, but I will start digging. The most important thing is to make sure you're out of harm's way," Miss Grey said as she navigated the car through traffic. Unfortunately, it was the start of rush hour, so it was taking her longer to get to Gabby than she'd hoped. "You stay there with the police and tell them I'm on my way. I'm going to hang up and make another call."

Miss Grey hung up and paused to think through what Gabby had told her. She had a suspicion about who might be behind this latest attempt, but it was a leap.

She pulled to the curb and spent a couple minutes clearing her mind. After thinking through the options, she pressed speed dial to call Andres. He would help her.

"Hey, babe," he said when he answered. "I was going to call you. We got word that Maxx has shown up at a security checkpoint outside of town. They didn't provide a lot of details about his condition, but we're heading over there now."

"That's good news," she said with a big sigh of relief. "Any word on Agent Hovis?"

"No, they said it was Maxx by himself. I'll know more in thirty minutes."

"I've got a situation here that I need your help with. Natalie, Maxx's ex-girlfriend, tried to kill Gabby. I'm on my way over to pick her up now."

"Damn, that's crazy," he said. "What can I do to help?"

"After you talk to Maxx, I need you to come back here and help protect her."

"You want Maxx and me to give up on the hunt for Li Jing and come back to Seattle? Maxx will probably want to come back, but shouldn't someone keep the pressure on Li Jing and Doctor Smith?"

She could hear the apprehension in his tone, despite the poor cellular connection. "No, I think it's best if Maxx stays in Afghanistan since he is the only person the Chinese said they trust."

"Won't you be able to watch out for Gabby?" he asked.

"I need to get there to help Maxx navigate the situation with the CIA. There is something going on that I can't put my finger on. Anderson is up to no good—I can feel it. I don't want to leave Gabby here alone for very long. I need someone here I can trust. And I don't trust anyone more than you, Andres."

"Okay, I see your reasoning. But with travel, that's going to leave both Maxx and Gabby without help for at least a day while we're switching places."

"Once you get to Maxx, can you explain the situation to him, then head to Bagram? I'll make arrangements for you and Glen to catch a flight back to Seattle."

"Are you sure Maxx will stay here when he finds out Natalie tried to kill Gabby? I don't think I'll be able to keep him off the plane."

She paused. She really didn't know what Maxx would choose to do. She assumed that he'd be torn between completing the mission and his desire to get back to Gabby. It wasn't an easy choice. "Have him call Gabby and talk it through."

"One last thing, because I know you're trying to get over to help Gabby. Wouldn't it be better if Glen and I stayed here to help you and Maxx? Surely you have someone at DHS or the FBI who can help her."

"She won't have confidence in them like she will trust you and Glen. She's distressed after the two attempts on her life this week. It really needs to be someone she and I both trust. And with CIA involved, I'm wary. I'm sure Maxx would prefer you and Glen watching Gabby over any other option, even me."

"You're right again. Stay safe and I'll see you soon when this is all over. Hopefully soon," he said, ending the call.

Before pulling the car back into traffic, Miss Grey made a quick call to the DHS travel coordinator. She arranged a flight from Bagram to Seattle for Andres and Glen. She also got clearance to use the DHS jet once again. It was still parked at McChord Airbase. She could be there within an hour after she was done meeting with Gabby.

As she thought through the events of the past week, she couldn't help but feel guilty about some of the choices she'd made. She'd manipulated things with Maxx to get him to Afghanistan. She wondered how that would work out. At least he was back at a relatively secure location, hopefully unhurt.

But Maxx's departure had also left Gabby in a position where she was almost killed. She didn't know if things would have played out differently had he been around. Regardless, Gabby was feeling abandoned and stressed. She couldn't blame her. But she had to keep in mind the greater threat wasn't losing someone she cared about. The greater threat involved losing everyone she cared about.

That was a risk she'd learned to accept and let go many times in the past. It didn't make for easy choices, but it did help make a choice she could live with, regardless of the outcome.

The matter that was burning in the back of her mind that she couldn't let go of was the uncertainty surrounding Anderson. She personally couldn't stand the man, but his motives were a mystery. She needed to at least trust that he wasn't working against her, or she needed to find a way to remove him as a variable. She couldn't be constantly watching her back while charging forward.

***

Maxx sat in the front seat of the command Humvee at the roadblock.

He had run through the desert for the better part of half an hour to cover the two or three miles of open ground between the abandoned house where he'd escaped from Li Jing and the coalition roadblock. It hadn't been a straight foot race, or he could have done it in half the time. With the Talibs chasing him, they'd tried to cut him off, so he'd had to find an evasive route around some of the gullies.

When he'd reached the areas dimly lit by the spotlights at the barricade, he identified himself as a US citizen, and they'd let him walk into the perimeter. There the soldiers had made certain he wasn't carrying any weapons or explosives. He'd then been given some water and a spare ChiliMac MRE and was told to sit in the vehicle while they checked out his story.

He hadn't been in the mood to eat anything except the teriyaki beef sticks and Twizzlers. He put the gum in his pocket for later. He was still reeling from the rush of adrenaline from his escape and didn't think he'd be able to stomach any more food. The last thing he wanted to do right now was get sick.

While he was gnawing the last cherry Twizzler, Lieutenant Weih opened the door and leaned in. "How are you holding up, King?"

The lieutenant was in a fresh uniform and looked like he'd stepped out of an ROTC ceremony. Buzzcut, stubble on the chin, Texas accent, and not a day over twenty-one.

Maxx nodded. "Been better, Lieutenant. Did you get a hold of Sergeant Zeller?"

"Yeah, I talked with him. Your story is wild, but it checked out. His team and your two buddies are inbound. ETA thirty minutes."

"Did you tell him that the FBI agent was killed?" Maxx asked.

"Yes, but I didn't give them all the details. I told them you'd fill them in when they arrived."

"They did ask about the Chinese woman y'all were chasing. I told them that after you'd escaped she'd driven through here alone almost an hour ago."

"Wasn't it a bit suspicious seeing a Chinese woman traveling alone out here in the middle of the night?"

"Heck yeah," Weih said with annoyance. "If our CIA contact hadn't had a call from someone from their office in Pakistan, we would have held her up. But they gave us her name and passport number. Said she was a scientist working on some project for the agency and to let her pass through lickety-split."

"Did you write down the name of the person calling?" Maxx asked.

"Yep, I have it right here," he said as he took a slip of paper out of his pocket. "Doctor F.U. Smith. Does that name mean anything to you?"

Maxx snorted and shook his head. "Yes, that's the person we're trying to stop. Smith is on the FBI most wanted list, and the woman is his right-hand person. She's ex-CIA. It figures she'd know the protocol to get by you."

"Damn," he said. "I guess we screwed up. Sorry, man."

"It's not your fault. We've been chasing those two all over the world. She's managed to slip by a few times, but eventually I'm going to catch up to both of them," Maxx said with scowl.

"Is there anything I can get you while you wait for the Green Beret team to arrive?" Lieutenant Weih asked.

"Do you have a satellite phone or cell phone that's got a signal I can use while I'm waiting?"

"Sure, there's a sat phone in the back seat that's all charged up. Just stay in here and make your calls," he said as he closed the car door.

Maxx pulled the phone case into the front seat and powered it up. He groaned when he saw the battery life was down to ten percent.

He dialed Gabby's cell phone and took a long drink of tepid water while he waited for the connection. After what seemed like long minutes, he heard her muffled voice. "This is Gabby. Who's calling, please."

"Hey, babe it's great to hear your voice. I was afraid you'd send it to voicemail if you didn't recognize the phone number."

"Oh, Maxx, I was wondering when you'd call," she said with relief. "Did you get my voice messages?"

"No, my phone got ruined, so I didn't have any way to contact you until now. Is everything okay?"

There was a long silence, then he heard what sounded like Gabby crying. "No, it's not. When are you coming home?" she said between pauses.

"I don't know when I'll be back yet," he said. "We've finally tracked Li Jing down, but she slipped away. I can tell we're getting close. I'm hoping we can capture her today, then I'll be on the next flight. Promise."

"Okay. But can't you head back now and let Agent Hovis finish the hunt?" she asked.

Maxx didn't want to mention to her that Hovis was dead. That would lead to more detail than he wanted to tell her on a call. The phone beeped to signal that the battery was down to five percent. "Why don't you tell me what's the matter? You sound like you're crying."

"I am a little. I was trying to be brave, but I'm really scared. Natalie tried to kill me," she said with a sob.

"What?" Maxx exclaimed. "Natalie, my ex?"

"Yes, she pulled a gun on me. She was going to shoot me, but she was shot by the agent first."

"I'm blown away. I know she's a bit psycho, but did she say why?"

"She wanted to know where you were. It is so mixed up, Maxx. I feel like we're in way over our heads. That's why I want you to come home now, so we can run away from all of this craziness and disappear into the mountains."

"First, let's make sure you're safe, then we'll figure out the next step. Are you with the police or Miss Grey?"

"I'm with the police, and Miss Grey is on her way. She was the first person I called when I couldn't get a hold of you. That's why I thought you'd heard my voicemail and were calling me back."

"Okay, I'm sure Grey will get a handle on this. Then I'll wrap things up here and grab the first flight out."

"I need you. Come home now, Maxx."

He was wracked with guilt. "I wish I could, but they need me here a bit longer. Hovis can't do this without me. I have to finish this, or running to the mountains won't be far enough."

"I'm begging you. I need you now, before one of us gets killed. I know these people won't stop until one or both of us are dead."

Maxx looked at the battery, down to three percent. He needed to call Miss Grey to make sure she was covering Gabby. And to let her know about Hovis.

"I'll be there, Gabby. You know I'll do everything I can to get there as soon as possible. I hate to end the call like this, but this phone battery is dying."

"Okay, call me back when you can. I love you."

"I love you," he said with a hitch in his voice as he hung up.

Gritting his teeth with frustration, he banged his hand on the dashboard. There was no good choice. Gabby needed him, but he needed to stop Li Jing and Smith in the next day or there would be hell to pay.

Maxx quickly dialed Miss Grey's cell. After the long delay, it went to her voicemail.

"Grey, it's Maxx. I'm at a roadblock near the Kush foothills. Li Jing is about an hour ahead of me. The lieutenant here tells me that the Green Berets, Andres, and Glen are on their way. After they get here, I'm planning on following Li Jing into the mountains. I talked to Gabby, and she said you're on the way to help her. I told her I'd get there as soon as I could, but to lean on you for now. Bad news about Hovis. He didn't make it..." he said as the battery on the phone died.

Maxx leaned back in the seat and looked out over the dark shadows of the mountains. He hoped Li Jing knew he wasn't going to stop until she was dead. He wanted her to pay for what she'd done to Gabby. She needed to feel fear deep in her black, little heart.

26

SMOTHERING DREAMS

The earth beneath the Kunlun Mountains had been silent for years, its deep secrets locked within the cold, hard rock. But on this fateful day, the silence was shattered. As dawn painted the peaks with a gentle golden hue, deep underground, where the pressures of the world converge, a seam in Earth's crust gave way.

At 07:39 a.m, without warning, the ground began to tremble. Li Wei, a local shepherd, felt the first subtle vibrations underfoot. He looked up from his flock, his eyes scanning the horizon for any sign of what was to come, but the mountains stood as stoic as ever. Moments later, the tremble escalated into violent shakes knocking him to the ground.

The Earth roared, a sound rising from its depths, as if the planet itself was groaning in pain. Li Wei's dogs barked frantically, and his sheep scattered in panic. Rocks began to dislodge from the slopes, tumbling down with increasing speed. The trees swayed as if caught in a tempest, their roots clinging desperately to the convulsing soil.

In the nearby village of Yushu, people ran out of their shaking homes, some structures already beginning to collapse.

Dust rose in clouds as walls fell, and the air was filled with cries and the clattering of crumbling masonry. They had lived through many previous earthquakes, and most of the unsafe buildings had been destroyed long ago. But there were always a few that fell.

Mei Ling, a geologist from Tsinghua University who was in the area to study the ancient geological formations, found herself gripping the ground, feeling the pulse of the planet through her fingers. Her camera, forgotten beside her, captured images of the chaos, frames of a world in upheaval.

She had received a special directive from her department chairman two days ago. She was instructed to arrive at this location last night and to plan to stay for a week doing research. She wasn't sure if her assignment to this place was luck or fate. But being this close to the remote epicenter would advance her career. Her only instructions had been to call and report any findings immediately to a government official in Beijing.

The quake's energy radiated outward, sending shockwaves across the region. In the nearest town, seismographs jumped, drawing sharp, erratic lines that scientists would later pore over. Mei Ling anxiously took photographs of the damage. Roads split like dry clay, and power lines fell, sparking briefly before going dark.

Villagers, now gathered in open areas, spoke in hushed tones, their faces etched with fear for what might come next and concern for family they couldn't yet reach. Rescue teams would take time to mobilize, but for now the people of Kunlun were on their own, facing the raw power of nature, a force that had reshaped their world in mere moments. The narrative of their lives had taken a dramatic turn – more dramatic than they could imagine – written by the quaking hand of the Earth itself.

Liu had been waiting in his office for the call from the geologist. He'd arranged to have a scientist from the university onsite in Kunlun to give him a first-hand report of the event that he was anticipating. He'd made the arrangements in anticipation of getting approval from the chairman to initiate the quake. He didn't want to rely on word of mouth or breathless media reports. He wanted the objective assessment of an expert, since his life hinged on the result.

The call from the scientist, Mei Ling, came before there were even reports on the radio or television of an earthquake. His initial excitement about the phone call quickly dissipated. The earthquake had a magnitude of 7.8, making it one of the most powerful earthquakes in China in five decades. However, due to the remote location, direct casualties and damage reports were limited. It was a notable event, but the effect on the surrounding area was so muted that the impact outside the scientific community would be trivial.

The geologist, Mei Ling, was also excited by the certainty that the event was going to be one of the best-documented examples of a supershear earthquake. The rupture speed exceeded the shear wave velocity of the rock, leading to unique patterns of ground shaking and damage. Mei Ling had been studying this area precisely because of the potential of a tectonic collision between the Indian and Eurasian Plates.

Liu rubbed his head in frustration after he ended the call. He wasn't interested at all in the scientific details that Ling droned on about. While the Others had technically delivered the event he'd asked for, it wasn't going to convince anyone that it was unusual or devastating enough to be considered a sentinel event caused by an alien force.

Even he had doubts that this was the event that he'd requested from Doctor Smith. He hoped it was only coincidental timing and there was more to come.

With the acid in his stomach churning, Liu dialed the phone number for Smith. He needed some answers quickly before the chairman called him or, worse, sent some of his personal security to escort him back to his office. Making guesses this time was going to get him more than a crack across the head.

Smith's phone rang endlessly. There was no voicemail, so he couldn't leave a message. He wasn't certain that Smith's phone was even getting a signal. All his previous calls had at least been answered by someone who would take a message. He was having a hard time catching his breath by the time his third call ended without being able to make a connection.

Liu brewed himself a cup of tea in the little kettle he kept in his office. It wasn't much, but it always calmed him when things became stressful. He sipped the hot tea while he waited for his next call to connect with Xi.

"I expected you'd be calling me as soon as you woke," Xi said as soon as the line connected.

Liu shook his head in confusion. "Why did you expect that? I don't recall arranging a call for us this morning."

"We didn't," Xi responded smugly. "But I am here at the Team Tacoma facility in Seattle, and they closely monitor any seismic activity around the world. It appears that Kunlun had a major quake about an hour ago. I anticipated you might call me to see if I knew anything."

"Yes, you guessed correctly. Do the Americans know anything about the quake's cause?"

"There was no activity from Thunderbird according to Mr. Green. I checked, and our team saw no unusual activity from the device at our facility in Beijing. From the information on hand, it looks to be a natural occurrence. Those do still happen quite often."

"That may be, Dr. Xi. Nevertheless, I think we should use the event to our advantage. Communicate to Thunderbird that it was a signal from the Others then pressure them again for assistance."

"You want me to lie to them," Xi said incredulously.

"I'm certain the event was initiated by the Others. I'm giving you an order from the secretary general himself. Tell them that the Others first threatened us and then sent a warning to Kunlun. Without some assistance from Thunderbird, the chairman is considering putting our military on standby. He needs a goodwill gesture from Thunderbird to proceed."

Liu could hear Xi on the other end of the call groan in exasperation.

"This is a dangerous game you are playing, Liu. Perhaps I should verify this with Chairman Jiang directly."

Liu held his breath. If Xi called the chairman, he may or may not back him up. He was caught in a trap and didn't see any way out except through committing to this lie. "That is your choice, Xi, but if you ignore his directive, you will never be allowed to return to China. We will tell the Americans you are a traitor. The XINXI program will be turned over to a successor we trust."

"I don't know how you can be certain that the earthquake was triggered by the Others," Xi said in exasperation. "We have no indication that they caused this event. If we tell Thunderbird we are certain it was the Others, and they know for a fact it was not, we will have ruined all our credibility with them and the Americans. We will be left standing alone."

Liu sighed. Xi was going to be more troublesome than he'd hoped. "I can't tell you how I know, but it was surely caused by the Others," he said with more certainty than he felt. "There is more to this than you know, Xi. I have the confidence of the secretary general, and I would recommend that you not overstep your authority. He is already questioning your loyalty, and this will cause him to conclude that you are not to be trusted."

The line was silent for several long seconds.

"Alright, Liu, you win. For now," Xi said. "If you are lying, it may end up with all of us in ash before the day is over."

***

Miss Grey recklessly swerved in and out of lanes in the rush hour traffic on I-5.

She had arranged for the last open seat on the DHS jet still housed at Joint Base Lewis-McChord. It had been previously scheduled to fly to Afghanistan carrying a group of agents from intelligence agencies representing the entire alphabet soup. The only downside of the arrangement was that she had to get there before the plane left on its tight schedule. With things expected to kick off tomorrow in Afghanistan, no one was going to wait for her.

She'd dropped off Gabby back at her condo with explicit instructions to lock the door and stay there. She was driving Andres's lemon-yellow BMW M3. She'd apologize to him later for not asking in advance, but she needed speed. She'd been exceeding the speed limit the entire distance from Seattle but still put on a wide grin every time she downshifted and accelerated past a car. She hoped the Washington State Patrol was not running speed traps, because she didn't have time to waste on a traffic stop.

She turned on the radio and sang along. One of her favorite songs was on, "Lady Marmalade," and it briefly took her mind off the craziness of the past week. She realized that she probably looked like a crazy woman singing and frantically driving in the fancy yellow coupe.

She'd tried to make plans to meet up with Maxx after she had gotten his voice message. But when she called him back, the call wouldn't connect. She could call Andres again, but he was already on his way to meet Maxx anyway. She'd see if there was a workable communication on the plane once it was in the air. For now, she was going into Afghanistan blind. She hoped she got there in time to help whoever was going after Smith.

The flight team had told her that it was an eleven or twelve-hour flight, which would put her at Bagram in the early evening of March 1st. It wasn't a timeframe she could control, so she'd need to be prepared to immediately adjust once she landed. It wasn't the first time she'd been in a high-pressure situation.

As she slipped around a Walmart semitruck, she spotted a car behind her trying to keep pace. In the dim light of the early sunset, she thought it was another of the want-to-be race car drivers that had been trying unsuccessfully to keep up with her since she'd left downtown. But this was a dark-gray sedan. It looked more like a vehicle from a government motor pool than someone's dream car. *Am I being tailed?* she wondered.

She wrote the worry off as a product of her anxiety, until she realized the chasing car was gaining on her. She stared at the driver in the rearview mirror when he started waving at her. It looked like he was signaling her to pull over.

A moment later, she realized the man looked familiar. She looked back again to verify her guess. *Mr. Green?*

He kept gesturing to her to pull off at the upcoming off ramp.

"Damn it," she swore loudly. She veered over to the off ramp and stopped on the side of the road. *Why hadn't he simply called her?*

Green parked his car behind her. He jumped out of his sedan, ran up to her passenger door, and pulled it open.

"We need to talk now," he said breathlessly. "It's critical. Nice car."

"Shut up, Green. Why didn't you call me instead of chasing me down the freeway? I need to get to McChord an hour ago or I'm going to miss my plane."

"Because this isn't the kind of thing I say on the phone, not even on a secure line."

"Then get in and talk to me while I'm driving. I'm leaving. The state patrol will get your car." She revved the engine to emphasize her point.

Mr. Green climbed into the passenger seat and slammed the door. Miss Grey accelerated at a breathtaking pace.

Green hurriedly put on his seatbelt and leaned back into the leather seat. "I don't mean to pry, but how did you afford a car like this on your salary?" he said with a smirk.

She gave him the side eye. "Don't be an ass. I'm borrowing it. What was so urgent that you had to chase me down the freeway?"

"Something is going on that I can't talk to anyone else about. I'm not sure if I should talk to you either, but I think you're a straight arrow. Just between us?"

"As long as it's legal. If you're going to tell me something illegal, I might pull over and shoot you. Fair?"

Green laughed nervously. "Honestly, I'm not sure it is legal. But I'm not the bad guy here, so no gunfire please. The senator asked me to do something that I'm pretty sure is crossing a national security line. I told her that I wasn't comfortable with her request, but she directed me to do it anyway with an implied threat."

"You've worked with her a long time. She'd a hard driver. Are you sure you're not overreacting?" she asked.

"I wondered the same thing at first. But as I prepared the data she asked, I had to go through so many security hoops that made it clear that I would go to prison for the rest of my life if I shared the information with anyone not authorized."

"What information were you pulling together?"

"All of our military data. Everything from troop counts to nuclear weapon status. It's the readiness data the Joint Chiefs review when they're doing their scenario planning."

Grey took her eyes off the road for a long moment and stared at him. "What the hell?" she muttered. "Did she tell you why she wanted that information?"

"That's the worst part. If it was for her eyes only, it would be bad enough. But she wants me to prepare this file for transmittal."

"Transmittal to whom?" she said in disbelief.

"Thunderbird," he said as he turned to stare out the window at the cars slipping behind them.

"I don't always see the bigger picture, but that makes no sense. Why would Senator Traficant want all the US military preparedness plans sent to Thunderbird. Did Thunderbird request it?"

"No, it was her idea."

"You know her better than I do. What do you think is going on?"

"I'm stepping out on a limb here. I've been on every interaction with Thunderbird since September 11th. Not once has she had a separate conversation with them using the device. And I would know. But I have this sense that there is some connection between her and them that I'm not aware of."

She pursed her lips. "That sounds weird. How would that even happen?"

"I don't know, but I can't help but feel there is something I'm missing after that conversation. For the first time, I have doubts about her loyalty."

"You think she has some special relationship with Thunderbird?"

"Yeah. I know it sounds crazy, trust me. But giving that information to Thunderbird isn't in the best interests of the US, and we have previously agreed not to give it to them. It's extremely risky sending that information to an ally. Allies today may be enemies tomorrow."

Miss Grey pulled to a sudden stop at the gate to McChord Airbase. After she and Mr. Green showed the security guard their badges, he quickly waved them through. She ground her teeth. She was cutting the timing close for catching the flight.

"That's an odd thing to say," she responded to Green. "What makes you think they may not have our best interests in mind?"

"I really shouldn't be telling you this. I'm putting my life in your hands. Thunderbird has privately revealed to us that their plan has been to bait the Others into attacking. They aren't trying to prevent an attack; they want it to happen."

Miss Grey shook her head. "They want us to be attacked. I thought the plan was to stop an invasion, not cause one. Aren't we concerned about winning?"

"Oh, they plan to win. They and the military have figured that we will lose fifty to one-hundred-thousand troops plus civilians caught in the crossfire. To them, that is an acceptable cost to engaging to eliminating the Others permanently."

Grey pulled up the BMW next to the tarmac. The airman waved at her to hurry over to the waiting DHS jet.

She leaned over, grabbing Green by the shoulders. "Green, you can trust me. I have to get on this flight right now, but I will help you somehow. For now – do not send that information to Thunderbird!"

27

FATAL ATTRACTION

Jane watched the lone man standing on her front porch, shifting from foot to foot.

With the bright lights on her porch, she could see he was alone. Tall and slightly balding, dressed in a dark suit, white shirt, and Yale striped tie, he looked like a million other government employees she'd dealt with in Washington over the decades. He was here because he wanted something from her, knew she was at home, and was going to keep pressing the doorbell until she answered.

It was after 9:30 in the evening. It was too late for a courtesy call, and he hadn't called first. His presence here and now meant trouble was in the wind.

Before she answered the door, she quickly checked her alarm system. She wanted to be certain there wasn't anyone else hiding beyond the bright porch lights. She'd had heat and motion sensors installed many years ago out of an extra sense of caution.

"Can I help you?" she said through the intercom on the front door. He jumped at the sound of her voice.

"Senator Traficant, Deputy Director Gutierrez from the

CIA. I hate to bother you this late in the day, but I need to speak with you."

"You folks don't have phones down there in Langley?" she said curtly.

"Some business is best done in person. Do you mind if I come in? It's chilly out here." He blew warm air on his hands as he rubbed them together emphasizing his point.

"You're going to have to wait outside a few minutes while I call and confirm your credentials. Hold your ID badge up to the camera."

Gutierrez took out his badge and held it up. The camera captured images of the ID and his face. She then uploaded the images to a verification portal at the NSA. Power had its privileges in DC.

After a few minutes, the identification check came back as positive. Guttierrez was indeed with the CIA and the man standing on her porch. That didn't mean she trusted him, but at least she was certain with whom she was talking.

She turned off the alarm. "Come in," she said after opening the heavy mahogany door.

The entry to her Georgetown townhome was an immediate plunge into grandeur with a touch of the unexpected. A chandelier appeared almost like a floating cloud of crystal, walls were covered in hand-painted silk wallpaper, and a large antique mirror with a gilded frame reflected this opulence, doubling the visual impact of the vestibule.

"Sit over there." She pointed to a chair covered in plastic.

"Umm, okay," he said as he looked back and forth between the chair and the door. He squinted in concern.

"I don't like strange people bringing germs into my house," she said with a shrug.

The overall effect Jane had tried to achieve with the décor was of decadent comfort, where every element has been chosen not for beauty or wealth but for the intimidation and curiosity it might inspire. The plastic-covered chair was the sole practical exception.

When they stepped into the living room from the entry, the atmosphere shifted from the historical to the eclectic. The furniture included a plush velvet sofa facing a coffee table that was a repurposed piece of art. The seating arrangement included wingback chairs upholstered in exotic animal prints or patterns that seemed to move as you looked at them. The centerpiece of the room was the fireplace, a massive structure of white marble with intricate carvings that might defy traditional style, depicting strange, alien creatures, and scenes from obscure folklore.

After Gutierrez sat in the uncomfortable plastic-covered chair, Senator Traficant settled into a wingback chair near the oversized fireplace. "Now tell me why you're here, Director."

"I presume you're recording this," he said. "Maybe we should press pause."

"I'll decide if I want to erase the recording after you leave," Jane said with the tilt of her head. "Simply to keep you honest, if that's even possible."

The deputy director cleared his throat. "I'm here on behalf of Director Anderson. He's unavailable tonight but asked me to relay some, shall we say, uncomfortable information."

Traficant stared at him a moment. "What does the director have to do that is more important than personally delivering some 'uncomfortable' news?" she asked.

Gutierrez squirmed in the chair. Whether his discomfort was from the plastic, or the conversation wasn't clear.

"He didn't tell me what he's doing. I simply know he was traveling today. Out of pocket."

"When he is back, then he can talk to me face-to-face like a man. Thank you for stopping by," she said as she brought her feet under her to stand.

"Wait a moment. Please," he said as he ran his hands over

his head. "I really shouldn't tell you this, but you'll find out soon enough. Anderson is on a plane to Afghanistan. I don't know why. He wouldn't tell me."

The senator relaxed back into her chair, glancing at the fireplace. Above it, instead of a traditional mantle, there was a large, custom-made clock that not only told the time but also the positions of several astronomical objects in real time.

Guttierrez followed her eyes. "I know we're under a major deadline, but Anderson said this was something you'd want to know right away."

"I'm tired of the games, Deputy Director. What is the information you came to tell me?" she said.

"The leader of Team Tacoma, code name Mr. Green, has been acting unusual this past week. We've had him under surveillance since September. He was selected for observation by the agency director because of the potential risk associated with his unique position. However, this past week we have noticed significant changes in his behavior."

Senator Traficant held up her hand to make him pause. She went to her computer desk and brought up a tracking website. Another perk from the NSA. She wanted to know where Green was at this moment. The software showed that he had entered the Team Tacoma facility thirty minutes ago.

"Continue," she said after she had sat back down.

"About two hours ago, we tailed Green from his office. He led us on a high-speed drive south on I-5. His excessive speeding dropped the trailing cars in the heavy traffic. However, previously we had placed a tracking device on his agency vehicle. He abandoned his vehicle on an offramp by Southgate after he had lost the cars tailing him."

"He left his car and did what?" she asked in surprise. "Walked, or did he have another car waiting?"

"Neither. He called the motor pool and requested a tow

truck. He told them the car stopped working, so he pulled over and was going to catch a taxi back to the office."

"Did you ask him why he went on this sudden high-speed drive?"

"No, we didn't want to alert him to the fact that we've been watching him. We've now increased the surveillance. We're very concerned and wanted to know if this sudden behavior is a surprise to you too."

"Don't be an ass," she said. "Of course, I don't know why the number-one person on this program suddenly goes racing down the freeway, especially this close to a critical point in the program."

"That's what Director Anderson thought you'd say. However, he wanted me to explicitly ask. He also instructed me to ask you if you trust Mr. Green."

"That answer is above your pay grade and none of Anderson's business unless I choose to make it his business. You tell Anderson to keep his distance from Mr. Green. I will address this in my own way."

Gutierrez stood and straightened his jacket. "Thank you for your time, Senator. Unless you have any questions or anything else you'd like me to relay to Director Anderson, I'm going to show myself out."

"No questions but a directive. Tell Anderson never to send a lackey in his place again."

Gutierrez turned a bright shade of red.

Jane followed him to the front door and locked it, setting the alarm behind him.

While this news about Green was a problem, it wasn't entirely unexpected. She'd known for several months that the CIA had him under surveillance. She had plenty of sources within all the intelligence agencies that were willing to supply her with information. For a price.

She had suspected that her push to get the confidential

military data to Thunderbird had been the last straw for Green. She had heard the resistance in his voice. In the end, it wouldn't matter, because in twenty-four hours it would be too late for him to resist or do anything that might get in her way.

She looked at the clock over the mantel. Less than twenty-four hours if the strange clock was to be trusted.

Green wasn't privy to the entire plan, so she wasn't worried about him divulging information that could be used against her. But it rankled her that he wasn't entirely trustworthy. She had enough dirt on him to ruin him, but that still hadn't stopped him from acting rashly. She wanted to know what he was up to. And with whom.

She didn't have time for this distraction, but knowing that Anderson was sniffing around was concerning. She disliked and distrusted him, but more than anything she knew he would do anything to get ahead. The man had no morals or ethics, only an insatiable thirst for power. Like her, except he wasn't as smart as he imagined he was.

First things first, she thought. She needed to find out where Green went and who he was talking to. That would give her the information she needed to act.

She quickly typed out a brief message on the secure email system. She addressed it to the head of security at Team Tacoma. Technically, he reported to Green, but in reality, he reported to her. A series of unfortunate gambling debts had helped make the decision for him.

Gene:

I am concerned about Mr. Green's continued support of our special arrangement. I need to know where and who he was with between four and eight this evening Pacific Time. Find out ASAP and email me the details. I believe he was on I-5, so get the traffic camera videos from Washington Department of Transportation. I suspect that our friends at the agency may be on to him too. Be cautious not to tip him or them off. JT

There was no one that she trusted to talk with about the true motive behind Thunderbird's actions. On the surface, their actions were congruent with what they had been saying for the previous six months. She'd gone along with the charade.

She had no illusions about her role. She was the real star of this drama. She'd only had to wait for fifty years for the final act to begin, and she wasn't going to let anyone get in her way.

***

Dr. Xi stared at the large shimmering cube behind the thick safety glass.

After he'd finished the telephone conversation with Liu, he'd contacted Mr. Green to ask him to meet in the large conference room adjacent to the lab that housed the alien communication device. He'd committed to Liu that he would contact Thunderbird and try once again to get them to provide the weapons.

Xi had his doubts about Liu's motives for asking, but it was impossible for him to refuse without irritating the chairman. He had no illusions what his fate would be if he ignored the command. It was better to remain silent about his suspicions for now and let Liu take credit for the success or failure of the request to Thunderbird.

Xi also couldn't on short notice determine the cause of the earthquake in Kunlun. Liu's assertion that it was a manufactured event and not a natural occurrence didn't feel genuine. There hadn't been enough time to scientifically validate the real cause. However, he believed the event was real and not a false flag produced by the party. There were plenty of unofficial stories and pictures available to validate the size and location of the earthquake.

He was jotting down some questions to ask the geologists when Green hurried into the room.

Slightly out of breath and bit disheveled, he said, "I'm sorry I'm late. I had to rush out for a moment."

Xi waved off the apology. "Not a problem, I understand you're very busy."

Taking his usual seat at the head of the table, Green took a few deep breaths. "So you want to contact Thunderbird and ask again for the weapons. Why do you think their response will be different now?"

"There was a very strong seismic event in China a short while ago. The Others have threatened us with reprisal if we help Thunderbird. My government believes that the earthquake was a warning from them. I was instructed to ask once more, otherwise we may have to stand down on our agreement to assist America in resisting the Others. We aren't a wealthy nation and are unable to absorb these kinds of cataclysmic events. We need Thunderbird's assistance in advance to block any acts of vengeance."

"I can't argue with your logic. However, I don't know that they will be convinced. Their response has always essentially been, 'You work for us—we don't work for you.'"

"That's true, but I was told to convince them. So, I will try."

Green pressed the button on the intercom. "Everyone, clear out of the device room. We're ready to initiate communication with Thunderbird."

Dr. Xi adjusted his glasses, his eyes immediately drawn to the object at the center of the glassed-in room — an artifact not of this Earth, referred to as the Mouth of Thunderbird. It sat silently on a pedestal, its surfaces shimmering with an otherworldly blue glow.

"Alright, team, let's start the initiation sequence," Mr. Green announced, his voice steady.

The cube hummed to life, its surfaces lighting up in a pattern that matched the initial signal's sequence. The cube absorbed the light in the lab, then after moments of tense anticipation it emitted a complex series of light patterns and pulse waves.

"It's time," Xi whispered more to himself than anyone else.

As the cube absorbed the controlled electromagnetic pulse, the device began to vibrate subtly, its glow intensifying. The room began to fill with the familiar smell of a summer thunderstorm, although they were deep in the Seattle underground.

The cube was communicating. "Why have you requested communication?" the flat alien voice intoned.

Green motioned to Xi to speak.

"This is Dr. Xi, the representative from the Middle Kingdom, or what the American's call China."

"We have spoken with you before, Xi. Again, why have you requested communication?"

"I am once again requesting that you supply us with some weapons to protect us from the Others. They initiated a destructive attack in our country a short time ago. They said it was a warning if we continued to assist your people."

"We saw the event. It is of no consequence to our plans. Additional weapons are unnecessary."

"What should I tell my leader then?" Xi asked with a hitch in his voice.

"Tell them that we will not provide weapons. This was a minor event compared to our response if you do not assist us. The Americans are prepared to engage the Others soon. Your country must get out of the way. Do not help the Others, as some in your government have planned."

Xi's eyes flew open wide.

"There is no such plan," he stammered. "We are aligned with you and the Americans."

"You are naive then," the voice responded. "Your leaders intend to position themselves as the global leaders once the Americans are distracted by the war against the Others. We will not let that happen."

"I am concerned that we have given you the wrong impression about my country's intentions. I will relay your concerns to our supreme leader. Perhaps he can better convince you that we are allies to both you and the Americans," Xi said insistently.

"Your leader will not convince us. We have been building worlds for millennia, and these attempts at duplicity are well known to us. Our directive is clear. Help us or stand aside. There is no third choice without suffering our wrath."

The alien cube went dark, leaving Xi and Mr. Green sitting in stunned silence.

28

CALL ME MAXX

The sun dipped low over the rugged terrain north of Kabul, casting a golden hue across the desolate checkpoint where Maxx stood waiting.

Maxx leaned against a sandbagged wall, his eyes scanning the horizon through the slits of the HESCO barriers. The stacked, dirt filled barricade topped with concertina wire, protected the outpost from bullets and any driver in a bad mood that might swing by. One of the loaner M4 rifles from Bagram rested in his hands, a silent companion in the early evening quiet that enveloped the post. The checkpoint was a lonely spot, a small patch of safety carved out amid hostile territory. Maxx had found out last night how lonely it was when he was chased by the Taliban through the surrounding scrub brush.

The radio crackled to life now and then, bursts of static followed by fragmented communications from Bagram and Kabul. Reinforcements were bringing Miss Grey, but the desert had a way of playing tricks with time, stretching minutes into hours, hours into an eternity. Maxx's thoughts wandered as he waited, Gabby's smile, Hovis determination as he'd been murdered by Li Jing, the majestic Olympic Mountains back home in Seattle, all starkly contrasting the bleak reality around him.

His fellow soldiers, Sergeant Zeller and the Green Beret team, were nearby, all dealing with the pause in their own way. Zeller was cleaning his weapon with meticulous care, perhaps more to keep his hands busy than for any real need. Lieutenant Weih on the other hand had his eyes glued to a set of binoculars, watching for any strays that might have escaped from the Taliban force that Li Jing had abandoned last night.

The checkpoint was quiet, too quiet for Maxx's liking. The absence of enemy activity was unsettling, a prelude to something more ominous, or so his intuition told him. He adjusted the helmet that the lieutenant had given him to temporarily wear while at the outpost. Feeling the weight of the helmet, both literally and figuratively, as he contemplated the likelihood of an attack.

As shadows lengthened, Maxx's vigilance began to fade. His ears tuned to every sound, from the distant call of a Muezzin to the soft rustle of the wind through the sparse, thorny bushes. He knew well the importance of this position, but he hadn't slept more than a few hours since he'd left Hawaii. It was a chokepoint, a strategic hold on one of the few roads accessible to the enemy, crucial for supply routes to the Hindu Kush and the gateway to where Smith was hiding in the nearby mountains.

Maxx sucked on another Twizzler left over from this evenings MRE of lasagna. He wasn't hungry, but it kept him from falling asleep on his feet. *Better dead tired than dead*, he thought.

Lieutenant Weih ambled over and offered Maxx a canteen. "Need a swig?" he asked.

Maxx sniffed the mouth of the container. "Nah, I'm trying to cut back on the hooch," he said as he handed the canteen back to Weih. "I still have a long way to go tonight."

The lieutenant raised his eyebrows. "I thought you were waiting for the federal agent and then going out tomorrow morning with the black ops team."

"Change of plans. We got some intel about the location of our target, and I don't want the trail to get any colder."

Maxx stood at the edge of the outpost, his eyes scanning the rugged, unforgiving landscape that had become his world for the past twelve hours. The sun was setting, casting long shadows over the rocky terrain, mirroring the conflict within him.

He had received word from home that Gabby was in trouble. Natalie had tried to kill her, and she no longer felt safe. His heart ached at the thought of her in danger, the same heart that had once beat with the thrill of the mission—a mission to capture or eliminate Li Jing and Doctor Smith, his "white whale" as he had come to call him privately. The mission was personal. Smith was responsible for countless attacks, including one last night when Maxx had lost a friend.

The desire to return home was strong. Maxx envisioned Gabby's smile, her laughter, the way she looked at him like he was her world. Andres had pleaded with him to leave now, take the next transport out. Yet duty weighed on him like a stone. The mission was close to completion, and abandoning it now could mean many more lives lost in the future, possibly even Gabby's.

Under the dimming light, Maxx made his way back to the command tent, his boots kicking up dust. Inside, the atmosphere was tense. Officers and soldiers alike were poring over maps and intel, the air thick with the scent of coffee and the murmur of strategy.

"Maxx, any more word from home?" asked Sergeant Zeller, noticing the troubled look on Maxx's face.

"No, all my calls are going to voicemail," Maxx replied, his voice steady despite the storm inside.

Zeller looked at him, understanding the unspoken dilemma. "We have the coordinates of the villages and tunnels in the area that that captured Talib gave us. It's a solid shot, Maxx. But if you need to—"

"I need to know the mission's status," Maxx interrupted, not wanting to voice his personal turmoil.

Zeller nodded, spreading out the map. "We're set for night. It's not just revenge for Hovis; it's about stopping him from using that communication device before it's too late."

Maxx absorbed the information, the decision weighing on him. If he left now, the mission might fail or be delayed, potentially costing lives. If he stayed, Gabby would face her peril without him.

That late afternoon, under the bluing Afghan sky, Maxx sat alone, cleaning his rifle, each part oiled and checked with precision. His mind, however, was far from the weapons of war. He thought of Gabby, of her strength, and of the promise he made to return. But he also thought of stopping Doctor Smith, of the purpose that had driven him here, the fate of the world.

As the team prepared for the mission, Maxx felt a resolve hardening within himself. He would save lives here, ensuring that Smith and Li Jing would kill no more. Yet in his heart he carried the hope that his choice would not come at the cost of losing what he cherished most back home. Gabby.

By dinner, with the mission looming and Miss Grey due to arrive soon, Maxx made his choice. He would stay. Sitting in silence, he sent a text to Gabby, his big hand shaking slightly. He didn't try to explain his decision, hoping that she'd understand. This was the last mission. Once this was done, he'd be home for good.

Finally, the silence of the dusk was broken by the distant rumble of engines. Maxx's heart rate picked up. This could be reinforcements, the arrival of Miss Grey, or something else entirely. He signaled to Zeller and the Berets, who immediately perked up, their faces reflecting a mix of relief and readiness.

Several vehicles approached, dust clouds trailing behind them like smoky banners. As they neared, the tension eased slightly. It was indeed the friendly convoy, armored Humvees and a couple of MRAPs, their shapes familiar and comforting in this alien landscape. The MRAP, or Mine-Resistant Ambush Protected vehicle, was a beefy, armored truck designed to shrug off mine blasts and small arms fire. It was becoming the vehicle of choice for commuting through the hostile areas in Afghanistan.

The makeshift gate opened, and the dust-laden vehicles rolled in, bringing with them not merely additional manpower but a palpable sense of relief. Maxx watched as soldiers disembarked, their faces weary from the road but alert. Among them was Miss Grey, a figure of calm authority, who approached Maxx with a crooked smile.

"It's nice to see a familiar face," Miss Grey said, her voice carrying the concern that made Maxx a little more relaxed. "Are they keeping you out of trouble?"

Maxx snorted. "Andres and Glen finally caught up with me early this morning. Unfortunately, it was too late to save Hovis. Thanks for making the arrangements for them to come over and support me. Unfortunately, it didn't work out the way we planned."

"It's awful about Hovis. He seemed like a solid guy," she said. "That woman is plain evil. I'm glad you got away. I don't know how I would have dealt with that news."

"She is evil. I'm going to put her and Smith down if it's the last thing I do."

"Keep some perspective, Maxx. Stopping the invasion of the Others is the objective. Taking out Li Jing and Smith are only a path to achieving that goal."

"We'll see," Maxx said noncommittally.

Miss Grey stared at him for a long moment. "You okay?"

"Nope," he said as he shrugged. "But we have a job to do, and I'll deal with that emotional crap another day."

"Fine. We'll talk about that when you're ready. I heard from Andres that you decided to stay here and sent him and Glen back to Seattle to watch over Gabby."

"Yeah, I'm worried about her, but I need to finish this. I trust Andres and Glen with my life. They'll watch out for her as well as I could."

"She needs you, Maxx. It's not about protection. She needs the support and to know that you are safe too."

Maxx pursed his lips. "Like I said, I'm staying. End of conversation, jefa."

"Alright, I hear you. What's the plan?"

"After Andres left to go back to Bagram, the Green Berets and I went back to the house where Hovis was killed to collect his body for shipment home. During our excursion, we ran into a few of the Talibs still hanging around. Before one of them died, I was able to get some information about Smith's likely location."

"Are you certain the information is accurate?" Miss Grey asked skeptically.

"He was in no condition to lie. I trust it's true. Smith is holed up in some caves, and the guy gave me a rough location. There are small hovels below the entrance. That's our first target. If we find that town, we'll find the right cave entrance."

"Did he know anything about the device?" she asked.

"Only that some weird stuff goes on the cave. Rumbling, weird lights. The interpreter had trouble understanding what he was talking about, but he said it was a metal box. It sounded like he was talking about the alien device."

"That sounds more promising than anything else we've heard in a while. In the meantime, I've tried to get some of the satellite images from around the time that Li Jing passed through the checkpoint early this morning. If she drove her car toward that village you mentioned, it will give us some precise coordinates to work from."

"Let's get you kitted up," Maxx said. "I'll introduce you to Sergeant Zeller and the Green Beret squad. They and the ranger squad that brought you here are going to be assisting us."

"Let's get this show on the road," she said. "Once we get on the trail, I'll update you on what's going on with the invasion."

"Do we have an idea when that's happening?" Maxx asked.

"It's already begun," she whispered quietly.

The wait for Maxx was almost over. The mission was going to continue under the vast, indifferent Afghan sunset.

***

It was very early morning in Seattle when the news broke about the military advance in the Middle East. The kind of news that made the air feel heavier, the gloom deeper.

Gabby sat on the edge of her bed, the yellow glow from the streetlights barely creeping through the thick curtains. She felt the weight of the world settle into her chest. Maxx was out there, somewhere in Afghanistan, and the war drums on TV were beating louder every day. The thought of him amidst the chaos and danger made her heart race with a fear she hadn't known before this week.

She reached for the phone beside their bed, her fingers trembling as she dialed his cell number, hoping against hope that he might pick up this time. The call went straight to voicemail, his voice recorded, full of life, now a haunting reminder of what might be lost. "This is Maxx. Leave a message..." She hung up, the silence afterward deafening.

Her mind was a storm of worry and fear, not just for Maxx

but for herself. Here in this city, peaceful after the turmoil last fall, whispers of danger had begun to circulate again. People she thought she knew, neighbors, old friends, suddenly seemed like strangers. Or worse, potential threats. The feeling of being watched had grown from a paranoid tick to a near certainty. The experience at Gas Works Park had shown that her fear was justified.

Gabby stood up, walking to the window, pulling aside the curtain enough to peer out. The street was quiet, too quiet, as if it was waiting for something terrible to happen. She let the curtain fall back into place, the fabric heavy like the decision she had been wrestling with the last couple days.

Going into hiding. The idea had been circling her thoughts like a shark smelling blood in the water. No one could know where she was, not even Maxx. The thought of leaving, of disappearing without a trace, felt like severing a part of herself. But the alternative, staying here where trust was as thin as the morning fog rolling in off the Puget Sound, seemed even more unbearable.

She moved to the kitchen, her feet silent on the cold floor. The coffee she made was bitter, mirroring her mood. As she sipped, she contemplated the logistics. Where could she go? Who could she trust? The more she pondered, the clearer it became that this wasn't about hiding from an unseen enemy; it was about surviving, about keeping the promise to Maxx that she'd be here when he came back. And for that to happen, she needed to be alive, not a casualty of this invisible threat that surrounded her.

She pulled out a paper map, old and crinkled, hidden beneath some sweaters in her dresser drawer. Tracing her finger over potential hideouts, remote cabins, distant relatives, places where she might be safe. Each location felt like a gamble, but staying here felt like betting against her own life.

The fear of running into the same situation elsewhere made her hesitate every time she considered her options.

Her phone buzzed, startling her. A text message. "Thinking of you, babe. Stay safe. I'll be home soon. XX" It was like Maxx sensed her internal turmoil from across the world. Tears rolled down her cheeks, not only from the fear but from the longing, the love that stretched across oceans and war zones.

"Stay safe," she whispered back to the empty room, the words feeling like a pledge. With a heavy heart, she began to place things in her backpack, essentials that wouldn't weigh her down, nothing that could betray her whereabouts. Only a worn map full of maybes. She was leaving behind the life she knew, the comfort of familiarity, for the uncertainty of the unknown.

As she locked the door behind her, the finality of it echoed in the quiet morning. She didn't know where she was going or what awaited her, but she knew she had to go. For Maxx, for herself, for the sliver of hope that one day, they'd be together again in peace.

29

EN PASSANT

Xi could feel cold sweat pooling on the back of his neck.

With Thunderbird's explicit response to the request for weapons – a flat no – he needed to pass along the decision to the Chinese leadership. The phrase "don't kill the messenger" kept circulating through his mind as he prepared for the uncomfortable call. In the end, he knew that what he believed wouldn't matter, because he was too close to the project.

He'd stayed behind in the conference room adjacent to the device. It didn't matter where he made the call from, because the Americans had been privy to the conversation with Thunderbird. The Chinese response would be evident within the next few hours.

"Do you want me step out and give you some privacy?" Green asked.

"No, I'd actually appreciate the support," Xi said as he bowed his head. "You've been helpful over this past week, regardless of what happens next."

"I'm happy to stay. I'm curious how your government is going to react. It seems like you're in a bit of bind."

"I've decided to take the honorable route and take the

responsibility for the failure. No matter what I do or say, in the end it will fall on my shoulders."

"That's true," Mr. Green said with a nod. "But I still respect you for stepping forward. I wish I had that much courage."

Xi nodded humbly. "I will call now," he said as he dialed.

Green pressed a button so the dial tone could be heard through the speaker system. The loud ringing was unnerving to Xi, causing him to wring his hands.

When the phone connected, a woman's voice answered in Mandarin. Green raised his eyebrows.

Xi responded in Mandarin, asking the woman to switch to English.

"You've reached the office of the general secretary," she said. "How may I help you?"

Green's forehead wrinkled as he raised his eyebrows higher.

Xi made eye contact with Green and shrugged as he answered, "This is Dr. Xi of the XINXI program. It is urgent that I speak with Chairman Jiang."

"He is busy," she shot back. "I can make you an appointment for next week at the earliest."

"That will not do," Xi said with more authority in his tone. "The general secretary gave me explicit instructions to call him with this critical information." Xi knew he was bending the truth slightly, but he planned to get this conversation over with before he lost his nerve.

"Hold, and I will ask him. I hope for your sake this is the truth," she said as she placed Xi on hold.

The line beeped every few seconds to let Xi know he was still connected. It was unnerving, like the ticking of a bomb.

After an excruciatingly long time, Xi heard Jiang's gruff voice. "Why are you calling me instead of your superior, Dr. Xi?"

"Thank you, General Secretary. I am calling because I have some bad news. and Mr. Liu asked that I pass the news directly to you." Another lie, but at this point Xi didn't see what difference it made. His head was going to roll no matter who gave Jiang the bad news.

"Liu is a spineless fool. What is the bad news he is too afraid to tell me?"

"I have spoken with Thunderbird. I once again requested that they provide us with weapons to protect ourselves after the earthquake in Kunlun. They have denied request."

Jiang was silent for a moment. "And their reason for denying the request?

Xi took a deep breath. This was the moment when he would seal his fate. "As I was instructed by your order, I told them that without their assistance, you will place our military on standby. They then said that they will not provide weapons, because our leaders intend to position themselves as the global military leaders once the Americans are distracted by the war."

Jiang was silent once more. "Who told you this was my order?" he asked calmly.

"Liu," Xi answered with gulp.

"How did they get the notion that we intend to undermine the Americans?" Jiang asked.

"I don't know. I vigorously denied it, but they could not be persuaded. It is my opinion that they do not trust us and will not provide us with any assistance," Xi said.

"I appreciate the update. Make every effort to convince the Americans that is not our intention regardless of what they have heard from Thunderbird. It is a grave misunderstanding."

Green gave Xi a thumbs up.

"Thank you, Chairman," Xi said with a sigh of relief. "I will tell the Americans and call Liu—"

Jiang cut Xi short. "Do not call Liu. I will talk with him directly. For now, you answer only to me."

The line went dead.

***

The morning was unusually quiet in Georgetown, the sort of stillness that precedes significant events. Inside her townhome, Senator Jane Traficant sat at her desk, the only light in the room emanating from a small lamp focused on the chaotic spread of documents before her. Her office was a fortress of secrecy, the walls lined with books and artifacts that whispered of the extensive reach and influence she had amassed over four decades in Washington.

Traficant reached into the back of the safe hidden behind an unassuming painting—a landscape of Mount St. Helens that she purchased during a visit to Seattle years ago. Her fingers brushed against the cold metal of a small metallic case. With practiced ease, she keyed in the combination, the tumblers falling into place with a satisfying click. Inside was a set of plans, dense with coded military strategy, encrypted communications, and detailed maps. These were the blueprints for Operation Anaconda, a military operation that promised to redefine the geopolitical landscape and more. It was the plan to stop the invasion of the Others in Afghanistan.

Anaconda's publicly stated objective was to destroy the al-Qaeda and Taliban forces that had been gathering in the area. She knew they were there to support the Others' landing. Set to begin after midnight in Afghanistan, Anaconda would focus on the Shah-i-Kot Valley and the Arma Mountains. Intelligence had pinpointed that locale as the probable site of the tunnels that Doctor Smith was using to hide his communication device. It was believed to be the epicenter of the coming war to protect Earth.

She pulled out another file, this one sent by Mr. Green, the director of Team Tacoma. The file contained Thunderbird's own plans, which she now needed to integrate with the military strategy. Senator Traficant was playing a dangerous game, one where the stakes were the very fate of Earth's interaction with the universe.

With meticulous care, she began to merge the documents. The first objective was straightforward: to block the Taliban, Al-Qaeda, and Iranian support to the Others. It was unknown exactly how the alien civilization was planning to arrive, but it was rumored to have already infiltrated portions of the Middle East. This would involve a coordinated military strike, cutting off supply routes and capturing what the military called "the device" from Doctor Smith.

The military mistakenly believed that the device was a nuclear weapon created in Iran. They didn't realize the device was much more dangerous than a bomb with Smith collaborating with the Others.

The secondary objective, however, was far more insidious. Traficant had arranged for Colonel Hanssen, a high-ranking military officer with a penchant for power and secrecy, to introduce a virus into the alien ecosystem. This bioweapon, provided by Thunderbird, was designed to incapacitate the Others, making them vulnerable. The virus was intended to have a delayed reaction so that the Others would unwittingly return to their home planets and infect the entire population. The strategic genocide of an entire alien civilization was a layer of planning only visible to her and her handful of co-conspirators. This was the root of Thunderbird's despicable military objective.

What remained hidden, even from Hanssen, was Traficant's ultimate betrayal. Thunderbird wasn't just looking to weaken the Others; they needed bodies, human soldiers, to continue fighting their wars in the cosmos. Their population had become decimated during centuries of continuous wars, and they needed a new source of combatants. The senator had agreed to this clandestine operation, where selected units would "disappear" during Operation Anaconda. These soldiers, along with selected nuclear technologies, would be transported off-world, disguised as Earth's aggression – vengeance for the invasion - fueling whatever interplanetary conflict Thunderbird was embroiled in.

Traficant's motives were complex. She envisioned herself no longer as merely a senator but as an emissary, a figurehead for Earth in intergalactic affairs. Her plan was to emerge from this operation with leverage, positioning herself as the sole human capable of negotiating Earth's role in the universe. It was the role she had imagined since she had first become exposed to Thunderbird's capabilities in the 1950s.

The clock on her desk chimed softly, reminding her of the time. She needed to move fast. Picking up her secure phone, she dialed Colonel Hanssen.

"Hanssen," said the gruff voice on the other end.

"Colonel, it's Senator Traficant. The plans for Operation Anaconda are ready for integration. I need your technical expertise and your discretion."

There was a pause, the weight of the moment hanging between them. "Understood, Senator. When do we meet?"

"Noon at the usual spot. Bring the necessary clearances for the integration."

Hanssen agreed, his tone betraying neither enthusiasm nor suspicion, which was precisely why Traficant chose him for this role. He was a man whose ambition could be manipulated, his loyalty to the military a mask for his darker desires.

Once the call ended, Traficant leaned back, her eyes scanning the room as if to ensure no shadows held secrets. Her mind wandered to the potential aftermath. If successful, Operation Anaconda would not only disrupt the Others but place her at the pinnacle of human interstellar diplomacy. A queen. If it failed, the repercussions could be catastrophic, not only for her but for humanity's standing in the universe.

Her gaze fell on a framed picture on her desk—a photo

from a recent family gathering. The faces of her grandchildren smiled back at her, unaware of the dreadful chess game their grandmother was playing. They were her anchor, her motivation. For them, she would risk everything.

She returned the original plans to the safe, ensuring all traces of her tampering were covered. The merged documents would soon find their way into the military system, disguised as an enhancement to Mr. Green's initial proposal. Colonel Hanssen would handle the digital integration, his skills in cybersecurity ensuring no trace would lead back to her. Green would be labeled as the source of the conspiracy if details were exposed. She smiled thinking about the possibility of Mr. Green, wearing one of his silly Hawaiian shirts, being led out of the Tacoma facility in handcuffs.

Traficant switched off the lamp, plunging her office into soft light of dawn. The morning outside was still quiet, but within her mind, the gears of a vast, interstellar conspiracy turned relentlessly. She knew the path she had chosen was filled with peril, but the allure of power, of being the one to guide humanity through the stars, was too intoxicating to resist. Not to mention Thunderbird's promise if she was successful. The temptation of alien technology to reverse the last forty years of aging and extend her life for centuries was too much to resist.

As she left her office, locking the door behind her, the senator felt the weight of her decisions. The future was uncertain, filled with shadows of both alien and human origins. But for now, she was the puppeteer, pulling strings in a play that could either save or doom humanity.

***

In the dimly lit corridors of the Team Tacoma facility, the air was thick with the scent of the granite-carved tunnels and the hum of hundreds of secure servers.

Mr. Green, with his slightly hooded eyes scanned each document. Dr. Xi, his gaze more contemplative, sat poring over military plans that Green had shared with him earlier. These were not ordinary plans; they outlined Operation Anaconda, the military operation in Afghanistan that was going to begin in mere hours. A devastating attack not just against the Taliban but the covert operation to repel the otherworldly civilization known as the Others. Earth's raiders.

"Xi, there's something you should know," Mr. Green whispered, ensuring his voice wouldn't carry beyond their small, secluded office. He leaned closer, his voice dropping to a barely audible murmur. "I've included the specifics of the alien virus deployment in the documents sent to Senator Traficant and Thunderbird." He paused, his eyes darting around, "But I've encrypted the location and access information with an AI-generated code. If Thunderbird can't be trusted, this information is as good as locked away in an impenetrable vault."

Dr. Xi raised an eyebrow, intrigued. "And the senator?"

"She's not aware of this locked back door. It pains me to say it, but I suspect her motives aren't entirely aligned with yours or mine," Green confided, his voice touched with caution.

As they continued their meticulous review, the silence was abruptly broken by the shrill ring of Green's secure line. It was Miss Grey.

"Grey, I'm feeling the heat here. I'm certain I'm being watched," Green said nervously as he picked up the receiver.

Grey's voice crackled through the static. "That's Anderson's doing. My NSA contact told me that the CIA has been tracking you for months. They got spooked when you chased after me down I-5. They're now worried you're going rouge."

"I haven't yet. I've sent the military plans to Thunderbird. It was unavoidable. The senator was pushing me hard," Green replied, his tone guarded.

"There's something else, isn't there?" Grey asked, her intuition sharp as ever.

Green hesitated then said cryptically, "Remember what I was drinking when you found me waiting at Maxx's condo?"

"No, why?" she asked puzzled.

"Some of the file information I sent is locked down. I don't trust Thunderbird or the senator right now. I encrypted it to buy some time or to use as a 'get out of jail free' card if I need it."

"Smart," she said. "What does that have to do with what you were drinking at Maxx's?"

"That's the encryption key," he said with a chuckle. "Ask Maxx about the name of the 'doctor.'"

There was a pause on the line. "Have I ever told you how weird you are, Green? But I'll ask Maxx. Stay safe."

After the call, the gravity of their situation seemed to weigh heavier on both men. "We need to move," Green decided abruptly. "This place isn't secure anymore."

Dr. Xi nodded, understanding the urgency. "Where to?"

"An undisclosed location. I've been preparing for this day. We'll disappear for a few days, give ourselves time to think, to plan. We need to help Grey, but not from here."

Quickly, they gathered what little they could carry, ensuring no trace of their digital or physical presence remained. The facility, with its myriad tunnels and secret passages, offered them a covert escape route. Mr. Green chose one of the lesser-known side tunnels, a relic from the building's more secretive past.

The stone tunnel was narrow, the walls damp and echoing with their footsteps, leading them to an ancient elevator beneath the historic Smith Tower. The elevator's metal grate clattered as it was pulled open, revealing the dimly lit interior where the brass floor buttons gleamed under the soft glow of an ancient bulb. As the doors closed, the elevator shuddered to life, the only sounds as they ascended were the creak of old machinery and their shoes squeaking on the worn linoleum floor.

Emerging into the ghostly lobby of the tower, they pulled their hats low, the brims casting deep shadows over their faces. The rain outside was a steady drumbeat, offering both cover and a sense of melancholy as they stepped out into the night of Pioneer Square. The sky was still quite dark, only the faintest hint of light visible on the horizon.

The streets were nearly deserted, the rain sweeping leaves and litter into gutters. They moved swiftly, blending into the early morning, their breaths visible in the cool, damp air. They had to vanish, not just for their safety but to ensure the delicate balance of their attempt to save the world wasn't disturbed by betrayal.

As they disappeared into the maze of Seattle's back alleys, the city seemed to close in around them, a secretive co-conspirator in their flight. Behind them, the lights of the Tacoma building dimmed. The operation was in motion, but the players were now moving through shadows, each step a calculated risk in a chess game with stakes higher than any before.

30

DULCE ET DECORUM EST

The corridors of the Zhongnanhai compound were as silent as a tomb, the air thick with the unspoken fears of those who navigated its halls. Liu Yuxuan, administrator of the secretive XINXI program, moved with a measured pace, his steps echoing softly on the polished marble. His heart was a drum in his chest, each beat a reminder of the precariousness of his position. Today, like every day, could be his last in favor.

The doors to Chairman Jiang's office were grand, carved with dragons that seemed to watch him with a cold, judgmental gaze. Inside, the office was a stark contrast to the opulence of its facade. Functional yet austere, the room was dominated by a large desk where Chairman Jiang sat, his meal before him, a simple bowl of rice and vegetables. The chairman looked up as Liu entered, his eyes sharp, betraying nothing of his thoughts.

"Ah, Liu. Sit," Jiang said, gesturing to a chair opposite him. His voice was calm, but there was an undercurrent of something dangerous.

Liu sat, his mind racing. "Chairman, you wanted to see me?"

"Yes," Jiang replied, taking a moment to chew his food, his

eyes never leaving Liu. “Dr. Xi called me. He said he had failed and was taking responsibility.”

Liu's relief was visible in the dim office light. If Xi was confessing, perhaps the brunt of the blame would land on him, leaving Liu to navigate the aftermath with less personal risk. “I see,” Liu managed, his voice steady but his mind racing.

Jiang continued, “However, Xi is missing. He has disappeared from the American facility. As his superior, I wonder if you know his whereabouts.”

Liu thought back over his most recent conversations, wondering if he’d forgotten something Xi had told him. “No, Chairman. I believe he was in Seattle last time we spoke.”

“You believe. I see. I believe he might have turned traitor and fled after his failure.”

The word “traitor” hung in the air, heavy with implications. Liu's relief morphed into alarm. “Missing? That’s...concerning. I could offer resources to find—”

Jiang cut him off with a dismissive wave of his chopsticks. “No need, Liu. Your place is here now. You will remain here as a symbol.”

Liu frowned, uncomfortable. “A symbol of what, Chairman?”

Jiang's gaze was ice. “Of your failure with the Others. Xi might be gone, but the consequences of your actions remain. You advised me to attempt to trick Thunderbird, did you not? To gain weapons from them? Instead, we've sown mistrust.”

Liu felt the ground beneath him crumble. He had indeed advised such a strategy, believing it would position China favorably in the global power structure. But the plan had backfired, and now, here in the Chairman’s office, the cost of that advice was becoming painfully clear.

“I... I believed it was for the greater good,” Liu stammered, his usual composure fleeing. “I believed outmaneuvering the Americans and the alien civilizations would be your triumph.”

Jiang set down his chopsticks, his meal forgotten. "Intentions mean little in the realm of outcomes, Liu. You have made me look weak, desperate. That is not the image I can afford to project."

The door behind Liu opened silently, and Mr. Fu, the chairman's personal security guard, entered. His presence was not surprising but ominous nonetheless. Liu's heart sank further. He still hurt from the last time Mr. Fu had beaten him.

"Chairman, I can fix this," Liu pleaded in desperation. "Let me rectify the situation."

Jiang shook his head in a gesture of finality. "No, Liu. Your time is finished here. You will take the blame for Xi's disappearance and the failure of the XINXI program. It is sweet and fitting to die for one's country."

Liu stood up and fell to his knees, his chair crashing back with a heavy thump that seemed to echo the end of his career. "Chairman, please—"

But before he could finish, Mr. Fu moved with a swiftness that betrayed his customary stoic demeanor. There was a flash of metal, and Liu felt a sharp, cold pain in his chest. He looked down, almost apathetically, at the blood spreading across his white shirt. The room spun, and as he fell, Liu realized the true cost of political games in the highest echelons of power.

Chairman Jiang watched dispassionately as Liu crumpled to the floor. He then picked up his chopsticks, his expression unchanged. "Clear the mess up, Mr. Fu. And ensure the news of Liu's death is handled appropriately. He died of a heart attack, overwhelmed by the failure of the XINXI program. Understood?"

Mr. Fu bowed slightly, his face a mask. "Understood, Chairman."

As the door closed behind the guard, Jiang's gaze lingered on the spot where Liu had fallen. The office returned to its eerie silence, the dragons on the doors now seemingly arrogant in their judgment. In the heart of China's power, loyalty was as fleeting as one's last breath, and the price of failure was often paid in blood.

***

Lieutenant John Weih gripped the edge of his Humvee's open window, his eyes scanning the rugged terrain ahead. The air was thin and cold, the kind that bit at your lungs with every breath. His platoon had left the relative safety of the checkpoint outside Kabul after sunset, now winding their way through the mountainous passes toward Shah-i-Kot Valley as part of Operation Anaconda. The landscape, stark and unforgiving, mirrored the mission's intensity.

The Humvees rumbled over the rough path, dust clouding behind them, a stark contrast against the clear Afghan sky. Weih, originally from Texas, had joined the Army in the wake of September 11th, driven by a mix of patriotism and a need to act. Now, as the new officer in charge, he felt the weight of every decision, every order given.

The valley opened up like jagged jaws ready to swallow them. It wasn't long before the first shots rang out, a barrage of sharp cracks that broke the silence of the evening. Taliban insurgents, hidden within the rocky outcrops, engaged them with sporadic gunfire. AK-47s but no rocket-propelled grenades or heavy weapons. Getting hit by an RPG would demolish their vehicles and ruin their day.

Weh could hear radio chatter up and down the convoy as the men reacted. The platoon returned fire, their training kicking in, but not before a couple soldiers were wounded. Weih shouted orders, his voice steady despite the chaos, directing fire and calling for medics.

After the skirmish, as the platoon regrouped and tended to the wounded, Weih received a radio call. "Lieutenant, what's the SITREP?" The voice from command was clear and urgent.

Weih nodded to no one in particular, his mind racing through tactics and strategies. "Situation report is unknown enemy strength. Firing from high terrain. Hostiles broke it off after we engaged. We could use some reconnaissance."

Command asked, "Causalities?"

"No KIA, two wounded. Ammo is green and gear is fully operational," Weih responded.

"We'll see if we can get you some intel. They're probing everywhere right now, so stay frosty. Out."

As the deep night fell, they set up a temporary perimeter. Weih shook off the latent effects of the adrenalin, his breath visible in the cold air. Trying to calm himself, he looked up at the sky. It was clear, the stars shining with an intensity only found in such desolate places. Suddenly, streaks of light began to cross the sky, one after another. A meteor shower, perhaps, or was it something more? The beauty of it momentarily distracted from the grim reality of their situation.

Weih's thoughts turned to Maxx and Grey, the two civilians who had been at the outpost earlier. Maxx, despite his narrow escape from the Taliban, with his sharp wit and steady aim was welcomed by the unit without question. It was strange to see a seasoned operator work in partnership with a Green Beret team. He didn't understand what their mission was, but when they took off into the mountains ahead of Operation Anaconda, he assumed they were doing deep reconnaissance into Pakistan. He was sorry to see Maxx go, because his confidence was a morale booster.

Grey, on the other hand, was the silent type, her eyes always scanning, her mind always two steps ahead, especially when it came to understanding the politics of the situation. She had told him that she was in country on an assignment from the Department of Homeland Security. Weih had never even heard of that branch of the government. She was intense, so he'd given her plenty of space. Here in Afghanistan, they weren't just fighting a war; they were part of something larger, something Weih was still trying to fully grasp.

The meteor shower continued, a silent fireworks display against the backdrop of potential carnage. Weih wondered about the irony of such natural beauty juxtaposed with human conflict. What were they really doing here? Was it about retaliation and security, or was there a deeper purpose, a connection to be made with these lands and its people?

The night was quiet now, save for the occasional whisper or the soft moan of the wounded. Weih knew that this calm was deceptive. The heavy engagement expected would test them all. He was prepared to do everything necessary for his country. But for now, under the stars, there was a brief, shared moment of wonder, a reminder of the world's vastness beyond the narrow lens of war.

He checked his gear one last time, the reality of their mission pulling him back from the stars to the ground. Tomorrow would bring its own battles, but tonight, under the meteor shower, there was a fleeting peace.

***

On that brisk March afternoon, Lower Senate Park, despite its usual tranquility, was the stage for a clandestine meeting to complete the final preparations for the ultimate betrayal.

Senator Traficant, a figure known in Washington for her decades of power and influence, frequently used this serene location for its privacy, away from the prying eyes of Capitol Hill. Her usual meeting place to direct her unofficial business. The cherry trees, on the cusp of blooming, were not yet a spectacle, allowing the park to retain a quiet dignity, the kind that whispers rather than shouts.

Colonel Hanssen, in his impeccably tailored gray suit, cut a figure both authoritative and enigmatic. Seated on a bench, his presence was like that of a hawk, his eyes scanning the park with a mix of military precision and underlying suspicion. The creases on his face from years under the sun and amidst the dust of conflict spoke of a life lived on the edge of danger. His posture, straight as an arrow, was a relic of his military upbringing, but there was something in his gaze, a glint that suggested layers of thought, perhaps even deceit.

As Senator Traficant approached, her demeanor was all business, her stride confident yet cautious. The senator, with her reputation for political maneuvering, regarded Colonel Hanssen with a similar mistrust. They met in person under the pretense of a casual walk, but their conversation was far from trivial.

"Colonel," Traficant greeted with a nod, her voice low to ensure their privacy.

"Senator," Hanssen responded. He stood and firmly shook her hand, discreetly passing her a small thumb drive that contained the information that she had requested.

They began to walk, their conversation masked by the sound of the wind and the distant urban hum. Hanssen began, "I've reviewed the data Mr. Green sent to Thunderbird. It aligns with our operational plans for Operation Anaconda, but there's an issue."

Traficant listened intently, her eyes scanning the park for any signs of surveillance. Only a solitary jogger traced the park's perimeter, their breath visible in the cool air. "What kind of issue?"

"The information on the location of the virus is encrypted. There is no evidence of a key, unless he gave it to you. If not, Mr. Green has made himself indispensable," Hanssen said with a hint of frustration. "What was he thinking?"

Senator Traficant's mind raced. The virus was crucial to her plan, which involved using Thunderbird's resources for her own ends under the guise of a military battle. "That's unexpected," she muttered, her gaze now fixed on the reflections in the central fountain. "What will Thunderbird do when they discover this?"

Hanssen's response was calculated. "They'll either seek to decrypt it themselves or demand answers from us. Either way, it jeopardizes the operation. They will be aggravated."

The senator needed to act swiftly. She pulled out her secure cell phone, dialing the Tacoma facility. She demanded to speak immediately with Green. After a tense few minutes, a rep explained, "Senator, Mr. Green is not answering either his phones or the overhead pages. There's no record of Mr. Green leaving, but it doesn't seem as if he's in the facility."

Her heart skipped a beat. "How can that be?" she whispered more to herself than to Hanssen. The plan was unraveling. Mr. Green was her linchpin, the one who knew too much but was also now indispensable.

Hanssen watched her, his expression unreadable. "Senator, if Green has gone rogue, or worse, if he's been compromised, we're facing a significant threat, not just to your plan but to national security."

Traficant's mind was a whirlwind of scenarios. Was Green playing a double game? Had he been abducted? Each possibility was more alarming than the last. Her political instincts kicked in, calculating the next move with the precision of a chess grandmaster. She was still the queen, and Green was nothing but a pawn. It would be sweet revenge if Green was the architect of his own demise.

"We need to find him," she stated without her usual conviction. "And we need to do it discreetly. If this gets out, the repercussions..."

Hanssen nodded, his face a mask of determination. "I'll

mobilize a discrete search. Meanwhile, we should prepare for the possibility that Thunderbird might react unpredictably."

Their walk continued, but the air between them had thickened with tension. Each step through the park was now a step into deeper shadows, where every leaf rustle could be a whisper of threat, every passerby a potential spy. The serene beauty of Lower Senate Park belied the storm brewing in the minds of Senator Traficant and Colonel Hanssen. A storm that could destroy their plans, their careers, and perhaps even the world itself.

31

NO REST FOR THE WICKED

Senator Traficant's office in the Senate building was a testament to her long and storied career. The walls were adorned with framed photographs, some black and white, capturing moments with dignitaries and past presidents. The furniture was old but well-maintained, a blend of traditional and sturdy, reflecting her tenure since her days as a congressional aide in 1957 when the first whispers of the Thunderbird Project reached her. Now, at seventy-two, her office was not just a place of work but a fortress of secrets, where the echoes of history mingled with the pressing concerns of the present.

She sat behind her mahogany desk, the leather chair worn in just the right places. Her hand reached into her purse, pulling out a small, unassuming cube known only as the Thunderbird device. With a practiced motion, she wrapped her hands around the small cube. Immediately, the overhead lights in her office began to shift. The fluorescent bulbs dimmed, casting an eerie blue hue in the corners of the room despite the afternoon light shining through the shutters. Closing her eyes, she focused, feeling the device cooling in her grasp, the sensation grounding her as time seemed to dilate around her.

Time itself began to drag, each moment stretching into eternity as she felt herself drift, weightless, in an endless void. Here, in this nothingness, she was not alone. The chilling presence of another entity seeped into her consciousness, its essence palpable and foreboding.

"You have called us forth," the voice reverberated through the emptiness, a disembodied entity whose presence enveloped the void in which she now drifted.

Senator Traficant, knowing the device sensed her emotional state, concentrated on the anxiety and fear that had been her constant companions since her meeting with Colonel Hanssen. "Something bad has happened," she repeated to herself, her apprehension growing with each silent recitation.

"Show us," the voice demanded.

Jane focused intensely on the mental image of a rusted, ancient door, its key shattered beside it. Beyond this barrier, in a thickening mist, was the coveted virus. "It's concealed, and the lock remains forever sealed," she whispered repeatedly, her voice trembling with a fear that clawed at her very soul.

The response from Thunderbird was immediate but chilling. The voice, though calm, carried an undercurrent of menace. "You have twenty-four hours to find the key. Provide the virus location or face the consequences. If you fail, you will burn with the fire of a thousand suns."

The weight of the ultimatum settled on her like she was being submerged. With a heavy heart, she opened her eyes, the room returning to its normal state, though the air felt colder, as if the threat had chilled the very atmosphere.

Her hand, shaking, extended toward the secure-line telephone perched on her desk. With deliberate, almost ritualistic movements, she dialed Anderson's mobile, aware of his distant location in Afghanistan. She murmured a silent prayer that the call would connect. The line crackled with static, an opus of conflict and pandemonium from afar, barely veiled by the encryption, each sound a reminder of the stakes.

"Anderson, it's Senator Traficant. I need your help," she said, her voice steady despite the tremor in her hands.

"Senator, what's the problem? Missing me?" Anderson's sardonic voice came through, strained by the background noise of gunfire and jet aircraft passing closely overhead.

"This is no time for joking, you ass. Green has encrypted the virus data location sent to Thunderbird. I don't have the key. Do you?"

"Of course not," Anderson shot back. "What did Green tell you when you asked him?"

"Green has disappeared. I need to find him. Can you help?"

"Damn." He was silent for a moment then replied, "I'm pinned down right now, but I'll have someone from the agency operations in Seattle track him down. What about Green's last known contacts?"

"He's been in the office since he disappeared during his drive down I-5. Do you know who he met while he was on the freeway?"

"He was chasing Miss Grey. Traffic cams show that when she pulled over, he jumped in her car. Then they drove to Joint Base Lewis-McChord."

Senator Traficant paused, her mind racing. "Is it possible he gave the encryption key to Miss Grey?"

"It's possible, Senator. I'll see what we can do from here. Grey is in Afghanistan heading toward me and Smith according to the Rangers escorting her. I'll be sure to ask her if I see her."

The senator gritted her teeth. "Get the answers I need from Grey, whatever it takes. And I mean whatever, Anderson."

"Fun," Anderson said enthusiastically.

The conversation ended, leaving Traficant in a silence that felt more oppressive than the noise of war. She leaned back in her chair, the Thunderbird device still in hand, its cool, smooth surface now a reminder of the precarious balance between power and peril. The clock was ticking. Her life's work, her covert plan, was teetering on the edge of failure.

***

In the cavernous depths of the Hindu Kush, hidden beneath the rugged terrain, Dr. Smith and Li Jing waited in tense silence. The air was cool and damp. The waterfall supplying power to the device lent an earthy, musty odor to the cave that clung to their skin. The cave system was vast, a labyrinth of history and secrets, now serving as a clandestine storage site for the communication device supplied by the non-human civilization known only as the Others.

Dr. Smith sat against the rough stone, his eyes periodically darting to the large, black device sitting in the center of the huge cavern. The device's skin flickered with surges of color, a sign of activity but not yet the clear signal they hoped for. His fingers tapped a nervous rhythm on his thigh, the sound echoing slightly in the quiet granite grotto. His usual controlled demeanor was slipping.

Li Jing paced the perimeter of their large, illuminated chasm. Her steps were soft but deliberate, each one echoing her internal battle between duty and desire to join the battle brewing outside the cave. She occasionally glanced outside, where the mouth of the entrance was barricaded by the Taliban. Her hand rested lightly on the Glock at her hip.

The valley beyond the tunnels was alive with the sounds of war. Sporadic gunfire broke the mountain's silence, punctuated by the roar of military jets overhead. The Americans were pushing hard, their intentions clear: to root out any form of resistance or alien contact in this remote region. The blockade at the cave's entrance was their temporary shield, but it was the knowledge of the tunnels leading toward Pakistan, and eventually Iran, that offered a sliver of hope for escape.

"We need those instructions soon," Li Jing muttered more to herself than to Dr. Smith. Her voice was steady, but the undercurrent of urgency was unmistakable.

Dr. Smith nodded, his gaze fixed on the device. "We'll get them. The Others wouldn't leave us without a plan. They need our assistance as much as we need theirs."

As he cleaned his glasses, his mind was elsewhere, wrestling with a darker thought. The idea of leaving Li Jing behind to manage the resistance while he secured his own escape had crossed his mind more than once. It was a survivalist's calculation, one he hoped he wouldn't have to make. Not because he was emotionally attached to her but because he felt safest with her by his side.

The device began to thrum with energy, pulling both of them from their thoughts. The monitor cleared momentarily, showing a fragmented message. Dr. Smith leaned in, squinting at the symbols. "I think it's coming through," he announced with a mix of relief and anticipation.

Li Jing stopped her pacing, joining him by the device. They listened as the toneless voice echoed throughout the vault.

"Await further contact. Prepare for multiple scenarios."

The flashing screen returned to a series of flashing lights. It wasn't much, but it was something. Li Jing sighed, her shoulders dropping slightly. "We need to be ready to move at any moment."

Dr. Smith nodded, his mind still grappling with his secret consideration. "Yes, let's prepare to relocate. We might need to move quickly once they give the all-clear, or if..." The unspoken possibility hung in the air like the dust and smell of gunpowder that was beginning to blow in through the cave's entrance.

Outside, the fighting seemed to intensify, the sounds growing louder, more desperate. They knew time was not on their side. They prepared their packs, checking gear and supplies. Each needed to decide what they were willing to sacrifice for survival, for the mission, for each other.

***

The village at the foot of the mountain was eerily quiet except for the sporadic bursts of gunfire that echoed through the narrow streets. Maxx, leading the joint force of Miss Grey, the Ranger squad, and Zeller's Green Beret team, moved cautiously. The intel that Maxx had extracted from the Taliban soldier earlier this morning had been correct. The cave system on the side of the mountain, where Smith and a mysterious device awaited, was about a thousand feet up the steep mountainside.

In the small village nestled at the foot of the towering, jagged mountain, the air was thick with the scent of dust and smoke. The village, typical of many in the region, consisted of mud-brick houses, narrow alleyways, and a bazaar now deserted due to the ongoing conflict. The structures, built close together for warmth and community, inadvertently provided perfect cover for guerrilla warfare.

As Maxx and his team moved through the streets, the only sounds were the crunch of their boots on the gravel and the distant sound of A-10s attacking remote positions in the valley. The A-10 Thunderbolts, affectionately known as Warthogs, were easily identified by the distinctive "brrrrrrt" sound of their Avenger cannons. The skirmish began abruptly, the silence shattered by the crack of gunfire from a concealed position.

The Taliban fighters, entrenched in the village, had anticipated the American approach. They were few in number, less than a dozen, but they knew the layout. They were armed with AK-47s and a fervent resolve to stop the Americans from reaching the tunnels on the mountain. Their positions were strategically placed — behind walls, from rooftops, and within the tangle of alleyways.

The Americans, comprising both the Ranger squad and the Green Beret team, responded with the precision of a well-oiled machine. They spread out, using the village's own architecture for cover. The Rangers, trained for rapid deployment and direct action, moved with speed and aggression. They flanked the enemy positions, utilizing the narrow streets to their advantage, their M4s spitting controlled bursts of fire.

The Green Berets, with their sound-suppressed weapons, coordinated with Gabby and Maxx to neutralize threats from higher ground. They tossed grenades into suspected hideouts, the explosions echoing off the mud walls, sending up clouds of debris. The air filled with the sharp tang of gunpowder, the acrid smoke obscuring vision.

The fight was fierce but brief, lasting no more than ten minutes. The Americans had superior weaponry, including night vision goggles for the heavy gloom and body armor that gave them an edge against the lighter-armed Taliban. Their small squad tactics quickly overwhelmed any remaining threats.

As the last Taliban fighter fell, the village returned to an eerie silence, save for the groans of the dying and the crackling of small fires. The Americans moved through, checking for any remaining threats, their movements now cautious, sweeping the area with an eye for traps or hidden fighters.

Miss Grey, though successful in the minor skirmish, knew this was but a prelude to the more significant challenge that awaited them on the mountain's slopes. As they pushed up the hill, the terrain became increasingly treacherous. Loose shale and jagged rocks made every step precarious. The hillside was steep, dotted with sparse vegetation and occasional rock outcroppings that offered fleeting cover from the gunfire still erupting from the mouth of the cave above. The air was thin, the cold biting, as they ascended, each breath a visible puff in the cold mountain air.

Reaching a small, flat section the side of the cave entrance, Maxx and Miss Grey, with Gabby close behind, found a momentary respite. The area was hidden from the tunnel opening by a large rock ledge, providing a shield against the relentless gunfire.

Here, in the middle of the Afghan mountains, they found Director Anderson sitting on a smooth rock with a satellite phone pressed to his ear. He had clearly been waiting. He was calm, almost expectant, as he finished a phone call with a chilling remark, "Fun." His knowing grin was bizarrely out of place on the side of a mountain with the sound of gunfire echoing around them.

"Glad you all could finally make it to the party," he said to Maxx and Gabby as he ended the call. "I've been waiting for reinforcements to arrive with explosives in order to breach the cave."

After brief introductions, it became clear that Anderson was the prevailing, although unofficial, leader of the small force. With the authority of his position in the CIA, he immediately began giving directions to the military units. "Climb farther up and to the sides," he instructed. "Make sure there are no hidden cave exits that will allow Smith to escape."

Turning to Grey, his voice lowered, he asked, "I was just speaking to the senator. She's concerned. Mr. Green has disappeared from the Tacoma facility. She wants to know if you know anything about his whereabouts."

Grey, trying to keep her face a mask of calm, replied, "No, I haven't heard anything from Green in days." Her eyes flickered, which Anderson caught immediately despite the dim moon light.

With the squad climbing higher up the mountain, their voices and footsteps fading into the thin mountain air, Director

Anderson's expression hardened. In one swift, silent motion, he pulled out a silenced pistol. The shot was a whisper against the backdrop of the mountain's silence, striking Maxx from behind.

Maxx staggered, his head snapping back with the impact. He fell face first to the stony ground, his head landing on the rock with a thud. His body went limp.

Miss Grey, frozen in shock, started to reach for Maxx, her instincts overridden by sudden fear. Anderson was quicker, intercepting her movement. With a cold, efficient grip, he disarmed her, pulling her rifle away before she could even grasp it fully.

"Don't make a sound," Anderson warned, his voice a low, menacing whisper as he redirected his weapon at her. "One word and I'll send both your bodies over the edge." His eyes, devoid of warmth, locked onto hers, enforcing the gravity of his threat.

"Have you lost your mind?" Grey demanded, her voice steady despite the terror gripping her.

"Far from it. I see through your lies and can finally do something about it. You and Green have been working together to undermine the senator's plans. I warned her about you."

"I don't know what plans you're talking about," she hissed. "I'm here to stop Doctor Smith, like you."

"Then give me the code that Green gave you," Anderson said, his eyes narrowing.

"I don't have any code," Grey lied, her mind racing as she glanced at Maxx, hoping he wouldn't wake up and recover enough to provoke Anderson further.

Anderson's composure broke. Exasperation and anger mingled in his eyes as he raised his pistol again, aiming at the already fallen Maxx. "If you don't give me that code," he snarled at Grey, "I'll put another bullet in him, and then we'll see how long you last under...persuasion."

Maxx began to stir, the fog of unconsciousness lifting. He

tried to rise, his movements uncoordinated, his mind still clouded. Grey gasped, her voice catching in her throat, "Maxx, don't—" Her warning was too late.

Maxx, barely aware of his surroundings, attempted to speak. Anderson, with a look of contempt, delivered a vicious kick to Maxx's ribs. The force sent Maxx reeling backward, his body unable to find balance on the uneven ground. He slid helplessly over the cliff edge, the darkness enveloping him as he fell. The sound of his body striking the rocks below was a grisly echo in the night.

Anderson approached the cliff, peering down into the darkness. There was no sign of Maxx. "Doesn't matter," he muttered, turning back to Grey. "That guy has been a pain in my ass since the first time we met."

Grey's facade broke. Tears streamed down her face, not only for the loss of her friend but for the dread of what was to come. She was alone with Anderson, too afraid to call for help. In this remote, hostile environment, survival was improbable, and death likely.

As the cold wind howled through the rocks, Grey realized that for the second time in a year Maxx had lost to a killer. But this time Andres was not there to save him. Or her. The mountain had claimed Maxx, and now she stood alone on the edge of the abyss.

32

STANDING ON THE EDGE

Gabby's footsteps echoed with finality through the empty TechCom office. With each step, she felt the weight of her decision, the air thick with the weight of her resolve. The office, once a place of innovation and collaboration, now felt like a frightening reminder of the unknowns the Thunderbird project had unleashed. She made her way to her desk, taking down the photograph of her and Maxx on the Bainbridge ferry, the frame catching the light from the window, a stark reminder of happier times. She tucked it carefully into her backpack.

She left her badge, keys, and computer on the desk, symbols of a career she was leaving behind. On the team whiteboard, she wrote, her marker squeaking, "Embrace today. Tomorrow is only a promise, not a given. - Gabby"

She turned on her phone, which she had silenced before leaving the condo, the device feeling like a dangerous connection in her hand. As she powered it back on for what she knew would be the last time, the message notification chimed. A text message from Andres appeared, earnest and melancholy. "Maxx sent us back to make sure you're safe until he finishes the mission. We couldn't find you at home. Security says you're in your office. OMW."

Her heart sank. Maxx, her anchor, had tried to ensure her safety even from afar. But he wasn't here where she needed him. With a heavy heart, Gabby knew what she had to do. She popped out the SIM card from her phone and tossed it into the trash can, severing her last digital connection. It was a small act, but it felt like she was cutting ties with her entire existence.

Peering out the front window, she spotted Andres and Glen, Maxx's trusted friends, pulling into the parking lot. Their arrival confirmed her fears. There was no time left for reminiscing. A wave of sorrow washed over her. The last six months had been a whirlwind, a mix of breakthroughs and breakdowns. *Will I ever see this place again?*

The elevator dinged, signaling its approach to her floor. The decision was no longer hers to ponder. She grabbed her backpack, heading for the stairs, her sneakers echoing a soft retreat down the concrete stairwell. Reaching the bottom, she pushed through the back emergency door into the alley, the cold and wet Seattle air biting at her skin.

Snow had begun to fall, each flake a gentle farewell from the city she loved. Gabby watched for a moment, the white specks dancing in the dim light, before she turned away, disappearing into the alley. As she walked into the snowy embrace of the city, she took with her only what she needed: her memories, her determination, and her hope for a future where she and Maxx would be together again.

THE END

AFTERWORD

Dear Reader: Below is a list of songs fueling my imagination as I envisioned the world and characters of Maxx and Gabby. I hope these songs add an extra dimension to your experience as you recall the world created in the book.

The complete playlist can be found on Spotify @ **Gabby & Maxx.**

"Masters of War" – Bob Dylan
Prologue: "Everything Hits at Once" – Spoon
Chapter 1: "All or Nothing" – O-Town
Chapter 2: "When It's Over" – Sugar Ray
Chapter 3: "Pop" – *NSYNC
Chapter 4: "Smooth" – Santana, Rob Thomas
Chapter 5: "Only You" – The Platters
Chapter 6: "Standing Still" – Jewel
Chapter 7: "Wherever You Will Go" – The Calling
Chapter 8: "Clint Eastwood" - Gorillaz
Chapter 9: "The Space Between" – Dave Matthews Band
Chapter 10: "How You Remind Me" – Nickelback

Chapter 11: “It’s Been Awhile” – Staind
Chapter 12: “A Long Walk” – Jill Scott
Chapter 13: “Breathless” – The Corrs
Chapter 14: “You Rock My World” – Michael Jackson
Chapter 15: “Butterfly” – Crazy Town
Chapter 16: “Hanging By a Moment” – Lifehouse
Chapter 17: “Drive” – Incubus
Chapter 18: “By Your Side” – Sade
Chapter 19: "One More Time” – Daft Punk
Chapter 20: “In the End” – Linkin Park
Chapter 21: “Fallin’” – Alicia Keys
Chapter 22: “Bittersweet Symphony” – The Verve
Chapter 23: “Yellow” – Coldplay
Chapter 24: “Let Me Blow Ya Mind” – Eve, Gwen Stefani
Chapter 25: “No Such Thing” – John Mayer
Chapter 26: "Blurry” – Puddle of Mudd
Chapter 27: “Lady Marmalade” – Christina Aguilera, Lil’ Kim, Mya, Pink
Chapter 28: “My Sacrifice” - Creed
Chapter 29: “Don’t Tell Me” - Madonna
Chapter 30: “Masters of War” – Bob Dylan
Chapter 31: “Hero” – Enrique Iglesias
Chapter 32: “I Will Remember You” – Sarah McLachlan

A NOTE FROM THE AUTHOR

A NOTE FROM JOHN H. THOMAS
Thank you for reading *Masters of War*!

I'd like to ask a favor: Would you mind taking a few minutes to review it?

Reviews help others find my work. Without them, my books would be buried in the stacks of all the great books available to read. With millions of books online, a higher-rated book becomes more visible, and then readers just like you can enjoy this story too! So please take a moment to share your thoughts with me and others. I'd greatly appreciate it. - John

Please rate or write a review on Amazon.

CREDITS

Cover Design & Layout
Nick Castle @ Nick Castle Design

Editing & Formatting
Jason Letts @ Imbue Editing

John lives in the Seattle area with his wife and the world's sweetest cat: Karmann. Raised in a nomadic military family, he is annoyingly curious, a consumer of whiskey, and a political junkie at heart, but his greatest interests are his family and their collective adventures. And, for the record, he enjoys swimming in the ocean — even if it's with sharks.

Printed in Dunstable, United Kingdom

64181876R10208